About the Author

Clara O'Connor grew up in the west of Ireland where inspiration was on her doorstep; her village was full of legend, a place of druids and banshees and black dogs at crossroads. Clara worked in publishing for many years before her travels set her in the footsteps of Arthurian myth, to Mayans, Maasai, Dervishes and the gods of the Ancients. The world she never expected to explore was the one found in the pages of her debut novel, *Secrets of the Starcrossed*, which is the first book in the The Once and Future Queen trilogy.

Clara now works in LA in TV. At weekends, if not scribbling away on her next book, she can be found browsing the markets, hiking in the Hollywood Hills or curled up by the fireside with a red wine deep in an epic YA or fantasy novel.

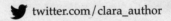 twitter.com/clara_author

Books by Clara O'Connor

The Once and Future Queen Series

Secrets of the Starcrossed

Curse of the Celts

Legend of the Lakes

LEGEND OF THE LAKES

The Once and Future Queen

CLARA O'CONNOR

One More Chapter
a division of HarperCollins*Publishers*
1 London Bridge Street
London SE1 9GF
www.harpercollins.co.uk

HarperCollins*Publishers*
1st Floor, Watermarque Building, Ringsend Road
Dublin 4, Ireland

This paperback edition 2021
First published in Great Britain in ebook format
by HarperCollins*Publishers* 2021

1

A catalogue record of this book
is available from the British Library

ISBN: 978-0-00-840772-8

This novel is entirely a work of fiction. The names, characters and incidents
portrayed in it are the work of the author's imagination. Any resemblance to
actual persons, living or dead, events or localities is entirely coincidental.

Printed and bound in Great Britain by
CPI Group (UK) Ltd, Croydon CR0 4YY

For Mrs Fitzgerald, the first to suggest that one day I could do this

Ms Young, who lured it into being

And to all out there wondering if they can

Do it. One life to live.

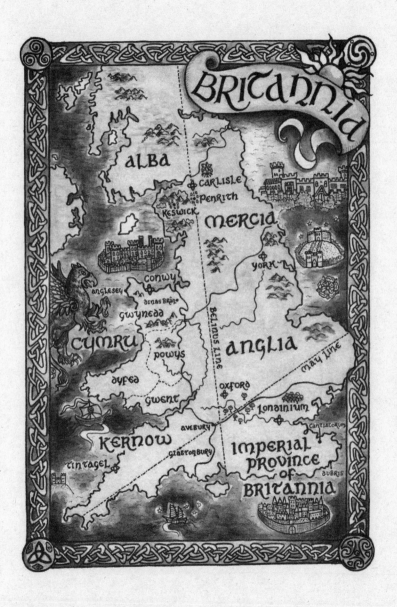

Part One

INTO THE ABYSS

I thought to die that night in the solitude where they
*   would never find me...*
But there was time...
And I lay quietly on the drawn knees of the mountain,
staring into the abyss.

I do not know how long...
I could not count the hours, they ran so fast—
Like little bare-foot urchins—shaking my hands away.
But I remember
Somewhere water trickled like a thin severed vein...
And a wind came out of the grass,
Touching me gently, tentatively, like a paw.

                                        — The Edge, Lola Ridge

Chapter One

Holy Isle, Anglesea

In the reign of Prince Llewelyn Glyndŵr of Gwynedd

The sparks from the pyres were released into the night sky, hundreds of tiny embers drifting up in the still winter darkness. So many pyres. The destruction that the sentinels had left in their wake was total, the mistletoe supplies gone, the groves badly damaged. The druids and those who had served them shed their bodies as their spirits lifted into the darkness. With Devyn.

He was gone. Here in his home, they had killed him.

I stood and watched while the druids prepared him, removing his clothes, exposing the hole in his chest that had ended his life. The rose and lakes he had tattooed over his heart were marred for eternity, the emblem of the Lakelands, my brother's sigil... My brother had never deserved him. On his upper arm were the meandering curves of the Tamesis, ending in a Celtic symbol, a symbol of us. I had traced it over

3

and over again; we had lost and found each other on the banks of that river. There our story had ended and started again. Now it was over, there would be no more chances. I could not follow where he had gone, not yet. I stayed by his side all day as the survivors and my brother's men bustled about building the pyres, tending the dead and the injured.

Occasionally the moans of those who had survived the attack found their way to me, but mostly it was just Devyn and me. His dark curls hadn't dried since he was pulled out of the waves. I tried to get the sand out but his locks had frozen, and my fingers didn't have enough warmth in them to melt the ice after a while. They left him until last; I could feel them hovering, waiting to take him.

"I don't have a photo."

"What was that, lady?" came the tentative voice from behind me.

It was hard to breathe through my mouth – my throat felt constricted. I drew a breath through my nose and exhaled, which only called attention to the pressing weight on my chest. I didn't have a photo of him. I pushed my fists into my eyes. Behind my lids flickered Devyn's face: his frown when I said something that annoyed him, his laughter over a cup of coffee back in Londinium, his serious expression cracking at my teasing of his indulgent citified tastes, his single-minded focus in all things, his frustration when I refused to let him push me away, his determination to see me back in the land of my birth; his eyes studying my reaction as I took in his Griffin tattoo the first time, the look that waited for me to appreciate and finally understand what the position meant to him. I would never see his eyes again – that dark warmth had faded. The intense gaze dimmed forever. And I would never see him again.

Bloody Briton, why had he never let me take a photo? Not

that I had a device to view it on out here in the Wilds anyway. I needed to take my fists out of my face. I was wasting precious time.

My next inhale expanded the pained void within me. Pulling my hands away, I lifted my face to the sky as I attempted to pull in air and not scream at the same time. Someone hovered closer, reaching out but hesitating to actually intrude. The concerned face of the young druid was barely visible, backlit as she was by the burning funeral pyres.

"Lady, we need to—"

"I know, I just want one more minute," I cut across her. I traced my fingers along Devyn's cheekbones, his arched brow, the peeking feathers of the eagle wings that spanned his back and curled slightly over his shoulders, not yet enclosed in the white cloth in which they had bound most of his body.

Hands helped pull me up until, in spite of my stiffened joints, I was upright. I shrugged them off, curling my fingers into my palms so hard that I actually felt something through the cold that had stolen away all feeling hours ago.

I felt lightheaded and too heavy to move as they wrapped him in the last strand of white cloth. Men stepped forward to lift him. I couldn't see through the blur but I trailed after them. I needed another minute. Hands pulled me back as they lifted him onto the last remaining stack of wood and wrapped around me, keeping me upright. There was a keening sound that tore through the night as the torch touched the winter wood, and the fire blazed higher and faster than any of the others had.

My knees were on the ground. That terrible howl finally stopped as my head was buried in wet unyielding leather. Sobs tore through me, doubling me over in their strength, and I was helpless against them. My mouth was torn wide by the raw pain that tried to escape in a never-ending gush.

I won back control and struggled to my feet in the sand, pushing away the intruder in my space.

Numbly, I watched the fire. The flames licked up into the sky, flickers of blue and green and orange. White smoke lifted into the night, obscuring the stars. The tang of sea salt mixed with woodsmoke as the flames consumed the bodies that had once held people we loved.

The blaze mostly hid the shadow of the body contained within, and after a while it started to crumble in on itself. In Londinium, bodies were cremated in a building created for the purpose. When it was all done, a neat little box of ashes was issued to be disposed of as the family decided.

What did they do out here in the Wilds once it was over? Did they just let the sea come in and take what was left? Was that why they built the pyres on the beach? Or should I take the ashes home to his father, or to Conwy or Carlisle? Where would he consider home? I didn't know. I didn't know anything. Devyn was the one who was supposed to guide me. He was the one who always explained how things worked out here beyond the walls. I should never have left. If I had stayed in Londinium, he would be alive. All these people would be alive. How would I tell Rhodri? His father had waited so long for Devyn to come home, had believed he was still alive long after everyone else had thought him dead... and now he was.

The fire burned down lower and lower.

Gideon ventured closer again. I flinched as his hand touched my shoulder. Everyone had gone inside, the pyres had burned down to glowing embers, but once I left this beach that would be it.

"Don't touch me."

6

I felt him leave. My brother sat waiting further up the beach, his heavy cloak drawn around him. He was watching me. He too had stayed by me all day – such a display of familial concern. Now he was worried, now he realised what Devyn had meant to me. Now, when it was all too late.

"Come." My brother's voice disturbed the night. "It's over."

I didn't respond, didn't have the energy.

"It's cold, you must come in," he spoke again.

What did I care? The heat from the pyre had long since faded.

Firm hands took my shoulders and started to pull me up.

"No." I tugged away. Who was Rion Deverell to tell me what to do or where to go? I was done with being told what to do. All my life I had done what was asked of me, what my parents wanted, what my society wanted, what Devyn had wanted. Where had it got me? My parents weren't even related to me and at the first sign of trouble had turned their backs on me; once I wasn't their obedient step up into society, I was no longer their daughter. The society whose code I had followed, whose prince I had promised to marry, that society had had its own plan all along, had stolen me from my murdered mother in order to use my magic, abilities I didn't even know I had until Devyn turned up. And Devyn, he had been the greatest liar of them all: he had fulfilled his destiny, lured me here with promises of love and family, and now I was alone. He was dead, dead because I had insisted he marry me despite the fact he had repeatedly pulled away from me. If Rion Deverell had just let us be, we would still be in Conwy, Devyn would still be alive, we wouldn't be here and I wouldn't be alone.

"You did this," I said, whirling out of his arms. "Get away from me."

Rion faced me in the night, his expression unreadable.

"You must come in," he repeated, ignoring my accusation.

"No," I said, turning back to the smoking embers on the sand.

"Get up."

I ignored his order.

He sighed deeply.

"Have sense. It's the middle of winter, you'll freeze out here."

"I don't care." I couldn't feel the cold. I couldn't feel anything right now. If I just left them to it, would he continue to have this conversation with this body? Could I just drift away to where people would stop bothering me?

"Gods! Get up, girl, or so help me I will drag your arse inside."

The great Rion Deverell, faultless King of Mercia, swearing at a grieving girl. What would people say? I felt his hands take hold of my upper arms to carry out his threat.

"Let go of me," I uttered in a low voice, "or I will—"

"What? What will you do?" he said tiredly. "What did you do today? Nothing. Heir to our mother's power and you did nothing."

I had done nothing.

When the sentinels had held Devyn and Matthias had killed him in front of me, I hadn't done a thing. I was supposed to be powerful but I hadn't been able to do anything. The drug had worn off now; I could sense that much. But even if my blood hadn't been laced with the drug that suffocated my powers what could I really have done? It had all happened so fast. I hadn't even thought to call it, had been frozen in fear, my only thought to get to him, to do as they asked... It had been over before I'd had time to think.

They had sailed away unhindered while he was lying in my arms. Useless, I had been useless.

I stared at Rion. Was this my fault? I had brought Devyn here and then I hadn't been able to protect him. I should have been able to protect him.

My brother lifted his hands out to me.

"I'm sorry." He paused. "I didn't mean… just please come inside, for your baby's sake if not for your own."

I nodded dumbly. I had forgotten about the baby inside me. Would the cold hurt her? The disconnection I felt, the pain that had clawed at me earlier, did she feel these things through me?

"The ashes," I said as I started toward him.

"What?" he asked. Perhaps my voice was too low. My throat felt oddly raw.

"I want to take his ashes home." Wherever that was. The hollowness inside me grew.

"I'll see it done," he promised, his hand going to the small of my back. I stepped away, beyond his reach, but followed as he led me to one of the houses still standing in the middle of the village.

There were several people inside sitting around the empty wooden table: long-robed druids and leather-clad warriors, and Gideon in his stained Midwinter finery. They all looked up as we entered. The room felt warm, the fire in the hearth small compared to those that had blazed all evening out on the shore.

Rion indicated a bed in the corner of the room before he spoke quietly to a warrior who exited to do his bidding. I didn't want to sleep, but I didn't want to speak with the sombre men and women who sat huddled around the table in the middle of the room.

An older druid brought me a cup of something warm and

set it beside the bed with a small nod. I didn't want it. I felt heavy in the heated room, but it was too much effort to take off my cloak, so I lay down.

Words drifted over from the occupied side of the simple dwelling. Worry over the mistletoe, loss of the dead, concern at the Empire travelling so deep into their territory, consternation that their weapons had worked so far north, basic tech though it had been. The words swirled around the room in a tangle, knotting around them all. So many threads around the golden-haired King of Mercia, to whom they all looked for answers. Gideon's eyes came my way time and time again. What did he want? What did he see?

I turned over, putting my back to them. I closed my eyes and saw Devyn's face, the moment when Matthias struck him imprinted on my shuttered lids. He had promised me he would always be here for me.

I felt again his body growing cold in my arms, the draining away of his life as the druid spoke words releasing the spirit of the Griffin. I opened my eyes and stared at the dark shadows playing on the wall. The words being exchanged in the room washed over me. I couldn't think about it yet. It was too much.

"Without the mistletoe, many will die this season," one of the druids was saying.

"There are no reserves?"

"Not here. Thankfully, half of it was sent to Conwy immediately after the harvest to be dispersed at Yuletide and there are other sites with some stores. That should last for some time, but after that we will need to source more until the next harvest."

"Why did they take it?"

People were ill in Londinium too. It wasn't just here in the Wilds that people had magic in their blood. In the city, too, people were sick and dying fast. Nothing and no one were able to prevent it, except for Marcus.

Marcus, who had come with us, whose father was still alive, had betrayed us. We thought we had escaped the reach of the council, that Devyn had triumphed in returning me home. But we hadn't beaten them. They had given us up, allowed us to leave so we would bring Marcus deep into enemy territory. Marcus, who now knew everything. It had been Marcus's idea to come to Anglesey, and no coincidence that the sentinels were here when we arrived. No. He had delivered us here.

How stupidly gullible. The praetor had engineered a similar deception when they had first caught Devyn, releasing him to see where he led them. Praetor Calchas had let him go a second time, but they had never planned for it to be permanent. The realisation trickled into my slow-moving mind. On setting us free, my return had already been set in motion and Devyn had been poisoned, not expected to last until midwinter. With him gone they would have expected that I would docilely return to the fold.

The man I had thought my friend, who had accused me of selfishness, of only seeing the world through the spectrum of my own needs – he had done this. He had planned it all. If it hadn't been for the surprise arrival of Gideon and Rion, I would now be halfway to Londinium.

"How did you know to come after us?" I asked as I turned back to the room.

The conversation stopped. A moment passed before Rion answered.

"Gideon found a note in your room. In it you said goodbye, that Marcus wanted to go to York now, and that you were leaving with him. I wouldn't have followed," he said, looking at the silent, scarred warrior, "but Gideon told me that it did not match what you had told him, which was that you had promised to return. Why bother telling me the story about York if you were actually going to Anglesey to marry?"

I absorbed this. I had been such a fool. Marcus had planned everything, had deceived us all along. Had he ever really thought his father dead? Had it just been another part of the lie he told us? The betrayal swirled in my brain until it too sank down into the numbness that filled me.

I carried Devyn's ashes back to Conwy.

How different the outward journey had been – the road a path bathed in moonlight, brimming with hope. I had thought all my dreams were about to be realised. I was going to hold Devyn's hand in front of a druid in an oak grove with waves lapping the shore and open starlit skies overhead. Instead a nightmare had awaited. The grove had been laden with dead bodies, not petals, and my intended groom had died in my arms. And yet I was married, though not to Devyn. The dark twist of fate tore a self-derisory laugh out of me, surprising both me and the warrior riding alongside me.

I supposed it was odd given the broken, grieving thing I had been yesterday. Today, I felt as though everything had happened to somebody else; none of it was part of my life. I was just unaccountably carrying a bag that contained all that was left of Devyn Glyndŵr. He had spent his whole life worrying about me, looking out for me, protecting me. Now he was gone, and it was as if he had never existed. Apart from my being here, riding along the coast of Cymru. If he had truly never lived would I now be in Londinium, preparing for a day of shopping and lunch, fussing over my darling husband, the wonderful Dr Marcus Courtenay? I suppose I would, and that version of me was probably happy, perfectly content, playing at life as a grown up until she did her duty and popped out the requisite children.

I also had a child, I remembered hollowly. How would I raise one out here? Did these people send their children to a school like citizens?

Of course, they did, though I supposed as a lofty royal my child would have a tutor – like Rion and Devyn had had Callum when they were young.

Marcus might be back in the city already. I had no real idea how long it took to sail down the coast of Cymru, around the awkward toe of the island, Bronwyn's ancestral home of Kernow, and along the underside until they came around and entered the Tamesis back into Londinium. Would they creep back in quietly or arrive with a great announcement and be hailed as heroes? There was the small inconvenience of Marcus's recent trial and labelling as a traitor to the city, but I had no doubt that Praetor Calchas would be able to explain that all away as part of the grand plan to steal a cure from the natives.

They would have to get Marcus a replacement bride. The void I had left would be hard to fill. Where would they get a new woman with so much magic in her blood to provide babies now?

Would my daughter have much power? She would certainly inherit mine. The power of the Lakes was inherited directly through the still unbroken matriarchal line. Unlike me, she would be trained in it from the beginning. She wouldn't stand uselessly on the shore while people she loved were killed. Drug or no.

13

Conwy rose up as imposing as ever, its grey granite walls a deterrent to all aggressors. If we had been here, we would have been safe. There were subdued throngs of people in the courtyard when we entered through the gates. News of the sentinels' attack on the Holy Isle would have preceded us. Dry words, conveyed by a messenger, not the kaleidoscope of blood and fire and bodies and violence that it had been.

Many people crowded the courtyard. Llewelyn would have called the townspeople in behind the castle walls when news of the attack reached him. Now, here they all stood, gawking at our arrival despite the heavy freezing rain. Did we look the part, the small group of smoke-grimed warriors and bloodied druids trailing in after the tragic King of Mercia and his newly recovered sister? What was my role? Was I still seen as the beloved Lady of the Lake returned to heal the land anew, or was I now reviled as the betrothed of the man who had caused the slaughter of the holy folk and stolen their medical supplies? Was Devyn part of my story to them, the disgraced Griffin, childhood friend of Rion Deverell, the Oathbreaker who returned with the resurrected lost lady? His role in the story was done – did they care that he would play no further part?

Did they know that my own path ended with him? I didn't know the road ahead. Where did I belong now? I had no home. Where did I go from here?

Hands reached around my waist and I blinked, realising that everyone had dismounted while I sat on my horse in the middle of the courtyard. I limply allowed the giant hands to lift me from my seat to the ground, holding carefully on to the bag that was hooked across my shoulder.

My body was small beside Gideon's and for a moment I almost succumbed to the urge to lean in. To hide from all these people. There was deep silence as they watched us all, the surviving druids in their bloody, dirt-stained robes, the warriors with their martial gear soiled by pyre building, never having raised so much as a sword.

I squirmed away as Gideon tried to pull me closer and threw my shoulders back. I was not entertainment. I was not here to be the object of those pitying gazes.

I stopped in front of Llewelyn, Prince of Gwynedd. His hair was soaked into his skull, the lack of curls making his head seem smaller. His partner, Rhys, had his arm around him.

"My lady." His eyes fell to the bag I now cradled in my arms. They all knew, then. Of course, a full report would have been conveyed to the ruler of these lands. After all, he was uncle to the dust I held – all that was left of Devyn. Llewelyn's eyes were dark too. I couldn't bear them.

I walked by him towards the entrance to the great hall. Stumbling against a tall man standing on the steps, I heard a growl from Gideon behind me behind me as the stranger put his hands out to steady me. I looked up to see the cold grey eyes of a handsome, older man directed at Gideon and a caustic smirk as he took his hands back in no great hurry.

I blinked in recognition as Oban extricated me from my dripping cloak, clucking at my wet hair and clothes where the fur-lined cloak had failed to protect me from the elements. He wrapped my bare shoulders in a warm woollen shawl while I held on to the bag. He had helped me into the ruined velvet dress that I was surprised to find I was still wearing. Had it only been the night before last that he had laced me into the beautiful gown for the Solstice festivities?

I stood there, unsure of where to go. With so many people inside the walls, did I still have the room I had left behind with the paltry possessions I had picked up since leaving Londinium?

Llewelyn appeared at my shoulder. He went to put his arms around me, but I backed away with an awkward step, straight into the ever-present hulking body of the dark warrior who seemed to have become my new shadow. I twisted my head around to glare up at him. He was not Devyn. He needed to leave me alone.

A huffed laugh had me turning to face the unfamiliar visage of the man I had stumbled against a few moments earlier, and I levelled a deadened glare at him too for good measure.

"My lady," Llewelyn called my attention back to him and without a further attempt to touch me, indicated that I should precede him into the great hall.

Rhys led the way, and I followed him through the hall, which was filled with the press of even more bodies. The damp heat rising from them was an ugly, foetid thing. They pushed back into each other to allow us to pass through. We went through the top corner of the hall, and down a corridor with which I was unfamiliar, until Rhys opened a door on the left. Inside the room was a study of sorts; a large desk had been pushed back against a book-lined wall to allow for chairs to be arranged in a circle.

Pulling back a seat beside Llewelyn, Rhys inclined his head to me to take my place before he took the seat on the Llewelyn's right side. Rion took the seat beside me while Gideon loomed behind me as other men and women took their seats. Some I recognised from the trial – the trial during which they had found Devyn guilty of being an Oathbreaker and had condemned him to death. Now that he was dead, were they glad? Did they feel he had got his deserved end?

Lady Morwyn – who had spoken at great length about how an Oathbreaker couldn't be trusted, no matter what the justification for breaking his fealty – didn't meet my eyes now. Neither did Lord Arthfael or Lady Emrick, who had also judged him. The High Druid, Fidelma, who had presided over the trial, sat opposite, her steady, sympathetic gaze making my bones clench. I wanted nothing more than to smash the jar in my hands into her gentle, judicious face. The had condemned him, and they were hypocrites all. A tremble went through the room.

Then Bronwyn was there, a whirlwind of dark hair and plush velvet wrapping around me. She smelled sweet and fresh, and the jar of ashes dug awkwardly into my ribs as she pressed against me. She pulled back, and her glistening eyes took in the bag I held, lifting them back to me for confirmation that what was left of her cousin was contained within. Her chin started to crumple as I averted my eyes and extricated myself from her embrace. Rion stood, pulling her to him and held her while she swallowed back her sobs.

I would not break down here, in front of what was clearly a gathering of the great and the good, which amounted to maybe a dozen people in all. This included the lords and ladies who had been here for the trial, some of the druids who had travelled back with us, and a few I didn't know – maybe they had been here for the Yuletide festivities and I just couldn't remember them. There had been so many people, all here to see the Lady of the Lake, newly returned from the dead. Rion was the last to take his seat with Bronwyn on his other side. She looked across at me, anguish clear in her eyes as she whispered urgently to Rion. He shook his head, quieting her, taking her hand in his. She was a lady in her own right, but I suppose she was doubly important now as the future Queen of Mercia.

Also seated in the inner circle was the man at whom Gideon had growled. He was tall but blocky, and had the air of a man who had little patience and expected his every word to be obeyed, immediately.

"Well, what bloody mess is all this?" he sneered before everyone had fully settled.

Chapter Two

Llewelyn threw him a dirty look before turning back to Rion, his hands splayed wide, his eyes red with grief. "What happened?"

"It appears that Londinium attacked the druids at the Holy Isle to steal the mistletoe harvest." Rion spoke for us. "They massacred the community to do so."

A number of the nobility looked to the robed druids for confirmation of what they surely already knew – as if Rion was making it up, or maybe because they just weren't ready to believe it. I could understand that.

"And my nephew?"

Rion cast a glance at me before he continued.

"It was bad timing. My sister, Devyn, and Marcus arrived as the attack was ending. Devyn was killed, and Marcus was taken."

I looked over at him dumbly. Bad timing? Was he hiding the truth, or was he simply not aware of it? I barely knew this man, but he had struck me as intelligent – high-handed maybe but not stupid. The effort it would take to correct them felt far away. And why should I. All these people and their judgement of Devyn, what would they say once they knew he had brought a traitor into their midst?

"You let them take Marcus Courtenay? He should never have been here in the first place. The Glyndŵr pup should have taken him to York. He'd have been safe there," the newcomer growled.

I bit my lip at the defence of Devyn that seethed inside me. Who was this man and what right did he have to call Devyn names? What did it matter now? My anger seeped away as quickly as it had surfaced.

"Why were they there? Why did you go after them?" Llewelyn asked, stiff-backed, as if the other man hadn't spoken.

He didn't know. Didn't see that it was my fault. *I* was the reason Devyn had been there. His face was grey and lined: he had lost the last son of House Glyndŵr, the nephew whose return he had barely had time to celebrate. He had been so happy – for himself and for his disgraced brother Rhodri who had survived long enough to see his son return to Cymru. Did Rhodri know? Would Llewelyn have sent word?

Rion's jaw locked, his eyes hooded when he answered.

"Devyn and Catriona were planning to get married by going to the Holy Isle where nobody knew I had forbidden it. We went after them hoping to stop their foolishness."

I hated him. I hated him referring to me by that stupid name. Hated him.

"We would never have been there if not for you," I said.

Rion drew a breath and Bronwyn laid a hand on his arm, quelling whatever he had been about to say in reply.

"How much of the harvest did they get?" Lady Morwyn asked, leaning back in her chair, her lips tight. She was less concerned about why we were there than the impact it would have on her and her people.

"More than half," the druid from the Holy Isle, John, answered him.

"Why were they even after the harvest?" Lady Emrick asked. "I saw no ill Imperial citizens at the last treaty renewal."

"The Mallacht is in Londinium too," the sneery newcomer said. "The illness inside the walls is rampant across the population this last year and despite all of their fancy medicine, the Romans have been unable to do as much as us. People are dying in droves, and they haven't been able to cover it up anymore. Riots in the streets, unrest in the province like they haven't seen in generations. As bad as anything that happened in the rest of the Empire over the last decades."

There had been a map on a college wall in Oxford that tracked the northwest progression of the illness from the central Mediterranean. I knew this much from the research that had been gathered in the library, if not from the news feeds in Londinium.

"The illness will be worse in Londinium because the ley line there is almost beyond repair," Fidelma added, and was ignored for her trouble by the newcomer, not showing even a modicum of respect for one of the most senior druids in the land.

"How do you know?" Rion asked Fidelma, when the man she had addressed failed to do so.

"It is inevitable. The Empire has hunted magic to extinction in line with the rise of technology. We tend the lines out here, holding back the decay and the corrupted energies, protecting the western and northern lines as best we can from Glastonbury," Fidelma explained. "But the line that passes

21

under Londinium has been deteriorating over the last two centuries, ever more rapidly in recent decades."

"How do you know there are riots?" Lady Morwyn redirected the conversation back to the lord I didn't know.

"I keep an eye on things. Ever since the lady was killed, we have been vulnerable. If they ever discovered she was gone, we needed to be ready, and I for one was not going to be caught off guard," he answered. His martial appearance said that he had been more than just keeping an eye on things. This man looked like the very embodiment of constrained violence; I imagined he had spent every day of his life, long before my mother had died, readying for battle.

"How did they find out we had something that treated the illness?" Llewelyn followed up. It was a good question. I hadn't been aware of how bad the illness was and I had lived in the city. The exchange of information between the Roman province and the rest of the island was even more limited. I had known next to nothing of what life out here was like, much less that they had a cure, until we had witnessed Rhodri being treated. But Marcus had known.

"No doubt they have their spies too." The newcomer's face twisted.

Guilt lashed at me. We had brought their spy home with us, brought him deeper than any Shadower could have come. How stupid, how impossibly gullible – it had never occurred to me that Marcus might betray us. But of course, he had never abandoned his position: he had only wanted to help the citizenry. If I wasn't such a self-centred idiot, I would have realised that Marcus would never desert the people of Londinium to save his own skin. I thought Marcus had fled the city for my sake to save two paltry lives. He had always favoured the many over the one, had always been the noble prince of the city, the devoted doctor. I was an idiot.

"How will we tell people that Londinium has stolen more than half the harvest?" Lady Morwyn moaned.

The martial lord stood. "How will we tell them that Londinium has stolen mistletoe? Damn the mistletoe! Sentinels came all the way here and attacked one of our holiest sites." His eyes narrowed. "How many of them were there? How were they armed?"

"Perhaps two or three centuries' worth," Rion assessed. "There were five maybe six ships. It was all but over when we got there – most had already boarded the ships. Only a handful remained."

"And yet you let them take the heir to the York throne?" the stranger circled back to his earlier concern.

I tried to summon the energy to correct them. I should correct them. Marcus was not who they thought.

"*Let* them?" Gideon's snarl came from somewhere behind me as he stepped forward. "There were half a dozen ships full of armed men, they held Devyn Glyndŵr under their weapons, and there were but eight of us."

The stranger stood and stepped up towards Gideon until they were eyeball to eyeball – no mean feat as the dark warrior was very tall. "Really? I just heard only a handful remained. And that you watched while they took the York Prince back to Londinium because they threatened the Oathbreaker."

Gideon glared at the other man. His jaw locked, a pulse in his forehead speaking to his barely contained anger.

"Gideon," Rion cautioned.

"Ah, is that why you failed? Was your leash being held?"

"No man holds my leash," Gideon said through bared teeth.

"No son of mine would have stood by while the heir to our throne was taken by thrice-damned sentinels," the stranger threw at him.

Our throne. Not a stranger. York. This man was Richard Mortimer, the Steward of York.

Gideon's face transformed, and his whole body relaxed before his lips spread in a smile designed to infuriate its recipient.

"Well, my lord," he said, inclining his head as he addressed his father formally, "as it happens, my priorities are not what they might have been."

The man clenched his fists as Gideon turned his back on him and sauntered over to the window where he took up a casual pose, leaning back against the wall, the taunting grin lingering on his lips.

"It wasn't how..." I finally found my voice.

The Steward's gaze turned from his insolent son to me.

"Ah, yes. Here she is. The long-awaited Lady of the Lake. This is what the gods have sent us. This child." He looked around at the assembled lords and ladies. "Her mother was a fool, taking her south, losing her to the Romans, leaving her untrained for years. What good is she to us now? I hear she has little command of the elements. What good was she when the Empire attacked?"

His eyes flicked to a shadowy corner of the room. There, behind the nobles gathered around the seated principles, was Callum. Returned to his master – to whom, it seemed, he had told everything.

There was muttering and shared glances between those who only two nights ago had gaily celebrated my return. But he was right. What use was I? To Devyn? To anyone?

They had all assumed that I had command of my

mother's powers; Bronwyn and Gideon had testified to my use of them. But my training in Oxford had shown me up for what I really was: I had no command of magic; it came and went of its own accord. I had no idea how I had called up a storm in Richmond, or how I had absorbed the energy that the Severn river had then used it to save us on the road north.

I sat there dumbly. Part of me screamed that I had been drugged. But another part sneered at my excuse. What of it? He spoke the truth: I had no control, no skill. I couldn't deny it.

Even if I hadn't been drugged yesterday, there was no guarantee I could have done anything to defend those people. Or to save Devyn. The truth was that I had been powerless to keep these people safe when Governor Actaeon had attacked. "Is this true?" Morwyn asked.

I looked down at the jar in my hands. Just yesterday morning he was alive. Now he was gone. I should have been able to do something. I was so tired of the events of my life, of Devyn's life being twisted and judged by others. Somehow this felt all too familiar.

"So blind. You all saw what you wanted to see. The Lady of the Lake come back to us. Deverell, you were there – they cut down her lover in front of her, isn't that right? And she didn't so much as raise a breeze in his defence," the Steward of York scoffed. "At least if the Oathbreaker were still alive, we would have had something. He'd lived for years amongst them, was adept in their technology; he would have given us some advantage with his knowledge of their defences."

But Devyn was dead. And all that remained was me.

"He's right," I said. "The Griffin's dead and I'm useless. I just stood there."

I turned to Llewelyn. If I just admitted my guilt perhaps

this would all go away. I just wanted to be alone. For all the noise to stop.

"I just stood there." I said again. "Devyn died because of me."

I made to leave. I couldn't do this. I couldn't just sit here.

"Sit," the steward ordered. "We aren't done with you."

Gideon began a predatory stroll from his position by the window back to his place behind me as Rion bristled but remained silent.

I faded back into my seat. What did I care if I came or went? It mattered not at all.

He's dead.

Dead.

I had done nothing.

It repeated over and over inside me. Was it my lack of training? If I had trained more, been better, would I have been able to get past the suppressant? Had I still been blocked? I hadn't even reached for it to save Devyn. It had all happened so fast. So fast. And yet I had to sit here as they went over it again and again. Absently, I noted that Rion's account of Devyn's death lacked some rather significant information – my pregnancy, Gideon becoming the Griffin and our hasty marriage withheld from the group. Rion had recounted everything else in detail – what he had seen, the numbers, the weapons, the damage done to the community who had lived there. All of those bodies, so many dead. Children, women, druids – peaceful people who had done no harm to anyone. All dead. Who mourned them? Did they have families across the land who even now were receiving word of the attack? Wondering if their loved one, the child, the brother, the sister who had dedicated their life to healing, to tending the land, was among those cut down by the sentinels?

The steward had again returned to yesterday's attack, tracing the sequence of events. "Marcus went to them first, while the girl waited for you."

"Yes, we were almost there before she saw they had Devyn," Rion agreed on my behalf.

"Why did Marcus go then?" Gideon breathed, understanding what his father saw that the rest had not. They were all so focussed on the theft of the mistletoe and the brutal massacre that they had not, like the steward, reflected in detail on the earlier sequence of events.

"Surely she had more reason than the Courtenay boy to save Glyndŵr's life if she was there to marry him," the steward pointed out for anyone who had failed to follow.

"Marcus *wanted* to go back to Londinium." I confirmed quietly. He had never intended to stay here.

"What will he tell them, of our magic, of our defences?" Llewelyn asked catching my words.

"Everything. He'll tell them everything." That had been the plan all along. I had been so blind, so stupid.

"Maybe he'll keep our secrets," Bronwyn countered, speaking up for the first time. She of all people should know better; Marcus had attempted to deceive her when they had met, and she had seen through him then. But she had seemed distracted throughout, not entirely focussed on the meeting. Her hands twisted in her lap, her eyes occasionally seeking mine before darting away. Now that she's had time to absorb the facts she couldn't even look at me. Did she blame me for her cousin's death, for not finding a way to save him somehow?

"What secrets? Why do you think he was here? How do you think the sentinels knew to attack the Holy Isle?" I asked incredulously. How could they not see it? "It was Marcus, it was all Marcus."

I looked over at the sneery Steward of York to see if he had finished putting together what they all seemed to be too blind to see. It was all so obvious now. As ever, the praetor had been pulling the strings, making us dance... from the very beginning.

"You have no secrets. Marcus knew you had a cure, that was the only reason he came here."

Bronwyn's head snapped back at the force of my anger. I turned from her to Rion.

"You think they don't know the Lady of the Lake is dead? Calchas has always known. They killed her." Somehow I had found my feet. Fury poured life into my veins, shaking me out of the stupor that had held me in its grip. The rage at finding myself once more manipulated by the praetor pushing me out of the mire of guilt and self-castigation. Turning that anger and blame outwards. "Think about it. I wasn't some random foundling they decided to marry to Marcus Courtenay. The city, you, you all wanted me to marry Marcus, to tie the powerful bloodlines together. That's why he did it, to take me. She was killed because of me."

My outburst hung in the room, the silence following my explosion drifting heavily down as each person absorbed the meaning of my words, the repercussions of these new realities. The heat of my anger seeped away, the emptiness inside giving it no purchase.

"They killed our mother and took you. It wasn't an accident." Rion's innate control cracked and he took a deep breath, pain and anger visibly vying for supremacy. "It was planned."

"They knew she was gone, all this time?" Llewelyn was disbelieving.

"Why haven't they attacked us, if they knew? Without the lady's magic, we have been practically defenceless for nearly two decades," the steward observed, the quickest to identify that the balance of power had substantially shifted long ago. Yet their enemy had not taken advantage of it.

The repercussions were evident to all. If the Empire had engaged at any time since the lady's death, the Britons wouldn't have stood a chance.

"Calchas knew. I don't think Governor Actaeon did; he would have wiped you all out had he known. But Praetor Calchas plays his own game," I said dully. Marcus's betrayal was nothing to the people in this room compared to my mother's death. But to me it was…

"Do you know what Calchas…?" Rion's question petered out.

Was he really asking me if I knew what Calchas was plotting? If I had known that, Devyn would not be ashes now.

"Will they attack now?" Lady Morwyn asked the obvious.

"They're too late. We have Catriona now; they've missed their chance," Rion said.

"Have they?" The military-minded Lord Steward asked, his lips tweaking in a downward moue that suggested he, for one, didn't think so.

All eyes turned my way. Even disconnected as I was, I squirmed under their attention, wishing I was anywhere but here. He was right. If these people thought that I would be of any use to them against the Empire's legions, they were sorely mistaken.

Mortimer rose and walked over to me, scanning me up and

down, his gaze reflecting all too clearly what he saw. A pretty enough city girl of little use beyond decoration.

"We need to prepare," he said, turning dismissively and addressing the room.

"For what?" Lady Emrick asked.

"War," he said grimly. "They will be coming for us."

———————

They argued for a while about whether or not the threat was imminent, occasionally pressing me for my reading of the situation. Before too long there was a common understanding that I had nothing of worth to contribute. I knew little of the politics of war, though if this was anything to go by it consisted largely of travel and food logistics. I sat numbly while they all droned on, cradling the bag on my lap.

The Steward of York, Prince Llewelyn, and Rion did most of the talking. Gideon's father pushed for attack before Londinium had time to prepare or to heal their ill, chafing to respond to the Empire's first strike. But Rion and Llewelyn needed time, not being nearly as prepared for war as Anglia.

The Lady of the Lake had been the biggest weapon in the Britons' arsenal for centuries. But not this time. I had been useless in battle, had done nothing when it counted. What if I had been trained? A thought blindsided me: Callum was here. He had tried to teach me magic and he had abilities himself. Perhaps it wasn't too late? Maybe we could fix this. Fix it all. I caught Callum's eye and jerked my chin towards the door.

This time, when I stood to leave, nobody stopped me.

Callum slipped out of the room moments after me. His great arms already lifted to embrace me. I raised leaden arms to fend him off as I stepped back stiffly.

"I need you to help me."

His eyes were sorrowful. "I am sorry for thy loss, child."

"I need you to bring him back," I stated baldly. "He promised he would always come back. I need you to help him. Bring him back."

Callum's eyes widened. He was silent as two people passed by.

"I don't know the castle, I've not been here in many years... Is there somewhere we can speak more privately?" His gruff voice was gentle.

I nodded and led him along the corridors until we came to the bedroom I had occupied before my departure, thankfully untouched since the night of the feast. It felt like so long ago.

He sat in the window seat and contemplated me quietly as I sat beside him.

"Well?" I prompted. What was he waiting for? Nobody could hear us here. "Can you do it?"

"It doesn't work that way," he responded gently. Everyone spoke to me like I was made of glass now, even the usually blunt professor.

"Why not?" I demanded. "You told me that with the right application your magic could do anything, that I could do anything. Well, this is what I want. I want Devyn."

"Devyn is gone."

"No." I frowned. "Everything is energy, right? Then the energy that was Devyn still exists, and you can bring him back to me."

"No, child. Devyn Glyndŵr is gone. He did what we all thought was impossible: he brought you home. He has left behind the legacy of which he dreamed."

"What? I don't care, I don't care about any of that," I rejected. "I want him. I need him."

Callum looked at me, the giant man with all of his knowledge, with all of his wisdom, was helpless. "He's gone."

"Stop saying that. There has to be a way," I pleaded. "Teach me, teach me whatever needs to be done. I'll do it."

He just looked at me sadly.

"Please. If I had trained properly, if I'd known what to do, I could have saved him."

"Magic cannot help you bring him back," he said. "But it *can* help you defend those you still have left."

I had no one. Devyn had been everything. He had been my future, the life I wanted to live.

"He promised me he'd always come for me," I said brokenly.

"I know, child." This time, when he reached for me, I let him. Maybe he could prevent the splinter inside me from splitting me wide open.

Everyone I loved had abandoned me. Except one, I thought, my hand creeping across my belly. I would protect her. She was all I had of Devyn, and I could make sure that I was strong enough that nobody could ever hurt her. Whatever it took.

The afternoon passed. I didn't cry, didn't weep, I just lay there, suspended, as Callum held me together, in his arms. The weak winter sun faded into night, and servants bustled in and out. Marina and Oban came in to check on me and sat in silence when I failed to respond. The flickering light of candles lit the room, and the fire began to crackle. Food sat uneaten on the table by the fire. I just lay there and let it all pass.

Time was empty and without meaning until our hideaway

was eventually interrupted. Marina checked with me before she opened the door but I didn't care, whoever it was, so the dark-haired girl opened the door wide, admitting the intruders.

"Callum," Rion acknowledged his former tutor.

"My lord," Callum said, though he remained where he was.

Bronwyn crossed the room to me and laid her warm hand to my cheek. "Oh Cass." She sighed, my grief reflected in her tone. I closed my eyes against the emotions in her face. I could barely contain my own pain.

"There are plans we must make. Callum, if you would leave us," Rion said.

"Cass wants him to stay," Marina objected on my behalf.

Rion raised an eyebrow at being addressed by the latent urchin I had helped rescue from the stews.

"This is not for debate." He turned to the Londinium pair. "We will let you know if the lady has further need of you."

Callum disentangled himself, propping me up in the window seat and, bowing his head, he left, taking the mutinous Marina and deferential Oban with him. Rion and Bronwyn sat at the table while Gideon, who had also entered with them, shut the door after the departing Callum.

"Have you eaten? How do you feel?" Bronwyn's concern was etched on her face. I watched the bustle in the courtyard below – some of the lords were departing, heading for home. To prepare their defences or prepare for war?

"You must eat," Rion said, and I could already hear the reminder of the baby that was coming. It was the tactic he used every time to bend me to his will.

"The baby will be fine," I managed to get out. My voice felt foreign to me, disembodied. The thought of food wasn't something I could contemplate. My mouth felt dry – the very concept of food seemed alien to me. I couldn't conceive of eating.

"You're pregnant?" Bronwyn gasped. The news apparently still hadn't been shared despite the hours of rehashing yesterday's events in Llewelyn's study.

Absently I wondered why he was bothering to conceal what would soon be all too evident. But then I hadn't shared anything beyond what they had figured out for themselves either. Maybe secrecy was genetic. Or more likely Rion had yet to decide how the information could be used to best advantage. Telling people I had been drugged and unable to use my magic wouldn't make a difference, worse than that, it felt like an excuse.

A twist of Rion's lips confirmed the news I had so carelessly let slip.

"What do you want?" Why were they here? In my space. Crowding me. Talking. Breathing.

"We need to be careful," Rion cautioned. "We haven't revealed everything that happened yesterday."

"What do you mean?" Bronwyn asked. "What else happened?"

"Devyn wasn't dead when he hit the waves," he began. "We pulled him out, but the wound was fatal. There was nothing we could do."

Bronwyn waved her hand, quieting him.

"I need to tell you something, about the relationship between... He was the last Griffin." Bronwyn stumbled over her message, her face tight with concern, her eyes never moving from me. "I..."

"Not anymore," Rion interjected. "Druid John performed a ceremony and the spirit of the Griffin was transferred to Gideon."

Bronwyn's eyes rounded, her head angling to take in the scarred warrior stationed in the furthest corner of the room. Gideon slanted her a wink in reply.

"Oh, thank the Gods." Bronwyn put her hand to her chest and ran the other hand over her face, exhaling as the room waited for her to collect herself. "That's what I needed to talk to you about. I didn't want to say it in front of everyone, but my mother is a Glyndŵr and she often spoke of the legends of her house when we were children. I was afraid for Cass. There is…" She hesitated, lowering her voice before continuing. "In the stories, the lady does not long outlive her Griffin, especially if they are together."

"What do you mean?" Rion asked.

"It's just part of the lore passed down by my mother. She has a romantic bent, and loves tales of star-crossed lovers. My mother said there has been a curse that originated in the days of Arthur Pendragon. The first Lady of the Lake to come to our aid, Guinevere, was rumoured to have betrayed her husband with his strongest knight. When he was killed she did not long survive her protector."

"There was no Griffin then," Rion interjected.

"No, the first Griffin came many centuries later and yet…" A line appeared between Bronwyn's brows. "When Jasper Tewdwr was Griffin he was killed in the border wars and the Lady Margaret did not long survive him. There were rumours of an affair between them even though she was married to his brother Edmund. They were not the first either: a previous lady who married her Griffin also faded away after he drowned. This is why there is a rule against the lady and the Griffin being together. That's why Llewelyn was happy to support Cass marrying Marcus, to keep them apart. The curse is something we have long speculated on in our house."

Rion looked murderous. "He endangered her like this?"

"I don't think Devyn knew," Bronwyn defended. "He was raised outside our house. There would have been no need to teach him the lore as we all thought the line of the lady had ended. I never... I thought they had ended it. Cass seemed to accept she would marry Marcus. But if there is a new Griffin, then all is well."

Rion exchanged looks with Gideon, shoulders slumped. "We have repeated Devyn's mistake."

"What? How?"

Bronwyn's eyes widened as she tried to conceive how I could already have attached to another Griffin. I had carelessly lost one, only to have become entangled with another so quickly. I almost felt sorry for her, but despite her confusion, I couldn't summon the energy to respond.

"You know the tethering effect of the handfast cuff?" Rion checked and Bronwyn nodded. Our inability to separate had been an issue on our journey north.

"Once Marcus boarded the Imperial ships and started to leave, Catriona... she was in pain. It looked like it was killing her – some kind of barbaric punishment the handfast inflicts for not complying with its edicts."

"How did you get it off?" Bronwyn looked to me, pulling short as pieces clicked into place. "Wait, how were you going to get it off if you married Devyn instead of Marcus?"

I didn't respond.

"There was a loophole. It seems it was some version of the contract charm," Rion said and the up-until-now silent Gideon grunted. "Any marriage will remove it."

Bron's eyes flicked between us. "Then... who?"

Gideon bowed sharply.

"Oh." Bronwyn's eyes were wide as she absorbed the latest revelation. "When York hears of this, he will not be pleased."

"We won't tell him." Rion surveyed the room to underline his command.

"What?" Bronwyn gasped.

"Any of it."

"Why not?" asked Gideon. "Anything that displeases the steward…"

"I don't know who we can trust," Rion said. "There has to be a traitor. Someone must have betrayed our mother. What Catriona said earlier, about not being a random match for Marcus. If she's right, then it was planned. We always thought it was bad luck. There was never any hint that anyone in Londinium knew our mother was dead. We assumed that whatever had brought her so close to the city, the sentinels killing her was just a case of being in the wrong place at the wrong time. But they knew."

"So?"

"So somebody must have helped them," Rion said. "We thought the sentinels came upon mother by chance, but what would bring them so deep into the borderlands? And they knew exactly where to find her. Somebody told them."

"How did Marcus send word to the Empire about where to meet us?" I summoned the energy to ask, suddenly sitting upright. He was right. "We didn't know where we were going when we left the city. Matthias bid us go to York, but Devyn wanted us to go to Carlisle. We were never meant to be here in Conwy. How did they know to come here? To get the mistletoe? They were near done by the time we got there."

I had thought only of Marcus, but he must have had help.

Rion nodded grimly at this further evidence of a traitor in our midst. "Until we know who it is, we keep Gideon's new status as Griffin, and as the lady's husband, to ourselves. Are we agreed?"

I shrugged as Bronwyn and Gideon concurred with Rion's plan.

I barely knew who I was anymore. I had already been struggling under the recently bestowed titles that still felt alien to me, and had been further bowed by discovering I was soon to be a mother, and now I was adrift without Devyn. This last I was not ready to face at all.

Wife. It felt incomprehensible.

Chapter Three

"There must be retribution," Richard Mortimer argued for the thousandth time. I had heard him repeat this over and over during the last few days, while I drifted occasionally into and out of the room which seemed to serve as the headquarters of their war council. "We cannot let such an incursion go unanswered."

"They will think us weak." Lady Morwyn supported the steward's argument. Caernarfon was not a natural ally of Anglia, but on many such points they agreed.

"We are not prepared to go to war with Londinium," Rion countered. "If we attack them on their own territory they will cut us down with their guns."

"Then we take out one of the smaller cities," Lord Richard said. "Venta Belgarum or Dubris, somewhere in the Shadowlands."

"You would attack one of these minor walled cities and what then? Kill innocent men, women, and children to show your strength," Rion challenged.

"Aye," said Lord Richard shortly, sitting tall in his seat and baring his teeth. He had waited his entire life for an opportunity to take on the Imperial province.

"Blood for blood," Llewelyn agreed.

"When they killed the Lady of the Lake, we did nothing. We repaid their insult not at all because we were afraid, afraid that without the lady we would not be strong enough, that the city would come at us and keep coming. I have spent the last twenty years ensuring that the next time they crossed the line, we would be ready. And by the gods, I am ready," the steward announced.

"I agree that war is coming, but we are not ready." Rion levelled a look at the steward. "Yes, I know *you* are prepared for war, but Mercia is not. We have always had the lady. It has been so long since the treaty. We are further away than you, and maybe that has made us complacent. We will need time to make ready for war.

"Gwynedd has already begun to arm itself; the attack was on our coast. I have sent word to Powys, Dyfed, and Gwent. If you say we ride, then we will ride. If you say we wait then we will hold until you are ready." Llewelyn directed his solidarity towards Rion despite his stated preference for retribution but he was apparently unwilling to ally with York. "What they have taken will only tide them over for so long. We cannot let them raid our stores or those in the other kingdoms. We must defend ourselves."

Druid John spoke hesitantly. "If the legions return we are vulnerable on the coast."

"We can send a guard," Llewelyn offered.

"If we are over-run again, we are too few already," the druid replied. "As the ley lines die, magic in the blood runs thin. We have just suffered a devastating loss. We cannot move the oak groves to a safer place. But if you can guard them, we will move the community inland." The druid looked to Llewelyn. "We thought perhaps Dinas Emrys in the mountains. We will be close enough to travel to tend the harvest, but the community will be safer."

"It's a desolate spot," Llewelyn observed. "We will send men to help you build."

The druid bowed his head. "We thank you, my lord."

When the talk returned to defences and the border and building up garrisons, I stood up and left the room. What did any of it matter?

Llewelyn promised me daily that Rhodri would arrive soon. I thought no further ahead than that. I ate meals as directed by Marina and Oban, who would sit with me to see it was done. When I could slip out I stood on the walls of the castle watching the coast road in the damp drizzle, waiting for him to appear. Gideon hovered in the shadows, always there.

The time slipped slowly by, and when night fell, and I could bear my own company no longer, I would curl up in the corner of Llewelyn's war room. On one such evening, I found myself the topic of debate.

"The mistletoe is nothing," Fidelma dismissed. "It treats the symptoms. We must go after the root of the problem."

"And how do we do that?" Rion asked.

Fidelma looked towards me. "The illness is a result of the deteriorating ley lines; the corruption of the lines has grown considerably in the last twenty years. She must tend the lines."

"She barely has enough ability to do the most basic magic," Callum said. He had repeatedly offered to teach me. I knew I needed to be stronger. I placed a hand over the small bump of my belly. I had to be stronger.

"That won't matter. She was born for this; her bloodline is

our greatest defence against the death of the lines. She must do this," said Fidelma.

"No, we need her powers to be honed as a weapon," the steward insisted to the room. "War is coming, the Lady of the Lake has always been our main weapon in keeping the Empire in its place. She is little threat right now. She needs to learn how to use her power. We need her to be ready to fight."

"The lines come first. The Mallacht spreads through the land and we know what comes next. We've seen the damage that happens once the lines fail," Fidelma looked weary from the days of arguing.

They were speaking like I wasn't here. Perhaps I wasn't. But I wasn't not here either. "What are you talking about?"

Fidelma came over and took a seat beside me, cradling my hands gently in her own. "You need time to heal, but we need you. The land has suffered while the Lady of the Lake has been absent. There is a network of energy lines that run under the ground, crisscrossing the earth. "

"Yes, I know." Even in Londinium we had some awareness of the lines, if only because fluctuations in the energy could interfere with our technology.

Fidelma continued. "For centuries we have tended them – those with magic in their blood can sing to the line, so that it runs true. Where magic has died out, and technology has become the only tool tended by humans, the line grows polluted and the energy corrupts. We are so few now that the lines across the continent are failing, and as they fail the knock-on impact of the pollutants gradually infects the land."

"Enough of this. If the Empire comes in and wipes us out, there will be no one to tend the lines." The steward cut across her.

Fidelma cut him a pitiful glare. "If there are no lines, then there will be no land to fight over. Everything will wither and die."

A hand slammed into the wood of the window shutters, silencing the argument.

"Who are you to decide the actions of the Lady of the Lake?" Gideon snarled.

I felt all eyes turn to my dark corner. I had vowed to myself to grow strong in order to take on the Empire, to hone what abilities I had so that they could never hurt me or mine again. And now here I was sitting uselessly while they braced for war, debating whether I should fight or heal the energy lines that I only vaguely knew existed. The words that Marcus had thrown at me on the beach replayed in my mind. That I was selfish, that I thought only of myself and my own needs and wants, and took no care of the greater good. If what Fidelma said was true then the higher purpose was to tend the ley lines.

I was only one person though – what good was I? To either side.

"Callum's right. I don't know how to do anything; I haven't been trained."

"I will train you," Fidelma said. "Come with me to Glastonbury and I will show you how."

I hesitated.

"No," said Rion. "She comes north with me. My sister is returning home."

I looked at him numbly. Home. What home did I have without Devyn? Did it matter where I went? My hand went protectively to the tiny life inside me. It did matter. *She* mattered.

"I'll come North too," Callum spoke up gruffly, not looking in the direction of his liege lord. "I can teach you how to handle the elements. You won't be fit for much more than that till the little one comes. I can show you the basics of how to wield your power, how to fight until you're ready for Fidelma."

It appeared the little cat that had escaped the bag of secrets we kept had wandered a little further. Had Marina told him perhaps? She was the one whose perceptive observations had alerted me to the pregnancy in the first place. I had told her to tell no one, but I understood if she had said something to Callum after seeing the large professor hold me. She may have assumed he was someone I trusted. My marriage and the new Griffin so far remained secret. We wouldn't have been able to hide the baby for long anyway.

"She's pregnant?" Fidelma's eyes snagged on my wayward hand. "When are you expecting to have it?"

"May. June. I'm not sure." I answered into my lap, from the corner of my vision I could see Rhys place his hand on Llewelyn's arm. I turned further away, back to the high druid. I hadn't thought what this would mean to Llewelyn. Couldn't bear to look up and see happiness.

Fidelma glowered at Callum. "We can't wait so long."

Callum looked at her, aghast. "You cannot be serious. Tending the lines takes a toll."

"It won't be as hard on her; she is the lady. Her mother tended them all of her life, was born to it and she never..." She waved a hand to indicate her own aged skin and silver hair.

"The lady did not tend the lines while she was with child," Callum insisted. "The lines have waited this long, they can wait a little longer."

Fidelma's golden eyes glared but she had been defeated. Callum's suggestion gave everyone what they wanted. I would learn to fight and tend the lines and be safely tucked away as far from the Empire as possible. I was too numb to care. If

Callum taught me how to fight, then I would tend the ley lines if they wanted me to.

"It's settled then," Rion stated. "Marina's brother has asked to remain with Catriona; Oban will come too."

Fidelma smiled tightly, accepting the consensus in the room, as I hastily exited before anyone could make more plans for my future. It was settled. I would go to Carlisle. I recognised that Oban joining us was evidence of Rion trying to velvet coat his iron-fisted control of me, and I was grateful that I would have a familiar face with me.

———————

When Rhodri finally arrived, I found I could not face him. I retreated to my room to keep the world out. When I went outside, it would be to say goodbye. I wasn't ready. I would never be ready.

I heard Callum's rumbling voice. Footsteps came and went. Rion insisting. Bronwyn pleading. I lay unmoving, watching the rain slide down my window.

"My lady," came Rhodri's trembling voice.

I couldn't answer.

I wanted to. Nobody else in all the world would understand my pain like the man on the other side of the door. But I couldn't speak over the shards of glass in my throat. Couldn't push off the heavy blackness that pushed down on me. I had thought it would get better, thought I must be over the worst of it, had functioned and walked and talked over the last few days. But tightness whipped across my temples, grinding me down. My chest felt as if it would splinter open and spit the ruined pieces of my heart out on the floor.

"If my presence offends you, I can leave," Rhodri said

through the door. "Llewelyn did not think... I wished to speak with you but I will leave. You may have the ceremony in peace."

His words floated in to me as his footsteps began to move away from the door.

Rhodri, the disgraced Griffin, would have received no welcome from my brother or the steward of York. He thought that I too blamed him for decade-old events. I sat up in the bed, still dressed in my clothes from yesterday – had I slept in them? I wasn't even sure if I had slept. There had been darkness and I supposed I might have.

I pulled open the door and stepped into the hall. Rhodri's hunched form halted. He turned back to me.

My chin trembled as my mouth opened uselessly and I compressed my lips together to contain whatever noise might emerge from within. I lifted a hand to Rhodri, and he haltingly returned along the hall.

I had thought him a ruined man the first time I met him. He was a shadow of that man now, despite his recent recovery from the illness. Yet as he drew me to him, his frail body gave me strength, gave me comfort.

I pulled back, gulping in air, and I dragged the heels of my hands across my eyes.

"I'm sorry," I eventually managed, my shoulders throwing forward in the effort of pushing the words out.

He looked back at me astounded. His brows pulled together in confusion.

"He came home to you," I sobbed out. "And I lost him."

Rhodri's eyes filled with the same tears that blurred my own vision as he took my hands.

"No, child," he sounded horrified. "He found you. He

brought you home to us. Our little Catriona. He found you, he found you."

My new name on his lips felt right for the first time, a recognition of what Devyn had achieved.

A tremulous smile broke across his face. "He is still with us. I thought my son lost to me many years ago. But Devyn brought you home. He came home. And home is where he will stay."

His hand caressed the side of my face, warm brown eyes willing me to hear his truth.

"They are all waiting," he finally said gently.

I nodded, and he took my hand in his. Oban appeared from the recesses and threw a cloak about my shoulders as we walked through the main entrance and took the path down to the coast. We stood together as the druid spoke words that I didn't hear and people whose faces I couldn't see sang haunting songs in a language I didn't know until the ashes flew into the sky and the wind carried them away.

"You leave in the morning?" Rhodri asked when we returned to my room after all those who had attended went their separate ways. Devyn's life and death was too challenging to be celebrated together.

I shrugged. I was unaware of the arrangements.

"You're with child, Llewelyn tells me," he said softly.

"Devyn's," I confirmed, in case he I might be under the illusion that Marcus and I had been together as we had pretended at Dinas Brân. Llewelyn's eyes had followed me since the revelation and his hesitation in approaching had finally dawned on me, when I realised the Steward watched me too. The baby's parentage was only obvious to those who knew better, others might be less certain.

"My son left us a child." His hand trembled as he covered

his mouth, his face sharp with fear and concern. "I must speak with you though. There is a curse…"

"We know." I interpreted his fear, his belief that I would not live long enough to birth my child.

His head bobbed tremulously. "You're young, maybe it won't come to be. Perhaps it is a legend only, we can't be sure. But I think there may be another. I don't know how but we must find him, your life may depend on it."

I looked up at him clear-eyed, reaching out and taking his hand this time to comfort the fear I saw there. Fear for me. Fear for his grandchild. Rion and his orders be damned.

"There is a new Griffin."

"Truly? How?" he asked, his eyes lighting up in hope, his newfound health apparent for the first time.

"Devyn knew he was dying and he insisted. There was some kind of transfer of the spirit of the Griffin, I don't really understand it."

His face broke into a smile as the sun through storm clouds. "Then, you will live."

He buried his head in his hands as if the weight had become too much for him. I placed a hand on his shoulder as it shook under the impact of the emotional onslaught – grief, hope, fear, relief.

"My child will live." I underlined again for him. "I will live because Devyn ensured we would. Even as he lay dying, he thought only of us."

"Who?" he asked, raising his ravaged face. "Rion?"

"Gideon."

"The York pup," he growled before his eyes warmed in rueful amusement. "Then I am to spend the rest of my days wishing Gideon Mortimer health and long life. Does his father know?"

I shook my head. "We have told no one. Rion thinks there is a traitor, someone who helped Marcus, who betrayed my mother. We don't want this news getting back to them. They didn't stop until my last protector was dead."

They had tried to kill Devyn before that morning in Anglesey – the poisoning. Marcus had denied being responsible; somebody must have given it to him in the city before we left. Or was the traitor someone we had met after we left the city? Someone we considered a friend – or worse, family?

If Devyn had never made it here, perhaps I would have gone back to the city with Marcus willingly. After everything, finding myself alone out here in the Wilds, without Devyn here to anchor me would I simply have let myself be pulled back to the life I had left?

"You knew?" My wayward thoughts backtracked to something Rhodri said. "You knew there was another. How?"

Rhodri's gaze was contemplative. "The morning your mother died, she received a vision before we set off for the stone circle she wished to reach. A warning. We had turned around; we knew we were in danger. She told me the oak had given her a warning, that without the Griffin you would be lost and when all was lost the Griffin would be found. She said she saw two Griffins in an entwined knot. We couldn't figure it out. There is only ever one Griffin, and there were no more males in my family, but she said if we kept Devyn safe then the other side of the knot would work itself out. As I told you before, she made me vow to keep him safe. She must have known that he would find you. He fulfilled his destiny… and now he is gone. But there is a second."

"She knew you were in danger?"

"Aye, I've gone over it in my mind a thousand times. If she

hadn't bound my vow that morning, if she hadn't acted so quickly, would it have turned out differently?"

"How do you mean?" I asked as he stood jerkily.

"When she came off her horse, I couldn't go back for her. If she hadn't bound it I would have gone back, for her, for you. We would all have been killed, but she had bound me to ensure his safety." He sighed. "Devyn never forgave me for what happened that day. I never got a chance to explain."

"I told him," I confessed. "He did forgive you. He understood."

"He did?"

I gave him a small nod. His whole body seemed to relax. That vow that he had kept hidden from the world, was known to the person to whom it needed to be known. Not an excuse. But the truth.

"I was drugged."

"What?"

"They think I didn't have enough magic to do anything. But I do. I do. I could have done something. But I couldn't. I couldn't reach it. Marcus gave me a drug, a suppressant. I couldn't do anything." The words tumbled over each other. Each word a shard set free. "I'm sorry. I couldn't do anything."

A hand came up and lifted my chin.

"Then you know."

It wasn't his fault that he had ridden away. It wasn't mine that when Matthias shot Devyn I had been unable to do anything.

I nodded.

"There is nothing more to be said."

I exhaled as he pulled me into his chest, melted into his warmth. It wasn't an excuse. It was the truth.

"Catriona," he breathed out the syllables of my birth name.

"Here. When you were last in my arms you were barely more than a baby yourself. I can scarcely believe this is real."

"I wish he were here to meet her."

Rhodri's eyes watered, and his voice wavered as he responded. "I am heart glad at this news. I shouldn't be. It was reckless of you both to be together; he should have known better."

"He did."

Rhodri raised a scandalised brow that reminded me the evidence would suggest otherwise.

"I mean, he didn't know," I said, flustered, my cheeks heating. "That is, he didn't know I was Catriona Deverell."

"Then how did you figure it out?"

The heat flared on my distressed cheeks. "Erm, after, y'know… We… uh… The bond clicked in. He was horrified."

Rhodri's face broke in the smile of a younger man as the event I couldn't put words to dawned on him and chuckled. "Was he then?"

"Absolutely. I didn't know what was going on. Suddenly I could…" I realised he was the one person who might be able to explain the Griffin bond. "Did you and my mother… could you feel her emotions?"

He sobered, his expression melancholy once more. "No. It's a known part of the lore, and you and Devyn already showed signs of it when you were a baby, but for most of us, we only sense when the lady is in distress, in danger. I only sensed it once."

A servant came in bearing a meal with Bronwyn following close behind her. She looked at us both assessingly and seemed pleased with how she found us.

"I'm not leaving until you eat – both of you," she announced, flipping her wild black hair behind her and throwing herself into a seat by the fire. "Now that you are well again, uncle, you need to get your strength back."

When Llewelyn came by to check on his brother, he found him regaling us with tales of Devyn as a child. It was a profoundly involved story regarding a neighbour's child, a boar, a holly bush, and a wooden sword. Llewelyn, who was familiar with the tale, soon joined in, adding pieces that had escaped Rhodri's memory but which were much relished details.

As the day sank into evening, the lights were lit, and more food arrived. I caught Bronwyn glance at the door and found that Rion hovered there, deeply engrossed in the story Callum was telling – a tale which included the mischievous young Prince of Mercia. His eyes flickered across the scene and met mine. My jaw hardened, I blinked, and he was gone.

Having delayed our departure for the funeral, Rion insisted on returning to Mercia the next morning. I said goodbye to Rhodri after breakfast in the great hall. Bronwyn promised that they would see me after the baby came, with a pointed look at Rhodri that if he had planned to fade away now that Devyn was gone, he had a new reason to live.

I entered my room to check that none of my few belongings remained and discovered that my shadow had returned, having been absent while Rhodri was around. Gideon stood leaning against the wall looking out the window.

"What are you doing here?" I asked coldly.

He turned and levelled a gaze at me.

"I wanted to check on you," he offered carefully. He had

hovered at a discreet distance over the last week, never engaging me directly.

"This is my room. You need to leave." I needed to be alone, needed time to prepare myself to leave the one familiar place I had here beyond the walls. to take the journey to the home to which Devyn had promised to deliver me.

"Leave," I repeated.

He took a step towards me. I put a hand up to fend him off.

"Don't touch me," I said.

He stepped back as if slapped.

"I wasn't."

My lip curled. "You weren't what? Going to try and touch a woman in love with another man against her will, another man whose body is barely cold?"

My words were cruel… and, I knew, untrue.

His face greyed, his head going back as if struck by a blow. "That's not what I was… that's not what happened between us."

"Isn't it? You think because we are married that you can step into Devyn's place. That you are the Griffin and the man I love. You are neither of those things. I can't feel you, I can't sense you the way I could sense him."

The thought terrified me. I couldn't bear the idea that he and I would share that bond. That I would have another connection like that.

"I'm not trying to step into Devyn's place, but we are about to leave for Carlisle. I only wanted to ensure that you have everything you need."

Rion had sent him then. Rion, who also only approached me in public. I had a vague feeling that I had said terrible things to him. He had earned them.

"No, I do not have everything I need," I said, making plain

53

that what I needed was not in his gift to give me. My face was hard, my tone hard too, as if I were encased in granite. I couldn't bear it.

But I had to move on. I had to leave here. I had to move on without him.

With Gideon at my side.

I was tied to him twice over, I realised. This stranger. I had let him touch me, had touched him in return.

"Griffin," I snorted. "You will never be him. You have the title but you are not the Griffin. We don't know that anything happened. You aren't him. We married to release the handfast, and that it is all. Stay away from me. The thought of your touch makes my skin crawl. I don't love you. I don't even like you."

Gideon stood unmoving, unblinking. I couldn't stop the words. I flung them like daggers across the room, each one laced with its own poison... as we had once thought he had done to Devyn.

"Get out," I repeated. "The sight of you just reminds me of what you aren't and will never be."

Gideon bowed his head. "My lady."

And then he was gone. I felt hollow, empty. Like the room I stood in.

Chapter Four

"You found it then?" Callum spoke from the doorway.

I turned away from the cradle I had just uncovered, in a room that had sat empty for twenty years. They must have sealed it off after Devyn fought to save it for my return. There was a broken stool in a corner, a casualty of the day a boy had fought off grown men in defence of an empty room.

And here I was.

Sort of.

I had drifted around the castle since we arrived in Carlisle. The servants watched me with the same awe and wonder as in Conwy. They so wanted to welcome me, to celebrate, but I was a ghost. I saw them, but it was as if they were on the other side of the glass as I passed by.

I hadn't asked anyone for help in finding the room. I had time after all, nothing but time.

I lifted my eyes to look at Callum. He had come north with us, leaving his life in Oxford to help me, and I wanted to train, I genuinely did, but I was tired. I sat in the rocking chair by the cradle and let its soft rhythm take me. I put a hand over my stomach, which had just started to show signs to all that there was a new life beginning within. I felt close to Devyn here, close to her – our daughter. For the first time since before Devyn died, I slept without nightmares.

They tried to make me move to the suite of rooms that had been prepared for me, the traditional suite reserved for the Lady of the Lake. But I felt comfortable in the old nursery at the edge of the Queen's rooms, so people bustled about and furniture arrived to make it fit for an adult. It didn't really matter. I mostly slept, and when I woke, I wandered around the grounds, uninterested in venturing further.

Beyond the castle gates lay Carlisle. The town had come out to meet us on our arrival, raising an overwhelming cacophony of sound, cheering and crying at the return of their lady. I had no desire to be on the receiving end of more of that; it was simpler to stay here. There was a garden and my room. Sometimes Rion came, but I couldn't summon conversation. What was there to talk about? I didn't know him and he didn't know me. When he had the chance to get to know me, he had been too busy trying to move me about on his chessboard. Now he had no power to move me. I was the most inert piece on the board.

Oban and Callum would sit with me for hours as I watched from my window. Oban would tell me of all he saw and heard as he found his place here, the way magic was used for things which were solved by technology at home – food preservation, light and heat, cooking even. Callum shared his knowledge of magic and the history of my new home, whether I listened or not.

As the snows started to clear, the sight of the first snowdrops appearing under one of the trees tempted me outside. So delicate, the green shoots surfacing through the frost-hardened ground, I felt my spirit soar. It lingered over the belled flowers, seeping into the roots below. The next day, when we returned to the gardens, I actually laughed in delight at the carpet of little white flowers that had appeared overnight. But the beautiful sight attracted whispering servants, so I didn't go there again.

There was a balcony from my room, which looked out over forests and sparkling lakes. The dark winter of the forest gradually lifted until one day I came out and it looked as if a magic wand had been waved over the spread laid before me, turning the world green. Vivid, vibrant green as the countryside burst into spring.

When Callum could lure me out to the gardens, he tried to get me to connect to the energy around me. But while I could sense it, I felt distant, never seeming to connect the way I remembered from before.

By March my pregnancy was visible to all as Callum persuaded me into an outing beyond the city. The countryside was expansive and lush, utterly different from the bare, craggy, wooded winter of Cymru. The browns of melting winter were replaced by the verdant greens and soft pastels of spring.

The journey meandered south under open skies and rolling hills along the River Eden that flowed serenely beside us, grass that grew greener than I had ever known possible under our horses' hooves. The great blue of the open sky was visible for miles and miles until we came to a place that felt as though it was the centre, a valley near Penrith that pulsed with an energy that called to me, at the centre of which was a circle of standing stones.

There were maybe seventy stones in all, including a tall red one that the high druid of the community there told us was called Long Meg after a Lady of the Lake who had lived centuries earlier. Her daughters formed a circle round her, some of the stones a reddish colour like Long Meg, others a blue-grey, while others still Callum identified as milky quartz.

"Oh," I said as I laid my hand on a medium-sized quartz stone and felt something vibrate through me. "That's amazing."

"No, no, no," Callum fussed, snatching my hand off the stone. "Don't touch anything. Maybe I shouldn't have brought you at all."

After checking no harm was done and once we were at a safe distance his curiosity got the better of him. "What did you feel?"

"I'm not sure… It was like a hum." A hum wasn't quite the right way to describe it though. A noise perhaps, or a sensation… both maybe. "Maybe an energy – not like what I pull from the earth, more like… it's charged."

He nodded. "That's the ley line. Some call it a songline, them what can hear the music of it. Others call it a spirit line. I'm told some feel different to others."

"Fidelma kept talking about them failing. But if I can feel it, it can't be that damaged?"

"This is the spring equinox. The stones here"—he pointed out some at each end of the circle—"are aligned to tune it to the ley, the community tends the line year-round now, but once it only needed tending at the solstice and the equinox."

"Solstice is the longest or shortest day of the year." That one I knew. "What is an equinox?"

"The spring equinox is one of two points at which the ecliptic intersects the celestial equator. The ecliptic is the sun's annual pathway. In spring the sun crosses the pathway going northward, then at the autumn equinox it crosses it going southward," Callum explained

I had no idea what any of that meant. I recognised the word 'equinox' – it was Latin in origin and meant balance. But after that, the words he had just put together failed to make sense to me.

Callum sighed as he took in my expression. Taking an apple out of his pocket he placed it on his palm and lifted it in front of my nose. "If your face is the sun and the earth was this apple, then the stem is the north pole. Right now, at the spring equinox, it is sitting exactly upright, so one half of the apple is in light and the other half dark for exactly the same amount of time," he said. "The rest of the year it is tilted and unbalanced, producing days of either shorter or longer duration, but today the light and the darkness are in balance with light on the rise."

"Okay, so the equinox is the most important day of the year for the ley lines."

Callum's bushy brows pulled up. "Well no. It is important, but it is the solstice really that is critical." He tilted the apple to its side. "The summer solstice is the day on which we have the most daylight, but it's also where the change happens, and we start to move back towards winter. At the turning of the tide, the leys are at their most vulnerable as good energies and corrupt ones ebb and flow into each other. If they are not directed carefully, the corrupt tide doesn't wash out but merges and comes back on the new tide."

"Right, I think I understand." At least, bits of it.

"It will all become much clearer once you get stuck in. There is a lot of theory and astronomic science to the leys which you may not need. Just think of them as underground rivers that circle the earth. At certain points of the year, the flow turns around, and at other times of year the river is at its fullest or lowest and this is when we can help clean them the most."

That I could follow. "And what is it now?"

"The river that runs beneath us here is at its lowest after the winter. The tides turn at the solstices."

"And those ceremonies take place here?"

"They are rites, and yes, they all take place here, but when Fidelma comes we will take you to the stone circle near Keswick. Its alignment is set up for the summer and winter solstices and it's one of the largest stone circles in the land, allowing you to focus your abilities better."

The rite took place in the late afternoon, and from the safe distance Callum insisted on, seemed largely uneventful. Druids came out, walked up and down, poured water at various points, which Callum informed me was largely ceremonial, and then three druids sat in the circle for a very long time while they tended the line.

The energy was a soft hum which floated around me. At Callum's direction I did my best not to engage with it, but it had the qualities of a trickling babbling brook and the temptation to let my fingers fall into it and watch the dance of water flow around them was almost unbearable. I could practically feel the sensation it would have. But I did as directed; there would be time for this after the baby came.

She came just before midsummer. The castle had already spent weeks preparing for the festival, boughs of greenery and flowers bedecking the walls and surfaces. The midwives clucked around worriedly, but it was a fast labour, as if she too was in a hurry to celebrate the longest day of the year.

My little flower – I felt like those first days were just us floating in a floral cocoon, the bright blooms that filled our room bringing the summer to her, the blue skies outside shining through the open balcony.

I still felt a little far away from everything, but one of the midwives assured me that that was only natural, especially in light of my loss. I looked down into our daughter's dark eyes, tracing her features with my fingertips over and over. She was so beautiful.

"Cat," a low rumble came from the door. Gideon stood there, taking up most of the frame. He looked freshly shaven and his dark hair was tethered back. He wore a soft white shirt and he was awkwardly wielding a bunch of meadow flowers. I hadn't seen him since our arrival here – he had done as I asked and stayed entirely out of sight. I had begun to wonder if maybe he had left Carlisle.

"I'd like to… meet her," he started tentatively, cautious in his choice of words. "If that's okay with you."

I looked down at the precious lace-clad bundle in my arms and felt such a flash of love that I couldn't find it in me to deny him access. She was a gift. How could I say no?

Gideon walked across the room, coming to a stop too far away from the end of the bed to see any more than he had been able to from the door.

I reached a hand out to him and beckoned him closer, my lips tugging up at the sight of the ordinarily cavalier Gideon so tightly wound. His face was carefully blank, his posture stiff. He expected rejection, was braced for it. This was my fault, I knew. I pushed at the fog from the last time I had seen him. What had I said to him? I didn't care to recall.

But he was responsible for having kept this bundle alive, in those terrible moments after... He had kept her alive against all the odds. He had saved her. His eyes flicked to the tattoo I had done on my left arm, the curve of the Tamesis, spinning out at the end into a triquetra design. He took my hand as I continued to hold it out to him, and I tugged him down to meet her.

"This is Féile."

He perched on the edge of the bed and his frame curled in closer to see her. His free hand lifted to touch her, but he halted, his eyes slanting to mine to check for permission. I nodded – at that moment I felt dizzily in love with this new person who had entered our lives.

His large hand traced her face gently, moving down to marvel at her tiny perfect little toes, with their clear miniature toenails, her rosy heels, and little rounded legs.

"Would you like to hold her?"

His gaze snapped up, his eyes wide with surprise, and a boyish smile spread across his face. It felt important that he have this moment with her. He took the bundle awkwardly as I showed him how to support her neck with his large hands. He soon had her cradled to his chest as if he had been born to it. He traced her ebony curls, no words needed to communicate his acknowledgement of her father, his entire body stilling as she stirred and grabbed his finger in her tiny starfish hands. I could see the joy in him as she opened her dark eyes and gazed up at him. The midwives assured me that she was too young to see anything much yet but from the sheer lovestruck expression of the large man locked in that stare with her, it would have been churlish to say so. And I wasn't entirely sure she didn't know exactly who she was seeing as we sat there admiring her.

Gideon eventually handed her back to me without another word and left the room, but he was back the next day and the one after that. I couldn't feel his emotions the way I had with Devyn, but there was a glow when he was in her presence that was unmistakably love.

I let her spend more time with him and as I recovered, Callum began to take me outside the castle, beyond the town with all its people, out into the hills and vast forests where I finally started to feel connected to earth, air, and water again. The longer I was in the woods drawing on its energy, the more I could really feel it again. Callum encouraged me to draw and release the energy – apparently this was the first step to wielding it. I had to be able to call it at will. It needed to become instinctive.

As the town prepared for the Lammas Fair in late summer, Fidelma came with Marina to train me in readiness for the autumn equinox in September. Oban was delighted to be reunited with his sister, even accompanying us out beyond the relative comfort of the city as we travelled across the fells and lakes to the circle near Keswick. It took only a few hours to ride there and we went the day before the fair.

All was green and blue, the sky an endless warmth illuminating the magnificent mountains that surrounded us as we joined the community of druids tending the lines at Keswick. In the middle of the Lakelands stood a circle of standing stones, fewer than at Penrith – more like thirty or forty – but the circle was wide and sat on a great plateau surrounded by mountains.

This time I was allowed to fully enter the stone circle and was drawn to one that stood just a little taller than me.

"Can you feel it?" Fidelma asked.

I placed my hand on the warm stone, which was speckled

with lichen and thrumming with energy; I could feel it, and it was a revelation. The babble of energy became a hum, a current of melody, but there was a slight dissonance, something not quite right. The flow should have been pure but it was tainted, slightly off key.

The pale-faced druids who lived there showed me how they tended and cared for the energies using the stones as they corresponded with certain lunar positions.

Today, the day before Lammas, Fidelma, Callum, and I sat in the middle of the circle and Fidelma talked me through what was required. Callum did not have the ability to sing to the line so Elsa, the high druid from the community who lived there, joined us to act as an anchor while Fidelma and I drifted down into the songline. It was glorious, the pulse of energy that flowed south. I was mesmerised by the beauty of it, crystalline and clear, and it welcomed me as it streamed by, clean and bright, its notes wondrous. Off notes and jarring pulses that felt wrong occasionally passed, but through Fidelma's instruction I found a melody, a cadence inside that I projected outward to harmonise and heal.

Eventually we surfaced, and the next day at the festival itself Fidelma had me join the circle as its anchor point, enabling me to experience the druids tending the line. I sensed them pluck and correct the flowing essence using lilting chords and mellifluous notes to calm the flow. Fidelma jerked and grabbed Druid Elsa when a strong undercurrent caught her, then brought about a calming resonance again.

When we surfaced, I felt drained, almost limp, as Elsa helped me stand and waited a moment while my legs steadied under me.

"What was that?"

"The corruption that flows from the decaying May line," Fidelma said, her lips pursed.

The May line was the ley that ran under a wide section of the borderlands. Though Callum had described the energy lines as rivers, some of the most important were more like channels, flowing in straight lines. The May line was one of the oldest and deepest, in the direction of the sunrise on May 8th. It was a spirit line that ran across the continent, through the borderlands to Glastonbury Tor, which Fidelma tended. The line that was tended here in the Lakelands was the Belinus line, which ran from the tip of Alba through to Vectis Island which Callum called the Isle of Wight.

"The Belinus line north of us is healthy, but now the pollution flows up from where it intersects the May line in the borderlands, and we must work hard to keep it well." Elsa's face testified to the immense strain that tending the line had been. "To have the Lady of the Lake back amongst us is a gift from the gods. I tended these lines with your mother – you have her gift and more. Even as a novice, you have helped more than the rest of us have done in years. You must be ready for Mabon. If you could participate in the autumn equinox, perhaps we can make a real difference."

After Fidelma and Marina departed to return to Glastonbury, I stayed some more days with Elsa learning techniques – both ones that she used herself and others she was unable to use but which she had seen my mother use; what she called singing to the line. When I departed, she gave me a gift of soap scented with summer flowers for my daughter.

As the summer ebbed, I visited again to learn more, in order to be ready for the equinox. I went regularly to Keswick, which was only a short ride from Carlisle. Time became irrelevant out there, the standing circle acting as a conduit that grounded the energies that pulsed laggardly through the land. Tending the lines filled me with a sense of belonging that was addictive in its pleasure and I showed a natural mastery. It felt as though I were a harpist from Llewelyn's halls, plucking notes, making it sing back to me. But on the more practical side, Callum despaired of my lack of progress in his lessons.

Callum and I still practised the skills of command over the elements, but it was tiresome. In contrast to singing to the leys, I did not enjoy the grinding frustration of my training, which never progressed no matter how hard I tried to control the magic my blood absorbed.

The leys, however, called to me. I could feel the land pulse with renewed health after our efforts, the glorious burst of colour that flared across the forests our reward.

For Mabon, the autumn equinox, we returned to Penrith. The currents were powerful, the taint deeper than I had ever experienced. The corruption in the line flowing up from the south was sluggish and murky and difficult to work with. I needed to go deeper, to sing harder to deal with it, and when we surfaced I felt a touch of the vertigo that had plagued me when I was younger.

My efforts at the equinox left me exhausted for weeks. A strange sensation similar to the disconnection I had felt in the months after Devyn's death started to grip me and refused to let go. I increasingly felt as if the world was leached of emotion, drained of colour. Callum asked me more often if I was well, encouraging me to take a break, teaching me to meditate, encouraging me to spend time with Féile. But staying away from the stone circles made it harder when I returned, and made the burden even heavier on the druids.

At night when I rested the same dream came to me again and again. I was sitting in a boat that was tethered to a pier in a lake. Reaching over the side, I could touch the water, but the water felt better, purer, away from the dock. The more corruption that flowed through the Belinus line, the more I allowed the boat to drift away, deeper into the songline. I knew there was a reason that the boat was tied to the pier, but the rope that held me frayed as I spent more and more time in the open elements floating free. I embraced the energy that the earth offered me, allowing the sun and sky to soak into me, fraying that tether more and more until one day I wondered if it just wouldn't be there anymore, and I would float deeper into the ley line, finding myself far from the lakeshore.

Occasionally I would look to the shore and check that it was still there. I could see the man caring for the baby, keeping her safe so I could do what I needed to do.

The wheel turned slowly to a harvest season that I was told was the best in many years. People who typically gave me wide berth now crossed intentionally into my path to bob and smile and thank me. Once the harvest was in, the townsfolk began to prepare for the Samhain festival. The oranges and golds of the countryside were reflected indoors as the decorations went up, and the halls of the castle were decked in a blaze of colour.

Bonfires were built across the countryside and candles were placed in windows to keep at bay the dangers brought by the night as the veil between this world and the next thinned. I could sense this weakening growing, and I reflected on how different I was from the girl who had arrived in Oxford only twelve months earlier.

Samhain also brought visitors: Bronwyn arrived, bringing her uncle with her. Bronwyn had written to me to give me advance warning that she would bring Rhodri at the time when Britons remembered their dead, not wanting him to be alone. She had asked for my support and to say nothing to Rion. I barely saw him, so this was achieved with no great difficulty.

They were met by Rion at the gateway to the castle, which I was alerted to by a breathless Oban. When I arrived in the courtyard, Bronwyn and Rion were in a standoff while Rhodri remained in the carriage, permission to lay foot on Mercian soil having been denied.

"Cass," Bronwyn greeted me with some relief. "Please inform your brother that we are welcome in your home, if not his."

I raised a brow. "Rion, you will not welcome Rhodri into your house?"

"He was banished for life. He is not welcome here," he replied stiffly.

Of course, Rhodri was the Griffin who had saved his son over our mother, the mother he had been gods-bound to protect. That was why Bronwyn had asked me to say nothing.

"He is my uncle," Bronwyn flashed back angrily.

"I'm aware," Rion replied in the calm, composed manner he had when his own emotions were heightened.

"He has a right to—"

"He has no rights," Rion said coolly.

He had come all this way though. I was already growing tired from the fuss Rion was making and was struggling to summon up the argument Bronwyn clearly expected of me.

Aid came from an unexpected corner, as Gideon strode into the courtyard, still armoured from training, his muscled arms glistening with sweat despite the slight chill of encroaching evening.

On his hip he carried a well-wrapped bundle and without so much as glancing Rion's way for anything approaching permission, he opened the carriage door. He spoke to the man within before handing the baby into the waiting arms.

Turning on his heel, he strode from the courtyard.

Chapter Five

B ronwyn's expression communicated carefully subdued triumph as she turned back to face Rion once more.

"You leave after the festival," he said, then he too left, taking a different direction to Gideon.

Greeting Rhodri as he carefully exited the carriage with his granddaughter I found him to be a good deal more robust than the last time I had seen him – though it looked like he would never regain the full health he would have had before the illness.

I was due at Keswick and left while they were shown to their rooms, returning some days later when obliged to for the feast. Callum and I were late, and we saw that bonfires were lighting the countryside as we made our way back for the main festivities at the castle.

I changed quickly out of the practical clothes I wore – boots and tweed trousers, with a woollen wrap tied with a Celtic brooch. They suited my life better than the fancy clothes that Rion had provided. Oban helped me into whatever he deemed appropriate, clucking over the dark circles under my eyes and dabbing colour on my cheeks. I discovered that the meal had already begun when I arrived, though thankfully I was not the last as some seats at the head table remained empty. I chose an empty place between Bronwyn and Rhodri, who looked up in surprise.

"My lady," he said, his head bowing deeply.

"My lord Rhodri," I nodded back. His gaze rested on my plate then looked at the empty seat past Gideon on his other side. "Perhaps it is right."

"What is right?" I asked as I ladled some of the steaming rich stew onto my plate.

"That his seat be by the York pup," Rhodri explained, or at least I suppose he thought he did. I knew well enough that the York pup referred to Gideon. Rhodri had never hidden his disdain for Gideon's parentage.

"Whose seat?" I asked, bewildered.

"We lay extra seats tonight," Bronwyn said softly in my ear as Rhodri resumed his meal. "For the dead."

I looked about the hall, noting that a large number of extra places had been set.

The same was true of our own table. Two seats of honour beside Rion – for my mother and father, and on the other side another place waited for me I realised belatedly. And I had sat here beside Rhodri, relegating Devyn to the other side of Gideon. I blanched at my error. I had unknowingly put Devyn in a seat lower at the table than Gideon.

The tall warrior on the other side of Rhodri was rigid, not acknowledging his awareness of the conversation beside him but not unaware either. He started to push his chair back, and the trembling hand of the older man came down, preventing him from switching seats.

71

"It is right," Rhodri repeated to the new Griffin. "You are not in his place."

Even my eyes were drawn to Gideon at that, as Rhodri had unknowingly rescinded the words I had thrown at him in my grief. Gideon's face didn't change, but the tension in him seemed to ease.

I felt dizzy, remote, struggling with my fatigue as I endured the multiple courses until I could excuse myself from the noise and brightness. I let the evening drift by me.

"My bond was such that I could only sense when she was in danger, which happened but once in her life, and I could do nothing," Rhodri was saying. "Some Griffins had great strength, others were fast or clever. Each is different."

"How did they know they were the Griffin?" I heard Gideon ask. Apparently at some point during the meal – or over the last few days – they had found better terms.

"Most realise in their teenage years," Rhodri explained. "My uncle, Ian, didn't discover it until he was in his twenties, as the lady he served was much younger than him. He was a great archer, my uncle. In lean times he kept the household's larders stocked high with game. But the Griffin is always the best warrior in the land."

"I was already the best warrior," Gideon said, his voice not boastful, just a statement of fact.

"Your gifts will come, boy," Rhodri continued. "The gifts are particular to the need. You are called to serve your lady, and as her needs are so shall your gifts be."

"I don't feel any different," Gideon said lowly. "Perhaps it did not truly transfer. I am not a Glyndŵr – maybe there is no Griffin."

I felt lightheaded. I had been angry that Gideon had been made Griffin, as if he had stolen it from Devyn, but the thought that there was no Griffin, that the line had died with Devyn, sent a cold shiver through me.

"If the gift had not transferred, Cass's place setting would have remained empty tonight," Bronwyn said, her voice low but filled with gratitude. A place had been laid for me, I realised; at every feast in all the years they had thought me dead, they had sat here with an empty chair for me even as I lived the life I had believed was mine as a citizen of the Roman Empire. I found some appetite and nibbled at a slice of the traditional Samhain apple cake in front of me, savouring the flavour.

"What were Devyn's gifts?" Rhodri asked, turning to me. He chose not to dwell on this moment, aware in a way that Gideon hadn't been that I had started to listen to their conversation. So often I felt too tired to partake in conversation and the endless chatter washed over me, but I smiled down at the empty seat beside Gideon. Devyn had never had the chance to tell his father this, I realised.

"He was able to appear other than himself," I said, recalling the insignificant boy who had sat in my classes. "When I first knew him you wouldn't give him a second glance; he was so unnoticeable that you would forget him as soon as he passed by."

"Devyn?" came Bronwyn's incredulous voice from the other side of me.

I smiled. "Oh yes, you knew him as he really was. Devyn Agrestis – as I knew him – looked like a strong gust of wind would knock him over. I started to see through it, realised he felt stronger, more muscular to the touch, than my sight relayed; there was something I couldn't quite figure out. When I took his tech, and he came after me, he was so intense, a force of nature. I couldn't understand how everyone didn't see him as I did. It drove me crazy. Sometimes he seemed like this weedy boy and then at others he was so much more." I laughed. "I thought I was losing my mind."

"A glamour?" Bronwyn asked.

I considered. Callum had explained glamours – something about using air to create an illusion.

"No, it was more than just looking different. He was muted – it was like he could turn himself almost invisible, like he could will people to overlook him. He could be in the middle of a crowded street, and people would step around him, but it was like they didn't even see him there."

"A useful gift for a Briton living in Londinium," Rhodri observed.

"Yes, I suppose so. He was also exceptionally gifted at technology, which didn't hurt either, allowing him to fund himself and to look for me in the records," I said, wracking my brain for other talents that could conceivably belong to the Griffin.

"Did you share the bond Rhodri was describing?" Bronwyn asked.

"For years, there was nothing. Devyn was pretty convinced that I couldn't be the girl he was looking for because he couldn't sense my emotions at all. We aren't sure why, but I was being given medication that suppressed my connection, so that could explain it. I had no magic at all during the years he watched over me."

"It is the one gift that is more or less standard amongst the Griffin's talents," Rhodri's tremulous voice agreed, a twinkle lighting in his eye as Bronwyn asked the inevitable question.

"How did he finally realise it was you, that you were actually the Lady of the Lake, the girl he was seeking?"

"I stopped taking the pills the city gave me to suppress my

abilities and one day it just happened." I quickly glossed over the how. "It was a shock. We could sense each other's every emotion. Our bond was so strong that it was even able to override the handfast cuff compulsion when we were together."

"What do you mean it just happened?" Bronwyn hooked on the one piece of information I had hoped would not draw further attention.

The heat came all the way up from my feet. By the time it reached my cheeks I must have been glowing like a beacon.

"Oh," Bronwyn said, figuring it out for herself and letting loose a whoop followed by a cackle of filthy laughter.

The sound of Gideon's chair scraping back was the only noise that broke across her laughter as she doubled over. I failed to meet Devyn's father's eyes as he patted my arm and I could hear him begin to wheezily chuckle too. When I finally managed to look up over my heated cheeks, Gideon was gone.

"Is he not adjusting well to being the Griffin?" Bronwyn asked as we watched him stride from the hall. I lifted my shoulders wearily. I had no idea, and had not given it any real thought.

"What news from Conwy? And Londinium?" I asked them, actually curious. Perhaps Callum was right in his constant nagging that I should eat better, socialise more; I felt somewhat restored after the long meal.

"Conwy readies itself for war. Representatives arrive for a war council that meets once a month. We share information, discuss the preparations," Rhodri said. I raised an eyebrow at this.

Rhodri glanced at Rion before lowering his voice. "Once they learned of the bound vow... I am not forgiven, but I am tolerated."

I nodded, giving him a small smile. I was glad for him. He had lived a half-life for decades.

"And from the Imperial Province? They have not attacked?"

"No," Bronwyn confirmed. "York has some word that there has been a change of leadership in Londinium. He reckons that once that has settled and the new governor has bedded in, then they will come."

"And we will be ready," Rion interjected from across the empty places where our parents should be.

As promised, Bronwyn and Rhodri left the next day. Absently I wondered at Bronwyn's departure as she said her goodbyes, recalling belatedly that she and Rion should have married long since, before Féile was born even. Had that not happened? Before I could ask, Devyn's father embraced me in farewell and the moment was gone.

"Will you come again?" I asked.

His lips twisted, his gaze going to Gideon who had brought Féile down to bid her grandfather farewell.

"I hope so. I should like to see the child grow."

"I'm glad you came to see her," I said, realising that I was glad. I should probably have made an effort to bring her down to Dinas Brân, or promise to do so again but there was so much to be done at the circles I wasn't sure I would be able to leave for the amount of time it would require to take her there and back. Perhaps Gideon could take her.

"My heart is full of her," he said. "In her Devyn lives on."

He cast an assessing look at the man who held her.

"The York pup cares for her," he said, "and for you. It does my heart good to see. When I meet with Devyn again, I will tell him you are well cared for. I will tell him that his last act, his choice in Griffin, was well done."

I cast my mind back. Had Devyn chosen Gideon? I had been half out of my mind. I recalled little of it. He was right though. Féile was well cared for by the dark warrior. As for how Gideon regarded me, if Rhodri saw something there that made him believe I was cared for then who was I to gainsay him.

"Yes, I suppose so."

Rhodri placed his hand on my arm. "So like your mother. I don't know how I missed it."

"Really?" I was surprised. I'd had the impression that Rion was the one who took after our mother.

"You have her determination, her stubbornness," he remarked. "You work hard on the lines – I think too hard. Do not give the land everything, or you will have nothing worth holding on for."

My eyebrows creased at his cryptic, typically Celtic advice.

"The ley line needs me," I reminded him.

"That's what your mother said." His eyes were haunted.

"That's why you went to the borders?" I asked. I had meant to ask before – the question had bothered me for some time – but I had almost forgotten to ask him now that he was here in front of me.

"Yes, she believed that the growing corruption came from a node in the ley that runs under Londinium, that if she could just resolve it…" He smiled sadly. "But we never made it that far."

"She was going to Londinium," I echoed in surprise. "But it was outside of renewal time – they would never have let her in."

"We had a pass; they knew we were coming."

"Then, why?" I saw again the sentinels coming for her. Riding her down.

"I have asked myself the same question more times than I have drawn breath since that day." His eyes were damp as they locked with mine. "Maybe they didn't want it healed, maybe the folk we dealt with were betrayed. Maybe you were their target all along."

"Cass, it's cold. You must let Rhodri go," Callum said gently from behind me. "Say goodbye."

Autumn faded and became winter, the hills and mountains reflecting the sun as the world I travelled in order to sing to the lines turned white with snow. Another feast, with ivy, holly, and berries this time. There was even a delivery of mistletoe that Rion cold stored, because the need in the country had declined.

Despite her position as High Druid at Glastonbury, Fidelma attended the winter solstice at Keswick, and after we had tended the line came back to Carlisle for the Yuletide festivities. She had helped, so I did not have to take the full brunt of the tide change myself. The winter solstice rite had been early in the morning, so there was plenty of time to attend the evening banquet, though as tired as I was I planned not to stay for the dancing, which could go on all night. Unlike a winter party in Londinium, there were no concerns here for transport across the city. Celtic celebrations, I had learned, were considered a failure if they ended before the sun rose.

Gideon followed me as I attempted to slip away after the

meal. I had seen more of him in the last few days than in previous weeks, obliged as I was to attend the festivities.

I occasionally saw him around the castle, always with the child. There she was now, in his arms, as he stepped in front of me.

I had long since moved out of the nursery and into my own rooms. Working with the ley lines was exhausting, and I needed my rest; there were many others all too willing to provide care for the next Lady of the Lake.

Gideon's face was carefully blank as he greeted me.

"I would like to speak with you, my lady," he said formally.

I drew in a deep breath. I knew what was coming, had felt his reproachful eyes following me in recent weeks.

"Do we have to do this now?" I asked, fatigue setting in.

"You are seldom here these days, and I would like to take the opportunity while you are."

He stepped to the side and opened a door that led to a small parlour where guests waited before meeting their king. I stepped through the door ahead of him, walking as far as the hearth before turning to face him.

He seemed to hesitate before starting to speak, choosing his words with care. "Cat, I've no wish to fight with you. I am aware you allow me access to your daughter when you do not care for my presence."

I gazed at him steadily, recalling the words I had flung at him in my anger and grief in Conwy. I shrugged – it seemed so far away now.

He seemed to struggle to find his next words before finally blurting. "Do you care for her?"

"Who?"

"Féile."

"Of course." I gave him a small smile to accompany my

words. Of course I did; I remembered the swell of emotion I had felt when she was born. The memory of it was still strong.

"When was the last time you touched her? Held her?" he asked, still in that same careful tone.

I thought back over the last days, weeks. I had been busy – in Keswick and before that at Penrith. I had little energy, and what I did have was needed to heal the land and hone my own skills. When I was here in Carlisle, I focussed on restoring that energy, on eating, sleeping, and studying.

"I may not be with her," I defended, "but I am doing this for her."

"I understand, but she is so young. She needs her mother."

"There are plenty of people to take care of her."

"They are not her mother," he said through gritted teeth, losing some of that studied calm.

"You are not her father," I flung at him. Who was he to say such things to me?

"Not husband. Not Griffin. Now, not father. That may be. But there is little evidence that you are her mother," he lashed back, his eyes dark with anger. They flashed to the door as it opened.

Fidelma entered with Rion following close behind.

"What is this?" Rion surveyed the scene, the pulse of Gideon's anger pervading the entire room, causing the child to stir in his arms. Rion gently transferred the bundle into his own arms with a quelling look when Gideon went to protest.

"Gideon tells me I need to be a better parent," I offered casually when no explanation was forthcoming from my accuser.

"The Lady of the Lake has a higher duty," Fidelma countered immediately.

Gideon levelled a dark, narrow-eyed gaze at the older woman who, I recalled, he did not like or trust.

"A child should have a mother," he said flatly.

"Not every mother has the luxury of being with her child as much as she would wish," Fidelma said. "Cassandra has the ability to heal the leys lines. You've seen for yourself the impact she has had on the land in just a few months."

"At what cost?" Gideon countered.

"Cost?" Fidelma's brows raised almost to her hairline. "The child is well cared for."

"What would you know of raising a child, druid?" he challenged.

"This is so much bigger than the needs of one small child," she dismissed, in a tone that nonetheless told of her sorrow for Féile. "It is vital that Cassandra trains and tends the songline. She is so late in starting and the lines are in dire need of her – you've seen the harvest, it's the best we've had in years. Not just here in Mercia, but in Anglia, Cymru, even Kernow. How many children are better off because of her actions?"

"The improvement has been incredible in the short time since the lady has returned," Rion concurred. "The lines are recovering, and once they are more stable, perhaps a better balance can be found. In the meantime, we are all here to help with Féile."

Gideon surveyed the room, his face carved in stone, stopping as he looked directly at me, questioning my silence.

"Don't you care at all?"

I felt a flicker go through me, a question, a longing, and with it a snag of pain, of the grief that had consumed me. Grief that had gripped me for a year, grief that had lifted, absorbed and washed away by the energy of the ley. I returned his stare with an indifference I couldn't and didn't want to overcome.

A pulse snagged in his jaw, and he strode from the room, pausing only to collect the sleeping child from her uncle's arms. He pivoted in the doorway, his glare landing first on me, then back on Fidelma, his jaw clenching before he turned on his heel and left.

Fidelma's hand rested lightly on my shoulder.

"You are doing the right thing," she said. "Once you have mastered your power, and the line is healthier, you will be better able to protect her. Then you will have time with her."

"Yes, I can be with her after," I said, then lifted my head in the direction of the music and laughter. "Shall we rejoin the party?"

Rion looked vaguely troubled but offered me his arm.

With another turn of the dial, the spring equinox passed, and the land bloomed again. Summer came and my daughter turned one. She was fine – Gideon watched over her, a protective giant as she tottered about on the grass, hovering, picking her up when gravity got the better of her.

The ley lines felt strong and healthy at the summer solstice when I travelled with Callum further south, crossing Anglia to visit Fidelma and Marina at Glastonbury Tor.

The solstice tide was different here, in the direct path of the corrupted May line. As the tide surged and turned, I felt the song change, the notes shifting almost imperceptibly but then more noticeably, and wisps of something other creeping into the line. It came from the south as the line reversed its flow, luring me from my boat to try and counter the dissonance coming in on the new tide. I could do more, clear more, if I went a little deeper, a little further into the depths. My boat took me further out and the rope in my hands frayed as we journeyed home.

Rion was furious when he learned how far south we had ventured. Glastonbury was far too close to the borders, but we weren't at war with Londinium, so it wasn't clear why he was fussing. Fidelma had looked well, and I had encouraged her to allow me to take on more of the burden that she had been carrying since my mother died. Now that I had become more adept, I could see how much more I could achieve before I became exhausted, and it made little sense for Fidelma to continue to overextend herself doing comparatively little. Marina's abilities were also impressive for a latent. Not only did she have command of earth and air, but her abilities to soothe and sing to the ley were astounding. She was increasingly picking up the primary duties at Glastonbury and encouraged me to return so she could show me Stonehenge on the borders, perhaps at the winter solstice.

By the autumn equinox, Callum felt I should take a break from the ley line and spend more time working on other skills. I still struggled to command the elements at his instruction. It seemed trivial compared to the ley lines, and I was more focused on keeping the song flowing through the land.

Another spectacular Samhain blazed by and I returned to Carlisle from Penrith too late to celebrate at the castle, for which Rion berated Callum on our return. If it had been up to me, I would have been happy to live at either one of the stone circles. I wanted to keep going – the line needed more and I needed to go deeper. In my dreams the tether was so thin now, my boat almost faded, the water's call irresistible.

I sat on the window seat of my rooms overlooking the bonfire blazing below. I rested my head against the cold stone walls. Occasionally, the little girl came into view amongst the crowd below – Gideon knew I was there, his movements stilted as he kept watch over the girl, holding the lead of her puppy.

His anger would be warm. I missed heat, I missed emotion.

The dark head finally turned to look up at me.

"Cassandra, you should be in bed."

"Yes, Oban," I returned softly, not wanting to break contact with the gaze that fired up at me from the courtyard. It was cold outside, but she was well protected against the elements. Her little hands were inside warm gloves, her sturdy shape bundled up in warm, rich clothes.

"You're freezing," Oban fussed, laying a wrap across my shoulders. I pulled it around me and looked back, but he was gone, and so was she.

"I think I need to take a day off tomorrow. I'm tired," I said as I moved back over to my bed, shrugging under the covers and curling up. Oban threw an extra blanket on the bed, muttering about how tired I was all the time. I wasn't here often now and it was a pleasure being back in a soft bed, under the heavy weight of the blankets. I recalled the first time I had stayed in a Briton bed in a freezing cold castle. Marcus had been there. I wondered where he was now. Had they curbed the Mallacht yet? I suppose they would have by now. He had killed Devyn to steal the treatment; I hoped it had been worth it. I should find out – maybe I would ask at dinner tomorrow.

I slept, and when I woke, I slept some more. Sometimes I woke to find Callum or Oban, and Rion came too. Breath came into my lungs but it took effort. Light hurt me and darkness was a blessed relief. I felt so tired, so weary, my bones and flesh ever less substantial. As everything else receded, my little boat somehow grew sturdier and the current stronger, as if it would take me away... not to the light of the depths, but away into the dark of the soft night.

That was okay. I had wanted to make them pay, I had planned to make it better, I had tried, but it was cold now.

"Cat." Gideon stood at the end of my bed, his tall frame outlined by the brightness of the fire behind. I smiled and lifted my hand. I hadn't felt anything in a while. I remembered the last time he had taken my hand. Féile, when Féile was a baby. He took my hand and sat gently at the end of the bed.

"Cat," he called again. "This is not how it ends. You need to get up."

He'd said that before.

Everything felt so far away.

I sucked in a breath; it came in jerkily.

"I'm cold."

Chapter Six

H is body warmed mine, heating it all the way through. His words called to me, coaxing me, berating me. I needed that. I needed his anger at me. It felt invigorating.

I dreamt. I dreamt in colour, music dancing through the boughs, my feet stepping lightly over the ground. Arms circled me, sweeping me around until I was giddy, laughing into almond-shaped dark black eyes, strong arms holding me close, the eyes warming in colour, becoming golden and sombre as they watched me.

I was awake. Gideon lay still on the pillow, his dark hair wild. His amber eyes were unwavering as they contemplated me. The tattoos that started just below his collarbone were a riotous swirling pattern, twists and spirals spreading across his skin. I recognised my brother's red rose and lake emblems and I reached out and traced the pattern. Devyn had had this one, too; he had placed it over his heart. Gideon had a different one there, the white roses and sword of Anglia, the different sigils entwined in a flurry of intricate Celtic interlacing. A newer tattoo sat above them, a butterfly. I traced it lightly.

"For Féile," he said softly. "In the language of the gaels, féileachan is a butterfly. She's like one, a summer baby; she brings colour, joy."

A wave of sorrow and longing flowed through me.

He caught my hand and held it still against his chest, the beat of his heart pulsed through my palm into me until I felt my own catch and answer his rhythm. Tears welled up and spilled over. The release was freeing, and I smiled tremulously at him. His brows drew together in bewilderment and I almost laughed out loud as Gideon's expression wavered between wariness and relief. Apparently I wasn't going to die. I felt stronger than I had in a long time. More in myself. Present.

I leaned across and pressed my lips softly to his. The room was gently warm from the still burning fire, I was aware that he had left me on occasion through the night to ensure the heat never dipped. I remembered him doing so, last night, and the night before maybe. My fingers curled up around the back of his head, holding him to me. The warmth of his kiss was intoxicating. Desire sparked to life within me. I was alive, alert, and I felt hope, joy. Me? Him? I wasn't sure, it was so long since I had experienced emotion. I felt like I had been on the other side of it, cut off, the world and people drifting by while I attended to tasks. My lips smiled into the kiss. I felt wonderful, strong.

I twisted so that I lay on top of him. I needed more, I needed touch. I pulled the soft silk gown over my head. Amber eyes looked up at me in consternation.

"Cat," his voice was a vibration in his chest. "What are you doing?"

I smiled in response.

"What does it look like I'm doing?" I bent to take his lips again. His response was still soft and gentle but I could feel his want, his need answer my own. The kiss became deeper, his tongue sweeping as he engaged. I teased him, pulling up, and he followed me, growling. He pushed up and rolled me under where I had no escape, no respite, as he kissed me deeper and deeper before he pulled away, and oxygen flushed in, lighting up my brain. I pulled him back down again, grinning, our teeth clicking as he responded in kind. He groaned again, and his broad hand splayed in the small of my back and pressed me to him. There was only the velvet whisper of skin against skin, my hands playing up along his sculpted arms, my head falling to the side as he kissed his way down my neck. Lower and lower, he was kissing and licking, nibbling as my skin came back to electric life…

I was a quivering mass of flesh. I was alive inside, fire and passion bursting out of me, his dark hair tickling as its fall followed his delicious, talented lips across my skin, stoking the fire, higher and higher.

He paused as his knee came between mine, dilated eyes meeting mine. He pulled me into him and then over until I was on top of him and his hands rested at his sides, his chest heaving, glistening in the flickering light, those saturnine eyelids heavy as he watched me. As he waited for me. The next move was mine; he would not lead. He had worshipped every inch of my skin, but this, this moment had to be me.

I bent down and took him in an open-mouthed kiss, manoeuvring until he was inside me and we were one. The rhythm built again, and we moved together until we splintered into dazzling pieces. I lay trembling across him, little skitters of electricity snapping and crackling through me.

I tumbled to the side, my head damp against the steady thump of his heart.

I fell asleep in his arms, but this sleep didn't feel like the end. It felt like the beginning.

I woke to find the room still in darkness, a dark figure stoking the fire.

"Gideon," I called softly.

The figure fell back on the wooden floorboards, dropping the poker with a clatter.

"No, lady," a familiar voice came across the room. "That is, it's Oban."

I smiled at Oban. I knew Oban. He looked like a little sparrow that was about to take flight, anxiously looking at me and the door, unsure what to do.

"Hello, Oban," I said.

He smiled nervously back, still half looking like he was about to jump for the door.

"Do you know where Gideon is?" I asked. Now I was the nervous one. Where was he? Why wasn't he here? He was angry at me. I had vague memories of him shouting at me, pleading with me to take more care of... It all felt so far away.

But last night felt very present. I stretched, the feeling of wellbeing flooding through me as I lengthened muscles and ligaments.

"Uh... he's at the ball," Oban answered, seeming to settle into being in the room, no longer looking like he needed to raise the alarm.

Wait... "What ball?"

"The Midwinter ball," he answered slowly like I was a halfwit. Which I actually felt like. Mid-winter? How could that be? It was November, wasn't it? How long had I been ill? What time was it? If I got up now, would I see her? Would Féile be with Gideon? I needed to see her. My heart felt like it was pumping again, rusty from disuse but working.

It was dark; had I slept through the day? No, if it was Yuletide I had slept through a couple of months.

"Can you bring me some warm water?" I sat up properly. Ah yes, no clothes. I pulled the sheet around my torso and swung my legs over the side of the bed. Here goes nothing. I stood and felt... steady. I took a couple of steps and, looking up, smiled broadly in response to Oban who looked like he was about to fall over as he took me in, his jaw practically on the floor.

He gulped and pointed to a jug that sat beside a large bowl and some cloths on a side table. Ready to give me my daily bed bath, I guessed. How embarrassing. Oban's cheeks flushed as he saw me realise his intended purpose.

"Um... I'll do this," I said. "Could you pull out something to wear?"

His mouth opened then closed as he turned to the wardrobe. I poured some water into the bowl and, bending my head, splashed some on my face. The liquid felt delicious in my fingers, soothing and cleansing, the cloth fine as I patted my face dry to find Oban returned and holding a brown cloth dress of some kind in front of me.

"Is there something more...?" I didn't want to offend Oban's once impeccable taste, but really, I couldn't go to a ball in that – I shouldn't even go gardening in that. Though that was what it looked like I had used it for, the hem still muddy. "I'd like to go to the ball."

"Go to the ball?" Oban looked even more shocked than he had been to discover me awake and then walking. I was going to end up damaging his health if I kept doling out the shocks this way.

"Yes, I... if that's where everyone is." I explained my motivation gently.

He nodded jerkily. "Yes, that is, everyone is at the ball. Well, almost everyone. I stayed with you. If you woke again we wanted someone to be with you. But it's Winter Solstice so they're all at the ball. You know what a big celebration it is," he clarified, his head shaking in wonder. "Not that I mind."

"Wouldn't you rather be downstairs dancing?"

"Cassandra, you're alive. I am dancing," he said, his broad grin finally meeting my eyes directly.

Oban looked down at the dress in his hand and then back at the wardrobe, his mouth pulling down as he turned back to me. "They're all like this."

"Oh." What to do? I could ask Oban to have Gideon come to me but suddenly I really wanted to see everyone. To be in the world. To dance. "Do I have any other dresses, in another part of the castle maybe?"

How odd. Had Oban really been dressing me in such clothes? Oban's lips were pursed, his tongue in his cheek huffily. "You threw them away."

I did? I had no memory of owning fancy dresses. No, wait, when I was pregnant, I had allowed Oban to dress me in finery, but afterwards it had seemed the height of foolishness while I trained with Callum and tended the lines to ruin the fine silks and satins. Rion had asked me why I didn't wear them, so I had gathered them up and let them flutter off the side of the castle, pretty coloured petals floating in the wind, carried away on the breeze.

"I'm so sorry, Oban, all your fine work. Is there someone else who might have something I could borrow?"

It was Yuletide – surely the castle was heaving with fancy ladies and their fancy dresses.

Oban cocked his head slightly to the side as he did a mental inventory of whoever was residing at the castle for Yuletide. I could practically see him check off the options, his eyes running up and down my figure as he thought of each possible candidate before he dismissed it. Running out of candidates, his brows drew together, and his mouth turned down before his eyes lit up. Then turned doubtful.

"There's no one. These Britons, they are all too big. You're small compared to most even back home, and the few who share your height, well, those ladies are a little... fuller," he finally said apologetically.

"There was someone that might do, though?" I asked. I had seen him think of a possibility.

His mouth opened, but he struggled to find words.

"The owner can't be that fearsome." I smiled encouragingly. Whoever it was I'm sure they could be prevailed upon to lend me something.

"It's not that," he said. "It's that, well, when we first came here, and you stayed up in the nursery, there were dresses here but I had them moved to the attics because they belonged to..."

My mother. These rooms had been hers. Tears sprang in my eyes, and I chewed on my lip as I struggled to contain the swell of emotion that came over me at the thought of wearing something my mother had worn. The woman I had never known, never mourned. By the time I had learned who she was and that she was dead, I'd had other things on my mind. Rion had told me a little about her when we met at Conwy but I had never asked for more information since we came here, to her home.

"They saved my mother's dresses?" I asked. At his nod, I ploughed on. "Do you know where they are kept? Could you bring me a couple?"

"Yes, they aren't locked up or anything. They were all kept by his majesty's father. Nobody ever touched them," he said. "I had them aired properly and put away in case you wanted to move into those rooms. They were in surprisingly good condition, perfect really. Perhaps there are one or two that would do, with a few small adjustments."

He was still muttering away to himself about the options as he headed out of the room. I cleaned myself as best I could with the basin of water. What I really felt like was a long bath, but it seemed I had already wasted enough time.

I waited impatiently for Oban to return. How long could it take to pull a few dresses out of storage? While I waited, I pulled my hair up into intricate braids, my fingers remembering how to accomplish the styles of which my mother, Camilla – my Roman mother – had been so fond.

I had nearly finished when Oban backed into the room laden with opulent gold and red and green gowns. There was even one in my favourite turquoise – had my mother favoured this colour as well, I wondered, or was it just one of many colours in her wardrobe? Oban had made me the most stunning gown of my life in that colour in Londinium.

I sighed.

It felt like everything I did tonight stirred a memory loose, tumbling through the spaces in my mind which had felt empty and void for so long.

"Were there many blue ones?" I asked him.

"Like this?" Oban knew precisely the one I meant, plucking it from the pile. "Not too many, lots of greens and a good many reds."

Her favourite colour had been green? I dropped the turquoise and pulled a deep forest-green satin from the bunch. It was off the shoulder and flowed like it was made of water, and it fit almost perfectly. Or at least it would after I put back on a few pounds – my bones were practically visible at the moment – but Oban fitted it with a few cleverly placed stitches.

"This would set it off perfectly." Oban, fully recovered now, seemed to have also raided my mother's jewellery, holding up a twisted golden torc.

Finally, I was ready. It was late though, too late for little girls.

"I'd like to see Féile first," I said, turning right to go to the nursery as we left my room.

"Uh," Oban hesitated, "she's not there."

"Where is she?"

"She's moved over to another part of the castle."

Oban said no more, and I was too ashamed at my ignorance of such a basic fact to ask why she had been moved. He led me up stairs and down corridors, the faint strains of music drifting along them until finally he came to a stop. I opened the door softly.

A woman sat reading a book under a low light at the foot of a bed. My daughter wasn't in a crib anymore.

As I stepped into the room, the woman stood up to send me briskly on my way but fell back as she recognised me. She dipped her head slightly as she backed up to her chair, her eyes going over my shoulder to Oban in the hallway. Whatever signal they exchanged seemed to reassure her, and she sat once more.

I made my way over to the side of the little bed, my legs giving from under me, and I found myself on my knees. Her little face was so close. So precious. My heart swelled.

Where had the time gone? She was a little girl almost. There were still traces of the baby I had held in my arms. I had missed so much. I felt like I could split into tiny sharp shards. Her eyelashes were dark half-circles resting on her dusky cheeks which were flush with sleep. A dark curl had fallen across her face and, unable to help myself, I reached down and brushed it back off her dew-soft skin.

I sucked in a breath. Tomorrow. I would see her tomorrow. My entire being felt tremulous and fluttery at the thought.

———————

The room fell silent as I stepped into the great hall. Dancers stopped as everyone turned to watch me enter the room. So much for slipping in unnoticed. I felt constrained by my dress, my heart fluttering against it.

Where was he? I saw Rion first. He was on the dancefloor, his partner stumbling over his feet as she caught sight of me. He turned and stilled as he took me in, his face whitening as he watched a woman in his mother's exquisite green gown enter the hall.

He looked like he had seen a ghost. Mine? My mother's? It wasn't clear.

A giggle formed and tumbled out – I couldn't help it – and when I looked back, the colour was returning to his face as he hurried over to me.

His usually composed face was decidedly discomposed, his expressions by turns disconcerted, hopeful, wary, and joyful.

"You really are well?" He engulfed me in a hug. "Gideon said... I couldn't believe... How is this possible? You nearly gave me a heart attack." His words tumbled over each other as he held me tight to him before pulling back to look at my face again to check I was entirely real.

Unsure what to say, I smiled crookedly back at him. We didn't really have a relationship, but I would be glad to find him alive too, I supposed.

I stepped out of his embrace, my eyes continuing to wander over the party. Where was he? He was usually easy to find in a crowd.

Movement in the far corner of the hushed ballroom alerted me to his location. He was still far away, watching me warily. My stomach sank. I had rushed down here like a fool; I didn't know what I was thinking, Gideon and I weren't... He and I didn't have any kind of... I just felt so amazing, and I had wanted to find him.

He drew in a deep breath and extended his hand to me. My breath caught, that gossamer thread spooled out across the dancefloor. Should I take it? Did I want to be pulled back in to shore? My daughter was there. I swallowed against the pain in my chest.

His hand hung in the air. The light in his eye dimmed. He was going to let it fall.

I took a step forward.

And another.

"How about that dance?" I stopped in front of him. "I promised you a dance once, did I not? In Conwy, before..."

I let the grief wash through me and float away as I stepped into the circle of his arms.

"So you did." He led me out onto the floor, and a tune began to trickle out from the musicians.

Guests smiled and laughed, and chatter rippled across the room as music played and we danced.

"How is this possible?" he asked.

"I'm not sure," I said honestly. I had no idea. I had been drifting away, but now I felt like I was firmly here for the first time in a long time.

"Last night," he began. I looked down, hiding my heated cheeks. "I need you to know… I didn't, I'm not the one…"

"Who started it?" I finished for him, my mouth open. Was he really making sure we were all crystal clear that I had initiated what had happened between us?

"Arse," I muttered, pulling away.

"Woah." He held on to my arm and swung me back to him. "Wait."

He pulled me closer and took a breath, twirling us back into the dancers. He was very good at this for such a large man, light-footed, with sure hands. My cheeks heated again at the memory of those talented hands. I tried to pull away again. This had been a mistake.

"Hold on. Let me try that again," he said in my ear. "Give me a minute."

We danced for a few more moments, and as we neared the open doors, he directed us through, and we were outside.

He pulled us swiftly across the snow and into the shadow of a tree, so that we were unobserved by the partygoers.

He looked down at me and shrugged off the jacket he wore over his dark tunic, leaving his tattooed arms bare as he covered my shoulders.

"I don't want to…" He paused before starting again. "I would like…"

"What?" I prompted.

He grimaced. "You've barely spoken to me in two years, you nearly die, we sleep together, and then you arrive at the ball and offer me a dance you promised two Yules ago. Give me a gods damned minute to figure out what to say without—"

"Without what."

"Without shouting."

"Shouting?" I echoed. "At me? You want to shout at me?"

He accused me of jumping him, and now he was angry at me.

I pushed him away.

"No shouting." I jabbed him in the chest. Ow. "No talking."

His lips were a thin line. He was furious, and Gideon wasn't really one to hold back his ire. But I felt alive, and pain-free, and I just wanted to hold onto it a little while longer. I took a breath.

"No. That wasn't fair." I bowed my head. He had been waiting a long time for me to hear what he had to say. I had abandoned my child into his care; he was livid on her behalf and he was entitled to express that.

He stepped closer and a finger tilted my chin up to look at him. Amber eyes searched mine, his breath a fog in the air before he groaned.

"No talking then," he agreed, and his lips came down, grinding into mine in a kiss that melted the last traces of cold that lingered deep within me. His kiss demanded... more of me. More life. More.

He tore himself away and stepped back. His chest expanded as he pulled in a deep breath, and another. Then he was gone, striding back into the festivities.

I followed, wrong-footed. I didn't know what to make of what had just happened. So many emotions swirled inside me. Pulling off his jacket as I stepped through the doors, I placed it on one of the tables and lifted a glass of wine to my lips with slightly shaky hands.

"Cass." I turned and was caught up in a fierce hug with someone closer to my own size though no less strong than the two previous embraces to which I had been subjected.

"You're not dying." Bronwyn's smile stretched all the way across her face, her dark eyes glittering. "Rion sent for me. He thought... they all thought... you were all but dead two nights ago and now look at you."

I shrugged helplessly; I had no explanation.

"Magic?" I offered weakly.

Bronwyn shook her head. "Not magic. They've had every druid, healer, and wisewoman from here to the tip of Africa in to see you. Nothing. No response. Then yesterday, Gideon comes out of there and says you woke up and you seem fine. Then you slept all day and all night, but you looked better, so much better."

Her eyes swept me from head to toe again. And she hugged me again.

"We thought we'd lost you."

"Me too."

"You knew how ill you were?" she asked.

"Yes. That is, no. Maybe." I shook my head. "It just feels like I slept for a long time."

Bronwyn eyed me strangely. "I was here at midsummer for Féile's birthday. You..."

"I what?"

"I don't know." She lifted her shoulder, her posture awkward. "You barely spoke to me or Rhodri. I thought that maybe you were angry with us."

"Angry at you? Why would I be angry at either of you?"

"I don't know, Cass." She shrugged. "You just seemed a bit distant."

"I'm sorry," I offered, though in truth I had little

recollection of their visit. I put my arm through hers as we swung out to face the party. "Let me make it up to you."

We danced and laughed. I went from group to group, everyone delighted at my recovery. Many of them I had no great memory of, though they seemed to know me. I was a very different version of me, each individual wary in their own way, stunned at the change in me. Gideon's gaze followed me all night, but he didn't come near me again.

Finally, I pulled off my shoes and made my way up the stairs, the cold flagstones a blessing to my tired feet. I paused when I got to the top of the first flight of stairs. The old nursery was to the left, my daughter's rooms to the right. Maybe I could sneak another peek of her.

I trod softly up the hall and across to her new room in the west wing. I pushed gently at the door, taking care to turn the handle all the way so it would create no noise to disturb her.

Before I could step inside, a manacle clasped my upper arm and pulled me back into a familiar granite body. He leaned down and whispered in my ear, his breath brushing the sensitive skin on my neck.

"Where do you think you're going?"

"I just wanted…" A hand snaked across the front of my dress and pressed me back against him. Oh.

"I wanted…" My voice was a little more breathless as I began again.

"Tsk, tsk," he walked us back to the other side of the hall and into the room opposite. His room.

His hand traced lightly up my arm and across the exposed skin before turning me around to face him.

"No talking," he whispered against my lips.

And there wasn't. Nothing decipherable, at least.

Chapter Seven

I woke the next morning to that same sense of wellbeing. The sheets felt incredible on my skin, the room was cold but it wasn't my room, nor my bed. I was in Gideon's bed, but yet again, he wasn't.

I lifted my head off the pillow and scanned the dark-wooded room. Gideon sat in the deep window, his heavy-lidded gaze entirely focussed on me. I reached out to try and get a feel of his emotions. If he was the Griffin, why couldn't I sense him? His face was set impassively as he failed to acknowledge that I was awake. Not a terribly good sign. For the second day in a row, I pulled the sheet off the bed, wrapping it around me before stepping out of bed.

I padded softly over to him.

"Hi." I felt absurdly shy and deeply unsure of myself. We had shared another night together, but last night had been different from the first night. Where our lovemaking had been tender when I woke from my illness, last night had been intense and mind-blowing. My cheeks heated when he didn't speak.

I reached out a hand and traced it across his collarbone, to his shoulder, my eyes caught and held by his swirling tattoos. My fingers traced down his wide upper arm. He adjusted, shrugging my touch away.

His eyes were closed off, devoid of all feeling. I stepped back from him.

"What do you want?" he asked flatly.

Our timeout was over, it seemed.

I shook my head, shrugging. I didn't know what I wanted... I wanted my life back. I felt as if I had been sleepwalking for the last two years. Now I felt compelled to live, to be alive, and I wanted to feel that way with him.

"I just want—"

"What?" he cut me off, his posture stiff as if he was holding himself back.

"I'd like to see Féile."

"If that's what you wanted, why didn't you say so? You didn't have to jump into my bed to see your child," he sneered. "No upfront payment required."

"I-I..." I flinched at his attack. "That's not what I was..."

"If that's not what it was, what were you doing? You've made it more than clear how you feel about me – as I recall, you said my touch makes your skin crawl. So I don't know what this has all been about. What game are you playing?" His jaw was locked as he waited for my response.

My chest tightened. I knew I had said terrible things to him, but I had been grieving. I didn't feel that way about him. In my giddy joy at being alive, he had been the one I'd wanted to share it with. He was magnetic and intense, and I had wanted to be in his arms.

He crossed them now, his eyes going flat as I failed to come up with a response. I took a breath.

"I want to see my daughter," I whispered to the floorboards at my feet.

"Féile," he said. "Her name is Féile."

"I know that," I snapped back. Of course I knew my daughter's name.

He clapped slowly.

"Well done, Cat," he said caustically. "What else do you know about her?"

I swallowed despite the dryness of my mouth. I searched my memories and came up with dismally few. Images of her in the distance, playing while Gideon watched, him carrying her about the place, his great strides taking her from place to place when her little legs tired. The two of them in the garden. An occasional closer encounter at a meal, though I usually ate in my room when I was in residence, where I saw them sometimes in the garden below.

"She has a puppy," I recalled desperately. There had been a little brown and gold pup in the garden with her over the summer.

Both brows shot up at this. It was weak, I knew that. I didn't know who had given her the puppy or when, or what its name was. What was the point in pretending? He knew exactly how little time I had spent with her since she was a baby. I couldn't understand... How had I done that? How had I just abandoned her? I felt nauseated, heat prickling my skin, my hands sticky.

"Please," I began through the lump in my throat. "I know I've been... I just want to... to... I want to make it up to her."

I heard him exhale. "What's changed? Why now?"

I couldn't explain why now. All I knew was that I had woken up yesterday and I had felt like me again. Restored.

Back to who I was before my world had been ripped apart. But that wasn't going to be good enough for Gideon.

"I don't know." I lifted a hand to him but it fluttered uselessly between us. I wanted to touch him, to connect, I wanted him to know how terrible I felt, how much I wanted to be better. But we didn't share that kind of connection and I let it fall to my side.

He snorted and pushed away from the window, stepping forward to loom over me, his lip curling in disgust. I disgusted him. I disgusted myself.

I took a couple of steps back and hit the poster of the bed. I braced myself.

"I… what can I do? Please, I'll do anything," I said. There had to be some way to prove to him that I could do better, be better.

His eyes flicked to the bed. My jaw dropped. Did he mean…?

He read my thoughts correctly, and his laughter was cold with an edge to it that would have sliced me open if it were a physical thing.

"Apparently you already have, sweetheart. You think that's how you get access to the child you've wanted nothing to do with?"

"No," I shook my head violently. What a mess I was making of this. How had I not stopped to think this through yesterday? I hadn't thought about anything. It had felt like I had lost so much time and I hadn't wanted to waste a second more. I had done it wrong. I shouldn't have gone near him last night. I hadn't meant to – I had been coming to sneak in one last look at Féile.

I put my hands over my face. I was trembling. *Think, think.*

"I'll do whatever you want," I offered. "We can take it slow. I'll only speak to her when you're there... I know I haven't..."

I trailed off as he turned his back on me and slouched casually against the window, watching whatever activity was going on in the courtyard below. I could be bleeding to death on his floor, and he wouldn't be less sympathetic. And if he could see into me, then he would know that I was truly bleeding to death.

The door pushed open, and there she was. Dark tumbling hair over her white nightgown, still rubbing sleep from her eyes. She stopped as she saw me in the room. Her big brown eyes were shy as she took me in before they flicked past me and she ran barefoot over the cold floor and jumped up into the safety of his arms.

This was why she wasn't in the nursery. She had been moved to sleep closer to his rooms.

Gideon looked at me stonily, pressing a tender kiss to Féile's forehead as she wrapped herself about him. I looked back at him, pleading with him silently.

"Morning, poppet." His gravelly voice was soft as he cuddled her close.

I felt like I was adrift, the gossamer thread from last night pulled taut. The tension was high and so close to snapping.

He ran a finger down her soft cheek, just as he had that morning after she was born. A wave of emotion washed through me, threatening to pull me down.

"Féile," he said, waiting until she lifted her little chin to look up at him. "Do you know who this is?"

She surveyed me solemnly, wide-eyed. How would she, in a castle full of people? I was someone she saw rarely and interacted with not at all. Devastation coursed through me that she mightn't even know me. My baby, Devyn's legacy, the gift he had left behind that I had failed to treasure.

"Dada," she turned into his neck.

Dada. She called him Dada.

The world exploded.

Gideon turned, huddling her into the wall as furniture burst across the room. I felt like I was coming out of my skin. I was a whirling dervish, a storm breaking, out of control, out of my mind with the pain and anguish that whipped through me.

He had stolen her from her father and from me.

"You're not Devyn."

The scream tore from the ragged pieces of my heart, merging and flying about the room as tangible to me as the broken furniture.

Through the tumult Rion's face appeared.

Then Gideon was there, taking my arms, pulling me into him.

Words – shouting, soothing, calming.

"Come back, hush, come back." Gideon held me against his chest, his arms around me like a band. Soft words murmured in my ear, a gentle touch on my hair, on my skin. "Shhh."

I went limp in his arms and the storm ceased.

The furniture lay in pieces around the room. I frowned at the damage. Had I done this?

"Féile?" I asked in a small voice. Had I hurt her?

"She's fine. Rion has her."

I pushed away from him. She must have been terrified. I couldn't focus, the anger still boiled through me.

"I want my daughter."

"Are you insane?" he asked, an eyebrow raising. "You think I'm letting you anywhere near her after that display?"

"She is not yours. Who are you to tell me that I cannot see

my own child? My child. Mine." Rage flowed freely through me in a surge that I was helpless to control. "You stole everything."

I hated him, with every particle of my being.

"You're not the Griffin. You're not her father."

Rion had come back into the room, his step faltering at the bitter, angry words I was throwing.

"So you keep telling me."

"You are nothing."

"I'm nothing." He stepped toward me, teeth bared. "Fine, but you, you are less than nothing. You're not a mother. She doesn't even know who you are. You are no one to her. And I'll be damned if I let you anywhere near her. Ever."

Rion stepped in now, pulling Gideon's arm. "Enough! Stop this."

Gideon stared down at me, nostrils flaring, my rage met and answered in his.

Bronwyn was there and she laid a tentative hand on my arm.

"Cass, darling. You need to stop. Please, Féile is afraid. You need to breathe." The storm had restarted outside, the windows rattling in the winds that were battering to get in, to answer my call.

What was I doing?

Gideon twisted out of Rion's grip and strode from the room.

The rage and everything else seeped out of me. Devastation flooded in its wake, inside and out. I lifted a trembling hand to my mouth as I took in what I had done to the room. What I had done to my daughter. What I had said to Gideon. I fell to my knees and sobbed in Bron's arms, weak from the morning's events. What had I done?

"Get me out of here," I said, depleted of all tears. I needed to get away.

Bronwyn nodded.

Within the hour, she had us both on horses heading to Keswick. A couple of days out in the Lakelands would give everyone a little breathing space.

We clattered slowly out over the cobblestones. Unable to resist, I looked up at Gideon's room. Was he there? I thought I detected a shadow through the diamond-patterned glass, but I couldn't be sure. My throat was raw as I swallowed.

The guards' faces were overly neutral as we passed by. The townsfolk's faces were less so. There was fear, signs of a recent storm visible in tumbled-over carts, cracked shutters, smashed slates in the streets. Had I done this? I would laugh if it was remotely funny. I hadn't been able to summon anything like this kind of power in all my training with Callum.

Where was Callum? He hadn't been at the ball. He was always by my side, but I hadn't seen him since I had woken up.

I waited until we were clear of Carlisle and on the open road before pulling alongside Bronwyn. Her dark hair was tied back, and a hood was pulled forward to protect her from the winter chill. I had pushed mine back as soon as we exited the town gates. I felt overheated.

"Where's Callum?" I asked as she turned her head in enquiry.

"He's gone to Oxford. He went a week ago. They had tried everything, and when they ran out of ideas, Callum went to see if he could dig up anything in the great libraries there."

"I don't have the Mallacht?"

I had presumed that was what afflicted me, that like so many others with magic in their blood it had finally caught up with me.

"No, you don't have the same symptoms. We're not sure what's wrong with you. You haven't been well for a while, don't you remember?"

I thought back to my last memories before waking up the other night in Gideon's arms. He had come to say goodbye. There had been others before him who had whispered words of love and regret. Mostly regret. I hadn't really given anyone a chance to love me. I shook it off. Before that, I had been tired, so tired. In the months over the summer, I had struggled to find the energy to do anything. No, energy wasn't right, more that I hadn't had the will to go on. It had felt so hard to move, to talk, to engage with anything. Not worth the effort to push on anymore.

I could barely recognise that now.

"I remember, I think." I smiled wryly at her. She looked well. "How are you?"

"How am I?" she burst out incredulously but not unkindly. "I'm well."

"You and Rion..." They had been engaged two years ago, but I had no memory of them getting married. "What happened?"

She cocked her head, a smile tugging at her lips in disbelief, but she managed not to ask me again if I didn't remember. I did remember the last two years. I sort of remembered everything, it's just that I hadn't really paid attention to anything outside of working on the ley line, Callum, and training, trying to get better, stronger in wielding the elements. If somebody had told me anything about Rion and Bronwyn, then it wasn't that I didn't recall, it was just that I likely hadn't been listening.

"I'm Llewelyn's heir," she said, as if that explained everything.

I lifted my shoulders. I didn't know what that meant.

"Llewelyn had always hoped that there would be another generation to carry his name but…"

"Devyn's death," I finished for her. Was she afraid of saying something that might upset me? Why would…? Oh, yeah.

"Yes, with Devyn gone, my older sister and I are the last of the Glyndŵr blood. My sister is heir to Kernow, so Llewelyn asked me."

She gave a small shrug, her brow furrowing at the fact that this was news to me. She sighed.

"I am heir to Gwynedd now," she said. "Marrying Rion before would have strengthened the ties between Kernow and Mercia. Now it would weaken Cymru, leaving Gwynedd without an heir as I would have had to move here to Mercia."

Not a good time to leave any part of Briton vulnerable. Kernow in particular was susceptible as it shared an extensive border with the empire. Mercia was an important ally but Cymru was their nearest neighbour, it's strength was their greatest protection. It made sense that Kernow would do whatever it could to shore up Gwynedd's politically. As it was, the Britons stood little chance of holding back the imperial forces once they made their move, given their depleted magic resources and with so many who had abilities ill and dying. The legions' technology might not be as reliable out here as it was in the city, but it worked, and they had the numbers and aggression. The borderlands were the main deterrent to them pushing north, the corrupted ley lines that ran through the country separating the southeast from the rest of the island acting as an effective barrier, the magic in there wild and unpredictable as ever.

Kernow was exposed though, as it sat underneath the ley line on the same side as the Roman territory. But Bronwyn would remain strongly allied with her family in Tintagel. If Gwynedd stood with Kernow, so too would the rest of Cymru. She was a good choice, and I doubted she would mind the broken engagement. She had never displayed that kind of interest in my brother.

"Do you know what happened to Marcus?" I'd never heard anyone mention him. He had betrayed me, betrayed Devyn. He was behind those walls, but they could not protect him forever.

Bronwyn ground her teeth before answering.

"Yes, some. His father is governor now – they overthrew the previous one. Or he faced a trial or something. Dolon and his son were hailed as heroes, saving all those within the walls while the last governor was blamed for the illness and not doing enough to counter it."

Calchas and Matthias had finally taken full control of the province. If Acteon had tried to eradicate magic then it seemed like Matthias shared Calchas's plan to control it. Or at least, he was sufficiently rewarded by his rise to the highest title in the city to allow Calchas to pursue whatever his master plan was.

"They will be running low on their supply by now though."

"Rion said there have been incidents?" I recalled from somewhere.

"Yes, they tried to land at the Holy Isle again, but we were ready for them. Shadowers also creep across the borders looking for other stores of mistletoe. The Steward of York mops them up and my sister sends troops from Tintagel to cover the eastern border. The oak groves are well guarded, and the mistletoe is only effective when it's been harvested with the correct ritual. The number of ill here and in Cymru has gone down, so the diminished stores mattered less than it might have."

As we drew closer to Keswick the sun was setting, and we found the community had settled down for the night, their lives much more dictated by the sun. They were up before dawn and went to bed soon after sunset, very different from life in the town.

Nonetheless, a couple of younger druids came out to welcome us and the small cottage that always remained ready for me quickly had a fire lit, and bowls of warming soup with great hunks of bread were provided for us.

Later, Bronwyn's breath was slow and even in the bed opposite but she tossed and turned, as unable to sleep as I.

"Bronwyn," I called lightly.

"Mmm."

"How did Gideon get his scar?"

A huff of laughter in the darkness.

"What's going on with you?"

"What do you mean?" I asked.

"What's with the sudden interest in Gideon?"

"It's not sudden. I-I mean, I'm not interested." I felt flustered. I had merely been curious. "I mean, why wouldn't I be interested? I'm married to him."

I could hear Bronwyn sitting up, soft balls of light popping into life, lighting up her incredulous face.

"You've been married for two years. Why now?"

I covered my face in my hands, mortified.

"I don't know." My voice was muffled from behind my hands. I knew so little about him – just that he was the son of the Steward of York, loyal to my brother... and a stonking great arse. Lingering annoyance flittered along my skin. Skin that he had kissed and caressed every inch of so carefully, so wondrously, the night I had woken to find him in my bed.

It had felt like a dream, the colour and warmth suffusing me even now. What if it had been a dream? Maybe he had never been there at all. Perhaps I had imagined it in my delirium. No wonder that he had found my behaviour at the ball strange... but no, he had kissed me and taken me to his bed. It wasn't all me, was it? Mortified didn't even begin to cover it. If only I never had to face him again. But that wasn't possible. He was the only parent my child had ever known.

And he was a good parent. He had tried to pull me back when I had started to drift away, had pleaded with me to spend more time with my daughter, to be a mother to her.

His own mother had left when he was young. No wonder he had been so angry at watching history repeat itself. He had tried to get me to be better – that was the last time I remembered interacting with him. That seemed to be his preferred way of dealing with things: if he couldn't meet it head on he would just avoid it. Or was that not fair? After all, I was the one who had told him I did not ever want to have to lay eyes on him, and he had done his best to ensure I didn't. *Fine, thanks for saving my life.*

"Why do he and his father not speak?" I asked.

Bronwyn tilted her head as I pursued my curious choice of subject.

"I think you should talk to him, hear it from him yourself."

"Right." Like that was going to happen. "Have you met Gideon Mortimer? We are talking about the same man?"

Another soft laugh.

"You do seem to like a challenge in a man," Bronwyn observed.

She was comparing my interest in Gideon to how I had felt toward Devyn.

"It's not like that."

"No?" came a wry tone. "Tell me, what is it like?"

Okay, so when she had arrived into Gideon's room this morning I had been dressed in a bedsheet. Maybe it was a little like that.

I groaned. "He hates me."

"Hate is a strong word. I don't think he hates you. It certainly wasn't hate last night, now, was it?" Her chuckle was full and dirty.

My cheeks flamed hot again at the memory of last night and discussing it in any manner with Bronwyn.

"Devyn was quiet – or not quiet, but he had secrets. He hid things from me." I shrugged. "So whether it was nature or a habit from keeping himself to himself for all the years he lived in Londinium, I don't know. I suppose I didn't know a great deal about him. I don't really know Gideon either, and I get that that is my fault. At least I think it's my fault, but he is a little intimidating."

Bronwyn was silent for a moment, figuring out which of those revelations she was going to touch, I guessed. I must be freaking her out. I had barely spoken to her, to anyone really, since Féile was born, and now I wanted to cover everything from the brewing war to the men in my life in my first day back in the world. I grimaced.

"If you ever want to know more about Devyn, I'm here. I have all the stories you'll ever need. And Rion does too – he loved Devyn. I know you can't forgive him but he would... you could talk to him about Devyn, too."

I nodded, unwilling to trust myself to speak. I didn't blame Rion for Devyn's death; there was nothing to forgive. Matthias Dolon had killed Devyn. I had never said that to my brother though. I had told him I blamed him, but it had all been so tangled up in grief that I hadn't been able to think straight. I never meant him to think—

What a mess.

Another person to whom I had barely spoken. He was my brother, but he too was someone I hadn't bothered to get to know in my new life.

"As for Gideon, well, he's sort of his own man. He's always been a bit of a law unto himself in doing and saying what he wants, which is, I presume, what got him that sexy scar over his pretty face," she moued, and a little laugh escaped. "You will really have to ask him how he got it. I don't actually know, not for sure. There are a lot of rumours: an angry father or brother of some poor seduced girl, a hell hound, a skirmish with Northmen on the Anglian coast. All I know is that he turned up at Rion's hall, a trained warrior, when he was twenty or so and he had it then."

"That would have been a couple of years after Devyn left," I calculated.

"Yes, about that," she concurred. "He picked the right castle to turn up at. Not that he had much choice. All of Cymru despises the Anglians – they've fought for years over the border. The Albans might have taken him in, although there is also a rumour that he slept with the king's sister there. But he chose Carlisle, which had a young king in need of a friend, and whatever else he is, Gideon has been loyal to Rion. Though as far as I'm aware he has never sworn fealty to Mercia, which is highly irregular. I've never seen him do something he doesn't want to do, but he is Rion's man all the same."

He might not have sworn an oath to Rion, but he had married his sister at his command. Even if she was the last woman on earth he would have chosen himself. Nor had it escaped me how many of these rumours included other women. I wondered how many he had been with while I... that wasn't any of my business. I had practically forgotten he existed. I had certainly treated him as if he didn't exist. He had married me to save my life, to save Féile's life.

I wanted to ask more, more about Gideon, more about Féile, but my head pounded at the thought. I couldn't. I didn't deserve it.

"I've been a terrible mother," I whispered, unable to look at my friend.

"Yes."

Her voice wasn't judgemental, just honest.

"Do you think they'll ever forgive me?"

I waited for her answer. I couldn't look at her, as she contemplated my question.

"Féile is young. Show her love, be patient with her, she'll come around," Bronwyn said. "Gideon, I don't know. It's hard to tell what he's thinking, but then his own past won't help matters."

"What do you mean?"

Bronwyn bit her lip.

"Please, Bronwyn, I... I've messed everything up so badly. I want to fix it. Tell me," I begged.

She sighed.

"You know his mother left him when he was only a child. To go off and train as a druid," she explained.

Talk about lightning striking twice. I had done to Féile precisely what had been done to him. I had deserted my child in favour of magic, of power. He must despise me.

"Oh." What could I say? I had no excuse; I had made my own bed. I felt incredibly alone. He had tried, when Féile was a baby; he had begged me to be a better mother to her, to spend time with her. More memories surfaced: he had tried to be kind, understanding of my grief, but I had been so focused on the ley lines. He had stopped coming by with Féile, had left rooms I entered. Avoided me when I showed time after time that I had no interest in the little girl I knew he adored. What few moments of guilt I had in those initial days had been soothed in the knowledge that Gideon cared for her. Once he loved, he loved deeply; if Bronwyn thought that he was utterly loyal to Rion, then there was nothing he wouldn't do for Féile. He would give up the afterlife if it kept her safe. No wonder he wanted me to stay away from her; I was the biggest threat in her life. There had to be some way to fix it. I would do whatever it took.

"She was all I had ever dreamed of. Devyn would be so proud of her, and so disappointed in me. How did this happen?" I had to convince Gideon to give me a second chance. We'd go back at first light.

After a few moments, when no more questions were forthcoming, Bronwyn got out of her cot and came over and pulled me into a hug, wiping the tears that slipped down my face.

I barely slept, so when dawn crept over the horizon I joined the druids tending the line that morning, I had missed the winter solstice, and felt I should stay and compensate for my absence. I could sense the off notes before I had gone too far down, how quickly the corruption had come this time.

The harmonies washed through me as I worked with the line, calming my worries and soothing the pain and tumbled emotions of the last few days. The frets and worries smoothed out as I tended the line. The cadence eased my troubles, the tones and rhythms in need of my care. I should have been here for the solstice. The discordant pollution was a steady undercurrent that felt distorted, murky. I stayed longer than a dawn service would ordinarily need. Bronwyn looked at me strangely when I informed her that we needed another day, which turned into two. But the line was much recovered when we returned to Carlisle.

Chapter Eight

On returning to Carlisle, I went upstairs to change while Bronwyn convinced Rion and Gideon to talk with me.

I met them in Rion's study, a surprisingly cheery room I hadn't been in before.

"Catriona." Rion smiled warmly as I entered, beckoning me to sit and join them by the fire, which was more than pleasant after a couple of days out on the Lakelands.

Gideon sat in the leather armchair a little back from the fire, the flames and shadows flickering across his impassive face.

"We understand you want to spend time with Féile," Rion began.

"I have some conditions," Gideon cut across him.

"Gideon."

"No, it's all right," I said calmly. "I understand."

Gideon leaned forward, his dark hair falling across his broad shoulder. He really was a very handsome man.

"You need to give her a little time, she's afraid of—"

I lifted my hand to quiet him.

Gideon exhaled. "I'm not saying you can't see her. I just need you to—"

"It's fine," I said across his explanation.

His brows drew together, and he looked at Bronwyn, then Rion, his lips thin as he sat back in his seat.

"What's fine?" Bronwyn asked.

"Everything can return to normal, so I'm not sure why you've called me here."

Rion looked stumped, as if he didn't know where to begin. How unusual for my composed king.

Bronwyn stood, agitated, then sat again.

"Cass, we love you," she began. I smiled at Gideon's snort, highlighting that not everyone shared the sentiment, but it was nice of her.

"Bronwyn, I'm not sure where this is going, but I'm fine," I felt some kind of intervention was coming, but I was tired. It was evening, and I would much rather be sleeping than listening to whatever this was.

"You're not fine." Bronwyn looked upset.

I stood.

"Sit down." My brother said in his best commanding voice.

"I'm going to bed. I am perfectly fine," I said, my voice colder and more cutting than I intended.

"Catriona, you got off your deathbed last week and bounced around like a giddy schoolgirl," Rion observed, "then nearly brought the castle down about our ears because you were upset, and now you're back to acting like we don't exist. This isn't right."

"It's fine. Take as much time as you need," I said to Gideon.

His eyes narrowed.

"What?" Bronwyn sounded confused. I had been beating

120

myself up over my failure as a mother two nights ago, but Gideon was a good father. Féile had everything she needed. "Don't you want to see her?"

"Not if it's a bother," I said mildly.

Gideon stood and glared down at me, his expression murderous. I raised an eyebrow. Wasn't this what he wanted?

He was out of the room in a few strides, and if we weren't in a castle the entire building would have been shaking from the slam he gave to the door.

———————

I arranged a slight smile on my face as I entered the study at their request only a week later.

What now? Bronwyn still hadn't left. Didn't she have a whole kingdom to learn to look after? Gideon sat in the same chair as he had the week before. His glowering had resumed.

I took the seat I had sat in last time, turning to my brother in mild enquiry.

"Is there a problem?" I asked.

"No, Catriona, no problem. We just wanted to talk to you," Rion said pleasantly.

I sighed. "I'm fine."

"They're right," came a voice from behind me. "You're not fine."

Callum entered the room, taking the seat that Bronwyn had recently vacated in favour of standing behind Gideon, her hand on his shoulder.

"You're sick."

"You may not have heard the news since your return, but I am fully recovered."

Callum tilted his head.

"So I see. What cured you?"

I shrugged. What did it matter? I was well now.

"Do any of you know what cured her?" He looked around the room, his gaze stopping at Gideon, who stared back narrow-eyed.

"We don't know," Rion said. "She went downhill pretty fast after you left. We thought... that is, we didn't think she had much time left."

Running out of time – a euphemism for almost dead. Why was that? As if we had an allotted amount of time given to us at birth and someone was keeping track on a stopwatch. Not that they had stopwatches here in the Wilds.

"Gideon?" Callum's bearded face was unwavering from its direction of interest. "Anything different about that last night?"

"I was there," he admitted in a growl. "I brought Féile in to say goodbye. Rion and Bronwyn needed to rest, so I sat with her."

"You sat with her all night?" Callum asked. How did he know that? Although sitting wasn't all he had done.

Gideon frowned. "What of it?"

"And she just woke up?"

"Yeah, pretty much."

"Cass, how did you feel when you woke up?"

I shrugged. "I felt good."

"If your emotions were colours, what were they like?

"Vivid, bright."

"And what are they like now."

"Shades of grey," I realised, examining my view on the world around me. "Washed out. Pale."

Callum sat back in his chair. "Aye, that'll be it then. Seems like there might be a symbiotic relationship between the Griffin and the Lady of the Lake," Callum explained. "He be her tether to this world. Cass, the energy of the ley line that goes through your body is elemental, raw – it washes out your emotion. With the way the line is these days, it's devastating on your emotional health. The more you treat it, the less you care about anything and anyone. You all but lost the will to breathe."

"You found record of this in Oxford?" Rion asked.

"No, it's just a theory." Callum stroked his great beard. "There is little enough in the libraries on the Lady of the Lake. Some pieces on her ability with the ley line, the impact she's had on battles against the Romans – not much though. Next to nothing on the Griffin. The best I could do was trace the bloodline – where the Lady of the Lake gift went in each generation. Even tracing the gift is a challenge from the twelfth century when the Lady of the Lake came to King Belanore. We know little enough about the Lady Evaine other than that she began the matriarchal line from which Cass is descended. Evaine's daughter married lower-born nobility and little record is kept of the lesser houses."

"But the early lady had no Griffin until after the sacrifice of Llewelyn the Great," Rion interjected.

"You do remember some of your learning then," Callum approved, in the same tone he used when he was proud of something I had recalled. Apparently even after twenty years since Rion was his student his pride hadn't dimmed. "We know something of Gruffyth ap Llewelyn, the first Griffin, because his father, Llewelyn ap Iorweth, had a great many songs and tales told of him after he died saving the then Lady of the Lake on a battlefield. But again, other than in the oral traditions of Cymru, little is recorded of the lady at that time."

Callum leaned forward, invested in the tale of his research.

"That is until the Lake bloodline is reintroduced into the Royal House of Mercia when Queen Blanche dies and her husband John marries the Lady Katherine. The Griffin at that time was a Glyndŵr. There is also a good deal on Owain Tewdwr, who was Griffin to the Lady Vivian Beaufort, because he married Catherine, the Queen Dowager. Their son Edmund married Vivian's daughter, Lady Margaret Beaufort, which pulled together the threads of the House of Lancaster and the Lady of the Lake to secure the throne. As there was such political turmoil, we know a good deal about her Griffin, Jasper. As the Union of the Roses swept south, pushing the Romans all the way back to the walls of Londinium, there are reports that Margaret would grow cold, uncaring of the outcome of the war at times, which I traced to periods where they were separated. Jasper was killed in one of the last great battles, and Lady Margaret died shortly after."

Bronwyn's lips pursed at this. I lost interest in the tangle of lineage and ran my eyes along the shelves of books behind Rion's desk. Perhaps I could take one or two with me when we were done here.

"The next generation is also well documented as the House Tewdwr saw the close entwining of the core branch of the Griffin and the Lady of the Lake." Callum ran a hand through his beard, pausing to take a sip of his drink. "Margaret's daughter married a noble in Anglia, a displaced family from the Shadowlands. Their second daughter, Anne, inherited the Lakeline; she married the High King's brother. There is some mention that she and her Griffin were not close, but there isn't a great deal more as they were all killed in the sacking of Richmond."

I tuned back in at the mention of Richmond, I had stood in

its ruins, seen through a whisper in time the sight of King Arthur's niece escaping the Imperial attack.

"The lady married the… but they were cousins, no?" Was I following this correctly?

"Such things happened and I suppose they wanted to keep the power close. Also, I believe Lady Anne was an ambitious woman," Callum clarified briefly. "When King Arthur's castle burned, the young Lady of the Lake, Elizabeth, fled north, and her marriage to Robert of Dudley ended House Tewdwr… and their son, Deverell, began a new house. His sister had the gift but married a commoner she met in the wars. The records can't help but chronicle the ruling families but tend not to hold too much of the lady herself beyond the basic facts, a precaution should Oxford ever be taken. Two centuries of war followed where again little is recorded of the relationship between the ladies and their Griffins. "

"There is no other record of the lady being ill like this before? Your theory is based solely on Lady Margaret?" Rion asked.

"It was the only thing that struck me in the records that might explain it. The lady has always tended the line that runs through Keswick and Penrith," Callum answered. "She may have on occasion gone south to the borders to bolster the fighting there, but her primary duty is always the lines. So Cass's illness couldn't just be the effect of working on the lines. There was something about Lady Margaret and Jasper. I can't quite put my finger on it. Tracking through the basic details of the Lake bloodline there was something else… Some ladies lived long lives, despite the early death of their Griffin, but there is something that makes me feel it is connected. And I worry that the reason Cass went so far may be because she is without the Griffin. But then that doesn't explain how she recovered."

Rion flicked a glance at Bronwyn, giving permission to reveal what we had hidden from everyone since Devyn's death. Rhodri knew but it appeared our other secrets from that morning had remained closely guarded, even from Callum.

"The Griffin lives," Bronwyn said. "After Devyn was killed, we saw no reason to reveal this, but the essence of the Griffin was transferred. To Gideon. Cass has not had to live without the Griffin that was created to serve her."

"It's true?"

Gideon lifted a shoulder. "We believe so."

Callum leaned forward, rubbing the back of his head, his brow furrowed in thought.

"Cass and Gideon are not as close as she was with Devyn. Most Griffins live in their lady's shadow." He seemed to remember that I was in the room and turned to me. "Mayhap that separation, combined with the woeful state of the line, is what nearly killed you."

"It's possible," I mused. Thinking back, I compared my recent experience with how I had felt when Devyn had been alive. "When I first started to show my abilities I was not well. I thought it was the episodes of magic use that were draining me. I was out in Richmond that summer but when Devyn was near, I didn't suffer from the same levels of exhaustion. Then when I drew power on the road to Cymru, after we left him, I was drained again."

Callum nodded. "There's no denying that there is a pattern. Was it enough for him to be close? Was there anything in particular he did that made you feel better, stronger?"

"Er... no. I don't think so," I said.

Bronwyn guffawed, drawing everyone's attention.

"Didn't you say that your connection with him appeared after you two..." She stopped, before adding delicately, "Did the deed?"

All eyes swung back in my direction in time to take in the damning blush glowing from my cheeks.

"You need me to replace him in her bed, is that what you're suggesting?" Gideon exploded, the veins in his neck popping out. Way to tell the room he most definitely had not been just sitting beside my deathbed.

"No, no, it is unheard of," Calum interjected quickly. "That is, there is no record of the lady and the Griffin ever having that sort of relationship before Cassandra and..."

"Devyn," Gideon finished for him.

"There might be no records, but it has happened," Bronwyn corrected. "Within my mother's house, it is believed that Lady Margaret Beaufort had an affair with her husband's brother, Jasper Tewdwr, who was her Griffin."

Callum gasped. "She died within months of him."

Bronwyn nodded. "According to my mother it is the curse is from the time before the Griffin line, a legacy of the betrayal of Guinevere Pendragon. It's triggered if the lady and her protector are more than... if they're together then their lives are bound."

"Yes, well," Callum cleared his throat, "I'm not saying that they..."

There was silence as Callum petered out.

"What are you suggesting then?" Gideon prompted tautly.

"What I was thinking is that it is more usual for the lady to be in the company of the Griffin more often. I think his presence is enough to restore her emotional balance, to keep her grounded." Callum turned to me. "Cass, you told me once that you felt a tether that prevented you from losing yourself in the ley. Might the Griffin be that tether?"

I shrugged. Saw again that golden line that had unspooled across the dancefloor when Gideon held his hand out to me at the Midwinter ball.

"You want me to give up my life to follow her around?" Gideon questioned, his brow raised. "No."

"Gideon—" Rion started.

"No, I'm not doing it," he returned. "I've given up enough. She's given up enough."

"Féile?" Rion asked, clarifying the 'she' that he was concerned about.

"You're going to take me away from her as well? I'm what she has, what she knows."

A spike of jealousy bounced through me. Of him? Of her? It was the first emotion of any kind I had experienced in days, I observed absently. A result of having been in the same room as the Griffin for more than a minute? Maybe, but did I want to go back to the chaos of last week? The highs and lows had been overwhelming. I didn't need a distraction like that in my life. I needed to focus.

"I don't need him," I said, having heard Callum out. "Nor do I have time for this."

"There has to be another way." Bronwyn tried to find an agreeable solution, giving Gideon's shoulder a squeeze. It was distracting. Why was she touching him? She had told me that Gideon didn't suffer from a lack of female attention – had that been some kind of tacit confession?

"If he won't give up his day, and she can't give up hers... then what about the nights?" Rion suggested.

"I just said no," Gideon snarled.

I felt a tad offended. I raised an eyebrow in his direction. He glowered back.

"Nobody is asking you to have sex," Rion assured him before turning back to Callum. "But they could sleep in the same room. Would that be enough to restore her?"

Callum nodded eagerly, delighted to have a reasonable suggestion. I shrugged. I didn't mind, though logic presented the argument that I didn't care right now. That was the point. I didn't have enough emotion to like or dislike the solution offered. After a few weeks, I might have a different view.

"Please just try it," Rion said to the snarly man in the corner. "Wouldn't you... Féile deserves a mother."

Gideon angled a narrow-eyed look at the King of Mercia, a mirthless smile acknowledging the hit to his weak spot. "One week."

"Catriona?" my brother asked. "Do you agree?"

"Sure." I shrugged.

"If she shrugs one more time, I will strangle her," came a dark mutter from the corner.

"Maybe we can find a room with separate beds," Callum suggested.

Gideon was sitting by the fire drinking when I entered his room. There was still only the single four-poster bed in the middle of the room.

I raised a brow at him.

"It's big enough," he growled.

My shoulders went to lift before I stopped them as his glare intensified. I was still smiling a little in amusement as I slipped between the sheets.

When I woke the next morning, there was no sign of Gideon, and no indication he had ever disturbed his own bed. I sat up and saw his long legs stretched out by the fire. Just as they had that morning when we had fled the hell hounds and ended up in that inn. He had saved my life. More than once.

"Do you feel any different?" his voice came from the other side of the chair. How could he tell I was awake?

"I don't know." I checked myself. "Not really."

I certainly didn't feel the joy for life that had overtaken me the morning after he had made love to me.

The door pushed open. Oh no.

Wary, dark eyes contemplated me from beside the door. Gideon stood up from his chair quickly so she could see him but made no further move. Féile looked at him then back at me, and then she padded her way slowly over to him without ever taking her big eyes off me. I didn't move.

Gideon lifted her up, still dressed in the clothes from last night.

"Morning, poppet," he said, dropping a kiss on her forehead, just as I had seen him do before. He started to walk to the door.

"Dada," she snuggled into him. He tensed but didn't look at me as he kept walking.

The door closed softly behind them. I lay back in the bed, my chest unbearably tight as tears squeezed out from my burning eyes.

Okay, maybe I did feel different.

I didn't see any sign of them all day. Callum refused to let me train. We needed to make certain my emotional balance was restored first, he said. Each night, Gideon slept in the chair by the fire.

On the sixth morning, Féile was accompanied by her small

dog who, despite no longer being a puppy, still had some behavioural issues. Gideon had paused long enough to get dressed before sweeping Féile out of the room. Curious at the delay, Snuffles came in to investigate and snuffled around the room until he got to my slippers. He promptly grabbed one and made for the door.

My yelp was enough to have Gideon reaching for Féile, whose giggle at her dog's antics had her meeting my eyes in shared mirth, causing my heart to flip in my chest.

That night, as I lay in Gideon's bed, he again sat in the chair by the fire, nursing a whisky, the amber swirl catching the light as he twirled the glass.

After a while, he slipped in beside me. I relaxed. He too had seen the benefits of our experiment, and if it was to become a permanent arrangement, he couldn't continue to sleep in a chair. My entire body unclenched. He was willing to do this for me, for Féile. I had to say it. I wanted to tell him that he was a good father but I couldn't force the words out. Couldn't take back the ugly horrible things I had said to him. I turned away, pulling the blanket tight about me, and finally sleep came.

Snows gave way to spring showers. Marina came north for the spring equinox to help at Keswick and Penrith in my absence and Oban joined her, leaving me to fend for myself as I grew stronger. The land became green once more as the small boat in my mind was gradually pulled back closer to shore. By Beltaine I was decreed strong enough to return to my long-neglected training, though I despaired that I would ever have decent control of the elements. Equilibrium had settled throughout the house too. I spent my nights with Gideon, though we did our best to pretend the other didn't exist. I might not be able to sense his emotions as I had Devyn, but he didn't exactly mask his feelings. It was exhausting being on the receiving end of the disdain that rolled off him in my presence. It was one thing to know he hated me, another to lie there next to that sullen resentment every night.

However, over the summer I was deemed stable enough to spend time with my daughter and Gideon unbent enough to slowly allow me to spend unsupervised time with her as she turned two.

My daughter's eyes glowed as her dark curls dripped with water, the apple gripped in her teeth. I beamed back at her, my heart filled to bursting. The castle burned bright on this night, the night the dead walked the land. I felt strangely close to Devyn, as if he stood at my shoulder, at peace with me, glad that Féile and I were better, even happy that Gideon was such a great father, showering our little girl with the love and affection he had never had the opportunity to bestow. It felt good, I felt good, stable, unlike the ley line, which continued to deteriorate. I had celebrated Samhain at Penrith at the request of the druids there – it had needed a lot of work. Tomorrow I would have to go out to Keswick because Oban had returned with the news that Marina was struggling. I couldn't let her continue to shoulder the burden alone.

The druids and I had tried everything. The wrongness, the corruption that crept along the ley line from the south was growing, as if someone was pouring a black sludge into it and the current was bringing it inexorably further up the line, corruption sucking the energy out of the land, turning everything grey in its wake.

Féile hopped up onto the bench beside me, and her warm body curled into me as the mummers cavorted their way into the room. Rion presided over the festivities with the same thoughtful consideration with which he did everything. Féile's head grew heavy against my shoulder. The painted laughing faces of the dancers and staff as the bonfires were lit flashed around me as my little girl fought sleep to enjoy every minute she could. Samhain had been eagerly anticipated for weeks. I breathed in the lavender scent of her hair, the shampoo that the druid Elsa had brought her from the summer meadows when she visited Glastonbury in Kernow.

A shadow fell over us as the tall, dark-haired warrior bent to take her to bed. I wanted to follow but knew I would be unwelcome. He had allowed her to stay close to me all day. My presence, even after all these months, was merely tolerated and always keenly observed.

I waited long enough to see Gideon re-emerge in the hall before I slipped away to sleep. Or at least to lie in bed... his bed. I felt like a ghost when I entered his room. Despite the months I had spent here, it bore no trace of me; it was still dark and masculine, wholly his. Swords and daggers hung high on the wall where his daughter's little fingers could not reach them. They were secured now so his crazy wife's tantrums couldn't send them spinning around the room. Luckily for me, they had been away for cleaning at midwinter, otherwise what was already one of my worst ever days could have been unspeakably worse.

I lay in the dark waiting. I couldn't help it. He rarely acknowledged my presence, but I felt wound tight until he arrived. Sometimes he didn't come at all, and I lay staring at the embroidered canopy until the early hours. I didn't know where he spent those nights – it was none of my business. He owed me nothing. But I was further punished on those days because on top of insufficient sleep the lack of time in his company inevitably led me to seek him out at training.

I paid more attention to my moods now, the ridiculous euphoria and deadly rage of those early days not something I wished to repeat. I worked hard to ensure that I maintained the emotional stability his presence gave me. It didn't matter if he ignored me, what mattered was that I remained me, a me who was able to hold her child, to show her she was loved – adored, if truth be told. She was an indomitable little thing. Entirely her own person, funny and bouncy like the curls on her head but stubborn as a mule when she wanted to be.

She wanted to learn how to fight, pleaded with Gideon to show her how to be a warrior just like him. Gideon was equally as stubborn, and horrified at the idea of his little girl holding a blade. He wasn't against the idea of women being able to fight. Just Féile. She was fierce, though. Maybe he was doing the world a favour.

Callum had taught me some more meditation techniques. I could feel the coil inside me wound tighter than usual, anticipation at heading out to Keswick tomorrow perhaps, or the sinking sensation that Gideon would avoid his room tonight. He hadn't come last night and I had been forced to spend half the day watching him train when I should have been preparing to head to the lakes.

He trained harder and longer than any other of the titled warriors, working with the master at arms to train the men and women of Carlisle for the war that now felt inevitable. I too needed to be ready. I had to be.

I watched as he held a blonde warrior, straightening her posture with his touch, his body long against her back as he adjusted her throwing hand. His skin glistened as he went through the paces with the better swordsmen. I brought books to study on the days when I was forced to track him down to be near him. He didn't like my being there, but what choice did I have? He never looked my way, but I knew he could feel my eyes on him, tracking his athletic body as he spent hour after hour in training.

The ley line this morning at Penrith had been draining.

He had to come tonight. He had to.

Chapter Nine

The door opened, the line of light from the hallway cutting through the dark. His purposeful stride ate up the floor, the creak of his chair indicating he had chosen to get his rest by the fireside tonight.

"Gideon," I said. I needed his closeness tonight. I was dreading tomorrow and I felt it like a hollowness in the pit of my stomach. I could feel the Keswick circle waiting for me, as if it called to me.

There was no answer from beside the hearth. I no longer felt the contempt he had thrown at me in those early weeks. I knew I had earned back some of his respect as I won back my daughter's love and trust. He primarily treated me with indifference, with more than a dash of disdain in it. Ignoring me mostly.

I was about to call to him again when I heard his sigh, followed by the rustling of clothes, then the dip of the bed.

"Thank you." I was grateful, the coil inside me loosening a little. The thread that bound me to shore felt instantly more substantial. I breathed easier, despite the intoxicating smell of woodsy male behind me. He smelt warm and alive and... full of whisky. I stilled. Gideon rarely drank.

I turned over to check on him, only to find myself inches from his eyes, staring straight at me.

"Are you okay?" I asked. He clearly wasn't. Interaction was not part of our agreement, but he did this for me and the least I could do was try to be there for him.

The tension in me mounted as he lay there watching me, unblinking. Was he...? What was wrong? I reached out to touch his shoulder. Maybe he was having some kind of dream, but... with his eyes open?

His hand shot out and caught me before I could touch him. I pulled my hand back, but he didn't release me.

His eyes shone in the light from the window, the light that was lit to protect us from the dead on this night. Maybe I needed more protection from the living.

"Let me go."

"You let me go," he said challengingly, his words slurred a little. How much had he had to drink, and why?

"I'm not holding you," I said. What was he talking about? I attempted to pull my wrist out of his grip again.

"Aren't you?" He wound my arm behind my back and used it to pull me flush against him. He wasn't wearing anything. I knew that already, because he never wore anything in bed.

"Is this better? Closer?" he asked, his head ducking into the corner between my neck and shoulder. He inhaled. "Hmm?"

I could feel his breath on my neck, his heat on my body. I could practically feel my eyes dilating. I shouldn't respond. He had been drinking, and he resented my presence in his life, in his bed. Responding would just make everything worse.

His lips brushed air in front of mine. I melted. *Please kiss me.* I wanted this, wanted him so badly.

"Do I feel like him?" His question was breathed into the dark.

"What? Like who?" What was he talking about?

"Is it the same, in the dark? Does one Griffin feel much like another?" His questions were a rumble in the dark.

"What? No!" Why would he think that? Did he think that I pretended that he was Devyn as we lay here night after night? Of course I didn't confuse them. They were nothing alike. Lying here with Gideon, all I knew, all I felt, was Gideon.

I leaned forward to kiss him, to show him that I knew who he was, that I was here with him, only him.

My lips touched his softly. I shouldn't be doing this. What was I doing?

But he responded, his kiss blazing as if the soft caress was tinder to a waiting bonfire set with touchpaper. I was pulled immediately into the inferno, a willing sacrifice to the flame.

He deepened the kiss, rolling on top of me, and my trapped arm twisted uncomfortably. I pushed up to free it.

"Gideon." I just needed him to ease the pressure to free my arm.

He stilled. His body froze over mine, and he breathed in before roughly pulling away and leaping from the bed as if it were a pit of snakes, and I the queen viper.

"What am I? A warm body to service the lady's needs?" he sneered from across the room.

Was he blaming me for what had just happened?

"That's not fair!" He had no right. He was the one who had pulled me in. But only after I had turned to face him and moved to touch him. Had I read him wrong? I had kissed him but it had felt like he wanted me to.

"Is it? What choice do I have in any of this?"

I couldn't breathe. He was right. This was all my fault. I was the one who forced him to stay with me.

"You can choose to be with whoever you want to be with. I'm not stopping you."

"Aren't you? Always there. Always watching."

My cheeks flamed. He knew, knew that I...

He was back on the bed in a heartbeat, pulling me against him as he knelt on the bed.

"Do you want me, kitty cat? Me?" his eyes blazed into mine, seeking an answer that I did not want to give him. I would not be humiliated like this.

"You can go and be with anyone you want to be with," I gritted out. "I don't care."

His laughter barked out in the growing cold of the room.

"And there it is."

He stood up from the bed, grabbed his clothes and was gone.

I sat shivering in the empty room, waiting for him to come back. I needed him, but obviously he had found another bed to warm, and it was none of my business. I had no right to hold him.

"Is there any way to free Gideon?" I asked Callum as we rode out through the Lakelands the next morning.

"Free him, from what?"

"From me? He didn't ask for this. There has got to be a way to allow us to live our lives separately."

Callum's eyes rolled over me speculatively. "There is someone else you would rather marry? Divorce shouldn't be too difficult to arrange. According to our laws, a mutual parting of the ways can easily dissolve an unsatisfactory arrangement. Your emotional health makes it rather more of a challenge."

Callum had been informed of the secret ceremony that had bound us legally as well as magically. After admitting that Gideon had been made the new Griffin, Rion had insisted on Callum being fully informed. But it wasn't the marriage that was the problem. Nor was it me who wanted out, but Gideon valued his independence and this had to chafe.

"The Griffin and the lady don't normally... You said before that usually the lady and her Griffin don't have anything more than the mandated relationship," I began. Did I want to be with Gideon because of the pull of the bond? Was that what he had meant when he asked if I wanted him... or the Griffin that dwelt within? "Do you think I feel... something because of Devyn?"

"Devyn?" Callum repeated, looking like he wanted to be anywhere but on the horse next to mine with no one for miles around but the few guards who trailed behind us. Callum screwed up his face so severely that he was in danger of being lost under his beard and shaggy hair.

"The transfer of the Griffin abilities to Gideon may have brought across some element of Devyn's essence, I suppose. Do you sense him?"

"No, no," I said, horrified. Did he think that I was only attracted to Gideon because of Devyn? That was so messed up. And also untrue. I hadn't been entirely unaware of Gideon's... um... charms before Devyn's death. Me and half the women in Britannia. He was undeniably attractive, mysteriously scarred, broad-shouldered, lean-hipped, long-legged, dark, and he had the whole brooding cavalier thing going for him... "Um, that's not, I mean, I wasn't asking about that."

Callum waited for me to gather my composure.

"I was hoping... that is, I feel much better now, but it's all a bit... messed up. Is there any way someone else could be Griffin?" Someone else that would mean a return to the traditional roles where instead of being trailed by guards during the day and sleeping with a man who resented me at night, we could put the world back in order. And Gideon would be free to be with whoever he wanted to be with.

"I'm not sure," Callum confessed. "I could look into it. The ceremony that was performed on the beach that day was unprecedented. I've never heard of abilities being transferred like that. The Lady of the Lake and the Griffin were empowered in a different era; magic was much stronger hundreds of years ago. It's a miracle that the druid John did what he did. If the power of the Griffin were gone, we would be in big trouble now."

Because of me. If there were no Griffin, then there would be nothing to ground me. I would be dead by now. Before Gideon and I had started to share more time in the same space, I had been wasting away from sheer inertia, from a lack of will. The will and emotion to enjoy life, to keep moving forward, that relationships brought, relationships with my daughter, my brother, with Callum. I still wanted to tend the ley line, to heal it if I could, but not at the cost of everything else.

As we approached the standing stones, I could feel it again. The wrongness here was so much worse than at Penrith, the hum so discordant, so out of tune. I saw the damage being done to the land as the greyness spread further north, that same lack of will that had gripped me. The land failing to thrive or to flourish as the seasons changed.

"I hadn't realised," I said to Callum. "How? You should have let me come sooner."

Callum pulled at his beard. "Aye, well, we had to be sure you were well. It wasn't as bad as this when I came last. Marina's message said that since Mabon there have been odd notes that they had never heard before."

I centred myself as we rode closer to the circle, the wide sky spread overhead from hill to hill, but it felt close, heavy. I felt tired already. Gideon hadn't returned last night and I hadn't managed to sleep much. I had to find a way to fix it, find a way to free him. And a way to fix the ley line as well.

Three silent robed druids waited for us as we dismounted just outside the circle of standing stones.

"Marina," I said, embracing the youngest of them as she pushed her hood back.

"Lady," she said formally. I frowned at her and the street urchin I had first met grinned back at me.

Elsa's outstretched hands enfolded mine.

"You are well?" she asked. "I know you were at Penrith. We would not have asked for you to come, but since the equinox, the song has twisted and the current is overwhelming. We are having little impact."

This close to the circle, the dissonance was already noticeable. I swayed slightly as I laid a hand on the table rock just outside the circle. The thrum was magnetically pulling in a strange rhythm, the cadence distorted. This was the worst I had ever known it.

I sat on the ground in a small circle with Elsa and Marina, the later taking the role of anchor. We each laid our hands flat on the ground and allowed our consciousness to become one. I could feel the thin threads they held out to me, binding me to them. I attached them to my boat, to the stronger rope that bound me to shore, as I let myself sink deeper and deeper.

I began the task of sorting through the notes, redirecting the good ones around me, ushering them on, while the jarring, offkey ones flowed through me, sinking down, distorted and mucky, before floating out the other side purified by whatever magic lay within me.

I could feel them coming, thicker and faster than before, worse than I was used to, similar to the ones in the May line Fidelma had taught me to deal with at Glastonbury, the ones coming through Stonehenge from beyond. From Londinium. The dark notes were plentiful, notes so dark and twisted that they hit me with force. There were so many of them and they took longer to deal with because there was little that was pure in them. The jagged dissonance wanted to be pure, to be clean, to flow, but these notes were heavy, resistant, and it was like trying to get water from oil. There was so much of it.

The threads were fraying; I needed to get away. The gunk stuck to one of the threads, corroding it, and I was being dragged me down. I was heavier than the current and I knew I wasn't going to be able to rise up to the surface again. The corruption slammed into me, forcing me deeper. I felt heavy. My tether was weak. I was so tired, and it was so dark.

It felt bad but I couldn't do anything. I couldn't help anymore. It wanted more, it was a cacophony demanding I do more. The flow was pulling me down, heavy, unctuous, corrupted. If I let it, it would take over everything. Deaden everything. Everything. Including the smell of lavender.

Beauty and light in the dark. If it stayed here, it would be smothered.

If I stayed here.

I was tired. It felt like I was drugged, but I held on to the thread that that sang of home, the thread that wanted me to surface. My daughter. I needed to return home.

I could hear Marina.

I pushed up to the surface. My eyes opened to darkness, but a darkness lit by stars.

"Callum," I said as I recognised the grizzly man leaning over me.

"You're back." He sighed in relief.

We were still in the stone circle.

"What's going on?"

"I need you to stand," Callum said. "You must stand and walk out of here."

"Why?" I didn't think I could stand.

"We haven't been able to touch you. You must move of your own free will. The land senses that you are being attacked and it moves to defend you every time we try to take you from here," he explained. The earth was torn and roots from unseen trees protruded from the ground.

"What happened?" It was an effort to speak as I levered myself up. I looked around and saw Elsa, blood seeping from her nose, lifeless on the ground beside me. I felt nothing as I looked at my friend, the woman who had spent countless hours helping me tend the songline over the seasons I had spent here. Her eyes were empty. She was gone.

Callum's eyes were sombre. "It was too much. The corruption pulled her down. Marina says she was trying to pull you back, put too much strain on the thread, and it took her."

"Marina?"

"She is well. But you must stand," Callum insisted.

I tried to push myself up.

Callum reached for me, and the earth between us started to

move. He pulled his hand back. There were other shadows in the dark beyond the stones. I could feel them all willing me to get up, the force of that will so much greater than my own. I felt so tired. The darkness was a softness waiting for me to fall back into it. Elsa was gone. My eyes closed.

"Cassandra, you need to walk from the circle on your own."

I couldn't imagine doing what he wanted me to do. It wasn't possible.

"Please, let me take you home."

There was a whisper of lavender on the wind. I looked at Elsa's glassy eyes.

I stood.

We clattered into the courtyard at full gallop. I felt almost outside of myself again. It was difficult to keep my eyes open.

I could hear Rion's voice demanding to know what had happened and Callum above me quickly explaining.

"Give her to me." Gideon.

Callum hesitated. All he knew was that I wanted out of the lady–Griffin dynamic. He didn't want to betray my wishes, but I needed Gideon.

My head listed back as I was handed down to him. I needed him now, and I didn't care. He could restore me. He was the link I needed to hold on to. My eyelids fell.

I came to in Rion's study. I could hear their voices above me. I was curled into the broad chest of the man who held me, his fingers tracing up and down my arm. I felt... Elsa.

"Was it my fault?" I asked softly, my lids slowly obeying my command to open.

Rion and Callum were half lit by the fire they sat beside. I lay cradled in the lap of the warrior most likely to throw me over the side of the battlements. I moved to sit up. Just being in the same vicinity was enough, he didn't need to hold me like a child. His fingers tightened around my upper arm until I ceased and lay back again. I didn't have the strength to resist. And I needed it. Just a little. Just for a few more moments.

"Did I do something wrong?"

"No, we don't know why... Whatever is corrupting the energy in the ley lines was too strong," Callum said. "Mayhap Fidelma has the right of it. The source is in Londinium and we need to fix it there."

"No," Gideon's growl came from above me.

Rion raised an eyebrow.

"It's too dangerous."

Callum met and matched the glare over my head.

"What's too dangerous?" I asked.

"No."

Gideon stood with me in his arms and was out of the room in a few short strides. He carried me through the halls and up the stairs, and I watched listlessly as the tapestries and familiar stone walls rolled by.

He laid me gently in his bed, tucking the covers around me. I felt like a child in Londinium again, protected, loved.

I felt the dip of the bed behind me, and the covers slightly lifting before a big arm came around me, securing me against him. It was like being sat beside a heat lamp for the soul, like he was sunshine and the grime and gunk that made me feel dark and empty and burned out was just melting away.

"Féile?"

"She's well. She doesn't know you're back." So she hadn't

146

seen me land at the castle door half-dead. Good. No little girl needed to see that.

I slept.

I woke to the smell of breakfast and my own ravenous hunger. A quick survey revealed food on the table and I was not alone. I pulled on the robe that was laid across the bed as usual. Less usual was to find the room's owner here come morning.

I padded barefoot across the room and sat carefully in the chair opposite. Was this food for me? Why was he still here?

"Eat," he ordered.

I rolled my eyes.

"Feeling better then, Cat?"

I nodded. I reached out and took a nibble of a piece of apple.

I looked up to find his gaze assessing me coolly.

"I'm keeping Féile away from you today," he said casually.

I shrugged. It was probably for the best. His lips thinned in reaction. What, wasn't that what he wanted?

I ate the rest of my breakfast in heavy silence.

"I'm going to sleep now," I said as I stood. He still hadn't moved when I reached the bed. I felt cold so I left the robe on as I curled under the blankets once more.

When I woke the light in the room was dimming, and I was curled like a kitten on a broad chest. What the...? I bounced up. Lazy eyes watched me as I backed away to the far side of the bed. Why was he still here?

A lip curled up in amusement. "So skittish, kitty."

I scowled at the play on my name.

He held a hand out to me. I watched it as if it were something that could scald me.

"Come here." His eyes dared me.

Fine. I took the hand he offered and allowed him to pull me back to him. I knelt facing him and our eyes met and held. Then he pulled his shirt over his head.

"What are you doing?" My mouth felt dry. I didn't understand what was going on.

"I need you to feel. We need you to be well. So hate me if you must, but feel," he said, drawing me closer into the heat of him. I let him, but I still wasn't sure. Lips touched lips. Oh. I startled away. Warm amber eyes held mine. Was he really doing this? Was I?

I exhaled a breath I wasn't aware I had been holding. Every muscle in my body was tense, ready to run, braced against... what? Him?

His lips descended once more, warm, teasing, coaxing, and I kissed him back. It felt good. It felt real. And I wanted it to be.

I let him draw me down, and fire started to lick through me, flames that whirled as flesh touched, as he took me higher and higher. Him, me, two, one, we spun out together.

I lay curled up in his arms, all thoughts melted away. His hand stroked up and down my arm.

"Gideon," I started, pulling in a shuddering breath before I managed to ask my question. "What was that?"

"Well if I have to explain I clearly wasn't doing it right." There was lazy laughter in his voice.

I elbowed the washboard at my back.

His arm came around me, and he held his hand out palm up. I stared at it. I had taken his hand earlier and look where it had got me. My lips twisted and I set my palm down on top of his and he entwined our fingers together.

He said nothing for a few moments.

"How do you feel?"

Right, like I was going to tell this man what was going on in my head right now.

"You did it right," I said primly. "If that's what you're asking."

He huffed behind me.

"Thank you," he intoned. "But that's not what I was asking. Explain to me how much you feel right now? More or less than usual?"

"Oh," I examined my emotional state. "I feel a little blissed out, like I could..."

He flipped me over to face him, his eyes still prompting me to finish, to trust him.

"I feel amazing, like I could fly."

His lips twitched. "Do you think you can?"

"I don't know. Maybe I should try." Jumping out of the window suddenly didn't feel like a bad option. I felt mortified.

"No," he growled. "Wherever you've gone just now in your head, stop it."

I looked up at him, and his hand swept down over my body, stoking the still fluttering embers back to life. His lips came down on mine again. Purposeful, demanding, enticing.

"What do you feel?"

"You know what I feel." I couldn't confess more, not to him, not to this man who hated me.

"I don't hate you," he said.

I tried to wriggle away, appalled that I had spoken aloud. He grinned down at me as he held me effortlessly until I realised that the friction was having the opposite effect to the one I desired. If I was trying to leave his arms, it was becoming clear that the movement of flesh on flesh was inspiring his thoughts in other directions.

I stilled.

"What are you doing?" I asked.

"I wanted to try something new."

"Being nice to me?"

"Is that what we just did? Something nice?" he teased.

I squirmed again. I really would feel better able to think if his naked flesh wasn't touching mine.

"Gods damn it, Gideon." I pushed at his shoulders, anger and frustration surging through me. Why was he playing with me like this? "Get off me."

He rolled off, palms facing up.

"Take a breath," he said in soothing tones. I frowned at him.

His laugh stopped as the handle of the door was turned, and then a knock came.

He got out of the bed and swaggered over to it naked. He couldn't answer like that! Everyone would know. Thankfully, he tugged a tunic off the top of the dresser and pulled it over his head before he opened the door. Then came the low rumble of his voice as he spoke to whoever was outside, his body lowering momentarily before he straightened and closed the door again.

He came back towards the bed, pulling off the tunic, his large muscled warrior's body lit by the pale morning light that bathed the room.

Why was he coming back over here naked?

"What is going on with you?" I asked, suspicious. What was he up to? "Who was at the door? "

"Féile," he answered, slipping back under the covers.

"You won't let me see her?" I felt crushed.

"I want you to tell me how you feel," he replied evenly.

"Piss off." That's how I felt. I was done with him asking me how I felt and dictating when and where I could see my own daughter. There was a rattle from the tray on the table as furniture started to respond to the emotion bubbling under my skin. He lifted one dark brow at the noise.

"The last time we did this, you weren't entirely stable after," he spoke softly, calmingly. "How do you feel, Cat?"

I took a breath, and another. He was right. I was all over the place. "I don't feel as crazy as last time."

"Well that's good. Replacing furniture gets expensive and I was quite fond of some of those pieces."

Tears sprang into my eyes. Damn it.

"Is that why you slept with me?"

"To save myself the expense of new furniture?" His brow arched, amusement lighting his eyes.

"Ah." I smiled weakly, gnawing at my inner lip. How could I put these thoughts into words. "To see... to experiment..."

His eyes narrowed. "You think I bedded you out of duty?"

"Did you?" Had they asked him to? Had they all decided it would be best if he became my bedmate in more than just proximity? All the better for me to serve the kingdom, to fix the ley lines. "The loyal Gideon, always ready to do whatever his king asks of him." My eyes swept him – I wanted to say they did so coldly, but they weren't cold. They were blazing. I was on fire.

His mouth slanted as he closed the space between us. He loomed above me, his big arms caging me.

"I live to serve..." His head lowered slowly and made for the vulnerable point at my neck, his kisses feathering their way up to take my lips possessively. By the time he lifted his head, all thoughts had ceased and I felt boneless and maddened once more.

"You think this is service?" he asked, his head lowering further, this time lavishing the same care on my breasts before teasing their way back to my lips again.

"You think I haven't thought of this every day," he whispered as his lips swept possessively over mine, "every night for the last three years?"

My breath trembled out of my throat as I wrapped my arms around his neck and let him sweep me back into the whirligig of touch and sensation.

———

When I awoke, the room was dark, and he was still there, curled around me. I felt safe, secure, whole.

"How do you feel?" his low voice came again.

I wet my dry lips. "Thirsty,"

There was movement as he stretched away and came back with a tumbler of water. I needed to see his face. The candles flicked into life as I lifted my head while he tilted the glass to my lips. I drank gratefully, water escaping down my chin onto my chest as I emptied the glass.

He put the glass back on the table and returned to lap up the escaped droplets.

"Tell me," he growled.

Could I tell him? Could I explain the feeling of wellbeing that surged through me? The balance, the sheer enormity of emotion? It was astounding. I felt so alive.

"I feel amazing," I confessed. "I feel like me. I don't know how to explain it." But I wanted to try, I owed it to him to try. "It feels like I'm in colour again." *That I'm whole again.*

Sometimes I feel like I'm a thin, pale ghost in a boat, tied to the shore by a thread. A thread you hold.

But I wasn't brave enough to tell him. How could I tell him that? He didn't owe me anything; he had already done so much. I didn't want him to know how badly I needed him, the miracle of how much better I felt right now because he had pulled me back.

I examined my emotions. Was I totally stable? I thought so. I still wasn't sure what this was though.

"Good," he said, satisfied, wrapping himself back around me.

"Why are you doing this?" Gideon had made his dislike of me clear, that he neither trusted nor wanted me near him, nor near the daughter I had abandoned. What had changed?

"Maybe I've just decided to embrace my fate."

And that was it. He said no more on it, but the next day we woke up together and the next night became the first of many such nights. Nights that warmed and restored me.

Chapter Ten

I looked up from the book I was reading, curled up in the window seat in Gideon's room, a smile of greeting already playing on my lips. I had seen him crossing the courtyard below a few minutes ago – he must have come directly here. He leaned down and tousled Féile's curls where she sat on the floor, concentrating fiercely on her latest multi-hued creation.

His lips touched mine in a promise I was never going to get tired of. My hand went around his neck and held him to me when he would have kept it light and sweet.

"Ew." I pulled away, the evidence of hard training lingering in his silky, wet hair and damp skin. He leaned further in, bringing us cheek to bristly cheek, rubbing against me in payback. He smelled of salt and leather. I inhaled, even as I laughingly pushed him off.

I shooed away the servants who brought the urns of water and helped him unfasten the leather body armour he wore.

"Anything good?" he asked, nodding at my abandoned book.

"It's a bit hard going," I admitted. Callum had brought

volumes back from Oxford, from ancient to more recent studies on the ley lines that ran under the land. They all held theories on the corruption of the lines and why magic was waning in the blood. He also had some dedicated volumes that House Glyndŵr had unearthed on the Lake bloodline and the Griffin protectorate. Gideon had read them but I hadn't yet. "A lot of stuff about telluric currents and electromagnetic grids and equinox lines. I'm not sure whether I'm under-educated in physics, magic, astronomy, or geography. It seems obvious that stresses on the lines caused by human contamination like technology are seeping through the earth and corrupting the— What's this?"

I traced the red mark blooming along his ribs.

"Hmm?" He glanced down. "Oh, that. It's nothing. Young Robbie is getting better with a sword; he got one past me today."

I frowned at the mark. Who was young Robbie? I was embarrassed to ask. All too often I was caught out by gaps in my knowledge, things which everyone presumed I knew that I had been too indifferent to take note of before. And if I was honest, I was so focussed on, well, my new family and solving the problem of the ley line now to be able to pay attention to anything else. I would have to go back out soon. The longer I left it the worse it would be. I looked down to find my fingers absentmindedly tracing the outline of the now all but disappeared bruise on Gideon's skin.

His dark hair fell over his shoulder as he too noticed the faded mark. His amber eyes were warm as he lifted my hand and kissed my open palm. How had I done that? I ground my teeth. I hadn't even thought about it and poof! Hocus pocus! I smiled at the memory of Devyn's face the day I had described the gifts of magic that way.

I slipped away from Gideon and went back to my spot in the window. What would Devyn think of this? Of us? Would he be glad? Angry? There had been no love between them, but I had to believe that he would... I let my hot forehead rest against the cooling glass. What could I know about Devyn's views on this? On anything? I hadn't known him, not really. I had been his mission, and once complete he had left me.

I looked up to find the Anglian warrior watching me in return. His expression was solemn before he returned to the job of wiping away the efforts of the day. I flashed him a small smile and returned to my study.

The books suggested that the nodes were where the energy flowed into the lines, which was why the ancients had built monuments atop them – stone circles, places of worship that centred and gathered the power before it flowed on. The main lines crossed through significant sites across the land. We had practically followed one that cut from Londinium to Oxford to Dinas Emrys, where the druids from Anglesey had now retreated to, in Cymru.

The Cern line, which ran from the eastern edges of the Mediterranean to the southwest islands of Eireann, intersected the May line at the tip of Kernow. Both lines were corrupted. Kernow had been forced to abandon its capital, Penzance, in favour of the ancient castle of Tintagel as the land began to fail.

The May line ran along a large section of the border between the Empire and Anglia. I wondered if the same was true in other parts of the world, if the boundaries between the technologically advanced Empire and the old ways were held by the lines of power that crisscrossed the earth. Was it more than mere coincidence that the May line was where the war had been fiercest? Crossing the borders under which it ran had deeply affected me and those with whom I had travelled.

There was another line further south that exited the Shadowlands at Stonehenge, crossing the May line at Glastonbury, but little was known of it because east of that the territory it ran through had been held by the Romans for most of the island's recorded history. This was the line that seemed most damaged.

But we knew so little of it. The barrier at the Tamesis had suffered tech fluctuations, as had Richmond. Perhaps it came close to the surface near those places. But without access to examine the line more closely, I found more questions than answers.

A small figure inserted itself between me and my books, little fingers reaching up to smooth the furrow from my brow as solemn eyes locked with mine – big doe eyes that broke my heart. Satisfied with her work, she turned around and presented her back to me. I had seen her do this to Gideon and her nurse a thousand times. I had even seen her stand just so in front of Rion at his big desk. She was shameless in her demand for adults to be put to use and read for her.

She occasionally came to me for a cuddle, but it had not escaped me that it was always when we were in company, and she felt most secure. My heart stopped as I looked up to find that we were alone. Gideon must have left the room while I was reading.

I gently put my hands to her middle and hoisted her onto my lap. I held my breath to see if I had interpreted her correctly. She turned her head towards me as I failed to start reading.

"Book."

I let out a small laugh. "Maybe not this one, darling."

I pushed the tome Callum had borrowed from Oxford out of the way and reached for one of the children's books haphazardly stacked on a corner of the table. There were several such piles in areas of the castle that the family commonly used. I picked up one I knew she had only been given at Yuletide.

I read to her as I had seen Gideon do, putting voices and drama into it. If I could impress upon her my abilities then maybe this would happen again. The feel of her body tucked against mine was simply the most heart-burstingly wondrous thing I had ever experienced in my life. I tucked my head against her curls, to see the bottom lines of the page, her hair tickling the skin under my chin. She smelt of Elsa's lavender soap and brisk air and pine cones and little girl. Her heart was a pitter-pat against my chest, her weight on my lap so singularly satisfying that it felt as if my whole life centred on this moment. How had I lived so long without this?

The spell was broken as the door opened and Gideon came back in.

"Dada!" She popped up and ran into his arms.

The knot in my throat was tender as I swallowed, biting my lip to keep the tremble from showing. She had come to me of her own volition.

Gideon lowered himself into his customary chair, my giggling daughter in his arms, flushed and delighted at his appearance now that she was no longer engaged in her colouring.

"Was Mama reading to you?" he asked her as he held her over his head.

She nodded, squirming delightedly.

He pulled her down to face him.

"Was she as good as me?" he asked her fiercely.

"Yes!" She laughed at his antics.

He pulled a shocked face.

"Was she better than me?"

"Yes." She cracked up, giggling at his dismay.

"What!" He growled. "Oh, how fickle is woman."

He laughed as he attacked her, tickling her in revenge at being cast aside. His eyes lifted to share the mirth with me but I was halfway out the door. I couldn't breathe. He had called me Mama and Féile had known he meant me. My head was swirling, the emotion making me lightheaded. I ran out of the room, unsure if I was doing so for their safety or for my own. They were making a place for me and I didn't think I would survive if I lost it again.

I felt incandescent, as if I would float away. I walked quickly through the hallways until I was outside and could turn my face up to the sky and feel the cool breeze on my face.

"Catriona." A careful voice called from behind me. I stilled, drawing in a deep breath, attempting to centre myself. They couldn't see me like this. I'm pretty sure my emotions were continuously monitored – Callum, Rion, even Oban always studying me to assess whether I was too low or too high.

"Rion," I responded without turning around. I just needed a minute.

"Are you well?"

He must have seen me. Why did he have to follow?

"I'm fine," I said, turning and casting him what I hoped passed for a stable smile.

His brow rose as if he was going to challenge my statement. I wondered if I looked as scattered as I felt.

His assessment was lingering and, based on his raised eyebrow, he was unconvinced.

"I just..." How to explain, so I didn't come across like a madwoman? They would limit my access if they felt I was spinning too high again. I bit my lip and willed my heart to slow down.

"I've never really had a family," I started, immediately stopping as his face shuttered. Of all the people to use that line on. I winced.

"I mean, I've never known..." I clammed up again. I had never truly felt loved by the mother who had raised me, and I had only tasted in a vision the love our mother had felt for me. Rion had been older than me when she died, had some memories of our mother, and by all accounts our father had loved him. He had just loved too much. Had been broken by our mother's death.

Rion waited for me to find the words I was so badly attempting to produce.

I breathed a laugh at my own witlessness.

"Féile asked me to read to her," I finally said, shrugging, but I could see the understanding in his eyes. He recognised the milestone for what it was. This was epic. I had abandoned her and frightened her, and for her to show signs of accepting me was a miracle of bravery and trust for a two-year-old child.

I also really wanted to tell him that Gideon had called me Mama and she had acknowledged me as such, but I was already inwardly cringing at how pathetic that sounded, even as my vision blurred with tears of sheer joy.

I couldn't keep the smile off my face though, and there was an answering one on my brother's.

"That's good. She needs her mother." It could have sounded patronising, but somehow it didn't. We had come a long way since we had diagnosed the effect the ley lines were having on me.

"How was it for you... after she left?"

He paused before he answered – the only sign of his

surprise at my showing interest in him, in his story. It had been three years and I rarely showed any sign that I recognised him as my brother. Much less that my pain at my lack of family, at the loss of the childhood that might have been, was his pain, his loss, too.

He indicated that we should walk through the garden, and I fell into step beside him.

"She was a force to be reckoned with," he began, with a slight smile tugging at his lip in remembrance. "Always calm, always controlled, everything ran according to her will."

Well, that didn't sound like me, but was not unlike Rion himself, I thought.

"Father was the heart, all heart. He didn't agree with her leaving that last time. I was barely five and I remember him yelling at her, but nobody gainsaid Mother when she was set on something... not unlike you." He smiled.

My eyes widened in surprise at this. The reference was light, but I knew he was raising the ghost that always stood between us: his edict, my defiance... all that had ended in Devyn's death.

"I should have known better. Father's heart and Mother's will wrapped up in a single being. I saw it and—" He stopped in the path and turned to face me.

This conversation was long overdue, but my head felt like it would explode as it came on top of the morning's events. I pushed through the kaleidoscope in my brain, reaching for something to say that would convey, if not my complete forgiveness, then at least that I too wanted to build a bridge.

"It was my fault. If I had been stronger, I could have stopped them." I was horrified at the words tumbling out of my mouth. That was not what I had intended to say.

He blinked. I'm pretty sure that wasn't what he had

expected either. The last time we had spoken on this topic, I had made it pretty clear that had he dealt the blow himself, that he couldn't have been more to blame.

"I know you wanted to do what was best for the country. As it turns out, your brother-in-law would have been a huge traitor, but that aside..." I waved off Marcus's betrayal flippantly. "You must have been so disappointed when you met me. If I had been better, stronger, had more control, then none of it would have mattered. You wouldn't have needed to marry me to an ally. If I had the power of a true Lady of the Lake I would have been enough."

He rubbed his hands over his face.

"Catriona." His voice was anguished. "You aren't... Mother wasn't as strong as everyone believes. The power has been waning for years. We've hidden it. Only our family and the Griffins knew it, but you are no less than our mother was."

"No, that's not true, she was trained from birth, maybe I'll never be... I can tend the line but what use is that if we are attacked again?" Perhaps he didn't realise how bad the situation really was. "Callum... Callum has been trying to help me. He knew her, he knew our mother, and he said she was incredibly powerful."

Rion shook his head. "Callum was a tutor here, from the House of York. He knew very little about what abilities our mother did or didn't have."

My mind boggled at this. I had spent the last few years killing myself to live up to the promise of my legacy, a promise that he was now telling me was wildly exaggerated.

"You mean that she wasn't stronger than me?" I asked.

His lips pursed and he gave a slight shrug. "I was young, and there was little need for battle-level powers because we lived in peacetime. Like you, she tended the ley; she and

Rhodri were close, so I have no memory of her ever being affected as you are. But you seem better now," he prompted.

"I am." *At his command,* the weaker side of me whispered.

"You and Gideon seem better," he tried again. What was he looking for? Surely he already knew exactly how we were.

"You would know."

His eyes flicked towards me. A horrified expression showed there and his brows almost hit his hairline.

"I most certainly would not."

The flush that started at my toes took its sweet time to recede again.

"Was it your idea?" I could have bitten out my tongue, but at least my colour was already high, my mortification already at full strength. But I had to know.

"Was what my idea?" He looked genuinely baffled.

"For Gideon to come and live here," I gabbled quickly, realising I did not want him to figure out what I was asking. When I had come back to myself, Gideon had been a lifeline, one I had grabbed with both hands. I knew why I was with him, but increasingly I felt curious about him. He had married me at Rion's command and saved my life. He had saved it again, and the thought that we shared a bed at his king's command was not one I contemplated often, but I would be lying to myself if I said it never crossed my mind. I couldn't bear to hear the answer. Not now, maybe not ever, coward that I was. I had tried to ask, but Gideon had avoided answering the question. Perhaps that was for the best. "When he left York?"

"Ah, no. In fact, he couldn't have arrived at a worse time. My father had died a couple of years earlier, and I was barely coping. I was struggling to master the elements. When I lost my temper, I would randomly absorb magical energies. The court was sure he was a spy for his father, here to assess how susceptible to attack we were." He swooped to pick up a stone before skimming it across the great pond at the bottom of the garden. It pulled low across the water, skipping off the surface several times before finally succumbing to the forces of gravity and sinking into the water.

I waited for him to continue as he scoured the ground for another suitable stone, his powerful frame bending to pick one up. It was difficult to picture him a lost and erratic teenager; he was always so kingly.

"But he wasn't?"

"Hmm?"

"He wasn't a spy?"

"No," he said, taking up the story again. "He wasn't. He just needed somewhere to be, and I needed someone to count on. Nobody really favoured our alliance, or indeed the bad behaviour we brought out in each other. But we got older and wiser... or married, in his case."

"You mean me?" I realised. "Are you implying I'm a steadying influence?"

"I'm not sure. He does seem to have taken on a bit more responsibility in the last few years."

Féile. My Féile was the reason he had changed. A change I was so profoundly grateful for, because it meant that she had been loved. Though if Gideon hadn't stepped up, Rion would have been there. *Was* there, I realised. My daughter had an uncle, and I had a brother.

"Why did you choose Gideon?" I asked. From all I knew of him he was an odd choice for the strategically minded Rion to have made that day on the beach. He was at odds with his father, the Steward of York, an alliance Rion had wanted to strengthen. I had some inkling of the youth he had shared with

Rion, making him far from the type of man to whom one married one's sister. He refused to swear fealty to anyone in a society bound together by such oaths. Any one of the Mercian soldiers on the beach that day would have been a better choice. "He cares about nothing and no one."

"He certainly works hard to make it appear that way." Rion eyed me speculatively. "But if that's what you think of him. Maybe the better question is, why did he say yes?"

I knew little enough about why Gideon did anything. Maybe if I knew more about him, I could figure it out.

"Why did he leave York?" I asked.

"You'll have to ask him." Rion smiled wryly.

"Why, because you don't know?" I tried again. Bronwyn's speculation that it was because of a woman was something that returned to me more and more often of late.

"No," he said. "I know, but it's his story to tell."

I frowned. "Thanks."

I spent most of my time with Gideon proving to him I was a fit mother or enjoying his company in other ways. The idea of probing him about his past was terrifying. He wasn't like Devyn who had been mysterious but open in his own way. Once I had got past his secrets, it had been clear what drove him.

Gideon was the Griffin by chance; it was not who he was, the way it had been for Devyn. What drove Gideon was less clear. He loved my daughter and slept in my bed, but what was in it for him?

Chapter Eleven

A s the first snowdrops began to push their way back into the world heralding the new season, Marina, who had shouldered the burden until reinforcements came not just from Glastonbury but Alba as well after learning of Elsa's death, was ordered to take a break and so she came to visit.

Her brother clucked around her, despairing of her druidic robes, delighted when she asked him to provide her with some of the more practical outfits he had rustled up for me. Loose tunics with wide belts and simple leggings, jewel-toned wraps with the intricate swirling patterns the Celtic region favoured, even adapting some of the Anglian preference for hard-wearing leather trousers, which she wore while training.

She had been enthralled at the sight of the Britons training for the war to come, insisting on working with Gideon. Rion joined them on occasion to round out her skills with the more magic-wielding side of battle skills. He had graciously lowered himself to teach her after learning she had a solid gift for two elements as well as a voracious appetite to learn everything. Freed from the ley duties she had shouldered since escaping

Londinium, she was a whirlwind of energy, a life-force bowling our careful steps out of her way in her boundless energy to take in all she could.

She had always been so careful and wise beyond her years – the poverty and danger of her early life behind the walls, the responsibility of the ley, which she had picked up without complaint – that it was hard sometimes to remember she was only sixteen.

"She just appeared on the battlefield?" I could hear Marina asking from where a near-collapsed Rion lay at the side of the training field.

Gideon nodded as I delivered Féile to him, swinging her in the air before setting her up with the wooden sword that our indomitable daughter insisted on learning to use.

"So legend has it. The Romans had us pushed back beyond Hadrian's wall; we had been losing ground for centuries—"

"But even without a Lady of the Lake there are still druids, still people like you and me who can fight," Marina interrupted the once impeccable King of Mercia.

Callum, who was waiting to start our own oh-so-frustrating training session, answered for him.

"Not like now. Guinevere had been dead for centuries. Without the lady to tend the ley lines on our island, the power in the blood fades, and there are fewer and fewer people with the druidic gifts, fewer latents. There are certainly no latents with the level of power you have, girl."

"So a new Lady of the Lake just arrived and beat the Empire?"

"More or less," Rion answered without opening his eyes.

"What does that mean?"

"Well she helped win the battle, but more importantly the Lady Evaine fell in love and married the *handsome* Mercian

King Belanore and her children inherited some of her powers. They eventually were slain in battle and their children continued the fight. Their daughter, Olwen, became Lady of the Lake, she was saved in battle by Llewelyn the Great and his son Gruffyth became the first Griffin and they pushed the Romans south."

Callum went to fetch our horses to head out and I took a seat – the Marina I knew of old would never be satisfied with this.

"What happened then?"

Rion groaned, levering himself up on an elbow and smiling at me in greeting. "Generations passed and magic grew stronger in the land. Mercia had given refuge to their Plantagenet cousins who had fled Anglia before the Lady Evaine came to us. The House of York spent its time raiding the lands they had once ruled, until the Lady Katherine, Evaine's descendent, married the widowed King Consort John and persuaded him to unite our houses, creating the Union of the Roses."

"Ooh, I know about this. They pushed the legions all the way south of the May line."

"Where they remain to this day," Rion summed up in a final tone.

I couldn't help the laughter that escaped me at his attempt to fob her off.

"But aren't you missing the bit where the Rose armies are defeated at Stratford and the valiant King Henry was slain without leaving an heir, thus breaking the line of the great Mercian House of Lancaster?" I had broadened my studies to understand better the history of my home.

Rion cast me a dark look, though I knew he would be pleased at my knowledge and at Marina's interest.

Marina's eyes opened expectantly. "What happened then? Did York take over Mercia?"

"Henry's widow, a princess who had fled Gallia, married the Griffin Owain Tewdwr. Their son, Edmund, married a Lady of the Lake, Margaret Beaufort, and together they founded perhaps the most celebrated House of Mercia."

"House Tewdwr." This was a Briton house that even the least educated child inside the stews of Londinium knew. "Was their son the High King Arthur?"

Rion chuckled at Marina's somewhat hero-worshipping expression. "Not yet. Their son Henry married the sister of Edward of York and their son Arthur becomes the first High King of Briton as he tied together some of the major bloodlines of Briton: the Lakes line, the Plantagenets, and through the Tewdwrs, House Glyndŵr."

United, the Briton tribes had pushed back the tide that had devoured Europe and northern Africa, all the way to the walls of Londinium itself. At least for a time.

"And his death started the two-hundred-year war, and pushed you back above the May line. But how come you couldn't defeat the legions again? Arthur did it in only a few years."

"The battles are not always as important as who leads," Rion explained as I made my way over to Callum, who had returned with the horses. "All those lines coming together created a king who everyone wanted to follow. When he was killed, we were splintered apart once more."

Callum tilted his head back and exhaled in frustration, pinching the bridge of his nose as he did when he was at the very edge of his patience. It was one of those little mannerisms more suited to the professor who lived on the inside than the bear of a man he appeared to the world.

"You need to have faith in what you do. Believe in the gift you've been given," he urged me for the millionth time.

I stared at the belligerent rock in front of me.

"Why won't it just obey me?" If I could smash it into gravel and throw it into the ocean to be ground down to sand it would be no more than it deserved.

"Obey?" Callum echoed, his mouth gaping in surprise at me. He let out a guffaw. "Obey? You are telling a rock what to do? No, no, it can't be as simple as that."

He pulled at his beard slowly.

"When you are dealing with the ley line, what do you do?" he asked.

"What do you mean, what do I do? I don't do anything. I sing to it, with it, I let the magic wash through me and the notes change, the harmony flows and continues on its way."

"And when you feel a storm rise when you are angry, how do you do that?"

I didn't really do anything, that was the problem. It just happened. I was aware of it and knew enough to release it if things hadn't got too out of control. When it took me with it, I usually needed someone to remind me not to be the storm. My heart stuttered a little at the flash of the first storm I had conjured, of Devyn's kisses bringing me back to myself.

"Cass," Callum prompted.

I shrugged. "I don't really do anything, it's just there. The magic comes in, and things happen."

"And when you tell the rock what to do?"

What did he want me to say? I wasn't able to do it. It was beyond me.

"Your best work comes when you just do what seems natural, no thinking, no weighing up the scenarios, just doing," he said. "Stop overthinking everything. Just do it."

The power was within me. I had everything I needed.

And the rock rose.

Callum swept me up in his arms, jubilant.

"I can't believe it. After all that," a broad smile stretched across his face. "You can do anything! You just need to... do it."

I beamed at Rion as I flopped into the seat in his study. I wanted to share my success with someone and as Gideon wasn't at training, the king was the easiest to locate. At this time of day, he was always in his study working his way through the large amount of paperwork that ruling the kingdom seemed to generate. My brother was nothing if not a man of routine.

My mood was not matched by his. Whatever it was he was reading was clearly not agreeable as he muttered angrily in response to what lay within.

An eyebrow rose in enquiry as I waited for him to acknowledge me. He finally laid his quill down.

"Why don't you use pens?" I asked. It was beyond ridiculous. How was dipping a feather in ink a better idea? I wasn't asking that they install computers in the castle but what harm could a ballpoint pen do?

He raised a brow across his papers. "When the Treaty was signed in 1772, the industrial age was just beginning. If truth be told, the new weapons that the Empire were producing were a large part of the reason we decided it was time for a truce. But a number of the delegates became ill during the negotiations; it's the reason we stay in the city no longer than a week. By the time we leave, there is always some signs of the illness. After we leave the technology behind, the stricken delegates usually recover fast enough."

"I always thought technology didn't work out here," I said.

"It works, though it can be unreliable. I wouldn't care to sail in a boat reliant on tech," he said. "It also doesn't agree with us. We have survived well enough without it."

"You think a ballpoint pen causes the illness?"

"I don't know what causes the illness. What I do know is that in Londinium, those with magic in their bloodline get sick, and when they leave they recover."

"Marcus's line is Plantagenet," I reminded him.

"How old was his mother when she died?" he challenged back.

I wasn't sure how old she had been. Marcus had been young though. "Maybe thirty or so."

"None of the Courtenays have enjoyed old age, as far as I'm aware," he said. "There was a reason I did not accompany Gideon and Bronwyn when you escaped the city."

"You were sick? But Bronwyn attended the Treaty renewal as well," I recalled.

"They had both recovered. I had never been to Londinium before." He shrugged. "I was drained for some weeks after. Anyway, you did not come here to talk about the reason we do not embrace technology."

"I lifted a rock." I grinned. "On purpose."

His eyes lit. "Most impressive."

Of course, he would have been slinging boulders about since childhood. I hunched my shoulders. It had taken me years to master this. I eyed his desk and, catching me, his hand lifted in warning as I poofed the air and all of his carefully stacked papers went flying.

Rion stood and watched as leaves of paper floated to the ground in every corner of the room.

"I cannot believe you just did that," he said, coming around his desk, making his way purposefully toward me. "Those contain important matters of state."

"Don't be so stuffy," I threw at him and, dodging his wrath, ran for the door. I was halfway down the corridor when I realised he had not remained in his study to tidy things. There was a slightly alarming glint in his eye as he stalked me down the corridor.

Fleeing out to the courtyard turned out to be a mistake as he pursued me across the lawn and captured me beside the ornamental pond, which he decided to make use of in a way older brothers usually got out of their system earlier in life.

I gasped as I resurfaced in the cold water before I sent a wave of water into the air and dumped it unceremoniously over the King of Mercia.

Which was the state Gideon found us in as he came careening around the castle.

"You're not being attacked?" he glowered as I took his hand and he pulled me out of the lake.

I glared at Rion. "I was."

"She messed up my desk."

"He threw me in the lake."

Gideon's jaw went slack, and he took a deep breath before turning on his heel and walking away, grumbling out loud.

"I lifted a rock," I called after him. At which my serious older brother burst out laughing.

Chapter Twelve

I tucked Féile into her bed in the new style she favoured, which involved her blanket being tucked in all the way from her toes to her neck "like a butterfly". More accurately, a caterpillar, but if that was what she wanted, then I was hers to command. My heart swelling, I pressed my lips to her cheek, and her eyelids fluttered over the eyes that danced their way through the day from one adventure to the next.

I entered Gideon's room, where he sat by the fire reading a book.

"Little butterfly asleep?" he asked without looking up from his book.

I nodded. *Do it.*

"Yes," I said aloud rolling my eyes at my own foolishness.

Do it. Have a conversation.

"What are you reading?" I asked.

He lifted an eye in my direction. "A military history of the last war."

"Ah, the one on the borders?" I asked, as I sidled over to the table and poured myself a healthy glass of red wine.

"Yes," he said, watching me as I took a seat opposite him.

"Is there anything in there that might help?" I cringed at the stupidity of my question. *Yes, Cass, that's how we will win if the Empire attacks, by reading about a war from four hundred years ago*, but I had to start somewhere.

He tilted his head, the firelight catching his scar.

"How did you get your scar?"

Oh wow. Apparently, I was going all the way on this don't-think-just-do philosophy. Looking at Gideon's expression, the change was a little too sudden.

"I mean, how did you come to live here? I was talking to Rion about it, and he said I should ask you."

"You were talking to the king about me?" he asked quietly.

I swallowed. I couldn't be making a worse job of this if I had come in here to annoy him on purpose. Gideon was somewhat intimidating at the best of times, and it was only as I asked him a direct personal question that I realised how little I knew of him. Titbits gleaned from others, mostly – his reputation as a warrior, and plenty of hints that before we had married he had had plenty of female companionship but nothing real. He was raising my child, and we shared a bed, and I knew almost nothing about him.

"Before or after he dunked you in the lake?" his lip twitched.

I pulled a face.

"No, I mean it wasn't today, that is, I... uh..." I shrugged helplessly. "I just wanted to get to know you better. I'm sorry, I didn't mean to pry."

I stood. This had been a bad idea. Gideon didn't like me. He didn't want to get to know me better, and he certainly wasn't going to tell me anything.

His golden eyes flickered as I stood feeling like a fish

flopping on shore. I was so profoundly out of my comfort zone. Just do? What a ridiculous plan.

His eyes dropped as he adjusted his position in his seat before he started to talk.

"My mother left when I was a child. She believed she had a greater purpose in life than to be a wife and mother. My older brothers were teenagers, but I was still young. I didn't understand that after the lady – your mother – died, those with the ability to tend the ley lines were needed. So little magic remained that she felt she had to do what she could. She trained in Anglesey, and occasionally took me along when she remembered. Then, when I was ten or so, she left for good."

I sat back down slightly dumbfounded that he was not just telling me something, but at where he had started. His mother had left him. Was he telling me this to explain why he had been so angry at me for not being there for my own child? I had wanted to make conversation, but instead I found myself jumping headlong into too deep water to find that the current was going to take me where I would have been too much of a coward to go myself. And what was even more shocking was that I had company. Gideon looked almost as taken aback as I was.

He smiled ruefully – at me, at himself, who knew? Nonetheless, he ploughed on.

"I was angry at her, angry at my father for letting her go, angry at the world for taking her when I still needed her. I was never high in my father's affections. You've met him. He's... well, he already had two sons and felt that the women of the castle were too soft on me. 'Poor motherless pretty-boy', he called me." Gideon said it in a way that felt like it was something he had heard all too often.

"Well, you are pretty," I said in an effort to lighten the

mood that had descended. He was undeniably attractive, even with the scar that ran across his cheek. As a child he must have been the object of every woman's tender heart. I had no doubt he had never lacked for female attention.

"I had a friend." He ignored my compliment. "She was the daughter of one of my father's friends, and we grew up together. We were close."

I raised an eyebrow at that.

"Not like that," he said. "Not then, anyway. Alice was my best friend, and the only person I cared for. Then, when she was seventeen, she was betrothed... to my brother. I was furious. They had taken away the one person who was mine. The one person I cared about. I was angry at them, and I was angry at her. Well, I was fifteen. I stomped around that entire summer and discovered the solace that can be found in the arms of women. In some ways, it was a most educational time." He smiled. "But their attentions just widened the hollow feeling inside, and twisted—" He exhaled deeply. "I shouldn't have done it. It was..."

"What did you do?" I prompted, as he struggled to get the words out. But even as I asked them I knew. "Oh no, Gideon..."

I could see it in his eyes, in his shame.

"You slept with her? But she was going to marry your brother," I said, aghast. "Why? For revenge?"

"Yes." The old Gideon was back, darkly defiant, indifferent to anyone else's opinion. I flinched in reaction to that look. How could he? He had used his face, his body, to seduce his friend and ruin her life.

He ran a hand across his face and groaned. "No."

I waited futilely for him to continue.

"If not for revenge, then why?" I prompted.

"I wanted her to pick me," he finally got out. "I suppose I thought that if we were together…"

"What happened?"

"Oh, my father discovered us." He shrugged. My heart ached for him. I was jealous of this girl, whoever she was, but mostly I was just sad for the confused, messed-up kid he had been.

"But wait, how did you get the scar?"

"I told you. My father found out. Loyalty, family, honour, these are not just words in the house I grew up in." A look of self-contempt flashed across his face as he ran a finger down the length of his scar. "Unfortunately for me, he wears a signet ring on his left hand."

I recalled him commenting on a cut on Callum's cheekbone when he had met us on the road in Cymru after letting us flee Oxford to evade the York troops coming for us. Gideon had said something about Callum having disappointed the steward.

"I dishonoured everything he believes in and he threw me out." He shrugged. "So here I am."

His eyes defied me to judge him.

"And the girl?"

"Oh, she married my brother," he said.

Who was I to judge anything?

"So you made your way to the Lakelands?" I asked.

"Eventually. I took my time getting here. I spent a while in Alba – my mother was from there and I had some notion of finding her. I spent some time in the Dùn Èideann court fighting and wenching until my welcome ran out. When I arrived here, my reputation preceded me, but Rion was going through a bad patch himself so he took me in and we had a wild time of it for a few years. Eventually, he started to become the wise and careful man we know today." He shrugged. "I had nowhere else to go, and he was... so I stayed. There you have it. My whole sorry story. Is that what you wanted?"

I stood, crossing to him. I leant over and, laying my hand on his cheek, kissed the other scarred one. I understood. He had loved his friend, as he had loved his mother, and she had left him. They both had. I felt twisted inside at his story. No wonder he looked at me with such contempt. I had been a terrible mother, as his had been. He had lashed out at this girl when she, too, had abandoned him. Did he still love her? Was that why he had agreed to marry me – because he couldn't have the woman he really wanted?

I eased away from him, but his arm encircled me and pulled me back down to his lap where he kissed me. The kiss was deep and true and searching, and I kissed him back. It wasn't chemistry or passion that fuelled it but something deeper, a connection beyond the physical, beyond the mystical. He was asking me a question in return, and I realised I wanted to answer it.

The book thudded as it hit the floor.

I deepened the kiss with the answers that eddied through me.

———————————

I made my way down to dinner early in the first thing that had come to hand in my wardrobe, weary after seeing in the spring equinox at Penrith. Working with the lines had become a constant battle, and turning back the tide of discordant, polluted notes was exhausting. I had thought Gideon would come as he now sometimes did but he hadn't and I was sorry that I hadn't asked him to. Now I was eager to see him, to simply be in his presence.

Today had been a bad day. I felt I had helped, but I was shattered and looking forward to being alone with my—

I stopped short and corrected myself. With Gideon and Féile.

They hadn't been in our rooms so I had embarked on a fruitless traipse around the castle, up and down halls and stairs, asking everyone I passed, but they were nowhere to be found. They ate in Rion's rooms sometimes, but his study had been empty. Given it was nearly dinner time, I returned to my room to tidy up and then took my place at the high table.

A couple of warriors came in, nodding to me as they took their seats lower down the table. I recognised Alec, Rion's captain of the guard. He was tall and thin-legged, even though he was often the first and last at meals. If the hall were ever to be attacked, it seemed it would at least have one staunch – if surprisingly skinny – defender.

The hall gradually filled up but I remained on my own at the high table. Rion was the punctual type, and it was late in the evening. Féile would have to go straight to bed.

Callum smiled at me a little tightly as he took his usual seat not too far away. Snuffles was at my feet, but there was still no sign of his tiny mistress. Dinner was served despite Rion's absence, and a number of the guard slipped away from their table, including Captain Appetite, who could hardly have managed to inhale his meal before leaving.

A strange tension snaked its way through the hall.

Snuffles poked at my feet with his nose, a trick that all too often earned him scraps from Féile's plate; I had spotted Rion handing down choice pieces of food on occasion with a wink to his niece who knew the dog was not supposed to be fed at the table.

The dog didn't usually try it with me, but he seemed insistent tonight. I lifted him onto my knee, and he immediately tried for my plate, which was strictly off limits.

"Hey, there, Snuffle-pup." I pulled back from the table and attempted to distract him by patting his silky hair, but he was insistent on trying to get to what was a great deal of food going to waste as I remained the only one at the table.

"What's going on? Has no one fed you today?"

I picked at a piece of meat, and he snaffled it down. He had never been the most discreet eater, which was one of many reasons why he wasn't allowed at table. Once he had eaten his fill, he turned his dark, melting eyes up at me.

"No, pup, I don't know where they are either," I said to him.

Putting him on the ground, I made for the door... where there were no guards stationed to ask. There were always guards at the entrance to the main hall, and they were somehow always aware of everyone's location. Sometimes I wondered if they had someone who went around giving and receiving updates.

They hadn't been there when I arrived either.

I made my way down to the main entrance.

A few scattered guards were making their way hurriedly across the courtyard. Not walking with purpose, nor running in alarm, but there was a stilted urgency, like they wanted to run but were restrained, and slightly directionless. As I watched, one man stopped and cocked his head before turning on his heel and heading back in the direction from which he had started.

"What is going on?" I demanded, intercepting him.

His eyes widened as he took me in, and he rocked back on his heels.

"Ah…" He looked around as if the answer might present itself or he would be rescued by one of his fellows who could deal with the Lady of the Lake, of whom they were all somewhat wary. My fault, really. I was often gone, and when I was here, I kept to my little family circle.

"My lady." He looked down at his feet, which he was edging off, one and then the other, uneasily. "We're looking for the little 'un."

"What?" His voice had dipped low and he mumbled the last. "The lit urn?"

That made no sense. Why would Rion be sending his men to look for an urn? Dread pitched into my stomach. The whole castle was out looking and Snuffles was still clinging to my heels. The pampered pooch who had never known hunger had not been fed.

"Where is my daughter?" I asked of the alarmed guard.

He shook his head, lifting his hands helplessly.

"How long?" I asked. "How long has she been gone?"

I could barely hear the words, directed as they were at the cobbles on the ground. "Since morn."

The world stuttered to a stop. It felt like every thought drifted slowly through my brain, time stilling to give me a moment to take it in. To think. She'd been missing since morning. Since morning.

I had come back just after sunset and she had already been lost for an entire day. How did a two, almost three-year-old get lost in a city that hummed around her existence? They had lost their last… She was doted on, watched carefully – on the odd occasion she scratched her knees I was subjected to reproachful looks for days.

From people I knew were half afraid of me.

How had nobody told me?

Breathe.

The guard in front of me backed away, nervously throwing his eyes skyward.

Breathe.

"Cass." Callum stood in front of me, holding my shoulders. At least I think it was Callum. The person touching me barely registered and I felt as if I would fly apart, my senses scattering as if to find her, each piece going in a different direction. "Focus, girl. Come back, come back. No good to anyone like this. Does thou hear me, girl?"

I needed to blink.

Callum.

I pulled each spiralling part of me back in tighter and tighter until I was present once more.

"Callum." I gripped his arm, hard. "She's gone?"

"Nay, lass," he reassured me. "Little 'un's just gone exploring, what a to-do, all this clatter and fuss. She'll be curled up like a kitten in some cosy corner at this hour."

"Right." I focussed. Of course. How far could her little legs go? They were all out scouring the countryside. Fools! She was here. Of course she was.

"I found Devyn before, with my mind... Can I do that?" How had I done that before?

"When? How?" Callum sounded skeptical.

"When he was on his way to Castle Brân we didn't know where he was and my mind was able to cross the distance to find him," I recalled.

"You were able to locate him without any indication of where he was?"

"Yes, I... No, I followed the druid. Madoc led me..." I trailed off. "What use is any of this if I can't help her now?"

Callum's mouth turned down. "Magic doesn't solve everything. But we will find her. All will be well."

I marched back inside and started in her room. She was so small. How far could she go? I knelt down on the hardwood floor and checked under her bed. It was tossed and ruffled, drawers already opened, wardrobe wide with clothes piled on the ground. Someone had already torn through here. Someone desperate. Why hadn't they found her already?

I picked up the clothes, in case she was under them.

They smelled of her, the summer breeze, flowers and hope of which she was made up. I buried my face in them.

I would wait. I would wait right here. Féile would be tired when they found her; it was nearly night time. I would wait right here. Last time... last time I had followed and that was why they had hurt him. To hurt me. If I hadn't been there, if I hadn't followed, maybe things would have turned out differently.

I sat on the little bed, her clothes, her smell all around me. This is where I would wait.

Minutes passed, hours, the sound of footsteps toing and froing in the hall. Voices, rumbling. None came in though. No one carried a tired little body with dark curls trailing messily down her back after her unexpected adventure.

I had to hold on. They would find her.

The door pushed open. My heart leapt at the sight of Gideon in the doorway. But his dark face was in shadow and his arms were empty.

"Where is she?" I asked calmly.

He shook his head, his shoulders lifting wearily in a shrug.

His energy was tense. That casual stance turned menacing, coiled, just looking for a target to unleash on.

"Why are you here?" I demanded. "Why haven't you found her?"

Gideon just looked back at me with flat eyes.

"Catriona, we've been looking all day and all night. She's gone," Rion said, entering the room from behind the dark warrior.

"Gone?" I echoed.

"We've been everywhere. We think she's been taken," Rion said the words like they were new to him, like he couldn't believe he was putting them together.

I whirled on Gideon.

"You," I snarled. "You are supposed to protect her, to keep her safe. That's your job. What are you good for if you can't...?"

Gideon, his eyes coming alive and blazing with unleashed rage, took a step forward, his instinct always to engage, to attack. He stopped, his lip curled. His eyes snagged behind me to the empty little bed. The bed he had tucked her into, where he read to her, so many nights, so many more nights than me. I hadn't kept her safe. All this work and I hadn't even been here. I hadn't been here when she needed me. Who had taken her?

I pushed that away. I couldn't deal with that yet. But I could take that stricken gutted look off Gideon's face. He didn't get to be wounded. There was no time for that. He had already had so much time with her. Now he needed to get her back.

I barged into Gideon's chest. He looked down at me as he fell a step back under my physical attack.

"I don't want to look at you. I don't want to see you until you have her. Go and get her, go and get her!" I could hear the accusation, the bile of jealousy and fear that soured my tone as I commanded him to do more. I could see every bit of trust, and whatever it was that had been between us, break and seep out of him. He had lost everything today. My daughter was gone from him and until he got her back, so was I.

Rion pulled me back to him and held me tightly. "Everything will be fine. You'll see, everything will be fine."

I shook him off, all my anger, all my hope, directed at the immobile Gideon.

"What good are you?" I demanded. "I hate you! You have failed. Again."

"You hate me?" His brow quirked as he stepped into me. "What an interesting way you have of showing it."

"Stop this." Rion stepped around me, putting himself bodily in front of Gideon.

"She's gone," Gideon said hollowly to his oldest friend.

"It's like you're cursed." I laughed, half beside myself, the thought coming out of nowhere. Gideon was beholden to no one, loved no one, and yet it seemed every time he did he lost the woman he loved.

Gideon's head snapped back. His eyes glazed over as Rion turned to look at me, horrified at my words.

"Doesn't that make us quite the pair." The scar pulled at his cheek as he smirked cruelly. "I have done everything so that Féile would have a mother. And what good are you now, despite everything?"

"Despite everything?" Despite all the work he had put in. I couldn't breathe. My throat felt as if it was closing in on itself. "You are only with me so that my daughter can have a mother?"

"I know what it is to be without one. She deserves more."

"Enough!" Rion roared. "Stop this. Tearing into each other won't help bring her back."

I whirled away, reeling, everything within me collapsing on top of the hollow void inside me.

It was a lie. When had I started fooling myself? Believing that he wanted me for me, that it was more than just a physical thing? I knew he had been forced into this marriage, knew he cared for nothing, that he'd had plenty of female companionship before I came along. I had thought, felt, as though he wanted me, as though he felt something for me in return.

What did it matter now?

I laughed and looked back at him with that warrior's body, the hunter's spirit, and that handsome scarred face. Amber eyes observed me insouciantly.

I was nothing but a tool, a weapon that could be wielded against the Empire. One that had become brittle, and he had merely done what any careful warrior did with a tool in preparation for war.

Now, war was here. And they had stolen my baby.

Rion sent word to York, Conwy, and Dùn Èideann that Féile had been taken from us. Gideon chafed at delaying pursuit.

"They are only a day ahead," he pleaded with Rion. "We can catch them. Féile will slow them down."

Rion looked thoughtful. "Whoever has her has not snatched her on impulse. They will have prepared for this; there is little chance we will find them."

"Dammit, we can try."

"At least it would get you out from underfoot," Rion

acceded. "Take no more than twenty men. The rest will be needed to prepare to march."

I drifted from Rion's study back up to Féile's room as Gideon gathered his troops and readied for pursuit. He knew I was here, as he had known the last time I had sat in a window over the courtyard watching the world I no longer felt a part of. No longer wanted to be a part of. Then, as now, he did not look my way.

As I watched, two riders came to the gate – not soldiers, farmers perhaps. They stopped and dismounted and spoke to Gideon, their gestures wild and urgent. A flutter ran through me. Gideon looked up at my window. What was it? What news had they brought that he would acknowledge my presence?

I ran along the corridor and down the stairs, my hand leaning on the stone walls, unsure my legs were steady enough to bring me to where I needed to be.

By the time I entered the courtyard, Rion and Callum were there. Why had they been summoned and not me? Had they found her? My mind flinched against the thought of bad news.

Rion turned as I approached, his eyes taking in my expression and giving me a swift shake of his head. No news of Féile then.

"A lake has appeared," Rion explained, the two farmers nodding wide-eyed, their mouths slack with the dazed reverence those meeting me for the first time often seemed to suffer.

What? A lake? What did that have to do with anything? With Féile?

"It appeared last night."

"Out of nowhere, my lady," one of the farmers interjected. "We thought the River Irthing had burst its bank first, but it's a great size."

I looked at Callum, my teacher. What was I missing here? Why should I care as much as these men all seemed to?

"The lake is many miles wide," Callum clarified. "There has been no rain, it is shrouded with mists, and apple trees grow on the shore."

"I don't understand. What are you telling me?"

"Apples are the symbol of Avalon, the home of Nimue, she who helped Arthur, and Evaine, the lady who married Belanore and started your bloodline," Callum explained. "I think it is an invitation."

"For me?" I asked. Of course it was for me. It had appeared the night Féile was stolen. "Why couldn't it have come before, why now, after?"

Callum lifted one shaggy shoulder. "Can't say. But it's there now. Thee must go. Speak with whoever waits below. Perhaps they offer help to get your girl back."

My eyes snagged to Gideon's. We may have flung vicious words at each other only hours ago but nobody else wanted her back more than he.

"You should go," he confirmed.

"You will go with her," Rion stated quickly.

"No," he protested, "I am going after Féile."

"These men can go after them. You know the chances of recovering her are slim," Rion reasoned. "Who else should I send with Catriona? You are her protector."

"Yes, my great gift as Griffin," he said, his lip curling. "What would she do without me there to hold her hand?"

Gideon bore none of the gifts of previous Griffins, apart from his ability to restore me. It was not evident that the spirit of the Griffin had transferred at all. He had never indicated before that it bothered him but then, I had never asked.

"Fetch my lady's horse," Rion commanded a nearby

warrior, dispatching another to find Oban to bring my travel cloak and pack.

"You must be wary in Avalon.' Callum looked concerned now that we were agreed I would go.

"Wary? I thought Avalon was an ally."

"It is, aye. Avalon has sent us great help over the centuries – weapons, sending the Lady Evaine who stayed and married Belanore – but the bloodline from Avalon has sometimes been less beneficent," Callum said as he fussed at his beard. "The lady has helped us to overcome our enemies, but on occasion, she has been the enemy within. For every Lady Guinevere there has been a Lady Morgana. Think on the Lady Guinevere a moment, her intentions were good but the curse you deal with comes of her actions, would have been cast by her sisters. In the records Rhodri sent there are indications that not all the women of the line were wholehearted. I came across a rumour that the Lady Anne may have been the one who destroyed the House Tewdwr."

Rion frowned. "Lady Anne, Lady Elizabeth's mother?"

"Mmm, she was Lady of the Lake but not very powerful, born into a dispossessed Anglian family. She married Arthur's younger brother Henry, and there is a school of thought that says she was ambitious, that she planned to overthrow Arthur and may have allied with the Empire to do so. Londinium killed them all and Elizabeth barely survived." His great brows drew together. "There is a treacherous aspect in the Lake bloodline. The gift is mercurial and only goes to one descendant in each generation. Power can be tempting, and the Avalon line seems to throw the occasional twist."

A Lady of the Lake marrying into the royal line of Mercia was not entirely unusual. My own mother had... Did Callum suspect that my mother had also been working with Londinium?

"Do you think I shouldn't go?"

He shook his head quickly. "No, you must go, but be careful. Things may not always be as they seem. Avalon is not of this world, and the rules that govern it are not ours. Weigh words carefully and offer nothing you don't have to."

Oban arrived bearing my fur-lined cloak as the spring was still cold, as well as my always ready pack. His face was pinched in worry as he wrapped his arms around me. "Be safe, lady."

I stepped back, and Rion also enfolded me. "Be careful, Catriona."

Gideon had already mounted, impatient to be away to get this errand done with as quickly as possible.

"Ride now," Rion said, giving me a boost into the saddle with his hands. "We will be ready on your return."

"Ready for what?" I asked, looking down at him.

"For war."

Part Two

MINGLED WITH THE RAIN

Mae'r hen delynau genid gynt
Ynghrog ar gangau'r helyg draw,
A gwaedd y bechgyn lond y gwynt,
A'u gwaed yn gymysg efo'r glaw.

The harps to which we sang are hung
On willow boughs, and their refrain
Drowned by the anguish of the young
Whose blood is mingled with the rain.

— *Rhyfel (War)*, Hedd Wyn translated by Alan Llwyd

Chapter Thirteen

W e headed east, towards Castlesteads just south of the wall that General Hadrian had built when he thought he could hold this land for the Empire a millennia ago. A heavy mist obscured the land as we approached the area to which the farmers had directed us. Gideon hadn't spoken since we left Carlisle, leaving me to my thoughts in the weighted silence in which even our horses' steps were muffled as we moved through the whiteness. The increasing regularity of apple trees was our only indication that we were headed the right way.

I picked over what little I knew about Avalon, which, given that two women had stepped out of myth to aid the Britons in halting the progress of the Roman conquest and one had started a line of which I myself was a part, was shockingly little.

The records spoke of the deeds of Guinevere and Evaine, but little was known of their origins. Avalon was known as the isle of healing, or simply as "the lake" but no one knew where it lay, or if it moved. Its appearance now seemed to prove the later theory. There were whispers of enchantments and seduction, and now it seemed, treachery.

The history of the line Callum had gleaned amounted to little more than genealogy, and I wasn't entirely sure what I was supposed to do here. Had the lake appeared in our time of need to offer aid, or did some trick await? In the tales, the Celts recounted in song and story aid arriving from the otherworld, and it was never as innocent as it seemed. Yet Avalon, in myth, had given aid in times of need and Féile was a daughter of Avalon. I had to believe that help was being offered. We weren't strong enough to take on the Empire, the ley lines were failing, and we stood little chance against the superior, sophisticated weapons of the city.

Finally, we came to the edge of the water, dismounting as two swans floated majestically out of the mists, a boat trailing in their wake.

Gideon looked suspiciously at the unmanned boat but managed to push down whatever it was that bothered him and handed me into the boat before pushing it into the water and jumping on board himself.

Gideon pulled the oars steadily until we were out in the middle of the water. The boat was insignificant, bobbing as it was on the water, fragile against the elements, but inside I was dry and safe. For now.

Gideon watched me carefully, his eyes as flat as they had been since Féile had been taken. I was going to get her back. I would be the storm that would rain down upon them. If what Callum told me was true then with the strength of previous ladies I would be as unstoppable as nature herself. They would be unable to flee, they would be helpless against my fury. That was my goal, that was my sole focus. The wrath of a mother was terrible, and I would ensure that they were ended.

"It will go no further." Gideon's words broke through my thoughts of vengeance, lifting the oars out of the water.

The mists receded as storm clouds gathered in.

There was no island visible, only water on all sides for miles, even though we could not be that far from the shore we had just left. I must have to enter the lake itself. I looked down into the dark waters. I could do this.

But if I didn't return, the warrior facing me would find Féile. He had to.

Gideon was elemental himself. His dark hair was being tugged by the wind that swirled up out of nowhere, his arms were bare, his dark Celtic tattoos swirling as if they were alive. New ink patterned his inner arms. Taking his hand, I turned it over to examine the tattoos more closely. He bore a dara knot, a rounded shield-like shape, a knot divided into quadrants. It denoted protection, survival, strength, destiny. Its weaving also contained echoes of lake and oak, fire and sky. It was a knot binding an oath, similar to the one that Devyn had worn on his heart with the Mercian symbols. The one that represented the oath that he had broken and the one he had kept. The swirls around it were heartrendingly reminiscent of the curls I had smoothed to help Féile sleep, her lively brain quieted by the soothing touch of a parent's hand. I held the hard calloused hand in mine, the hand that had learned the trick to help her rest and taught it to me.

I ran my fingers lightly over the still red, inflamed skin.

"What did you do?"

"I made a vow."

Gideon the warrior, who would swear no fealty in a land built on it, despite his ties to some of the most powerful families in the land, the Griffin who would not make a promise to the Lady of the Lake, had made a vow.

"I can see that," I responded. "What was the vow?"

What had he done? She was *my* daughter; I was the reason they had come for her and I would be the one to get her back.

"I will give my life's blood to see her safe."

I met his gaze directly for the first time since she had been taken. Devyn had made a similar vow, and once it was realised he had died. I could not see Gideon's life-force ebb away before mine. I would not survive another loss. He had no right to make such a promise. He needed to wait for me. I would come back wielding enough power to put the city on its knees and bring my daughter home. He had to wait for me. He was my anchor, the only one left who could call me back.

"You are the Griffin first," I said, in a hard voice. "Your first duty is to me."

His head tilted slightly, in revolt; he did not plan on waiting. He would be gone as soon as I stepped off this boat.

"We all agreed this was the plan. This is our best hope," I said.

"No, *you* all agreed. You and Rion and Callum. *You* decided. *I* did not agree. I am going to find her. I will not leave her to them a second longer than I have to."

"You think I don't want to go after her?" I seethed. "You think I want to delay? That I'm not terrified at how scared she must be right now? That every breath I draw is a breath too many before we go and get her?"

He quirked a dark eyebrow up. "Then why are we here?"

"We wouldn't make it across the borderlands."

"Devyn did."

"Devyn slipped in as a child by way of Calais, not as a strapping great warrior tattooed to the hilt, taking the most direct route on the heels of thieves. It was a dozen years after the fact, and even then it took him years to find me, and we were almost killed trying to escape," I reminded him. "What chance do you have?"

He shrugged. "More chance than if I sit here doing nothing."

I shook my head and placed my palms on either side of his face. Rain began to slash down from the grim greyness of the sky above, the weather worsening as I continued to ignore my invitation.

"You are the Griffin. Your first duty is to me," I said again to him.

His lips tightened, and he wrenched his head free.

"I'm the Griffin?" he scoffed. "When did you decide that? Now, when it suits you?"

He pointed an accusing finger at me, raising his voice as the storm heightened and the boat rocked furiously in place.

"You've never accepted me as Griffin. I'm the medicine you take to keep you whole, I am the caretaker you tolerate to ensure your daughter is looked after. And now you want me to do your bidding and wait for you on shore?" He laughed, his eyes glinting. "I am not your—"

He paused, his mouth full of ugly words that he wished to pour out at me.

"She is my daughter, and I have vowed to do whatever it takes to get her back." He thrust his clenched fist towards me, inner arm upward with its new tattoo. "I will not break my oath."

Unlike Devyn, were his unspoken words.

He was resolved. But so was I.

I smiled at him, baring my teeth. The energy from the storm filled me; it was raw and pure, free and wild.

I took his offered arm, grasping it in the upper arm clasp of the Celts, a clasp that brought our wrists into contact. This was the traditional pose for a reason; this was where the blood flowed closest to the surface of the skin, the blue veins of my wrist pressed to the pumped, healthy veins of his darker skin.

"Your oath is my oath." I spoke clearly, not shouting as he had against the storm, but as one with the storm. Its power and purpose was clear to me now. "My blood is your blood."

His amber eyes burned as they held mine, widening as he, like I, felt the scalding fire down the inner side of our clasped arms.

Did he understand what I was saying? That the promise made was ours together, that the blood I was binding him to was that of the child he had sworn to protect, her blood to his. He was her father.

He swallowed and nodded as he accepted what I was offering. His oath I could take, but my daughter had to be accepted – a fact he seemed to understand. A feeling, a rightness came over me. The ease of a piece clicking into place.

Releasing his arm, I moved closer to him in the rocking boat, which remained precisely on the spot to which he had rowed us. The shore was distant and hidden in the mists.

"I need you to be here," I said softly.

I looked up into his eyes. He was my tether. If he left, if he was not here for me, then I was already lost. He was right. I had never accepted him as Devyn's heir. It felt too much as if I had allowed the universe to replace the irreplaceable. The energy of the ley lines had scrubbed clean the wound in my soul, and this man's touch I had allowed to smooth the joins of the scar. But I had never let him in. He knew it, and I knew it. His role as Griffin had been reduced to its basest form. He had allowed me to do that to him because that was what I needed. And it had kept me alive. I felt unworthy, late to the realisation party again.

"Promise me," I urged. I felt incandescent with power, but I could not compel this of him. If he could not do this, we were ruined before we began. I wished for once to share with him the bond I had with Devyn, to let him feel the conflicting emotions swirling within me, my regret and sorrow for how I had used him, my anger and resolve to find Féile, my gratitude and acceptance of his role in both of our lives.

I watched the battle rage in his eyes, the resentment, the pride. How had he humbled himself so low for me? Why? I knew enough of his background now to understand the damage he had overcome, the lack of trust, the scars of betrayal that went beyond me, all the way to his core. And still, he had been there. For Féile. For me.

"Please," I begged. I could sense a bending in him, a chink of hope that I would not disappoint him again.

"For Féile." His lips thinned, but he nodded his agreement. Not a promise, not a vow, but a statement that he would be here.

I looked down at the tattoo, a mirror to his own, that now glistened under the rain on my arm. Magic had shared his vow, and his tattoo. A thought glimmered in the shadows of my mind. Was it possible?

I eyed the leather body armour that encased him. The storm intensified. I needed to go. They were waiting.

I tore at the buckle of his body armour, pulling it off him. A brow rose, his eyes questioning, but he did not resist and he did not question me. The ties of his tunic were next, loosening them until I could pull the wet cloth over his head.

I placed one palm over his heart and wrapped an arm around him, placing the other hand flat against his back.

I looked up at him. "You are my Griffin."

A searing pulse went from one palm, through him to the

other, spreading across his back, and he arched toward me, his head flung back as the tender nerves of his body were assaulted. His torso was taut, yet I managed to hold him, whatever flowed through me holding him in place. I saw the black ink appear over the edges of his shoulders.

I knew what was there – I didn't need to look. It would be a copy of the intricate Griffin tattoo that Devyn had done just days before his death. His had been a choice, the artist human. Who the artist of this was I had no idea. Devyn himself, perhaps? Who had guided my hand?

Gideon sagged as the pain faded.

"What did you do?" he asked.

"You are my Griffin," I repeated.

I pulled his head down. He was too drained to resist, his muscles exhausted.

I pressed my lips to his firmly. I laid a light finger on the tattoo of the butterfly which fluttered above his heart.

"I will come back," I said. My promise to him. The waters surged restlessly. I needed to go now. If I tarried any longer my window would close, and Avalon would not have me.

"I will be here," he said on a heavy breath.

I gave him a tremulous smile and stood up.

Avalon awaited, I hoped, otherwise I was going to drown and nothing would save my baby.

I stepped over the side of the boat into the waiting waters.

Chapter Fourteen

I plunged down into the turbulent waters, the cold of the lake a shocking slap as my impetus carried me down. I slowed, and the breath in my lungs began to seep out of me as I went further and further into the murky depths. I couldn't see anything.

My lungs emptied, and still, I slid down ever deeper. Bubbles of panic started to rise through me as I denied my body its desire to kick for the surface.

It seemed brighter somehow, as if the storm above had stopped. The water was blue instead of black and I felt at peace with it, its calmness seeping into me as the silken tide pulled me along, my limbs growing lighter and sensation more and more distant. The light grew closer and brighter, and then she was there, her glowing hair floating around her, her head tilting to the side as she examined me.

A slight smile tugged at her mouth as she extended her hand.

"I'm Viviane," she said. Her lips didn't move, but her lilting voice was welcome in my head. Assuring me of friendship. Of acceptance. Of belonging here, with her.

"Where am I?" I asked, because I was no longer underwater.

I had washed up on a beach, the sand pale and sparkling, water lapping against the shore the waves seeming to delight in tripping over each other, little mischievous spouts of water playing like dolphins in the surf. A green valley stretched in front of me, the air shimmering as if with heat on a summer's day, yet it was neither hot nor cold. A gentle breeze drifted off the coast and up into the valley, which seemed suspended in that glorious moment in between spring and summer. Lush and deliriously full of flowers, it was a paradise that seemed untouched but welcoming. A place to stay.

"Water is seductive. It lures you in. Initially there is a shock of awareness that it is not your natural environment, that you are not safe, but then it feels silky on your skin, invites you to play, and the temperature becomes more welcoming as you adjust to it." Her soft words were lyrical, lilting along with the playful breeze in which floated many coloured butterflies, their paths crossing that of a swallow which soared, twin-tailed, into the blueness of the sky. "So too with Avalon. You must remember that you are not safe here, no matter how alluring it seems in the moment. Do you understand?"

"Mmm," I said. I understood – or thought I did. I blinked as I attempted to decipher her warning. I needed to accomplish what I had come for and get back to land, back home. Back to Féile.

"I came for your help. Will you help me?"

I would help your daughter," she assured me gently, "if it was within my gift, but regretfully it is not."

Daughter. My attention snagged on the word. I examined her more closely. Did she...? Was it possible? No... She had said her name was Viviane. I searched for my mother's name. She was referred to as the Lady of the Lake. Or Mother. But I felt I had heard it somewhere. Viviane... Was it possible?

She had pale skin and pale blue eyes which looked at me kindly. There was something of Rion in the way she held her head, as if she were continually contemplating the board. Preparing her next move. Assessing how best to position others.

She took my hand gently in hers.

"You must focus, Catriona," she said. "You do not have long before Avalon tests your will."

I pulled my wayward thoughts together. It took a concerted effort to remember why I was here. How long did I have?

"I need help to get Féile back." I identified my task. "I'm not strong enough. I need to be able to wield more magic."

"You are strong." She smiled. "You were weakened in the years you lived over the Strand line. I would have healed it if I could, but I was betrayed. It has become corrupt, desperate, and it leached off you, weakened you, so your magic shielded your inner self. You must trust."

"Trust who? Trust what?" I felt deliciously languid, as if my limbs were weightless. I relaxed on the couch beneath me. It was hard to retain any urgency while my body felt so good. When had we arrived here? A perfect white tent shielded us from the warmth of the sun, the sheets fluttering in the barely there breeze.

"Trust yourself, trust the power. It needs you, but you resist. You are afraid. It gives what is needed, and in return you must offer it what it needs."

Ugh. Celts and their mystical non answers.

"No, you don't understand. I need to help Féile. I've got to be able to access more power, the kind of power they say the Lady Evaine wielded."

She laid a gentle hand on my chest. "You are afraid. I was afraid when I left you, and that is what you feel, that is what you remember when you feel the power gather within you. It is why you have more success allowing the power of the ley lines to flow through you and be cleansed but why you gather little to yourself. You do not believe, you do not trust."

"Trust what? Believe what?" I sat upright, shaking off the languid sensation that had come over me, recalling my urgency, recalling the need for aid. I couldn't begin to process that this woman might be my mother when what I needed so urgently she wasn't giving me.

"Believe yourself, trust those you love."

Believe myself? What, that I was more than some stupid girl being handed from one manipulative set of circumstances to the next? Trust those I love? Like her, like the people I had called my parents, like my lover... all of whom had left me? Right.

I could do those things later. For now, what I needed was to have the ability I hadn't had when they came for me, when they came for Devyn, when they came for my daughter. I needed power to obliterate my enemies.

"Tell me how to gather more magic. Show me how to wield more," I demanded of the woman who was speaking of healing when what I needed were weapons.

Her eyes creased in confused concern.

"You can gather all you need," she repeated.

I pushed her hand away.

"I can't. You did this to me. I knew no connection for too long," I accused.

Her eyes opened wide. "I cut the bond between you and the Griffin to save you pain. I could not let you and him suffer the separation with it intact. I sought only to spare you."

That was why Devyn and I had not been able to sense our bond, because she had severed the connection before she died.

"That's not what I meant. I grew up behind the walls. They made it so I couldn't touch magic. I started to learn too late. I'm not strong enough." I would never be as adept as those who had gone before me. I struggled to achieve the connection that my predecessors must have had during the wars, when the great and feared Lady of the Lake had saved the Britons. "I need to—"

"You need to do what I failed to achieve. You must heal the ley line of the corruption." Her blue eyes locked with mine. "You are ready."

"Ready for what?" This was not what I needed, yet I couldn't help but follow where she led.

"I tried before but I could not. The balance must be restored." She lifted my hand and turned it over, baring the tattoo so recently carved there. You are the key," she said, her fingertip tracing a new pattern, three curls looping out from a central point, each chasing the one in front of it. "Present in belief, past in trust, future in love, held by courage."

"I don't understand," I said, frustrated, the sensation of her touch as she traced out the new tattoo lingering.

"My present," she said, smiling, absently cupping my cheek. "My sweet gift. I tried to give it then, to spare you this, but it was too early, and the circle was not complete. It was always meant to be one other than the first; the second is as true, but he had to be bound to the circle once the first was gone."

She was making no sense. I winced at the flash of pain on my arm. I looked down and discovered the three spinning curls of the triskelion she had traced had appeared beside the new oath knot.

"Hurry. Time is running out."

I felt a feather of a kiss on my cheek.

And then I looked up to an empty space where my mother had been. Had that really been my mother? I felt her loss. I also seemed to be alone once more, and no further along in achieving my goal. I had come here for aid and so far had been told what, to be ready and various bits of nonsense that I would never be able to unravel?

I stood and returned to the shore. How did I return to Gideon from here? Did I need to swim? Which direction was I supposed to take? There was nothing but sparkling blue water in any direction.

And then another woman was stepping out of the crystalline waters of the lake. This one looked less human than Viviane. Long silver hair moved in a nimbus around her, water sprites bobbing in the water nearby as she stepped out of the waves. Her skin was almost translucent and glowing.

"I am Nimue." Her voice was so soft that it barely seemed to register in the air. It was possible she hadn't spoken at all and that her words, her name, merely fluttered in my mind.

"I am Cass… Catriona."

"You are all this and more." Her eyes were a luminous violet, and they shone with a kind, accepting light.

"Can you help me?"

"Perhaps. What is it you seek?"

I seek…" I hesitated, wary of this woman in a way I hadn't

been of Viviane. Callum had warned me to choose my words carefully. What was asked for might be granted but it didn't mean that I would obtain what I wanted. Asking for power did not mean I would get Féile back. "They have taken my daughter."

"What would you have of me, child? Do you need a weapon? Or would you simply have us get her back for you?"

"I'm not sure what I need. You have provided weapons before, but I can't just choose Féile. The land is dying and I would help if I can. Is there something I can ask for that gives me both?"

She arched a brow, a smile tilting her lips.

"There is. Excalibur is ready, but I don't think you need a sword. I think you have everything you need," she said. "You must have faith."

Need. Rhodri had once said that the Griffin was whatever the lady *needed* him to be.

"Is Gideon the only way I can be restored?" What if I could free him from the bond that ties him to me so completely?

"Do you need him to be?" The silver of her hair floated in the air as if she were underwater; it was mesmerising. "The Griffin responds to necessity."

"I don't need him?" I heard myself ask abstractedly.

"Need, want, they are two sides of the same coin, or two coins of the same side, are they not?" She took my hand in hers and walked us along the beach, the waves lapping at her feet, endlessly reaching for her.

"Can you help me?" I asked again. Had I asked that already?

"The land grows weak in magic. Until the balance is restored, this is as much as we can do." Her violet eyes dimmed in sorrow. "It is already too much for some – my sisters would prefer we hold on to what little is left."

She stopped and placed her hand over my heart. "So strong, so hurt, you have all you need, and you need all you have. It is up to you how you use it. Choose wisely, as we can help no more."

My heart suddenly felt whole. The scars that lay on it were mine, were part of me, and the way forward seemed so clear as I looked out across the water. I lifted my arms and twirled in the sheer joy of the moment. The lightness of my soul, the freedom of my body, the sun on my skin. I felt as if I were a water sprite pirouetting and dancing in the surf, captivated by the rush and ebb of the white water.

A figure caught my eye.

A dark shape in the distance drawing closer.

He ambled through the dunes toward me, his eyes dark and warm, fixed on mine as my eyes devoured him. Was this possible? Could it be? I waited until he stopped in front of me, afraid to move, afraid to look away in case he disappeared. Had Nimue left? I couldn't take my eyes off the man to scan the beach to find out.

I lifted a hand to trace it down the side of his face. He was real. His lip quirked up in acknowledgement of my disbelief.

"You're here."

He smiled. "I told you I would always come back for you."

He kissed me lightly.

"We can be together," he said as he wrapped his arms around me under the golden sun. "Stay with me."

Everything was perfect. He was here. We were together.

No. Something was missing.

She was… missing. Taken.

"You're not real." I pushed him away. It had to be a lie.

Devyn, my Devyn, was a being constructed almost entirely of duty and honour. He would never try to convince me to stay, to abandon the people who were counting on me, to abandon the destiny that had been lost and was now regained.

"Why go back?" he asked. "Stay here with me. You'll be safe. We can finally be together. Isn't that what you want?"

Was it? It had been once. I had given up my world to follow him, to go where he led. I had defied my family, old and new, to be with him.

He pressed his lips to mine. The familiar movement was honey lazily drizzling on the arid wastes of my soul. The light and golden liquid melted across my heart. More than anything I wanted to revel in its luxuriousness; it was comfort and joy.

But it wasn't real. And I wasn't alone. I wasn't alone. There was a thread that called to me, that led me home. That thread was real. It left the light and went into darkness, but it was anchored and it was true. I needed to follow it.

"Not Devyn," I muttered against the lips that touched mine. This wasn't real. It was a temptation to stay here in this beautiful, peaceful place with the man I had loved. With the man I had said goodbye to far too soon. He was gone, though, and I had said goodbye.

I was needed elsewhere. I breathed, forcing my focus onto that thread. At the other end were people I cared about, people who needed me: Gideon, the surly warrior; Féile, my beautiful daughter. Féile. My heart burst with remembered pain. And then butterflies floated around us, fluttering into the blue.

This was not Devyn. Devyn would never try to keep me from going after my daughter. Our daughter. They had stolen her. She would be afraid.

I grabbed onto that thread.

The lips moved more forcefully on mine and I felt pressure

on my chest, air filling my lungs. Lips pressed forcefully against mine.

"Come back," he whispered.

I pushed him away.

"Not Devyn," I managed to say.

The darkness surrounded me.

And then I spluttered and rolled onto my side as water spewed out of my lungs.

Chapter Fifteen

I lay exhausted in the damp ground at the edge of the lake.

It was evening. Had I been gone for that many hours? I scanned the shore in front of me. Gideon sat glowering at me in the gloaming. His once customary sneer was an unexpected yet nonetheless welcome sight.

I smiled in relief – a smile that remained unanswered.

"Hey," I managed croakily.

"Hey," he echoed in palpable outrage.

What was I missing? I had done it, I had survived.

I pushed myself up to a sitting position. My clothes were wet and clung to me in the cold night air. It was freezing.

I felt the strange aftereffects of magic – not the clinical emptiness I usually felt after wrangling with the energy in the ley line, but tingly. I pulled myself over to the Griffin, tucking myself into him. He was hunched, his expression shuttered, but he pulled me close and held me there stiffly.

I had seen Devyn. But had it been real? Or had it been an illusion of Avalon? I thought I had been on dry land, but maybe I had been in the water this whole time. Viviane had warned me against the seduction of Avalon. Had Devyn – or the mirage of Devyn – been nothing more than a lure the water had sent to keep me there? If I had stayed longer would I have forgotten to leave?

"Forgetting and remembering," I whispered out loud. There had been something I needed, that was what had brought me to the shores. Did I get it?

"You're cold," came a growl above me and I was hoisted off the ground by strong arms lifting me over to a fire crackling in a clearing a few feet from the lakeshore. My teeth were chattering violently when he put me down, and I huddled as close as I could to the fire. He stripped off my wet shift and wrapped me in a heavy cloak. He left me without a word, striding back to the shore, his back tense, braced as he watched the sun slip below the horizon. Some of the tension seemed to leave him and his shoulders dropped, his head bowed, before he returned to me. He sat behind me and wrapped himself around me.

As always, I felt comforted and renewed in his substantial presence. I soaked it in until I noticed he was tense and unyielding. I peeked over my shoulder, taking in the locked jaw and thinned lips.

We had been better earlier, before I had gone into the water; it had felt like we had reached a new understanding. He was the Griffin, and he wore Devyn's tattoo... Had I dreamed it? Twisting around more fully in his arms, I pushed his tunic back. The feathers of the Griffin's eagle wings curled over his collar bone. I hadn't imagined it.

I moved behind him and untucked his tunic. He tensed against my touch as if it were something he endured rather than enjoyed. I needed to see all of it, and there it was, the same but different. Where Devyn's Griffin had been poised to protect, Gideon's was positioned to attack. I traced the arc of the wings and the powerful haunches. There had been no curl of tattoo on the Devyn who had kissed me in Avalon.

"Not Devyn," I whispered. Devyn was gone, Gideon was here.

Or at least, he had been as he shrugged my hand away and leveraged himself to a standing position in one fluid motion.

"Where have you been?" he growled.

"What?" He knew where I had been. My hair still lay wet and bedraggled about my shoulders.

"I should have left. She is alone." He scowled down at me, his powerful form backlit by the fire that lit up the circle of the glade and its rough camp before the dark became dominant once more. I surveyed the glade more thoroughly. The camp was not the work of a few hours whiled away waiting for me. There was a stockpile of wood and a substantial shelter – not the quick assembly of branches and leaves and cloth that I had become accustomed to when a journey took more than a day to travel. This was not like the quick camps of the Britons that borrowed from nature in a light-touch way, that could quickly be constructed and deconstructed, leaving little trace of the overnight presence. Further signs of extended habitation filled the clearing: another fire pit, a buck hanging from a tree.

It was cold too, cold in a different way than a March evening would be. I had become more aware of weather out here in the Wilds than I had been behind the walls. In Londinium, the urban environment was dominant to the point where summer or winter barely changed the shape of the day. Here in the north, where once I would have dismissed the cold as merely another northern night regardless of the season, now I could feel the difference in the atmosphere – the additional warmth imbued in the land that came from summer, the mellower feel to the evening of early autumn, the early fall of summer gold and russet leaves that I picked wonderingly from the ground around me. How was this possible?

"Where were you?" he asked again, his voice demanding an answer that I wasn't able to give. His jaw was darkly bearded where he had been clean shaven this morning. Gideon suffered from evening shadow, but this was more than that, substantially more.

"Did you forget about us again? That seems to be your speciality. Did you find somewhere better, somewhere you preferred? A place where small considerations like your daughter didn't matter? Again." His glare suggested he expected no more from me. Forgotten? Had I forgotten?

"No, I was... It's only been a couple of hours." It was dark, I had left in the morning.

But it was no longer spring.

"Ha," he scoffed. He stepped closer to me, looming above me as he gripped my shoulders. Gideon wasn't just angry, he was furious, and he was blazing with an unrestrained fury. It was suppressed and constrained no more. "I told you I would stay. But what about Féile? How could you do this to her? She will have given up hope by now. *If* she's still alive. I don't even know that much. Nobody has come; I've had no news. What if she's dead? What if Rion attacks without us? What if they think we are dead?"

I wilted under the barrage of questions and circular thoughts of a man who'd had nothing else to do but wait and fume and wonder at the events unfolding far from this lake – events that he would be desperate to be part of. I could scarcely believe that so much time had passed, but for him to have waited here while Féile was out there somewhere was impossible to swallow.

"Why didn't you leave?" He had sworn me no oath. He had said he would wait, but there had been no vow, no promise. For him to have remained as day after day passed, while Féile, was out there alone... He had sworn to find her. I couldn't imagine that there wasn't a law of man or nature that he would not tear asunder to get to her.

His teeth ground together audibly.

"I could not leave."

My gaze flickered to the buck by the tree. He'd clearly managed to go hunting.

His eyes tracked my gaze. "I can hunt at night but when dawn breaks I am here again."

His hand encompassed the glade and the lakeshore. "The Griffin has been well provided for one way or another while imprisoned here, awaiting my lady's return." His tone was off, as he bowed his head in mocking subservience. To me or to the bounty provided for him, it wasn't clear. Both probably.

"How long?" I felt a horrible tension. How long had Féile been waiting for us to come? How long since she had been stolen from me?

"Twenty-three weeks," he ground out, despite the incredulity in his eyes.

Almost six months!

I gasped for air. I had only been there for a few hours, and I hadn't even managed to find the cure I had been promised. Callum had been wrong, there had been nothing waiting to reveal itself to me. Nothing that would allow me to descend on Londinium with the well of power available to Evaine's heir overflowing and ready to rain down fury on those who had dared to challenge me, to hurt my child. Half a year.

"You'd better be ready now," Gideon stated flatly, as if he could sense the truth and was not ready to hear it. How could I tell him the truth of the months he had given up? All those months for nothing.

I had nothing to show for the time I had been gone.

———————

The buck was lowered from the tree, and a store of berries and nuts packed as Gideon stiffly moved around the camp, demolishing it as he went. A few long-legged strides carried him into the forest and when he hit the edge of the clearing, he looked over his shoulder at me where I still stood, uncertain of what to do.

"Are you coming?" he ground out.

I scurried to catch up but was happy to trail him from a safe distance. Close enough to keep him in sight in the falling dark but not so close that I had to absorb the waves of sufferance at my company that were rolling off him.

We had walked a reasonable distance before I got up the nerve to speak.

"Where are the horses?" I asked. It was not an entirely outrageous question. We had ridden here from Carlisle; was he now planning for us to walk back?

He stopped ahead, rolling his shoulders back before he responded.

"They wandered off." His tone was sour.

"You let them go?" We really were going to have to walk the whole way home.

"I thought you would be back in a few hours," he said. "I let them wander. By the time I realised that you weren't coming back, it was too late. "

"Too late for what?" I was almost afraid to ask.

"Too late to fetch them."

I frowned at him. I was not following this explanation.

Gideon sighed in exasperation. "When I went to gather them that first afternoon I discovered that while they might not be tethered, I certainly was."

"How?"

"I could walk for an hour or so in any direction before I would wind up back at the camp."

"Oh." I was horrified, that he had been trapped this way while also learning that he had tried to leave me, after promising he wouldn't. My stomach sank. It was ridiculous to be disappointed. Of course he had tried to leave; it had been months. He must have been going out of his mind with worry for Féile, not to mention boredom. While the entire country prepared for war, he had sat beside the lake waiting for me to return. Day after day. I cringed.

He opened his mouth then shut it before finally adding. "Turns out that was the least of my problems."

His jaw set, and he turned his back once more and continued on his path.

I followed without any further attempt at conversation, despite his cryptic comment. We took a break after a while, at which point he silently handed me some of the food he had brought from the camp. He set a gruelling pace, and when the sun went down on the grey day he pushed on, our way lit by what moonlight filtered through the trees. After I stumbled over a root for the tenth time, he waited for me and took my hand in his before continuing, pulling me up and preventing me from falling as we powered on. As if I was a small child being tugged along by a hurried parent.

Which he was. How would Féile be? She would have expected us by now. Had she given up? I had been gone the whole summer... She was three now. Who had her? Had they celebrated her birthday? Did anyone care for her? Had they given her to a family like they had with me, and told her to forget us? Or was she locked in a cage with no one to read to her? With no one to tell her it was going to be all right, that she was loved...

The thoughts went round and round in my brain as I kept pace with Gideon's longer legs, breaking into a little skipping run every now and then to keep up with him. I felt as if my feet were on fire but fuelled by thoughts of my daughter no pain or exhaustion would keep me from her.

I had been frantic when she was taken, but it was nothing to the agony I felt now. I couldn't bear to think of her believing we were not coming for her.

Gideon came to an abrupt stop – at least it felt abrupt as I had been entirely focussed inwards and not paying attention, but realised now that he had been slowing the pace for a while.

"We'll sleep here."

"I'm fine," I protested. We didn't need to stop. We needed to keep going. Féile needed us.

"You'll be no good to anyone if you can't walk," he said gruffly.

"We can go for a little bit longer," I said. I was fine. My feet were sore, but they had toughened up in the years since I'd left Londinium, I was no longer the tenderfoot who had made the journey north with feet that only had to see a road to start to blister.

"No," he said. "We're nearly out on the moor. It'll be warmer here under the trees."

I nodded my acceptance and went to sit down but, still holding my hand, he pulled me over to sit under a tree. I pulled my hand from his and went a small distance away to relieve myself. On returning, I found he had piled the leaves together and was lying down in a mound of autumn leaves. I felt absurdly shy. I had slept with this man for the last year or so, but his anger made me loath to go near him.

"Are you going to stand there all night?" he asked in the same derisively mocking tone that he had thrown at me in the past. I hadn't deserved it then but I did now. It was my fault we had come here. I had thought that the Lady of the Lake would offer me stronger magic, a way to guarantee that no force could stand in the way of my reaching Féile. Instead, I had wasted months. Months.

I lay down next to him, unresisting as he pulled me closer. It was cold now that we had stopped moving and I was grateful for the heat. For his proximity.

"I didn't know," I offered into the dark.

Silence.

What did I expect? Every day for him must have felt like an eternity. For me it had been hours but for him it had been half a year. I lay there with his arms wrapped around me, as I tried and failed to subdue my shivering.

"Sleep," he rumbled in my ear.

How had so much time passed?

"Maybe they already have her?" I whispered, a small flicker of hope inside me bursting to life, hope that they had somehow managed to catch her, or had already got her back from the city.

"No," he said shortly.

"How do you know?" I asked. He had been tied to the lake; he could know no more than I did.

"They have waited for you at York."

"How can you be so sure?"

The silence stretched so long that I momentarily wondered if he had gone to sleep, but I was familiar enough with the feel of his body and the tempo of his breathing at night that I knew he hadn't drifted off. He was coiled tight, every muscle and sinew in his body taut, ready to continue the journey. We had stopped for my benefit alone, and I couldn't relax enough to sleep either.

"Without you, there is no chance." He had waited so long to speak that I was momentarily confused, my thoughts having drifted back to my strong-willed daughter. Would she be free to roam the city as I had been? It had been the only thing that had kept me sane, those brief glimpses of sky and green pockets of park, a relief from the stifling urban environment in which I had grown up. How much harder would it be for Féile who had known nothing but freedom and open skies, green hills and forests, her whole life. My chest constricted just thinking of it.

I pulled my thoughts together.

"No chance of what?"

"Without you, there is no way through the walls, no way into the city," he said. "We are not strong enough. No matter how many men have gathered, we cannot defeat them. Their technology has grown strong."

"While our magic has grown weak," I finished for him. He was right. In the centuries of fighting, the balance of power had never been more firmly in the Empire's favour. They would have waited for me, and when I arrived, I would have nothing more to offer them.

He'd had months to think this through. I had only had the few hours that we had been trudging across the moor.

"The moor…" There was no moor on the way to Carlisle. It was all hills and mountains and dales. Our journey to the lake hadn't been that far, and we had already walked through half the night. "Where are we going?"

"York," he said in clipped tones. "Rion and his men left Carlisle months ago."

"But how can you be so sure?" I asked. "Maybe they waited at Carlisle."

"They didn't."

"How do you know?"

He was silent so long I thought he wasn't going to answer. His arms tightened about me.

"When I said before that I could only leave to hunt, that wasn't all of it. At first, I thought I dreamt it, that Avalon provided the game that turned up in the camp. That in my dreams alone did I take to the skies and roam the forest as a beast. Night after night. I began to direct my dreams, to soar on eagle's wings to Carlisle where I watched the banners assemble and march south to war. I could reach York in a night, but if I didn't return before the sun rose, I would wake in agony. I learned the boundaries of my dreams," he recounted tonelessly. "Until I no longer believed they were dreams."

I lay unmoving in his arms. Was he telling me at night he transformed into... an actual griffin? I pushed at his arms.

"The sun has set, Cat." His tone was indecipherable. I turned to try and see his face, but it was in shadow.

"You can turn into a griffin?"

"Something like. At least, aspects of; I could fly like an eagle, roam the forest as a lion." His chest expanded as he took a deep breath and exhaled. "Or could. Whatever it was seems to have stopped now."

"Oh."

"Yes. Indeed," he said shortly.

"You were able to stop it from happening."

"It just didn't happen tonight." He didn't sound like he knew why. "Now, rest."

His arms tightened around me, and there, clasped in that band, I somehow drifted off for a few hours.

———————

"Cat." Gideon's voice pulled me from my sleep. I lifted my eyelids to the sight of my Griffin and our two horses in the grey dawn light.

"What? How?" I asked in astonishment. After all this time they had come back and found us. No saddles or bridles, of course. Those had remained uselessly behind at the lakeshore camp.

Gideon cast a sour look at the empty landscape.

"A parting gift to see us on our way, it would seem," he said, patting the side of his stallion's neck who shied away nervously until his whispered assurances seemed to calm the beast down.

"But how?" I asked again.

He cast me an incredulous look. After the revelations of the night, this was the thing I found hardest to understand.

"What does it matter? It gets us to York faster, does it not?"

Right. I stood, brushing off the worst of the leaves as his heavy cloak fell to the forest floor. I gathered it up and gave it back to him.

He waited for me by my horse, hands cupped to help me mount. I tied the cloak about my neck and accepted his help.

"Thank you," I offered quietly as I put my foot in his hands. A slight thinning of his lips was my only acknowledgement as he hoisted me up and we set off for York at a brisk pace.

Chapter Sixteen

We rode hard for two days, making camp before sunset each night at Gideon's insistence. His lingering edginess as night fell cost us the extra miles we could have travelled in the twilight. I could barely breathe when I thought of my daughter; the fear and guilt at having abandoned her for so long was crippling. I couldn't think, I couldn't move, so I focussed my swirling thoughts on my companion.

Gideon barely looked at me. As we rode, it was a blessing not to have to deal with him. I knew I had never done anything to earn his... well, anything, really. When I had met him first, he had been mocking of the city girl, and scathing of my relationship with a man he held in contempt as an Oathbreaker who had hurt Rion, his best and most loyal friend. He had married me at his lord's command and had loved my daughter as a father. My lack of care for her must have galled him, but my appreciation of anyone's emotions when I had been so devoid of them myself was low. Since I had come back from the brink, as it were, our shared love of Féile – not to mention our physical relations – had created at least a

225

friendship of sorts between us. Before I had gone into the water, there had been a moment where the chance of something more had seemed possible.

Now though... The man I had come back to was not my friend. What he had been through while I was in Avalon... His need to get to Féile matched mine. If he hadn't had a use for me, I suspected he would have been more than happy to leave me behind. As it was, he barely slowed down enough for me to keep up. But keep up I would; the faster the pace, the sooner Féile would be back in my arms.

We climbed hills and over dales as we made our way south. On occasion, a farmhouse would appear, and Gideon would stride off and return with food. The first time he had done so, I had attempted to follow, but the glare I received had stopped me firmly in my tracks, and I hadn't tried it a second time.

On the third evening, Gideon dismounted, taking both horses' reins, indicating that we should continue. My legs felt heavy, the evening was dark, and I struggled to keep up with the tall figure in front.

Watching the ground to pick out where it was safe to step forced me to concentrate only on putting one foot in front of another. He wouldn't leave me behind, I was sure of it. Well, I was almost sure of it, but it made me feel better to keep telling myself so.

"We'll stop in Ripon," came a voice from the other side of the horse.

The yelp that escaped me was unfortunate.

"We're stopping?" I asked. The pace had been relentless and he had gone from being caged to ruthless in his determination to reach York as quickly as possible. If I hadn't been slowing him down, I had no doubt he would already be there.

"Aye, York is another day on. We'll get fresh horses in Ripon and be in York by lunchtime tomorrow."

"We have no money," I couldn't help but point out.

"We're in Anglia now. My name will get us what we need," he said grimly.

A name he bore with no pride but which he was willing to use if it got him where he needed to be quicker.

The town was small, a cluster of stone houses around a wide market place with a large inn on the south side of the square. Gideon stooped as he stepped inside and dealt with the innkeeper who hurried to assist us before Gideon even gave his name. Clearly we were not his usual type of customer.

I had never really paid attention to how others reacted to Gideon. For the last few years, it had been because I had been so indifferent to the world in general and, more recently, because I was so busy dealing with my own reaction to him. But now I watched him as he interacted with the innkeeper, taking notice of his impact on the room in general. He was magnetically attractive. His features shouldn't work together like they did, carved as they were with a brutal hand. His eyes were golden and framed by dark lashes, his brows arched, his cheekbones lethal in an almost over-long face. The scar added a counterpoint to the beauty that he clearly dismissed himself. Female eyes followed him about and a few male ones, too. He often projected a lazily amused air, yet there was an aura about him that kept most people at a distance. He let few close to him, and fewer still did he welcome into his proximity. Where Marcus's charisma had brought people to him like bees to honey, there was something about Gideon that warned that, like flickering flames, what drew you was as dangerous as it was beautiful.

His eyes flashed in my direction before moving coldly on.

Flames? The man was walking frostbite. But I was tied to him regardless.

The innkeeper noticed the interaction.

"My apologies, my lord. I assumed…" he stumbled over his words. "I have many rooms available. I can have a second made ready."

"Is that so?" A dark brow arched. "One will suffice."

I cut him a glance. I had a strong preference for a second bedroom myself. It would be nice to have a moment to myself out of range of his resentment and anger.

"I want a separate room," I said, the moment we were shown to a surprisingly large room above the bar. The beams on the roof were dark, catching the flicker of the merry fire that danced in readiness of our arrival. The staff must have prepped it while we ate our hearty but silent meal downstairs.

I felt full and warm for the first time in days, and it made me strong enough to insist that I did not have to put up with whatever this was.

"No."

"No?" I echoed. "I'm not sure when you think I started taking orders from you, but let's put that to rights."

I headed for the door but a firm hand encircling my upper arm ended that act of rebellion.

"Let me go." I glared up at him. "Enough."

It was all enough. The manhandling, the mood, everything was enough. I whipped around.

"What is it?" I demanded. "What is wrong with you?"

"Nothing is wrong with me," he said. "We are in a hurry. You may have forgotten, but there is a war about to start, and we don't want it to start without us."

"Forgotten?" I echoed. "Forgotten that my daughter is in Londinium?"

How dare he imply…!

"You were gone a long time," he threw at me. "Who knows what you care about?"

He couldn't really believe I had abandoned my daughter a second time, could he? My breath came fast as I struggled to rein in my temper. I had more control than this, even as I felt the winds respond to my agitation.

"What is that supposed to mean?" I dared him to say it, dared him to say that I didn't care for her, that I didn't love her, even as the guilt at the delay gnawed inside me. What would she believe?

"You were gone for a long time," he levelled at me. "You have pulled in a lot of power – I can sense it in you. You get a little less concerned about others when you handle that much magic. Did you just forget us? Tell me the truth."

What power? The tingle. I…

He was right. More energy than I had ever held simmered through my veins without my even noticing it. It barely registered. But I'd had enough of his accusations. "I have told you the truth. I didn't know that it had been so long. It wasn't like that for me."

He pulled me into him, and his mouth descended on mine, far more softly teasing than I would have expected given his mood. It was a leisurely exploration and I responded tentatively, unsure of him. I wanted him to believe me, I wanted to be with him, but something wasn't right.

He lifted his head, his amber eyes glinting down at me speculatively. "Tell me the truth."

I was confused. I was telling him the truth. What was it about my kiss that confirmed his suspicions that I was lying?

"I am telling the truth."

"Dammit, Cat. However damned this relationship is, you have at least always been honest. What aren't you telling me?"

I shook my head and his lips flattened grimly.

"Do you know what it's like for me?" he asked lazily, his hand lightly brushing hair away from my face. His mood was mercurial, slipping from one thing to another and I couldn't follow what was happening or where this was coming from.

I shook my head. "What what is like for you?" I asked.

"I married you to save your life," he reminded me.

"Yes, I know," I said, when the silence lengthened way beyond what I could withstand. "Thank you," I offered lamely.

"Thank you?" He huffed, repeating my words. "I slept with you to save your soul."

My mouth dried. Was that how he saw it? That I was using him?

I felt sick. It wasn't like that.

"No thank you this time?" he asked mockingly, reverting to the Gideon I had first met.

I stood there stricken dumb. Did he really want my thanks?

"It wasn't like that..." I began.

"Wasn't it?" he asked. "Do you know what it was like when you came to me all those times, when you sought out the Griffin after magic had sucked the soul from you?"

I thought about the first time we had slept together when I had been ill. It had felt as though he had wanted me as much as I did him. Gideon had a reputation with women – he had certainly been far more experienced than me – but it had felt reciprocal. My stomach folded in on itself as his words came back to me. He had done it because it was his job as Griffin.

"You think I..." But the words stuck in my mouth – my mouth that felt too dry from horror to produce noise. "You felt used?"

His head went back in surprise. He blinked as he looked down at me.

"No, you little fool. I never... that's not what I'm saying." He shook his head. "When we came together I... you drank me in like I was oxygen. Like my touch was a living elixir that you were starved of and needed for your very existence."

I nodded. I knew what he meant. It had felt like that to me, like I was scorched earth after a draught and he was rain. I hadn't been able to get enough of him.

He ran a finger across my lips.

"You don't kiss like a lady who has been absent from her Griffin for too long," he said speculatively. "Yet it's been months."

I flinched. It hadn't been long for me, but maybe that really had been Devyn in Avalon and he had been there to help keep me on an even keel even as I absorbed the extra power, more power than I had ever known before.

"Not for me," I said, but not fast enough. "A few hours, no more. Not months."

"There's something else," he accused. "Whatever has been between us, it may not be love, but it's always been honest. Now, tell me what you are hiding."

I lowered my lids and hid my eyes. He could see through me, he'd always been able to see right through me, and he was right, I couldn't lie to him.

"Devyn was there."

His breath caught, and his face turned to stone.

"Okay."

He moved away and started to unbuckle his leather body armour.

I stood there uncertain, still braced for the storm that should be headed my way in the face of that confession. But he had no right to be angry, and I wasn't even sure it had been Devyn. At the time, I had convinced myself it couldn't be.

I climbed into the bed beside him. His arms reached over to the edge where I lay as far away as possible from him and pulled me against his chest.

"Go to sleep," he grated as I lay stiff in his arms.

"I don't understand," I whispered into the dark.

There was silence. I had only just managed to force my body to relax and enjoy his closeness when his deep voice came as I was on the edge of sleep.

"If he was there..." he paused, "then I'm grateful that you came back. For Féile."

He thought I would have chosen Avalon and Devyn over my daughter, over him, and he was saying that he understood. I'm not sure I did. I hadn't just come back for Féile; I had come back because I had to, because I had needed to. Not just for my daughter, not just for Britannia.

I had come back for him.

I wanted to explain, to correct him, but I was so tired and being here in his arms I couldn't help myself as sleep overtook me.

———————————

The next morning the horses took us swiftly to the walls of York, which loomed up before us. Fortifications in Anglia were taken seriously. I had thought that Llewelyn's castle at Conwy was built to withstand attack but here in York it wasn't enough to fortify the castle. Gideon told me the entire town was built with attackers in mind, and the defences were many and varied. The great stone walls surrounding the city seemed almost as high as the walls of Londinium itself, and they made Carlisle's walls look flimsy in comparison.

"Anglia has spent centuries preparing for this war," Gideon said as we waited for entrance at the heavily guarded gate.

"Clearly," I said, craning my neck to appreciate the feat of engineering such a task would have been. I still on occasion forgot the advantages of magic, which such a wall would surely have required. There were makeshift camps further along the walls on both sides, a small, ramshackle town sheltering beneath the immense walls. "If an attack comes, are they allowed inside?"

Gideon frowned in the direction of my gaze. "The camp has been growing for months. When I flew over, I couldn't tell at night who was in it."

I realised as I watched the sentries at the gate shoo away a family ahead of us.

"The ill."

The mother and one of the children looked feverish and they were shivering. The scene reminded me of the crowd outside Bart's Hospital when I had visited with Marcus. People desperate for aid stayed close to where hope lived. Even when denied entry they lingered in the belief that being nearby salvation, even if they could not access it, was better than returning to where they had come from, where there was no hope at all.

"Why are you not letting those with the Mallacht inside?" Gideon addressed the sentry as we reached the top of the line. "It's not contagious."

The fresh-faced soldier shook his head, his expression troubled. "Orders, my lord. They get some treatment, but we been told for them to be kept out."

"No entry for nobody without papers," said a more weathered-looking soldier beside him.

I looked at Gideon. What kind of papers?

"We don't need papers," Gideon said in his most arrogant sneer from his relative height.

The grizzled sentry was entirely unfazed.

"No papers, no entry," he said, his hand going to his weapon. "Move along."

Gideon smiled and didn't move one inch. The sentry recognised trouble and nodded up to the discreetly placed archers above the gate.

"I said, move along."

"I am Gideon Mortimer," he said, leaning down. "I suggest you let me pass."

The man's face dropped and he looked Gideon up and down. He didn't step aside until he was satisfied that the dark-haired warrior in front of him was at least potentially the steward's youngest son.

"And who's she then?" He nodded toward me.

"She's with me."

The man's eyes flickered in my direction, and I could see the moment he worked out by whatever reasoning my actual identity. Where he had remained somewhat unimpressed by the menacing son of his liege lord at my side, the Lady of the Lake was another concept entirely, and he stepped back immediately. The abruptness of the move took his younger companion by surprise as he stepped into him.

"My lady, my lord," he said, his head bobbing. As we nudged the horses forward, I could see him inform the younger man who took off at a run. I pulled the hood of my cloak further around my face. Heavily populated places were something I had grown less comfortable with since my celebrity. As Marcus's bride, I had started to become a known face in Londinium, though I had usually only been recognised when I was actually in Marcus's company. Since I had been introduced as the Lady of the Lake, however, I seemed to command more attention than the caesar himself, at least among the Britons.

Walking around Carlisle had become something to be avoided, despite Féile's frequent entreaties. The faces turning, the whispers, the eyes following me about had made me uncomfortable. I didn't know what people expected of me. Did they judge me? Did they expect something more? I didn't know, so I avoided crowds of strangers whenever possible. The castle and the communities at Keswick and Penrith were different. They were more used to me, I supposed, and I could go about my business with less fuss. People still watched me, but they were more discreet, and there were simply fewer of them.

I trailed after Gideon through the cobbled streets of York as we made our way to the castle – winding being the operative word. It seemed like we weren't so much crossing the city as we were crisscrossing our way through it.

"Isn't there a more direct route?" This was ridiculous; it was going to take us longer to cross the city than it had to get here at the rate we were going. I could occasionally glimpse the castle over the rooftops, and it didn't look like we were getting any closer.

Gideon looked back over his shoulder, a smirk lifting his brooding features.

"Welcome to York," he said.

I pushed my horse up alongside him. "Is there no quicker way?"

"The city is designed so that the castle, the defence of last resort, is the hardest place for an attacking army to reach if they breach the walls," he explained.

"What is the point of that if it takes all day for your own people to get there?"

"The defending army and townsfolk take a more direct route," he said, nodding towards the narrow alleyways that cut between the shops at intervals.

"How long will that take?"

"Oh, not more than fifteen minutes on foot."

"Right," I said, and slipped from my horse.

"What are you doing?"

"What does it look like I'm doing? It's taken us long enough to get here. "

"So it has." He descended from his horse and taking the reins of both, quickly handed them to a young boy with instructions, and we were off.

With permission to hasten, Gideon did just that, and despite the years since he had lived in York, he led the way through the warren without ever hesitating.

It was ingenious and I pitied the army that ever breached the walls of York. For surely they stood no chance in these dark, narrow passageways. The advantage would be entirely with the defenders who knew the territory and were able to pick off those foolish enough to take on the labyrinth.

The alleys were not entirely empty, though those who crossed our path were quick to make way for the oncoming cloaked warrior. There were also those who could not step aside – low huddled beggars, coughing, fevered men, women, and children. The reports Rion had related to us had mentioned the growing impact of the corruption seeping northward, but I hadn't imagined anything like this scale. The

Mallacht was here in force, in far greater numbers than in Carlisle, or even in Londinium when I left.

When we arrived at the castle gates, the guards, clearly prewarned, immediately stepped back to let us pass. Beyond the castle walls, there were perhaps twenty steps before we had to go through another interior wall. The Anglians didn't take the threat at their southern border lightly. Callum had told me that Anglia had been a place of refuge for rebels fleeing the reach of the Empire for centuries – Saxons, Vikings, Normans. All the strongest and most defiant of the tribes of Northern Europe had either fallen at the hands of the Empire or had made their way here. Wave after wave, generation after generation. Not only was the kingdom of Anglia always on alert against the force to the south, but their very blood was made up of those who itched to tackle the oppression of the Roman Empire. Anglians, and especially those from the capital of York, merely waited for the day when they would be unleashed. Conwy was defensive but life there was about so much more; Carlisle, meanwhile, seemed relatively oblivious to the threat of the south, the castle airy and sympathetic to the beauty around it. York and the land it sat upon were not like that; it was stark and ready for the inevitable conflict to come.

A solitary figure in dark martial clothing waited by what appeared to be the main entrance to the castle. Not grand like Carlisle, but the only way in.

"Father sent me to fetch you in," the tall man greeted us.

"Henry," Gideon acknowledged the other man, his face impassive.

The man grunted in response and walked back inside without waiting to see if we followed. Was this the brother Gideon had betrayed? It was impossible to tell; both men had an impressive capacity for conveying indifference.

"Where have you been?" I had barely stepped inside the room before I was enveloped in my brother's warm embrace. I allowed myself to sink into it for a moment. "We thought you were—" He halted. "You were gone so long."

"I can explain." They had thought I wasn't coming back, that I was dead even, that I had failed in my attempt to reach Avalon.

"Yes, please do." The voice came from across the room where Richard Mortimer, the Steward of York, sat at the head of the table. Llewelyn was there and a few of the Gwynedd lords and ladies I knew from my time in Conwy, as well as some large and fierce looking men and women I didn't know – Anglians, I presumed. Why did they always look like they were either coming or going from a battlefield? Martial, dour, stoic, and grimly ready to take the head off the next person to cross their path. No wonder Gideon was the way he was. The Griffin leaned casually against the wall by the window. What was I thinking… Gideon must have made them crazy.

Rion pulled out a seat for me and took the one beside it while Gideon remained standing behind me, a silent predatory presence.

The steward surveyed me and then his son, his lip curling in a characteristically cold manner.

"I believe congratulations are in order."

Chapter Seventeen

"**D**id you find Avalon?" Rion asked quietly, ignoring Lord Richard's provocation. He was positioning my answer to be one of strength, not the defensive one into which the steward would have forced me.

"Yes, I found it; that was the easy part." Getting in had been easy, too easy; leaving had been less so. Rion didn't react to the flicker he saw in my eyes, but I knew he had seen it. *Later*, I promised him. I would need to tell him more than I would share with this gathering.

"Who and what did you find there? Were they able to help?" Llewelyn asked. He looked older than when I had seen him last, and there was no sign of Rhys who must have stayed behind.

"I was met by Nimue and others, and they have supplied me with greater power." I hadn't even been aware of it when I left. But Gideon had been right; there was a well of power inside me now. A well that waited, deep and wondrous, for me to call upon to do as I willed. And what I willed was to get my daughter back.

CLARA O'CONNOR

"Call up a breeze now, can you, girl?" Richard Mortimer asked, all too ready to remind me and all present of my failure to save Devyn the last time I had been attacked. Back then I had been drugged, cut off from what little magic I could command, but the truth was that calling on magic had not been instinctive then. It was now. I allowed myself a moment to picture the things that the power inside me would allow me to wreak upon this tiny, fragile man.

"Yes." Whatever he saw in my eyes seemed to convince him without having to resort to a demonstration that would have left him substantially less sneery. Because I could feel it now when I contemplated what I could do. It was waiting for me to beckon, a possibility of what could be. No longer did I need to draw from without to build potential within; it was just there waiting, ready.

"Catriona." Rion touched my arm to bring my attention back to the waiting room. But it was the hand at my shoulder that centred me, that allowed me to turn away from the mesmerising pull of energy that had come with me from Avalon. I drew a shuddering breath. That had been unexpected. Was that what Viviane had meant by time running out? Not that the power would leave me, but that if I didn't loose it sooner rather than later, I would leave the world behind for the power... and the power would consume me. This was why the power of the Lakes was different. The lady mostly allowed power to flow through her, to sing to the ley lines. When she did draw power, she didn't allow it to deepen within her, because it became everything. The grip on my shoulder tightened.

I focused on Gideon's hand on my shoulder, focused on each long, capable finger through the layers of clothing that separated us.

240

"What?" I asked, blinking. There was no pretending that my attention hadn't left the room.

"What did they teach you?" Rion asked.

"Nothing." I smiled wryly. It was the truth. Beyond riddles I couldn't decipher, I realised that what Callum had taught me was enough. I had fundamental control over the power I could draw in from nature – what Avalon had given me was beyond that. Enough for what needed to be done. Enough, I hoped, to bring Londinium to its knees and take back my daughter.

"Nothing? But we've waited for months!" Lady Morwyn protested at this information.

"It wasn't months for me," I explained, as I had done for Gideon, hopefully to a more receptive audience here. "Time moves differently there. For me it was only a few hours."

"We delayed for nothing," Lord Richard said sourly.

"Not for nothing. I did not leave Avalon entirely empty handed. If your forces are assembled, we can go now."

My eagerness was not reflected in the uneasy rustling as the assembled lords and ladies looked around at each other.

"Catriona, we can't take on Londinium alone. We are not enough," Rion explained.

"Who else is coming?" I asked, confused. Those at the table represented Cymru, Anglia, and Mercia. Bronwyn sat beside a woman who could have been her twin and an older man, so House Cadoc of Kernow must be here too. Bronwyn smiled at me stiffly in greeting.

"Alba," Llewelyn pronounced determinedly.

"They will fight with us?" Everything I had been told of Alba had been of their independence. The Romans had never stepped foot on their land in nearly twenty centuries. They had a reputation for fighting, but they had never had to take on the Empire, content in the buffer provided by the southern kingdoms. That they would do so now was unexpected but welcome news.

"If Alba will join, then there is a chance that Eireann will send forces too," Rion explained softly.

"That's great news. How long before they get here?"

Rion's lips tightened. "We were discussing the terms before you arrived."

Ah, that explained why they were all assembled here. Of course they hadn't known that Gideon and I were on our way; we had been expected months ago.

"What's to discuss?" If the kingdoms of Alba and Eireann could be persuaded to join us, then we would be unstoppable. If we got the Romans off the island before reinforcements could come, we stood a chance of not just retrieving Féile but pushing them off the island for good.

"They want Féile," Rion said.

"What?" Had I misheard? He couldn't possibly be suggesting that the cost of getting my baby back was to lose her again.

"Not now." Bronwyn spoke up from across the room. Her face pinched. "When she's grown, they want to marry her to their princeling."

My daughter was being bartered just as I had been, her choices in love taken away. But if we rescued her then she would at least have some remaining choices – in how she lived, and that she lived at all, for what did we really know about what the praetor wanted with her? Worry for her squeezed my heart until the lack of oxygen made me weak.

"I see. You have agreed to their terms?" My priority was getting her back. The Albans were a better option than those who had her now. So she had to marry an Alban prince. She loved Gideon, and he was half Alban; maybe she would end up in an arranged marriage she didn't mind so much. I glanced over my shoulder; I didn't mind so much myself, I realised.

"No." Lord Richard's response was loud and final. "We'll not exchange one threat to the south for another to the north."

"Why would the marriage make Alba a threat?" I asked. Apart from a stronger tie to Mercia, it wouldn't overly shift the balance of power.

"She would have to live there," Bronwyn said.

"No, that's not right. The lady resides in the Lakelands; her husband must join her there." I looked to Rion for confirmation. It was rare for the lady to travel outside Mercia; she was the great bogeyman in the north, kept far from Londinium, not just as a threat but to do her duty. The lady's primary responsibility was the ley lines and to be most effective she needed to tend the stone circles in Keswick and Penrith.

"How would she tend the lines from Alba?"

"In previous generations the lady has lived further away, and visited only at solstice and equinox. They are prepared for her to travel down a number of times a year. The Mallacht has arrived there too. It's the only reason they are willing to take on the Empire," Bronwyn explained. She seemed to be representing the Alban offer at the table; she must have been the one they sent north to ask for aid.

"The Albans seem to have come to the conclusion that while they can live with the Romans on the island, they are less happy to suffer the corruption of the lines," Rion said. "They benefited from the vitality you restored to the Belinus line which travels on into Alba, and they traced that change back to your return. It's got much worse since you left. The land failed to thrive this summer. Throughout the midlands the crops were as poor as those in the Shadowlands. Hundreds will starve this winter. Next year the reserves will be gone and it will be devastating. The Albans sent word that they would negotiate. They fear the slow death that comes with the corruption of the land, and they will act with us to save the lady's heir, but then they want her for themselves."

I met Bronwyn's concerned face. What choice did we have?

"What if we refuse?"

"Given that we've seen sentinels use technology outside of the walls…" Richard Mortimer, who had spent his entire life planning for this fight, shook his head and then smiled. "How many of them can you take, girl?"

I had no idea. Could I bring the walls down? Could I rain storms down on the city for weeks on end? It felt possible, but how many would die? My power would kill indiscriminately; it was a force of nature. I could send a hurricane to Londinium but I would have no control over what happened then. Hundreds of thousands of innocents lived behind those walls, including my daughter.

The largest force ever assembled on this island would surely be a better option.

"I'm not sure." I stood. "I'll think on it. If you'll excuse me, we have travelled hard to get here."

"You'll think on it?" came a jeer from behind me. "You think you get to decide our fates?"

I stopped and didn't turn around as I said clearly. "I do."

Having made such a bold exit, I realised as I arrived in the hallway that I had absolutely no idea where to go from there.

A familiar touch on my back propelled me forward.

"You would truly give Féile to Alba?" came the growl from above me.

"Better Dùn Èideann than Londinium," I snapped back.

There was nothing more. Gideon guided me silently through the hallways of his old home.

"Where are you taking me?" I finally asked as we took a turn up into a tower well off the more open areas of the castle.

"My rooms," he said, trying the handle on the door in front of us, as if unsure it would open.

He looked inside before swinging the door wide and indicating I should enter.

I looked around. There was an abandoned air to the rooms which nonetheless had a somewhat familiar feel to them. The colour scheme and arrangement of furniture was not unlike Gideon's rooms in Carlisle.

"These are your rooms, but it must be…"

"More than ten years," he supplied for me. "My father is more sentimental than he appears."

"That's not saying much," came Rion's voice from behind us. He and Bronwyn had followed, it seemed. Bronwyn wrapped her arms around me.

"I'm so sorry," she said, her face reflecting her guilt at selling my daughter to the Albans and relief that I was there at all to be angry at her. "Are you all right? No, of course you're not all right. We were so worried, we thought something must have happened. We only responded to Dùn Èideannout of desperation. The steward won't attack without them; he says it would be suicide."

I stepped back and put my hand up. I wasn't able to deal with her sympathy. I needed space; I needed a moment to think.

"Has there been any word?"

"Of Féile?" Rion asked. "No, the city is impenetrable. We relied on word from Shadowers, but few are let into the cities now and certainly not ones from regions we trade with. Others got sick and they had to leave. Security inside the walls has never been higher."

"What happened in Avalon?" Rion asked, all too aware I had limited what I revealed to the group assembled in the hall.

"I was met by two women. I think the first might have been our mother, and the second was Nimue, the first Lady of the Lake, and they knew why I had come." I drew the sleeve back on my dress, showing them the tattoo she had given me.

"She gave you that?" Bronwyn asked, her eyes widening at the dara knot and the oath it symbolised.

I looked at Gideon, remembering again that moment we had shared before I descended. We had been of an accord, and it had felt so pure, so clear to me. Would we ever get there again?

"No, I had that one before I went. But Viviane added the second one." I traced the curls of the triskelion. "The arms I think represent past, present, and future, and perhaps the Griffin is the centre that holds them, or I am... She spoke in riddles."

"And Nimue?" Bronwyn asked.

I shook my head. "More riddles. That I had what I needed and needed what I have."

"And there was no trickery?" asked a gruff voice from the door – Callum. I went to him and sank into his fierce hug.

I pulled away. "Devyn was there."

I didn't have to share an emotional connection with Gideon to feel the shift in that predatory vibe that seemed so close to the surface since the Lake.

"He tried to get me to stay," I revealed.

Bronwyn gripped my hand; she knew that this was not a temptation from which I would have easily walked away.

"It can't have been him," I said. It was a statement, but I needed them to tell me I was right. "Not Devyn. He would never have asked me to stay while Féile was in danger. Right?"

"Not Devyn," Gideon echoed.

Bronwyn gasped. "I don't know. They say that in the afterlife, worldly concerns drift away. Perhaps he had forgotten."

My heart twisted inside me.

"Maybe if you had stayed you would have forgotten too," Rion added.

It could have been him. Really him, there in my arms. If I had known, if I had believed, would I have stayed?

What had Viviane said, believe in the present, no... present in belief. If I was in the present I had to have belief in what the present gave me. I frowned at the riddle, the words rolling in my head. Féile was the present. Gideon was the present. I was the present. This me. With these people. Devyn had got me to where I needed to be, I had to trust in that past. And believe in this present.

"Catriona." Rion had crouched in front of my chair and gripped my shoulders. "You had to return to us."

I blinked and smiled widely at him. Another gift of the now: my brother.

"I know." Impulsively, I gave him a peck on the cheek. "I think it was a test."

Rion pulled back in surprise, a flush appearing along his cheeks. I flushed in response from secondary embarrassment until I realised that it was probably the first time I had showed him any affection. I had spent so much of the last years tangled up inside myself, pulled and pushed by events over which I had no control and which all too often had dictated my emotional state – the wear of the ley lines, the handfast cuff, and my connection to Devyn. I supposed, while I thought about it, the meds that the council had used to suppress my magic had also cut me off from a core part of myself. Now I felt whole, and wholly myself.

"I'm glad you passed," the usually fastidious Rion said, sitting back on the dusty floor.

"Me too," I said, locking eyes with Gideon across the room. And I was glad.

"What else happened?"

I shook my head. "I'm not sure. I thought, at first, nothing, but over the last few days I have felt more magic running through me than I thought was possible."

There was also the strange experience Gideon had endured.

"There's something more," Rion prompted. Gideon narrowed his eyes at me; he was not ready to share what had happened to him.

"I asked her if Gideon could be freed," I threw out, in order to satisfy Rion's suspicion that there was something left unrevealed. "It is unfair that I need him the way I did."

Gideon was straight backed as he looked out of the window and I couldn't gauge his reaction.

"You no longer need him?" Bronwyn asked lightly.

"Maybe not. I feel more whole than I did before. She... they both said things about the Griffin's relationship with the lady being subject to need, that... oh, I don't know, it was riddle after riddle. I thought I had come away with nothing." I wasn't sure what had happened. The whole piece about my need for Gideon was not something I really wanted to discuss in public, or with Gideon most of all.

"We could test it," Bronwyn suggested.

"Cat stays with me." Gideon turned to face us, his jaw set. "The castle is full of strangers." He cracked his neck. "Besides, somebody told my father that we are married."

He glared at Rion.

"It wasn't Rion," Bronwyn defended him. "It was me. During the negotiations with Alba, they said they wanted the fully grown Lady of the Lake, who obviously isn't available."

She looked at me before offering the room a shrug. "It has been almost four years."

With so many people packed inside York, many of the council were not present in the great hall as we made our way to dinner that evening. The princes of Cymru in particular were noticeably absent.

"Where is Llewelyn?" I asked as I walked to the high table with Rion.

"The princes of Gwynedd, Powys, and Gwent, and Richard Mortimer tend to stay out of each other's paths. They have always shared an uneasy border. It doesn't help that when Mother died Richard was so vocal in his demands that Rhodri should be executed, which he very nearly was. Llewelyn does not forgive easily."

I eyed the table ahead of us. The steward sat in the middle with Bronwyn on one side and two empty seats on the other. I had a bad feeling that I was expected to sit beside him in the position of honour at his right side, while Rion sat with Bronwyn.

"That is one of Gideon's brothers?" I nodded to the dark-haired man at the end of the table.

"Yes, Henry, and his wife, Alice," Rion confirmed. "The eldest, another Richard, has gone to Eireann to beg further aid."

Of course, it was. The steward had the praetor's inclination to make mischief, it seemed, or perhaps he just enjoyed making everyone as uncomfortable as possible.

"Lady," the steward greeted me as I sat down. "Or should I say, daughter?"

"Lady is fine," came a dark growl from behind me as Gideon lowered himself into the seat on my other side.

The steward's lip thinned. "It appears you all failed to tell us the full truth of what happened that day on the beach. Married, and made the Griffin?"

"Yes," Gideon said shortly.

"You've finally made something of yourself, boy."

Gideon rolled his shoulders and leaned back in his chair, a smirk easing his features as he met his father's gaze. "If you say so."

"I wasn't aware that sleeping with the lady was part of the Griffin's duties," Lord Richard prodded, knowingly or through luck making a direct hit on the most sensitive part of our relationship.

Gideon took my hand from where it was reaching for my wine glass, in need of a healthy mouthful. He lifted my hand to his lips and laid a lingering kiss on the backs of my fingers before directing a burning amber gaze directly at me.

"A terrible hardship," he agreed, flicking his heavy-lidded gaze back at his father.

"What new skills do you bring to the field apart from your prowess in bed?" he asked before looking past Gideon. "Not that that's new."

Alice and Henry both stiffened at the jibe and Gideon's face tightened, visibly sustaining a hit from his father's attack. This dance had a familiar rhythm, but he had a new partner.

"What new skills did he need?" I asked. "My understanding is that I married the strongest warrior in Mercia."

Not Anglia. The steward's eyes narrowed; he did not like to be reminded of this fact, despite having kicked Gideon out.

"Not exactly your choice though, was he my dear?" Lord Richard's eyes gleamed in triumph as I failed to protest, and he redirected his gaze to his youngest son. "Second choice again. Unwanted by your mother, unwanted by me. Your wife and her brother would give you up for the real Griffin in a heartbeat. You as the Griffin! What a travesty. You care for no one but yourself. Devyn Glyndŵr had more duty in the soles of his feet than you have in your entire body."

My breath was taken by the sheer unprovoked viciousness of the attack. If the steward had set out to hurt his son, he had to know he had drawn blood.

Gideon leaned across me. "But at least I have a wife."

His smile was a malicious gleam as he swiped back at his father, before pushing away from the table and strolling out of the hall.

Is that what he thought? That I didn't want him? I rose to follow him, throwing his father a dirty look… and caught him watching Gideon's exit with a look that was at odds with the words he had spoken. He looked as if he would eat every word he had just flung at his son.

I frowned down at him.

"Then why?"

He didn't pretend not to understand as he looked up at me.

"I did not intend…" He pulled a weary hand over his face. "A pattern, once formed, is hard to break. I spoke badly. He goads me and then I hear worse things coming from my mouth."

I was all too familiar with the pattern. I sat back down, unwilling to make the situation worse – and having both of us leave his table would be worse. The steward, however, withdrew into a morose mood after delivering the only glimmer of sympathetic nature I had ever seen from him. This left me to the slightly awkward overtures of Gideon's one-time lover, for which I found myself very particularly not in the mood.

———

Despite his words at the table, Gideon did not spend the night in my bed. In the morning I finally tracked him down to the stables where he was busy saddling a horse.

"You're leaving?" Was this his response to learning that we might no longer be shackled to each other?

"Nothing so dramatic," he said, continuing in his task. "I'm going for a ride."

"You didn't come to your room last night."

"Did you miss me?" He slanted a leery look my way.

"Gideon, please."

"Please what, Cat? What is it you want?" he flung at me, his mood shifting, "You don't need me anymore, isn't that right? So I stayed away. Yet here you are. Why?"

"I thought…"

"What? What did you think?" He turned, hemming me in. "That you got what you needed from me? And now I'm discarded, no longer of use."

I frowned. I had given him his freedom back.

"Was it what your father said?"

"My father didn't say anything I didn't already know."

"Then, why?" Why was he angry? Why had he left me alone last night? He had already known that I had seen Devyn in Avalon, had been okay with it. What had changed?

"You asked the lady to take back the one thing you needed from me as Griffin," he said into the horse's neck.

"No." I went to him and placed a hand on the hunched muscles of his shoulder. "I asked her to give you back your freedom. You shouldn't have to be tied to me like that. It's not fair."

"And am I free? Do you not need me now?"

"I don't know," I said. "She told me that needing you was a choice. I don't know what that means but I feel restored now. Whole."

He nodded to himself and shrugged off my hand before turning towards me in a way that made me feel like I was the prey he was stalking.

He bent his head and his lips grazed across my collar bone as I stayed frozen in place.

"What do you want?" he asked into my ear. It was a mere whisper, a breath that urged my confession. "Tell me," he said as his lips brushed across mine. My body melted as my brain swirled, trying to find an answer to give him. Or hide from the one I wasn't ready to face yet.

His hands reached and tangled with mine by my side before twisting them behind my back as he pulled me into him.

"This?"

I was molten liquid. I looked helplessly up into his glittering eyes in that darkly brutal face.

What did he want me to say? My mouth felt dry, and my

heart was pattering like a butterfly's wings in the cage of my chest. Did I want more? Was he offering more?

At my continued silence, his hot gaze cooled, a flicker of what might have been disappointment crossed his face. Nodding tightly, his body was rigid.

Then I was suddenly free as he mounted the horse and left the stable without another word.

He clattered out of the courtyard and I turned to find that the stable was not as empty as I had thought. Two pairs of sympathetic eyes peered around the corner of the last stall.

Bronwyn, and Gideon's sister-in-law, Alice. Of course.

"Great." They must have heard everything. I leaned my head against the stable wall and closed my eyes.

"Puppies," Bronwyn explained, holding up one of the offending articles that had brought them to their hidden spot in the stables.

I blinked the extra moisture out of my eyes and walking to her, lifted the liquid-eyed pup out of her hands, cuddling him to me. I was unable even to look at Alice. Rubbing my cheek against the silky softness, I closed my eyes and drew it in to myself, allowing it to restore my equilibrium.

"Gideon didn't love me, you know."

Or not.

If I kept my eyes closed, maybe she would stop.

"Not like that. We were friends, but his mother left him and then I was leaving him too. He begged her to stay. He used his body to try to get me to stay. He uses it as a weapon. He does not give his heart easily and he doesn't care for people lightly."

Wow. That was a lot of information from someone I didn't know.

But I guess she had just learned a lot too.

"It's not like that between us." I squirmed uncomfortably,

finally opening my eyes to meet her earnest ones. "I don't know you or anything about you other than that you are the reason he bears that scar."

She waved dismissively. "That's what I'm trying to tell you. That scar is nothing to the one his mother left when she abandoned him. He was a sweet child, and after... He won't love easily, and he will never ask you to stay."

"I think you may have misunderstood our conversation."

"Have I?" she asked. "He will never put himself out there first. If you don't hold on to him, he will not hold on to you. He will let you go. He expects you to leave him, to not want him."

"You aren't hearing me. Gideon feels nothing like that for me. For Féile, yes, me not so much. We're married because Rion commanded it, that's all."

"You think Gideon does whatever Rion orders?" Bronwyn said, amusement at Alice's forthright approach hovering on her lips. "Like bringing Devyn north unharmed?"

I saw again Gideon throwing that knife at Devyn, his uncaring attitude when Bronwyn pulled him up on it. My first impression had been that he cared for no one and did no one's bidding. Had I really seen anything that suggested otherwise?

"He does follow orders. He was a parent to Féile when I was unfit," I threw back.

"That was his choice. No one commanded he do so."

"He slept with me," I managed to get out, mortified.

Bronwyn's eyes rounded and she exchanged glances with Alice. "You think..." she spluttered. "Why on earth do you think that?"

I cringed, hunching my shoulders and wishing they could all leave me be.

"He didn't want to share my bed, but he did it because Rion ordered it."

"Cass, I was there. He was ordered to share his room, and if things got cosier after that, that was his choice, and yours."

I shook my head, rubbing at the tension in my temple. I needed this conversation to be over.

"He didn't seem all that pleased that you tried to free him when you were in Avalon. Nor does he seem to be in a hurry to kick you out of his room now," Bronwyn went on.

"We fight all the time."

Alice laughed. "Henry and I fight all the time. From the moment we married we fought, we made up, and we fought some more. You know who I never fought with? Gideon."

"I fought with Devyn," I said, to no one in particular.

"What did you fight with Devyn about?" Bronwyn asked.

"Mostly him and his bloody duty." I huffed out a laugh.

"What do you and Gideon fight about?"

I gnawed my inner lip as I thought back to some of the choicer moments when we had clashed, unwilling to share the details with the room.

"I've witnessed one or two of those fights," Bronwyn said, leaning towards me. "You two, when you fight, it's personal. You both make the other bleed. This is not how people who are indifferent to each other act."

She leaned back against the straw behind her, eyeing me speculatively.

"Do you want him? If you do I'd wager he's yours."

"I'll take that bet!" Alice laughed. "The way he watches you..."

"It's his duty to watch me."

"Not like that. If people went around doing their duty with that look in their eyes there'd be riots in the streets."

Were they right? I rested my head against the wall, the puppy a warm bundle in my lap. Was I more to Gideon than his duty? Was I his choice? And if so, what was he to me?

I had never chosen this. I had never chosen him.

But what if I did?

Chapter Eighteen

At lunch, Gideon took a seat beside me with no indication of our earlier fight. I understood that whatever else was going on between us, in front of his family, specifically his father, we would maintain a united front. We had only just finished the meal when a young girl ran into the hall and whispered in the Lord Steward's ear. Whatever she said caused his face to darken.

"It appears we have company," he said curtly, and sat back, watching the door.

The druids entered as a group, long robes flowing white, the epitome of everything I had imagined this world to be before I had arrived here. Having worked alongside them, I knew them to be no different from any other type of people. I knew quite a few of the group: Zara was head of the new settlement at Dinas Emrys and she had a sly humour that was always expressed under her breath; John, the druid who had saved my life that morning on an Anglesey beach, had come north to Keswick since Elsa's death and he was the most earnest person I had ever met in my life. He gave everything he had to purify the ley lines and took each added wave of corruption as a personal affront.

Marina was at the back of the entourage of druids entering the room. I saw her smile cheekily to someone lower down the hall and realised with surprise that Oban was here and that he had company – Snuffles sat at his feet. At least one of us was convinced Féile would be with us again soon. The druids strode through the hall with purpose and energy. It was unusual to see so many gathered outside of their own community. The druids were called upon when a higher power was needed in matters of law or health, and it was quite clear from the black look on the steward's face that he had issued no such invitation.

They came to a halt halfway up the great hall.

Lord Richard rose from his seat and strode to meet them as if halting their progress through the hall would prevent them from being fully arrived.

"What brings you to York?"

"I do," a voice from the middle of the group came, and the druids stepped aside to allow the white-haired Fidelma to appear. "You need our help, Richard."

If the steward had looked displeased before, he looked positively thunderous now.

"How dare you step foot in this house," he spat at the older woman. "Leave your lackeys if you must, but you go now."

"The time for games is over, my dearest," she tutted back at the furious man. "I have done all I can to be ready and now we must stand together or fall."

"I want you gone from this house," he roared.

"No."

Richard Mortimer was not the most diplomatic of men at

the best of times but he was a militarily minded one. We needed every bit of help we could get.

"Fidelma," Llewelyn intervened in the scene that was unfolding in front of the entire castle. "Zara, John, perhaps we can continue this discussion elsewhere."

The most senior of the nobility present and some key members of their household exited the room. As we made our way to a more private location, Rhodri greeted me discreetly. I hadn't seen him the night before and now he gave my hand a gentle squeeze. I understood I shouldn't call attention to his presence, lest someone object, and nodded at his request to speak later.

Reassembled in a smaller room which appeared to be where the council of war met most often, Fidelma smiled across at me.

"They treated you well in Avalon, child?" She could sense the power that pulsed inside me. At times it felt so strong that I wasn't sure why everyone passing couldn't detect it.

Lord Richard refused to take a seat, instead appearing behind Fidelma and placing a hand rather too firmly for her birdlike bones on her shoulder.

"We need to talk. In private," he growled down at her.

"That won't be necessary," she dismissed him.

"I insist," he said, his fingers now definitely gripping her too tightly. This wasn't right; he couldn't treat her this way. I opened my mouth to intervene when I felt Gideon's hand on my own shoulder, his reminder that this was his father's house and that it was not my place to interfere.

I was disinclined to agree.

"Really Fidelma, you're happy to speak openly?" Richard challenged, his eyes flickering to the man behind me.

"Perfectly."

"After all this time," came the dour response.

"After all this time," Fidelma threw back tritely.

Their little contretemps was odd and the tone far from what one would expect for anyone, no matter how prominent, to have with the most senior druid in the land. Especially in front of such an assembly. Rion's face reflected that my assessment was right, and if Rion couldn't mask his surprise, then we really were in strange times.

"Shall we speak openly then?" the Lord Steward's tones were even more dour and authoritarian than usual.

"Let's," Fidelma responded, wrinkling her nose in a fashion I wanted to call flirtatious. Druids weren't celibate, but Fidelma was as old as the castle walls, and the steward was not a man you teased.

A flicker of annoyance wafted over his face.

It was a familiar expression that I recognised from Gideon – the first time I had noticed any familial resemblance beyond their shared stature. Arrogance aside, physically they were not terribly alike, unlike the steward's middle son who was a life-size younger copy of his father.

The steward drew a breath, his lips thin. "What do ye in York?"

"You are preparing to take on Londinium, and we have come to offer what assistance we may," Zara answered, while Fidelma's eyes glinted at the head of the table.

"We don't need your help," Lord Richard said. The lords and ladies around the table all turned to stare at him. We were vastly outnumbered, and currently begging assistance from neighbours who had little inclination to get involved, and my daughter's life was at stake. Féile might mean little personally to the company here, but they were each and every one clear that the next Lady of the Lake being held in Londinium would not end well for them. And the steward wanted to refuse the magical advantage we had over the technologically advanced weapons Londinium would throw at us.

"Are you gone mad?" Llewelyn spoke for the room.

The steward faced the assembly, and the looks he met there seemed to convince even his mighty will to bow. If the druids were in then what possible reason could he have to refuse them?

"Fine," he said begrudgingly.

"Why don't you catch us up?" Fidelma smiled impishly.

Llewelyn looked between the druids and the steward. When the later made no further move beyond staring at Fidelma with a locked jaw, he outlined the current status of the gathering armies.

"Winter is closing in. Alba will join us in the spring."

"Spring will be too late," Fidelma announced.

What did she know? Could she see something? Was Féile in danger? Was it already too late?

"Why?" asked Rion's measured voice.

"The line through Londinium is on the verge of collapse," John explained. His thin face looked up and to the left in the direction of the distant southern ley line, his fingers tapping at the table in front of him. "We must get to it now; once it is gone, we will never restore it."

"We can't risk going sooner," Llewelyn said. "We'll be massacred."

"If the line dies, we're all dead anyway," Fidelma stated softly.

The room erupted, as those who understood the ley lines and those who understood war attempted to explain to the other their position and the impossibility of the other option. The ley line was failing. I could barely comprehend what that meant. I had spent much of the last two years healing the ley that ran from the south to the north. I could see the impact of the growing corruption in the Belinus line on the land. The further south we went, the more ravaged the land, and the higher the number of ill. But for the line to collapse entirely... And never be restored...? That line ran from east to west through Kernow. I met Bronwyn's ashen face; her country would be uninhabitable within months of the line collapsing.

"Can't we do something?" I asked Fidelma.

"I have spent years doing what I could. What I can offer is no longer enough. Your mother knew it was failing and she tried to do something about it."

"What? You know why our mother was in the borders? You're saying that she gave Catriona up on purpose?" Rion asked.

"Yes – at least she meant for her to be there. It was not part of the plan for Viviane to be killed," Fidelma said. "She believed that she could heal the line. She had a vision: mother, daughter, and Griffin were vital to heal the line. She was impetuous, and she believed that they would hear her. The Strand line in Londinium must be healed. The corruption caused by industrialisation, technology, the loss of the old ways, and it being abandoned for so long without anyone to tend to it has been catastrophic. The corruption has slowly been seeping north from the intersection at Glastonbury. Your mother could feel it in Carlisle; it nagged at her endlessly. She had to do something and she had a vision that she believed in. The triskelion was the key: each loop springs from the centre, and she believed that she and you were two arms and the third would be created in Londinium. She thought if she could just get closer she would figure it out, and the final pieces would fall into place."

"But she never got closer."

"She should never have gone," the steward said, scowling at the elderly druid. It was clearly an argument they had trodden before. "She left us vulnerable; she had no right to make such a decision."

"She saw what was coming. She saw what had happened across western Europe and northern Africa, line after line failing, people growing ill, the land growing weak. She had to act."

"Like you? Aye and much good it did her."

"I followed the path, once she was gone. I had no choice."

"There is always a choice," Richard roared.

The room silenced at his outburst. The exchange had been heated on the steward's side at least. Rion placed his hand on my arm, acknowledging our pain at finally discovering why the lady had risked her life by going south.

"I did what I thought was right," Fidelma stated quietly.

"Oh aye. Well done," Llewelyn threw at her, his tone caustic on discovering she had more insight into my mother's motivation that she had failed to share previously in defence of Rhodri. "And where has that got us? No Griffin, a lady with no training, the next lady in the arms of our enemies, and the line failing before we can get to it."

"But there is a new Griffin." Lord Richard smiled, thin-lipped.

"What?" Fidelma looked around to spot a new addition to our group.

"*My* son," Richard indicated Gideon with his chin. "Husband and Griffin to the Lady of the Lake."

Fidelma's face was shocked. "But how?"

"The morning Devyn died," Rion began, before recounting

the events on the beach, including the crucial elements he had chosen to omit the last time they had heard this tale.

Fidelma's face was grey. "Why did you not tell us this before?"

"We were concerned that there might be another traitor in our midst," Rion explained. "Turns out we were right."

Whoever had taken Féile at least did not go back to Londinium with the information that Gideon was the Griffin and that we were married. There might be rumours in Carlisle that we were lovers but given Gideon's reputation that he had slept with half the single women in the city, that didn't mean much. Still, only half a dozen people in the world knew the information we were now revealing.

"You are the Griffin?" Fidelma directed her question directly to Gideon.

He nodded, no more pleased to be forced into having to deal with Fidelma than his father had been.

"It's not possible. Devyn Glyndŵr died. The Griffin is dead."

Some of the Anglian lords and a number of the druids started to agree that the line was extinguished, even though John himself confirmed that he had performed the rite of transfer. They were all too ready to believe that Gideon was lying.

"It's true," Rhodri said, coming forward. "He bears the mark of the first Griffin."

A number of the company frowned. The lore of the Griffin was mysterious. The Glyndŵrs kept the knowledge to themselves as a defensive measure, as the abilities of the Griffin, like that of the Lake bloodline, varied wildly between generations. By not sharing the knowledge with the world, others simply assumed that the powers passed down were similar and as strong from one to the next.

"What mark?" Rion asked.

"Pup," Rhodri stepped forward from his discreet spot in the back of the room and instructed Gideon to stand with a lift of his head. The steward bristled at the sight of the old Griffin under his roof. I struggled not to roll my eyes.

Gideon stood reluctantly, then a glint came into his eye, and he unhooked the clasp on his dress tunic, slowly revealing his chest. He threw Bronwyn a wink as she gave him an admiring glance, her expression quickly clearing as her gaze extended to include me.

"Wife," he tossed me the shirt which was still warm from his skin as he turned and displayed the image drawn across his back to the room.

The room hissed at the image, the predatory eagle intermingled with the proud lion. The tattoo that Devyn had worn had been a work of art, but it had been manmade. This drawing, by contrast, was undeniably otherworldly. I had only seen it briefly by the lake, had not had a chance to examine it up close. Now, my fingers lifted to touch it, to trace it from the finely wrought wings to the pads of the lion's hind legs perched above the tree that I knew swirled up from his right thigh.

Fidelma crossed the room. Her hand hovered above Gideon's shoulder as he turned back around and stilled to find her so close. She stepped backwards, her breath exhaling in a hiss.

"What are your gifts?" she asked, almost as if she had forgotten whom she was addressing.

Gideon's face closed over. She met his eyes and her own welled up as she stepped back nodding, as if to herself.

"Time is running out on the ley line?" Recovering faster from the news he had already previously absorbed, Rion returned to the main subject of concern.

"Yes," said Zara, "we have a few weeks at most."

"We won't get inside the walls in time," Richard said.

"Oh yes we can," Rion replied, already two moves ahead on the board.

"Not without Alba, and it will take weeks for their army to get here."

"We don't need the Albans," Rion offered. "We have an invitation."

"What?"

"We attend the Treaty Renewal," Rion suggested calmly, as if we weren't on the brink of war with the opposite party of said Treaty.

"Just walk right in?" the steward scoffed.

"Yes, why not?"

My jaw dropped. "I can't just walk right in. They'll have me in moments."

"No, they won't," Fidelma said, and her face started to change, her skin smoothing out and her hair darkening until it was a black waterfall down her back with broad streaks of white. Her face was almost smooth, though still lived in, wrinkles by her eyes and across her forehead from where she clearly raised her eyebrows a lot. It was a characteristic gesture that was so familiar to me, as were her high cheekbones and her golden eyes that were clear now the film of age had lifted.

A ripple of reaction went through the hall. The hand tightening on my shoulder shook me out of my shock at the revelation sooner than everyone else as I turned to the man behind me. Gideon's smirk was in place as the room reacted to the transformed Fidelma. There was the sound of a crashing chair as Henry Mortimer stood, turning to take in his father's reaction, but the steward also seemed less surprised than the rest of the room. Then Henry looked over at Gideon's amused face before striding from the hall, Alice going after him.

I turned back to Fidelma, who was watching the retreating warrior leave with regret. She squared her shoulders before turning back to the top of the table where Lord Richard glowered from his seat. He squashed down his own visibly strong reaction, only to scoff at what the transformed druid seemed to be proposing. "You're suggesting we send in our strongest asset protected only by a child's trick."

"Yes," Fidelma answered him with a challenging smile. "An illusion... and our son."

Our son. This was Gideon's mother.

I blinked. "You knew?" I asked under my breath.

"Suspected."

That explained his antipathy to Fidelma, the odd jibes and his refusal to be alone with her.

"I agree with Rion," Gideon stated. "If we go, we can check on the ley line and search for Féile."

"How do you plan to do that?" the steward challenged, his features pinched. He was not enjoying the afternoon.

"Devyn went to Londinium to see if he could find the lady, and find her he did." Rhodri reminded us.

"He tracked me down because I was matched to Marcus Courtenay, and he hacked the city's records to see if the pieces fit. It was logic and technology, not mystical powers." I corrected him.

"He went straight to you and stayed, even after all evidence suggested he was wrong," Rhodri insisted stubbornly.

"He tracked you down," Gideon repeated. He exchanged a

look with Rhodri across the room, and a wide grin split the older man's face.

"Of course."

"Care to share with the group?" Bronwyn asked, when neither said anything further.

"Nimue told you that the Griffin is empowered by necessity," Rhodri said. How did he know that? I looked back at Gideon. Was this where he had spent his morning?

Gideon looked at the ground, contemplating the wood before surveying the room, his gaze coming to a stop on me. "I've had some six months of honing my hunting skills."

Six months at the lakeshore shackled to Avalon, every night transforming from a man into one of the Griffin's forms, hunting endlessly for prey. What if the torment had had a purpose? What if our need was answered?

"Do you really think...?"

He shrugged. "Maybe being Griffin still has its uses."

"You are not the child's Griffin," Lord Richard said, helpful as ever.

"I believe I can find her."

Rion looked from one to the other of us grimly. "That's good enough for me."

"We are agreed then?" I asked in disbelief. Years had been spent planning for this war, all of which would be upended here after a series of revelations and half-hidden truths.

"Agreed."

Chapter Nineteen

On the second day of journeying south, the landscape started to change, the fields gave way to woods and the hills were rolling. But they had a sense of abandonment, and I could identify now what I had barely sensed the last time I had crossed the borderlands.

There was a ley line here, the May line, running from Land's End in Kernow through the Chiltern hills and across Europe. It wasn't corrupted in the same way the Belinus line was, or the way I expected the one that ran through Londinium was. When I tended the Belinus line, I noted there were two types of wrongness: one was a twisted sound to the notes, discordant off-key notes that waved through at certain times of the year, and I could sense that same problem here in the May line; the other was more physical, like a sludge, a heavy weight that overtook the water and polluted it. Yes, that was it, one was corruption, the other was pollution.

The borderline was sickened with the dissonance of twisted corruption. The power that Avalon had given me pulsed to be released, to spread and heal the wrongness here.

I dropped back beside Fidelma, seeking a distraction from that call I felt to heal the line – her new appearance would take some getting used to.

"Why did you do it?" I waved my hand at her face.

Her mouth pulled down. "I wanted to do my work without the burden of being the steward's wife. To tend the line, to be part of my new community. To attend the Treaty Renewal as a druid, or wisewoman, and no more. I hoped to avoid bringing pain to my family by simply ceasing to be the wife and the mother I no longer was."

"Seems to me like they were the only ones to figure it out," I commented.

An eyebrow directed at Gideon's back was my only response.

"Should I call you Elizabeth now?" I had had trouble adjusting to my new name, and had had to accept what others chose to call me. The least I could do was offer my friend the dignity of her own choice.

"I have been Fidelma a long time," she said in answer. "Elizabeth was a different person."

"Is this all the truth or part illusion?" I asked. Some of the signs of aging made her appear older than other women her age.

It was odd to speak to someone I knew, who had overnight become a complete stranger to my eye. Though not to Gideon it seemed, who had all but disappeared in the days spent in hurried preparation to get to Londinium at the usual prescribed time for the Treaty Renewal. He had barely tolerated Fidelma when he had suspected her of being Elizabeth Mortimer. Now she wore his mother's face once more, he avoided her presence when at all possible. And as I had been in consultation with Callum and the druids while I still could, I had barely caught sight of him or Rhodri until we assembled to leave. I had felt relieved not to have to face Rhodri, even though he too knew the pain of a lost child. I couldn't bear to meet him until I could put his granddaughter back in his arms.

"Ah," she pulled at the silver-streaked braid that came over her shoulder. "The truth is that working with the ley lines after your mother was gone has been taxing work. It took its toll on my body."

Was it vain to worry that my hair might be white in twenty years?

She laughed at my expression, sensing my concerns.

"No, child. You are the lady, you were born for this." She cocked her head. "Can you feel it?"

I raised a brow. Of course I could feel it – or rather, hear it. It was a hum that sang and keened as we climbed each hill and passed each tree. It was in my throat, on my skin, a flicker in my eye.

We were weeks off Samhain but there was something here of that otherworld. What I had experienced the night I crossed the borders with Devyn and Marcus had been terrifying. The borders had writhed with the dead and battle-fallen. It wasn't like that now, but there was a note of it that tumbled through the breeze.

"I can hear something." I started to describe my previous experience.

Fidelma nodded. "Aye, the battles here raged for centuries. So many dead. Thousands and thousands, of us, of them. Generation after generation, this was where they bled, where they died. So many trapped here."

"Trapped?" I asked, confused. "I thought they crossed over on one night a year."

"At Samhain? Yes, that's true everywhere else. Here it is something different. They are caught here, so many souls damned in the place they fell."

"The people who died here? They're all still here?"

The flickers that had started a while back were more frequent now. Was that what they were? Ghosts manifesting and flickering in the veil as they struggled to get out? Flies in a web, caught for all these centuries.

"I'm not too sensitive," Fidelma said, "but I worked with a druid who spent many years at Glastonbury Tor before me. He would sing to them, for hours and hours until his voice gave out. We all tried to get him to stop. He was a young man but he wore himself out in only a few years. Couldn't bear to listen to them, he said. He said that they called to him in their agony and that his songs soothed them. He wouldn't abandon them, and then he joined them all too soon."

"He died?" Marina asked from the other side of Fidelma.

"Yes, he poured every part of himself into helping them." Fidelma looked out across the countryside. "They are all still here."

"It's their cries." I gasped. "That's the note, that's the wrongness. It's not the ley line itself, it's their calls of pain, their screams. That's what's wrapping itself about the line here; that's what's corrupting it."

As I said it, I could feel the rightness of what I was saying, the truth of it.

"Where are the power nodes?" I asked. There must be stone circles like at Keswick where it was easier, or more effective to treat the corruption.

"Half a day's ride west, there's a stone circle at Avebury," she said.

Gideon swung his head, all pretence of being oblivious to

our conversation abandoned. He knew where I was going with this, what I was offering.

"You can't do this," he said.

"I have no choice." I didn't. There was no way I could pass through the borderlands and not do something to help the twisted souls bound in pain and torment here.

"You want to stop and treat the May line?" Fidelma asked.

I shook my head, my skin prickling in excitement, the power fizzing underneath, effervescent inside me.

"I'm going to free the spirits."

Fidelma looked at me in astonishment. "The spirit line... You think that the ley line has held them and that you can convince it to set them free?"

"I'm sure of it," I said, the excitement bubbling in my voice.

"It would take a mighty amount of power to do this," she said, concerned.

"I've got to try."

"Our priority is to restore the Strand line," she reminded me.

"And get to Féile," Gideon said. The warrior cared less about the failing ley lines; his sole purpose in attending the Treaty Renewal was the opportunity to get behind the walls and locate Féile. His entire being was focussed on the small chance of recovering her before we resorted to waging war on the very city she lived in.

"We can do both," I assured him.

"Avebury has the largest circle on the line; if you are to succeed it will have to be there," she said thoughtfully.

"Gideon, tell Rion we need to go west." Rion was up at the front and due to the protocol and protections I was forced to ride in the centre of our caravan of thirty odd delegates. Fidelma was smiling in amusement as her son bristled at the command in my voice. We needed to go – why hadn't he told Rion already?

"Please," I added belatedly. Was that what was wrong with him? I hadn't asked nicely enough? I looked to the right and saw a path winding into the forest. I pulled out of the train; there was no point continuing if there was a path right here.

Gideon ground his teeth then nudged his heels into his horse and rode off to the front of the train. Riders passed us as Fidelma and I waited on the side of the road for them to come back.

They weren't all that far in front – maybe twenty riders and a couple of vans. I could see Gideon's dark cloak and three more riders coming off the path, talking urgently.

What were they talking about?

I could see them now, the flickers in the forest, gathering, waiting. Glitches in the shadows, keening, calling for help. It wasn't a hum here like in the north, but a croon, their melancholy entreaties that they not be left here, trapped for eternity.

Hoofbeats indicated that the others had arrived, but I was transfixed by the calling, twisting shadows. How could I have ignored them before? They had played games with Devyn and Gideon tricked them and taunted them, but they hadn't done anything to me really. Because I had the power to help them? The last time I was here, I'd had some of the praetor's drug in my system and so I hadn't heard them. The hell hounds had tracked me, had followed me far beyond their territory... was this why? Had I run in fear because I didn't understand?

I could hear Fidelma explaining. Could hear them argue.

"We can't delay. We are due in Londinium."

"It will take too long. There is no good road west; nobody ever goes that way."

"Nobody ever goes this way."

"We can't waste power here, we must save every advantage for the war to come."

"It's too late for them, we have to save hundreds of living men."

I pulled the hood of my cloak up. If I was going to ride the road through the flickers I could see milling in the shadows, I needed to do this now. There were more and more of them gathering every minute we delayed.

They could feel me – or maybe what they could feel was the power that Nimue had given me. This had to be done.

Gideon listened to the argument; I knew his instinct was to preserve the power running in my veins for the battles ahead.

"Will living men fight for us knowing we abandon their souls to this fate?" he asked, surprising me.

"We need all the power we have to attack Londinium," the steward objected.

Gideon levelled his dark gaze at his father, then looked to Rion and whatever he saw there confirmed it.

"We ride for Avebury."

"What about the Treaty Renewal? What about your daughter?" Richard demanded.

My heart pulsed in pain at the unnecessary reminder that my daughter lay south, not west. But I had no choice I could not reach her any sooner, or make her any safer, by not doing what was needed here.

"If just a small group goes, we'll catch you up before morning," Rion suggested.

"You're surely not intending to go with them?" Richard Mortimer blustered, knowing he had lost the fight but not quite ready to concede.

Rion smiled wryly at me. "It appears I am."

Fidelma came back up to the group, accompanied by an older woman who doled out bags with supplies to keep us going until we rejoined everyone in the morning. I almost whimpered in my impatience to be off.

And then we were, and the flickering spirits followed us, were ahead and to the side of us, more and more of them. The shadows grew longer. I gripped the reins, my eyes darting from one movement to the next.

Gideon snatched the reins out of my hand.

"What are you doing?" his eyebrow rose, his lips thinned. I blinked at his odd appearance, the spectre of something other hovering over his features.

By this stage, I was twitching at every flicker, the cries and offness making me jittery in my very skin.

"I can't," I started, and flinched as a grey burst went off over his head. "I can't... they're everywhere."

"You can see them?" Gideon asked, surveying the forest, his amber eyes predatory, that odd impression of otherness increased as he pulled closer as if to shield me bodily.

I nodded, averting my eyes from a flicker that floated around my knee.

"This is why you've been riding like a..." The otherness faded as he sighed aggravatedly. I was pretty good at identifying the noises he put on particular things that annoyed him about me and this one seemed unfairly high on his scale. He reached an arm out to me.

I looked down at it, then back up at him. I couldn't see his face in the shadows.

"Ride with me."

I hesitated. It felt like that would be closer contact than we had shared in a while. In York he had arrived late and left early, preferring the chair to the bed for the few hours we shared his room at night.

"I won't touch you," he reassured me, reading me all too easily.

I hadn't meant to imply that I hadn't wanted to touch him... I had just been surprised, that was all.

The others had stopped up ahead to wait for us. I took his arm, and he swung me across, tethering my horse to his saddle. The horses were almost as jumpy as me, and we couldn't be sure that she would stay with us, as well trained as Rion's horses undoubtedly were.

I held myself tightly as I sat in front of Gideon, but I eventually relaxed, turning my face into his chest. Sitting stiffly on a cantering horse with your eyes closed is not something I would recommend. But given the alternative, this was a significant improvement.

As the sky turned red with the setting sun, an avenue of standing stones appeared to the south, heading west into the sun, until we came to Avebury circle.

"It's enormous."

There were possibly one hundred stones in a circle at least three times wider than I was used to. We halted at the wide ditch that surrounded it.

There was a nervous energy all through the clearing where the spirits swelled and called. A tremor ran through me as a familiar howl ripped through the night. Avalon's power rippling through my veins had drawn them. I saw Gideon tilt his head, that predatory aura surfacing again. We were too small a group if the hounds attacked. I shook it off; I needed to focus.

I had to do this. I could do this.

I let myself float out a little, to get a sense of the ley line beneath me. And quickly pulled back into myself.

My breath got shorter. I wasn't ready. It was so deep. If the ley line that ran through Keswick was a river below the surface, then this was a river at the bottom of a gorge, a gorge whose depths I could barely sense, but it was deep, so deep. What if I couldn't find my way back? I wasn't sure.

A hard warmth settled behind me. With the hounds so close he would not like being too far from me.

"My presence won't interfere?" he asked his mother. To my knowledge, it was the first time since her unveiling that he had spoken directly to her.

Fidelma looked over, her eyes lighting at the mere fact of him addressing her, despite our dire situation. She nodded. "It is not the custom, but I don't suppose it will interfere."

I was surprised that she permitted a civilian to remain in the circle for such an important rite, and wondered briefly if she would have permitted anyone else. But I felt better having him there. Marina and Fidelma took their positions further away than usual to accommodate the size of the circle.

A hand appeared at each side of my waist. Palm up, calloused, strong. I entwined my fingers in his, all too happy to accept his offer.

"I've got you," came a gravelly whisper in my ear. He barely spoke to me for days on end, but when he did, he sure knew how to make it count. Some of the tension inside me eased.

I closed my eyes and leaned back into that strength and let myself push out and over.

Down, down, the energy wafted through and around me, drifting past. So deep, deep to pull away from the pain above it, snagging at the tune, twisting it off key. It needed to be righted. I sang, freeing some of the energy from the Lakes, the calm, throbbing warmth of it slipping into the ether, spreading, pulling me deeper, deeper.

I felt loose, calm, and I smiled into the energy. My song encouraged it to move up above us, to go to the pain, to free the souls tied to the ruined land, land that had lost its connection with the ley line that ran so far and deep beneath it. The power pulsed out of me, a comfort, a light spreading out wider and wider high up above me.

The energy here had receded from the surface, twisting away from the pain, but the mellifluous wave washed across it, harmonising, soothing, the gift of the Lakes spread wider and wider. I let myself drift along. The May line here had little of the pollution from the ley that intersected with Londinium further west. But Mabon was coming and the autumn equinox would change the direction of the flow.

All of me felt incandescent, like I was the light, but my hands, I could see my hands. I looked at them. My hands were holding something... a thread, a connection. I couldn't be here. Everything was all right, but I had to surface, I should not go any further. Enough. Enough now. It was all right. The lake's gift was given. I had to surface.

I felt pressure on my hands, I felt touch.

Gideon. I needed to go back now. Everything was light. I floated back up and up, and the ley line was with me, around me.

I was warm and safe. Strong arms were wrapped around me.

My eyes opened.

The moon had risen, and the clearing was bathed in silver light.

Fidelma's eyes were open and rounded and Marina's

shimmered with unshed tears. We were all back. They had held the door open, and Gideon had called me through. A sense of wellbeing filled me, filled the circle.

The atmosphere was changed. The flickers were no more. They had coalesced into tiny bubbles, pinpricks of light. There were hundreds of them, thousands, floating up into the moonlit beams of light. And all with a miraculous sigh of release. They filled the sky, all the pain, all the misery gone.

A hound stalked at the edge of the forest, but as I watched the great white beast transformed and it too was light, another of those tiny brilliant lights floating into the sky.

The horror and pain of being tied here to the battlefields where they had fallen was over. And they were gone upwards, melting into the moonlight above. The last thing I saw as my eyelids drooped was Rion and Fidelma watching the sky in wonder.

I woke to find myself in a caravan trundling along, the sound of the wheels on the rough road unmistakeable. There was a lightness to the outside, the sound of birds calling, and a smell of warm earth after a rain. And the cedar and leather that was Gideon's own particular smell wrapped around me.

Fidelma looked down and beamed into my no doubt sleep-creased face.

"Good morning, lady." She inclined her head in a way that communicated her honour to serve.

I blinked, uncomfortable.

"I didn't do anything," I said hoarsely. "I just carried what was needed."

"If you say so."

She looked over at her son who rested on the other side of me, but I could feel the solidifying and flexing of hard muscle which indicated that he was awake.

"That was one of the most singular moments of my life and I am honoured to have witnessed it." She took my hand in hers. "Now, you look well. Do you feel all right?"

I ran through my body, checking for the usual signs that my emotions, my will, had been thinned out by such intense contact with the energy at a node. I made a small moue.

"I feel fine." Actually, I felt unbelievably fine – tired, but nothing like I had felt in the past.

Gideon shifted behind me and with his finger tipped my chin round to look at him. His intense scrutiny surveyed me up and down and then he nodded back at his mother in confirmation of my assessment.

"And the power?" he asked.

I hid my eyes from his. How could I tell him that I was not as strong as I had been. He had paid such a price for this power, months stuck waiting for me when he had wanted to find Féile.

Was giving up some of that power a betrayal of the price he had paid?

There was a rustle as Fidelma exited the caravan and jumped down, leaving the two of us alone. She already knew my power was less. How could she not, when yesterday I had been bursting with it?

My mouth felt dry as I confessed. "It's not what it was."

I tested it, felt around it. There was still more than what was my natural gift, much more, but would it be enough?

"It was well done, Cat." My startled eyes flashed up in time to catch the end of a nod not dissimilar to the one his mother had given – a bow of the head that said way more than I was ready to receive.

"I... don't..." I stammered but he was already levering himself up.

At the entrance of the caravan he reached for me, his cavalier smirk back in place. He picked up my hand and placed a kiss on the back of it before he swung out into the beautiful borderlands day.

Part Three

THE DAYS OF GOLDEN DREAMS

But, when the days of golden dreams had perished,
And even Despair was powerless to destroy,
Then did I learn how existence could be cherished,
Strengthened, and fed without the aid of joy.

Then did I check the tears of useless passion —
Weaned my young soul from yearning after thine;
Sternly denied its burning wish to hasten
Down to that tomb already more than mine.

— *Remembrance*, Emily Brontë

Chapter Twenty

We had agreed that while Gideon could attend as Rion's senior attendant, I would pose, ironically, as Gideon's wife. Given that we didn't yet know what impact the proximity to the dying ley would have, Rion and Gideon had insisted that we continue to assume I needed Gideon. And if the ley line was as dire as had been reported, I could not take the risk of being here without him.

The walls of Londinium were far higher than any of the castle and town walls I had experienced across Briton. I had never truly seen them before, I realised, as from within the city you never really saw the wall, not as such. You caught pieces of it where a building wasn't pressed against it, and as you passed through you could appreciate the width of it, given it took over a dozen steps to pass through a gate. But from outside, approaching underneath from the borderlands, it was beyond credulity that man could have built something so vast, and above it like a twinkling jewelled crown were the towers of the city itself.

My stomach had been heavy with dread when we had fled

that night from the White Tower, and I had never thought to be behind the walls again, never planned that far ahead. That I was back and Devyn was not with me was a jag through my heart that would never heal. However, I realised its existence caught me by surprise now, it was no longer a pillar of pain around which I existed as if tethered.

Féile was near. I couldn't sense her the way I could her father, but I knew that we were close for the first time in months – an eon of time for a small child. Would she have forgotten me? The breath was stolen from me at the idea. We had been together for such a small amount of time. What if she didn't even recognise me? She would be three and a half now – how far back could a small child remember?

The noise of the crowd seeped through the wall as our procession entered the city. Riding as I was at the tail end of the line of Celts, Anglians, and Mercians, I had time to brace myself before we left the sanctuary of the wall and entered into the pandemonium of the crowd.

The Anglians around us looked dead ahead, chins raised, mysterious and aloof in expectation of the turn out that their arrival usually engendered. I knew what it was to be on the city side of the crowd – not out here by the walls but further in where the elites awaited our arrival.

I remembered it feeling more festive than this – I could sense a sullen, dark feeling from the crowd watching us pass. Gideon nudged his horse closer to mine and stepped a little in front.

There was a chain of sentinels in front of the corridor of citizens and they weren't here for decorative purposes or to watch the foreign delegation. They faced inwards, watching the citizenry. The crowds were not happy to see us here. They were not here for the usual spectacle, for the pageantry of the festivities surrounding the Treaty Renewal. Instead, they watched us pass with sullen eyes.

We finally arrived at the great square in front of the Governor's Palace, where the praetor and the Council stood facing Richard and Rion and the other more prominent members of the delegation while they waited for the rest of us to arrive. There was no sign of the new governor, which was an insult to the delegation but one I was happy to accept if it meant not having to set eyes on Matthias Dolon yet.

Once we had all dismounted and our horses had been escorted from the square, the praetor stepped forward. He surveyed the arriving Britons in front of him from his position above us on the stairs. My heart skipped a beat as his gaze passed across where Gideon and I stood. While they snagged momentarily on Gideon – who, to be fair to him, with his height and beauty was reasonably eye-catching – they passed seamlessly over me.

I wondered what he saw when he looked at me. Fidelma said that the illusion existed only in the mind of the person looking at me. While Gideon and the rest of the Britons still saw me, everyone else would see someone entirely different. The illusion she had maintained on herself for years had been much more holistic; it had taken years to cement it in place so that everyone saw the same thing when they looked at her. The glamour I used was a surprisingly simple piece of sorcery – one even those with a modicum of magic could do. Maintaining it for longer periods, as Fidelma had done, took greater skill. So while I felt utterly exposed out here with the whole city watching, the lack of reaction from Praetor Calchas reassured me that my identity remained concealed.

A sentinel approached the praetor from behind and whispered something in his ear. Calchas showed no reaction beyond a small nod, and he took a couple of steps further down the stairs.

"My lords and ladies, I welcome you into the city," he began effusively. "We are so grateful to receive you."

He stopped in front of the Steward of York, who had been the most prominent of the Britons to regularly attend in the last few years, that I was aware of. The lady traditionally never came, remaining a silent threat in the north. Rion had participated in the last one as prince, maintaining the Briton deception his parents still lived, but that charade was done with and he now attended as king – making him technically more senior than the Steward – though I suppose Londinium had yet to be formally informed, whatever they actually knew unofficially. Kernow sent minor members of House Cadoc; the princes of Powys, Dyfed, and Gwent were present but slightly lower ranking, Bronwyn alongside them given her new status in Gwynedd. Alba never sent anyone as they were not signatories of the Treaty, and barely acknowledged that they shared the same island as the Romans. However, I knew from Callum's history lessons that they had occasionally participated in the wars over the làst millennia or so. Llewelyn and the higher ranking Kernowans' absence seemed unremarkable, thankfully, as they slowly followed behind with the army we had raised.

"Especially in light of that bad business a couple of years ago," Praetor Calchas was saying as he clasped his hands to his chest penitently.

The steward raised an eyebrow at Calchas's choice to speak so directly and openly about the act of war that had been committed in Anglesey.

"We wish to continue to honour the Treaty that has kept the peace on this island for so many years," Lord Richard said in return. I couldn't begin to imagine the effort it had taken for him to get that out.

"I am most relieved to hear that," Calchas said, one hand indicating that the steward should precede him. "Most relieved indeed. We have much to discuss."

With that, we trailed after them up the stairs. We passed through the great marble lobby and into a room where warm drinks and bowls of water awaited to allow us to wash the worst of the journey off.

We had stopped outside the city to wash off the dirt of the road before entering the city, but this reception seemed to be part of the welcoming ritual. Senators' wives greeted the delegates and helped them clean off the dust of the road.

Marina caught my eye from across the room, her air of druidic calm not quite hiding the gleam of mischievous amusement at being tended to by some elite citizen when only a few years ago she would have been less than dust beneath her expensive heels.

My breath stopped as I recognised my former friend in the citizen who approached us with a bowl and cloths draped over her arm. A ring sat on her hand... she was married then – presumably to a senator or some other senior official. That match would have pleased her.

Ginevra offered a cloth to me without so much as moving her eyes from where they lingered on my husband's face. He was a good foot taller than her so her notice wasn't the most discreet, but at least we knew my glamour was convincing up close.

Her eyes flicked to the pendant Gideon wore around his neck, a slight crease appearing between her brows in vague recognition.

"I like your, ah... charm," she offered when she realised her attention had been noticed. "I had a friend who wore something similar once."

She remembered the charm Devyn had given me to protect me from the pervasive cameras. We all wore one, Calchas would no doubt be quick to spot them too, but there was no point overplaying our wide eyed pretence that all was well.

Once I had cleaned my hands and wiped them on a cloth, I began to step aside but paused as I did so. Ginevra still wasn't shy in her appreciation of a handsome man and her attentions were starting to ever so slightly grate on my nerves.

"Allow me, my love," I said, dipping the cloth in the water before taking one of his hands in mine and slowly drawing the wet cloth from the heel of his hand through the hollow of his palm and across his sword-calloused fingers. I took my time, lingering on each strip of skin as I passed the cloth across first one hand and then the other.

I looked up at him through my lashes and caught the snag of his tongue as he wet his dry lips.

"Thirsty, husband?" I asked as I dropped the cloth into the waiting bowl. His amber eyes glinted down at me. I smiled up at him for the sake of our overly attentive host but even with an audience my eyes skittered quickly away. I had never flirted with him before. He had barely spoken to me since Féile was taken, and I had waited until we stood in the very jaws of the lion waiting to chew us up to start.

The prickle of awareness that floated between us centred on where his hand touched my spine as he guided me to the side of the room where he would not have his back exposed to the enemy. I felt him tense as his hand took and gripped mine in warning.

Surveying the room, it didn't take too long to spot what had set him off.

Marcus.

There he was. My former friend. And once, my future husband.

At first glance, he looked the same: broad shoulders, elegant outfit, chestnut hair sweeping across his head. He looked a little older maybe, and there was a gauntness about the cheeks and a slight stoop in those strong shoulders. There was a fracture splintering that charismatic prince-of-the-city aura that he gave off.

My mind blanked as he looked in our direction, but his focus went straight to Gideon and his eyes hooded as he recognised the Anglian warrior who had accompanied us on the road north. He didn't acknowledge the acquaintance before his eyes moved on, searching the room, sticking when he got to Bronwyn before moving on again. He scanned back again when his eyes failed to find his target.

Me.

My mouth turned down as anger rolled through me. The room became a tad darker as the sky outside clouded over ominously and we became reliant solely on the candles which had been lit around the room – no doubt, in preparation for the effect the Britons' presence typically had on electric lighting. Which I now realised had been unaffected until this moment. Until I had used magic.

But I remembered from my childhood instances where the Britons' presence had left the whole city without power. Did it only happen when magic was in use? But the Britons were forbidden to use magic inside the walls. My awareness of my effect on my surroundings slipped away as Marcus stepped further into the room. Closer.

He had killed Devyn. His father had pulled the trigger but Marcus was who I really blamed. Dolon had just been following his nature. That he had shot Devyn once he no longer had use for him had been inevitable. You couldn't kick a dog for barking. Marcus though, Marcus the white knight, saviour of his people, healer of the masses. My friend. He had betrayed us. He had lured us there. He was the reason Devyn was dead.

"My lady," came Gideon's urgent voice.

If I killed Marcus here in front of everyone, would I still be able to find my daughter? What if he was the one who had her? I felt sick. It was possible. He was a doctor, obsessed with curing the illness. If anyone knew where my daughter was with her power, he would.

Gideon stepped into my personal space, his finger running lightly down the bare skin of my neck. He lowered his head and whispered in my ear under the guise of nibbling kisses.

"Stop," he hissed. He pulled my lower body into him, bringing me more securely into his warmth where I couldn't fail to notice his presence. I blinked and inhaled the smell of sweat and horse and man. I put a hand up onto his broad chest as I centred myself and released the power that had fermented under my skin and pulled the clouds into the sky.

"Let's get you out of here," he said in a low voice and escorted me out of the room before I did something stupid.

We arrived back out in the lobby where liveried servants waited and, despite our somewhat earlier than expected exit from the reception, they showed us to our allocated room.

The room was beautiful, classically lined with intricate mosaic work on the floor and an open window that looked out over one of the great avenues of the city facing west. The reds and oranges of the setting sun could still be glimpsed between the towers above us.

I took a deep breath as I felt rather than heard Gideon come to a stop behind me.

"Are you all right?" he asked softly.

Was I? I wasn't too sure I was. I hadn't expected to react so strongly to Marcus.

Gideon curled his body around mine, placing a large palm over my stomach as he drew me close. He made me feel protected and safe. I drew strength from his closeness, it grounded my body and soul in a way that only he could give me. But Avalon should have freed us, I thought. I shouldn't need him like that anymore.

I drew a shuddering breath and pulled away. Turning around, I saw his closed face, and how he watched mine in the lengthening shadows. I don't know why I thought that moment downstairs and his closeness here meant anything but I had, and that closed-off expression was like a slap in the face.

"I don't know what came over me," I found enough voice to say. "Thank you."

He pushed his fingers back through his hair, rolling his shoulders as he made his way over to the bed where he casually stretched out his length.

I rounded and flexed my own shoulders to shake off some of the tension that threatened to snap my bones in two.

"Why do you do that?" I asked the question into the quiet evening. My hands clenched as I waited for his answer.

"Do what?" he asked lazily.

"Kiss me, touch me," I clarified. "Even though you hate me."

"I don't hate you," he said so coldly that if his tone were a physical thing, it would have given me frostbite.

He exhaled.

"I don't hate you," he repeated, this time in a tone that was slightly more in tune with his words.

"Right," I said and, wrapping my arms around myself, turned to look out over the city once again. The lights twinkled in the growing twilight. The rest of the city, I noted, continued to operate, only the Governor's Palace struggling technologically from my recent release of energy.

"Sometimes it seems like touch is the only thing that will refocus you," he said, finally answering my question. "I suppose I saw your last partner do it."

Devyn. It was a technique Devyn had used, particularly in the early days when I had struggled to pull out of magic once I got caught up in the energy, in the flow and pull of it. Sometimes I sort of forgot I lived in a body.

"There must be another way," I conjectured. "I'm sure previous Griffins didn't use this technique."

"Ah, and here I thought you were worried about me." He huffed. "You would prefer I didn't touch you?"

"No, that's not it," I started, but I stopped, not sure what to say. I felt so in my head all the time, overthinking everything, or outside of myself, tackling the ley lines which left me adrift. I lived for those touches. He was the only person who ever touched me now that Féile was gone. Merely being in his proximity was enough to keep me grounded, but today he had touched me, put me back in my body when I had been at risk of revealing myself in the middle of the reception.

The truth was that I missed his touch.

"Do you think she's close?" I asked, desperate to change the subject and turning to the other topic that pulled my thoughts in a never-ending cycle of worry.

I turned when he didn't answer. He shook his head slowly.

Right. I knew better. Historically, the Governor's Palace,

like the White Tower which was the praetor's residence, wasn't under the same level of surveillance as the rest of the city but we had agreed to be circumspect even with the charms. We couldn't be sure the city wasn't listening.

He extended a hand in my direction. Confused, I took a tentative step forward and placed my hand in his. He pulled me toward him and I found myself with one hip against the bed and my hand on his chest.

"What are you doing?" I asked, a betraying tremor in my voice.

His hooded gaze looked up at me, a slight upward tug at one corner of his lips.

"If you don't recognise it I must not be doing it very well," he said with a distracted air. His free hand traced a pattern on the oath tattoo that sat beneath the sensitive top layer of skin of my inner wrist. We had shared purpose here. He had sworn to find Féile, the only oath he had ever given as far as I was aware. His touch was having other effects than a simple reminder of his vow, as he knew only too well.

"You expended a lot of energy yesterday," he remarked, his lips mesmerising as they formed the words. "You don't need this?"

He was doing this to check on me, to see if after my efforts at Avebury I needed him. I pulled my hand away.

"No, thank you," I said smartly, tugging on the hand he still held.

There was a flash in his eyes, and then in a single manoeuvre I was no longer beside the bed but on it, rolled under him, his muscular body caging mine as he hovered above me.

"No, thank you," he repeated mockingly. "The lady declines?"

He pushed his hips into mine teasingly, tauntingly. I pushed back. I hated it when he called me by my title – I had from the moment we first met. It didn't matter that he did so now only because we couldn't risk anyone using my real name. Either one of them. And he had failed to use the name they had given me since we got here.

"Yes, I decline," I grunted trying to push him away.

He raised himself higher, granting me space but not escape.

"You don't need this?" he asked.

Need it? No, I didn't need it. I didn't feel the hollowness that used to pull me down after a bout with the ley lines. Perhaps using the magic Avalon had gifted me rather than raiding my own resources didn't affect me the same way. Or perhaps Nimue had granted my request and made it so I didn't need him like before. But did I want it?

"You've barely spoken to me in weeks."

His mouth twisted in a strange smile.

"That's never bothered you before."

I turned my face away. "Well it bothers me now," I said as I pushed at his unmoving broad chest again.

His fingers caught my chin and turned my face back to his.

"Why?" he asked. "If you truly don't need me anymore, what does it matter?"

My eyes watered as I looked up at him. I didn't know why. I didn't, I insisted to myself. But whatever he read there seemed to satisfy him, and his mouth swooped down and claimed mine. His body relaxed. I could escape if I wanted to. This kiss was the only thing that held me now.

I kissed him back deeply, thoroughly. Not need this? I would die if I didn't have it, if I didn't have him.

He pulled back in the dark, lifting his tunic over his head, giving me a moment of space, of time, to consider my next action. Time I used to pull free of my own clothes.

He helped push my dress down over my shoulders and then we were together in the dark, skin against skin, hand to hand, mouth to mouth, moving, seeking, finding. I needed everything.

In that moment as the world exploded, I felt complete, body and soul united, the fractured mess that walked and talked through my life was simply whole.

We lay there afterwards, wrapped in each other in a way that reminded me of the time before. Before Féile had been stolen, when I had thought briefly that maybe, maybe there was something more than duty and service between us.

"How do you feel?" he asked, in an echo of other times, times when I had been broken into pieces only he could put together.

"I feel…" I bit my lip, "good."

"Just good? No desire to fly out of windows?" He arched a brow at me.

"That's a good thing, no?"

He didn't answer as he turned on his side away from me. I traced the branches of the tree that wound over his hip, worrying at the Celtic patterns that lay there, then up across the magnificence of the creature on his back, to the wings that splayed across his shoulders.

Gideon's behaviour was a mystery to me at the best of times but he had been behaving oddly since I came back from Avalon. I had thought that it was because of Féile, or the strangeness of his months at the lake. But maybe Alice and Bronwyn were right. Was he not pleased that I might not need him? That I might not need this closeness to restore me?

"I wanted you to be free," I whispered into the darkness.

The darkness ate my words until finally he responded. "I've always been free."

I slipped easily through the crowd in the forum, which parted to make way for the two Celts in their midst. The forum was one of the few public places where the delegates were permitted, making it the most natural location for us to make the switch from Briton to citizen. We made our way to the tent where Fidelma read the palms of the city's elite. She had reported that the queries they had about their futures now lent towards health rather than wealth or whatever more frivolous concerns had occupied them in the past. She had initially protested at resuming her old position as the wisewoman, but when she finally acquiesced she had insisted on keeping the face of Elizabeth Mortimer, much to Rion's frustration.

Our first day here, Rion had insisted we keep strictly to our assumed roles within the delegation to establish ourselves before disappearing for periods to explore the city. Gideon and I, as minor players in Rion's entourage, were able to slip away quite easily while Bronwyn was too visible as she now represented Gwynedd. Llewelyn had stayed with the army, leading them as far as the borders in readiness while we waited for the Albans to come south, hoping they would arrive before winter but not satisfied to wait in York for them.

Fidelma looked up and indicated to the screen behind her current client, who was just departing.

I changed quickly, loathe to leave Gideon alone with Fidelma for too long.

When I emerged, his stony face explained the heavy silence.

He took the neat pile of clothes from his mother and we exchanged places.

I stood in front of one of the mirrors on the tent wall, my fingers nimble as they pulled my hair up into the intricate styles that were the custom here. It was amazing how my fingers remembered how to do it, when I hadn't done anything more than a loose tie or braid in so long.

Fidelma nodded her approval, admiring the outfit Oban had supplied before we left him behind in York. He had been unable to travel into the city as, despite his sister's power, he didn't even have the smidge of latent magic it would take to keep from being recognised.

"Tonight," she said, "I'll take you to where I believe the main node is. We can see if we can gain access."

I shook my head. "I've spoken to Rion. We're making Féile our priority."

"What? No, the ley… we must…"

"Fidelma," I said, taking her hands in mine to soften the blow of the change in our power dynamic. "I sense the corruption but the line feels strong to me. It's not dying. You must sense it too."

Her brow creased. "I don't understand. When we were here last time it was worse. The level of corruption reaching Glastonbury indicated… I assumed the line must be fading."

"I believe you." And I did. Recalling how weak I had felt in those final weeks here, no longer taking the state-sponsored suppressant, I had been susceptible to the line drawing on me, but that drag was much fainter now. Rion and Bronwyn concurred, they had both suffered from the illness on previous visits Rion particularly but so far they felt fine. The line could wait – we had to find Féile.

Gideon emerged from behind the screen freshly outfitted

in another of the looks Oban had whistled up. Our resident tailor had done himself proud. The clean lines and sharp tailoring managed to emphasise style and diminish the impact of Gideon's physique, as requested, to an astounding degree.

"How on earth did he manage that?" I asked, running a hand down the lapel in admiration of Oban's craftmanship. My breath caught as I sensed a shift that I recognised, a disorienting adjustment between what my eyes were seeing and what my touch told me was the truth.

I raised surprised eyes to amused amber ones. I stepped back and the predatory wolf in Roman clothing wavered and became once more an urbane, average-looking citizen.

"Oh."

"Rhodri helped me figure it out," he said simply.

So that was what he had been doing while we were in York.

I looked again at my reflection in the mirror. It was unnerving. My delegate appearance as a brunette, pale-skinned Mercian stared back at me. Fidelma appeared at my shoulder nodding approvingly as the image wavered until a dark-haired, olive-skinned citizen blinked back at me.

"What do you see?" I asked Gideon curiously.

"You," he said. "I see you."

He bowed his head in the formal manner of the elite, and, straightening, offered me his arm, a devilish glint lighting his eye.

"Shall we?" he asked, mildly flirtatiously.

I wrapped my arm in the disconcertingly un-muscled one offered to me just as a new client entered the tent.

"I do beg your pardon," the woman said on seeing us there.

I froze. The woman nodded at us politely, her reaction the same as she would have offered any citizen.

"Yes, these people are just finished," Fidelma said, ushering us out. "Please come in."

We made our way through the forum, weaving between the people in the porticoed corridor.

"What now?" Gideon asked as we stepped through the forum gates, unhindered by the sentinels waiting by the transports that were for the sole use of delegates – mainly used to ferry us from the Governor's Palace to the forum – and out onto the bustling street.

"We wander, I suppose."

We strode along the streets, the sights and smells at once so familiar to me and yet also newly foreign.

The projections from shop windows flickered as they attempted to boot up avatars with the latest fashions in front of us, but glitching when they failed to identify our faces and stored preferences. The twirl and dance of other pedestrians' avatars, as well as the neon monitors flashing advertisements and news from the feeds, threatened to overload my senses. How did people think with this constant bombardment? But that was the point, I supposed. Who had the space to think, to ask questions, to challenge the status quo when there was so much coming at them all the time?

In the end, I was surprised at how easily and quickly I was able to tune out the bombardment and simply absorb the wider world of the city.

I noted the familiar grandeur of the great buildings, their styles reflecting eras of prosperity and austerity side by side in the towers that twined upwards ever higher. I felt the thrum and vibrations of understood rhythms of life here wash past me: the worker dashing to get the last train, the huddles of children walking home from school, the candlemaker hawking his wares in the window of intense trade that only came every four years with the Briton delegation. There was something about the higgledy-piggledy architecture of this city that had been my home that called to me, that whispered in my ear of ages past, of histories known and forgotten. The sights and sounds were so different to what I had become used to during the last couple of years: the song of the ley line, the vast expanse of fingers of light breaking through cloud over the valleys of Cymru, the rushing waters of the rivers and brooks, the mesmerising reflections on the lakes outside of Carlisle, the defensive huddle of houses in York.

Maybe Londinium wasn't the home of my soul now, but it was a home I had once loved nonetheless. It didn't sing to my soul as the wide-open spaces did. But neither could I deny the rhythms of life to which I was again responding now – sounds and sights I had grown up with. Just as in the north I knew the familiar sound of Gideon's footsteps in the hall, Féile's giggle as she played with Snuffles, the harmony of the Belinus ley line at the stone circles in good periods. Here too there were things I knew and that were a part of me.

Gideon trailed at my side, his mild-mannered façade blending seamlessly into the city streets, but on taking his hand and getting a closer look I saw the signs of stress. His sharp eyes missed nothing, scanning the streets as we walked along, but there was a lot more to take in than he was used to. He looked like the men one occasionally saw at the annual sales in the shopping districts: overwhelmed and in shock. I was struggling with the assault on my senses, senses which were nowhere near as sensitive as Gideon's must be, especially as the sights and sounds were new to him. I curled my fingers around his and scanned the busy street for somewhere to give him some respite.

I pushed through the door into the relative calm of a coffee shop. Soft music and the nutty, caramel aroma of freshly ground beans enveloped us as we left the city behind. I could feel Gideon relax instantly.

"Thank you," he said quietly, even as I winced at not having seen the signs earlier. I set him in the quietest corner and hurried to place an order.

"Here," I said, handing him a small coffee. His entire face screwed up in protest at his first sip.

"Are you trying to poison me?" he spluttered.

I was utterly horrified. I had brought him into one of Devyn's favourite places and served him his favourite extraordinarily strong coffee. I had just done the very thing Gideon had been hung up about for years.

"I'm so sorry. I didn't mean to…" My voice cracked.

"It's all right. I'll survive," he hurried to reassure me before pausing as he took in the full extent of my distress. "You came here with him?"

I gave a small nod. "I'm sorry. I wasn't thinking. It doesn't mean anything."

"I know."

"What?" It was that easy.

"I've been thinking about him today," he said softly. "I don't know how he did it. How he lived here all those years. Day after day. Never sure if he would find you."

"Oh," I said against the knot forming in my throat.

"Walking a mile in another's shoes is… educational." His eyes looked tired.

"Have you sensed anything?"

He shook his head wearily. "It's a lot, turning on my hunting senses here in the city." He rubbed a knuckle into his temple. "I know she's here, but it keeps slipping away. Every time I sense her... all the digital things, the transports, the noise."

"We will find her."

But two more days of walking, crisscrossing the inner city, gambling that the Council would keep her where security was tightest turned up nothing. On the third, I ventured out alone, despite Gideon's protests. But I had recruited Rion and Bronwyn to insist he take a break; Gideon could barely hold the glamour anymore, much less extend his senses to seek out our daughter.

The days were slipping by so fast. I stepped out of the forum onto the crowded street I wasn't entirely sure what use I was on my own but I couldn't just sit at another trade discussion. I needed to try.

Time was running out.

Chapter Twenty-One

"**D**onna," a voice hailed me from behind.

I walked on, sure I must have been mistaken.

"Donna," it came again, insistent. "I want to help."

My breath became short, but I refused to turn around. I had only just started my search today. How had I been identified so quickly?

An object was pressed into my palm. I looked at it and stopped short. It was a charm, sewn onto a wristband – not the one I had given to Marcus, an older shabbier model. I pulled the charm and twisted it to reveal the Celtic symbol that sat hidden on the reverse.

I lifted my eyes to the crooked smile and lined face of a man I had never met before.

He placed his hand over my own and activated the charm.

"I'm Linus," he said. "Devyn's friend."

"Right," I said warily. He could be Linus, or he could be anyone.

"There is somewhere we could go, talk more freely, if it please you, donna," he said, catching my sense of caution.

I needed a friend in the city, someone who could help in my search. Someone who could move about more freely than I could. I squeezed the hand that held mine before releasing it and examined his face. Trust was not something I gave too freely these days. I gripped the charm in my hand. Could I trust him?

Could I afford not to trust him?

"Okay," I said.

His crooked smile broadened and he took off, turning once to check that I was following him before he barrelled onwards, ducking down alleys and dashing up connecting walkways that all led east. We passed through Bishopsgate, him always staying a few feet in front, within sight but never so close that we appeared to be together. I pulled my cloak close around me, hiding the fine cut of my clothing as best I could. Luckily my cloak was nondescript enough not to attract unwanted attention.

Finally, he dodged into a familiar doorway and up shabby stairs to wait for me in an open doorway to a room that was filled with memories: shouting at Devyn for deceiving me, laughing in jubilation after we got Marina out, kissing him... I closed the lid on the box that threatened to spill over, its contents something I could not deal with right now.

"So, you're Linus," I said.

He waved me over to the seat by the wall.

"I am, donna."

"Do you know who I am?" I'd had time to think on the way here – he shouldn't have been able to recognise me.

"I do. I don't know if the boy told you how we met. I'm able to see past illusions and glamours and suchlike." His face clouded. "He's gone, they told me. I was so sorry to hear it. He was a good lad."

"How did you find out?" Rion had told me that the flow of information across the walls was squeezed tighter than ever these days.

"I was still in the Shadowlands when word came out of York. Tales of an attack and the Griffin dead. I didn't know what that was rightly, but the Briton folk, they were full of tales of the young lad what run off to find his lady. I knew right off it had to be him. He found you, didn't he? Said he would. Never knew anyone in my life more like to make the stars do what they were told."

I smiled thinly, recognising the man I'd loved in the young boy Linus had befriended. Even as I cursed the stars that had betrayed us so terribly so soon after we left here.

"Why did you come back?" Surely he would have been safer in the Shadowlands, and to come back to his old flat seemed particularly foolish.

"I had to. People need my help. I couldn't just see myself safe."

"You know that the praetorians tracked Devyn. They may know about this place."

"It has been four years. Devyn put heavy charms on this place that make it safer than anywhere else so I had to get it back when I returned. And most importantly, I am not the same man." With these words, his face changed appearance. "I am a latent. My only skill is in glamours. That was how I met Devyn – I saw through his."

"I can't stay long," I said. "I have to be back for a banquet this evening."

"I won't keep you, donna, but I wanted to tell you who I was and that I'm here for whatever you need."

"Do you know where my daughter is?"

"Daughter? Is that why you've come?" His brow crinkled. "I thought, maybe you were here to help."

"Help who?" I asked, curious. He had risked a lot in approaching me, and apparently it had not been just for my sake.

"The latents what are ill," he said slowly. "I thought you might help us with getting them out."

"No, I'm sorry, Linus," I said slowly. "But why do they need to get out? There is medicine now. Aren't they able to come forward, get the medicine?"

His eyes widened at this, his crooked mouth twisting.

"Those meds only go to the elite. Nobody from here ever sees the stuff they brought in a few years ago. "

After everything Marcus had done, all of his so-called purer motives, he had failed them. Just as he had failed me. Bitterness ran through me, deep and unrelenting.

"What's more, nobody from round here would put their hand up to try," Linus continued. "We're locked in like mice in a trap, no way out, not for us in the stews. No papers good enough to get you through the gates these days unless you've got a clean bill of health, and there's nobody from round here that ain't got some taint in 'em."

"Taint? Magic, you mean?"

"I mean in the blood. Ain't just latents they take now. Anyone what's got a smidge of Briton blood seems to fit the bill."

"Fit what bill?"

He sighed, pushing his hair back with his hand. "We don't know. Can't figure it out. Even the hackers, they've tried everything, but there's no sign of it, no sign of the truth anywhere."

"What truth?"

He looked at me as if I were the one speaking in tongues.

"Where the disappeared go."

The disappeared. When I had helped Devyn smuggle Marina out of the city, it had been to flee the mysterious arrests and disappearances of latents who surfaced because of the illness, signifying the magic that lingered in their blood from their Briton ancestry.

"Are people still disappearing?" I asked. In light of how many ill there were now, surely there was safety in numbers for those who hid real abilities?

"Yes, donna, so many."

"They can't all have magic."

"Just so. Seems like they don't need to have magic nowadays to be a target. Like I says, a smidge of the taint, and off you go," he said. "That's why nobody can get papers. To get papers you got to do a test, see how many genetic counters you have. People with a high count, they never make it to the gates – never make it home some of 'em. As for the rest, in no time they get picked up."

"How many?" I asked.

He shrugged helplessly. "Hundreds from this area alone, maybe thousands across the city. All from 'tween the old wall and the outer wall, of course."

Devyn had never been able to figure out what happened to the people who mysteriously disappeared. His leading working theory had been that Calchas was taking them away and somehow using them for their magic.

"How is he getting away with this?"

"Away with what, donna? Nobody knows but a few of us who managed to piece it together through our network. All the mob knows is the feeds, and the Mete, and shopping and working. So maybe a neighbour ups and leaves, it's only one

311

person here, one there. Why would a normal person think oddness of that? Ain't nothing in the feeds or in the gossips about such carrying on."

Thousands. What was happening to them?

"We didn't know."

"Nobody does, donna. We've tried to tell our friends in the Shadowlands to leave now before it starts out there, but they don't believe us neither. Though they are good folk so they still help what few we can get out."

Thousands. My mind was reeling. So many lives were at stake and I had come here in search of one. But she was my one.

I stood. I needed to leave – had stayed too long as it was. "You have no news about my daughter then?"

"I'll reach out to my network to see if they've got any word of her. What are we looking for?"

"Devyn found me because the records left a trail that he followed, perfect records, but there's always a mistake. Her name is… was Féile. They maybe call her something else now. She was three at midsummer. She was stolen just over a month before Beltaine, so she's been here six or seven months, no more. She has Devyn's black curls, and her skin is a lighter bronze than his was. Look into Marcus Courtenay; I believe he may know where she is. I've got to go. Thank you, Linus." I pressed his hands in mine. "I don't know how to help you, but I will if I can."

I looked around the small, shabby room, farewelling its ghosts as I stepped out into the hall. I saw Devyn turn to me in the shadows by the window, his intense features willing me to listen, to believe.

"You need me to see you back?" Linus asked.

"No," I blinked. "I know the way."

I stepped out into the dirty street and took a breath. The area had been poor when I left, but there was something new in the air, an added hopelessness. Maybe people didn't know what was happening, but there was an undercurrent of worry, of fear. They knew someone was coming for them, and they were helpless to fight it.

I was late for the banquet, the rest of the delegation already leaving when I hurried down the hall to my rooms.

The door opened, and a formally attired Gideon halted in the doorframe. His amber eyes glowed down at me, the question in them easily read. I might not be able to sense his emotions, but when it came to Gideon, reading exasperation and annoyance in all its varied nuances was something of an art form for me at this stage. There was more than a touch of relief there too, and I felt terrible for the worry I had caused him. He walked and talked like the same devil-may-care warrior I had first met but the pinched look in his eyes, the slight tightness of his lips, spoke to his constant worry for Féile. His every waking moment was consumed with finding her.

On impulse, I stretched up on my tiptoes and planted a peck on his mouth.

"Later," I whispered as I pulled away. In both interpretations of the word.

His eyes glinted down at me.

"Do hurry, my little cobblestone," he said. "I shall keep a place for you."

Despite everything, his nonsense made me smile. He had overheard a senator calling his wife a little cabbage in the fashion of the Gauls. It had amused him, and in our role of husband and wife, he had taken to calling me equally outlandish endearments.

I paused as I put a dab of colour on one eyelid, a green that went wonderfully with the brown eyes reflected back to me in the mirror. Our role of husband and wife. We *were* married, so why did it feel like playacting here in Londinium? My shoulders dropped. Because we were happy. Not happy happy, obviously, as Féile's absence consumed our thoughts, but in the sense that with our joined purpose we were united as husband and wife in a way that felt novel and not dissimilar to happiness. It was different from the tentative, cautious emotions when I had been recovering, different from when we had started sleeping together, which had felt more like an exploration. This had purpose, connecting us, making us more sure of each other. I sighed, finishing my makeup and throwing on the dress that Gideon had laid out on the bed; Oban himself would be impressed at his choice.

The great hall of the Governor's Palace was a picture of lavish decadence, the table piled high with delicacies and delights from the four corners of the Empire and beyond. The merchant's daughter in me surveyed the heaving banquet with an assessing eye. There was dragon fruit from the Orient, corn and squash from the Americas, and olives from the Med scattered around the gleaming roasts. The aromas indicated a liberal use of spices from Africa. I had never attended this event before so had no way of measuring the excess against previous years, but given the strained relations on the island right now it felt like a point was being made here.

I wove my way between the tables and glittering company over to Gideon who rose and pulled back a chair for me.

"Why, how very civilised of you," I batted up at him.

"I can be civilized." A brow quirked in his darkly menacing face before he took my hand and laid a lingering kiss on the backs of my fingers, a delicate, barely there kiss. My heart swooped in response.

"You're feeling better?" Bronwyn asked from the other side of Rion's captain of the guard who stayed close to us, on his lord's orders no doubt. I greeted Alec before answering, mindful that my lateness would have been explained somehow to the citizens at the table. Alec nodded gravely even as he excused himself, no doubt to pile another mountain of food onto his plate, a look at Gideon indicating his duty was being handed over until he returned.

"Much," I smiled faintly, the better to give the impression that, while improved, my reason for being absent, whatever it was, had not been agreeable.

"Terrible things, headaches," Bronwyn commented. She looked lovely tonight with her black hair glossily free to flow down her back and a scarlet confection of a dress, which somehow managed to look whimsically Celtic and vaguely martial at the same time. There was something to the cut of it that suggested the wearer was ready to fight should events overtake them. Subliminal messages were everywhere, it seemed.

Rion and Richard sat at the table of honour with Calchas and the new Governor Dolon who looked at least as impressed with his new title as anyone else in the room. A title bought with the blood of a man I had loved. A squeeze of my hand alerted me that my emotions were conveyed all too clearly in my expression.

I lifted an olive off the plate piled with food in front of me, popping it into my mouth after the cursory check I gave all food and drink before I consumed it. A simple technique

Fidelma had taught all of us with magic to ensure we didn't ingest the suppressant while at our host's table.

"Whatever happened to Acteon anyway? Did anyone hear?" I asked softly.

Not softly enough as my question was answered by a familiar voice behind me.

"He sickened with an untreatable illness some years ago," Marcus said, pausing at our table. He nodded in turn to Bronwyn and Gideon in recognition. I gripped the hand that moments earlier had been alerting me not to give my emotions away. I needn't have feared. Gideon was all too good at hiding what he felt behind a languid mask. You would be hard put to tell that Marcus wasn't a complete stranger. Bronwyn, on the other hand, had no such mask. Her face had tightened into an expression of complete and utter contempt.

"May I join you for a moment?" Marcus asked, indicating Alec's empty seat.

Bronwyn sat frozen as the man she blamed for her cousin's death casually took a seat beside her. Marcus's father may have struck the blow, but Matthias Dolon was nobody to her; Marcus was the target of all of her anger, and plenty of mine as well.

"Untreatable illness?" Bronwyn asked silkily, recovering. "And you such a clever healer."

Marcus gave her his easy smile. "If only I could cure all the ills and damage in this world."

"If only." Bronwyn's smile was thin as she directed her gaze to where Governor Dolon sat holding court. "But then there are such rewards to be had from the gap left behind."

"So true," Marcus agreed amiably, his head turning to encompass Gideon and me in his response. There was a flicker as his gaze dropped to our entwined hands. I momentarily forgot how to breathe. Did he know? "Some damage creates gaps that can never be filled. As a healer, there is a line that I cannot cross."

Bronwyn's eyes flicked to mine for an infinitesimal moment, as she also felt she heard or saw something beneath the surface of Marcus's casual chat.

"Is there?" Bronwyn responded icily, after the silence went on slightly too long.

"As a healer, it is my life's work to keep families together, if I can," Marcus answered before changing the subject. "I would like to repay some of the hospitality I so poorly returned when I visited your lands. If you and your friends would like to visit my hospital and see my work, I think there is much that could be gained by helping each other."

Bronwyn's eyes narrowed at him.

"That sounds interesting," she said cautiously.

"I trust it will be very educational," he said, rising, as Alec now hovered behind him. "I will send my man in the morning."

My chest felt tight as he walked away after flashing us his charismatic grin – a movement of teeth and lips that hid the traitorous, deceptive, shrivelled-up soul beneath. There was a roaring in my ears and I closed my eyes to shut out the sensory overload and focus on the chaos inside me.

I hated him. He had been my friend, and now I hated him with every particle of my being. Marcus had lied and deceived and had me lure Devyn to his death, using bait he would have known I would be unable to resist: the promise of a future… a future in which I married the man I loved, the father of the child that grew within me. Marcus had known I was pregnant, and now they had taken my child from me. A flash of memory slivered its way through the maelstrom of bitterness and grief that consumed me. During our escape, I had told Gideon about the baby in an attempt to persuade him to let me have the future I had thought awaited us on the other side of that moonlit ride. I had been filled with hope and dreams for a future that was at my fingertips. But I had caught an expression on Marcus's face that had seemed so out of place in that moment. He had looked sick... because he had felt guilt at what he was doing?

"He wants to help," I whispered.

"What?" Bronwyn asked, unable to hear the words that I had uttered half to myself.

"We should go," I said brightly. "I'm sure a visit to an imperial hospital will be fascinating."

"No," said Bronwyn and Alec as one, even as Gideon said, "Yes."

"He has her," Gideon said.

"Could you smell her?" Bronwyn whispered, vaguely horrified.

His lip curled up slightly as he shook his head. "It's not like that. But he has been with her. Recently."

Had Gideon been so focused on sensing Féile that he had failed to see what I had? Had I imagined it? That flicker that went to our hands? Marcus had given no indication that he knew me, acknowledging Gideon but speaking only to Bronwyn, and so why the interest in our relationship?

"We are already behind the walls. What does it matter whether we are in the palace, or touring a public facility in another part of the city?" I asked lightly.

Bronwyn frowned and then nodded. "She's right, and he promised it would be educational. Let's see what the city boy thinks he can teach us."

The next morning, we were met in the great marble lobby of the palace by Praetorian Kasen, who I had last seen lowering the watergate at the White Tower. He had been Senator Dolon's man then; it seemed odd that Marcus would send him to fetch us if I was right about his intentions. Kasen introduced himself, showing no sign that he might be more familiar with me than the face I presented to the world.

A town car whizzed us across the city to Bart's hospital. A military vehicle trailed us – for our own security, Kasen assured us; there had been some trouble in the city the night before, and it didn't hurt to be extra careful with the visiting delegates, especially with one of Bronwyn's status amongst us. Rion had wanted to come, but we had persuaded him that Bronwyn and a couple of companions attracted significantly less attention than the King of Mercia would.

The car brought us directly to the door, no sign this time of the less fortunate people of the city – those with symptoms of the sickness unable to afford treatment but lingering here in the hope that help would be offered. Instead, it was almost eerily silent as we stepped out of the vehicle, the populace giving the building a wide berth.

Marcus stood waiting in the entrance, two sentinels positioned either side of him.

"You came," he said with some relief to the four of us, as Rion had insisted Alec accompany us. "I wasn't sure."

He exchanged glances with Kasen who indicated to the red-cloaked sentinels that they might step back a few paces and allow us some space.

"Yes," Bronwyn said acerbically. "I brought some of my

people. I hope you don't mind. It's not seemly for one of my station to travel alone."

Marcus looked toward Gideon and me for the first time. His eyes were lidded and slightly averted. He nodded courteously at Alec, before his eyes flicked back again.

"I hoped you would bring—" He pulled up short, swallowing with effort. "Please, this way."

"As you can see, we are equipped with all that modern medicine offers," he said in a more confident tone, striding down the shining marble and glass corridor. He pointed out different aspects of the facilities as he gave us a grand tour. There were remarkably few occupied beds.

"A hospital with no sick people," Bronwyn eventually remarked. "How clever."

"We are fortunate that so many of the world's more serious diseases are practically extinct within the Empire," Marcus said in a formal manner.

"Not all illnesses," Bronwyn cut in shortly.

Marcus bowed his head, and when he looked up again, his eyes were hollow. "No. Unfortunately not. As you are aware, we gained a treatment which manages the Maledictio... at a high cost. We developed it and have made it spread as far as possible. Those who can afford it live comfortably and have no need of a hospital. Those who cannot have no reason to come here."

"Where do they go?" I asked. Where were they, the masses he had traded Devyn's life to save? Where were the ill Linus had told me were disappearing?

Marcus's eyes slipped to the sentinels who waited at a discreet distance behind us.

"I must show you our genetics labs," he said in place of an answer. "I think you'll find it most illuminating."

We followed him down more sterile, empty halls until we came to a busier section of the hospital. Here, white-robed men and women bustled busily about. Marcus handed us white lab coats and masks which were needed to cover our noses and mouths.

"It is important to minimise the possibility of contamination," he explained. The sentinels were not provided with any.

"We'll be just in there; you'll be able to see us the whole time," he told them, pointing out a room which was visible through the floor-to-ceiling glass. It was a sterile white room with glass fridges full of vials of blood and a bench on which sat microscopes.

Marcus stood in front of a panel which used some biometric measure to identify him and then the door opened. Kasen positioned himself outside the door as we entered behind Marcus. Gideon gestured to Alec to stay outside too, to guard our exit from outside.

"The lab is where we test for the genetic markers which... uh, may indicate a patient's likelihood to contract the illness which has plagued the Empire over the last few decades," he explained. His tone was much less confident than it had been now that his audience had been reduced. He was hesitant almost.

"There are particular markers found in the native genetic lines that increase the chances of being a carrier of the illness." He swallowed. "Many of these indicators have been bred out of the gene pools across the Empire. In citizens here, we've found that there are a lot more of these markers, perhaps due to the greater dominance of the Britons and the high incidence of intermarriage prior to the introduction of the Code."

"You believe the illness is caused by being Briton?"

Bronwyn challenged. "That's ridiculous. Our blood is no less mixed with other European and African gene pools than yours."

"This is true," Marcus agreed, pulling out a sample from the countless vials of blood on the countertop. "The difference is that on your side of the border there are more of the genetic counters that indicate latent or present magic."

"This sample belongs to someone identified as a latent with late-stage Maledictio." He indicated that we should look through the darkfield microscope to see for ourselves. The blood on the platform of the microscope looked like any other blood – a red splotch on a glass plate. But through the magnification and illumination of the device, it was different to what I had seen blood in biology class before. The balls of red blood cells held a dark shadow, which must be the illness. But that was not what caught my eye, dancing through this sample was a vague shimmer.

"You're investigating magic in the blood?" I asked.

"Yes, they… we have made great strides in locating the presence of magic in sections of the population. The rise of the illness surfaced a great many who we would not otherwise have been aware of. It is impossible to test everyone, but as people fell ill, the research was able to go faster and we could identify them sooner," he said, stumbling over the words.

It was true then, what Devyn had suspected. The Empire had used the Mallacht – or Maledictio as they called it – to identify and target those with the illness, but why then had Londinium gone to such lengths to get a treatment? A treatment that they then only made available to the wealthy elite… or was the answer that simple? One world for the poor, another for the rich.

He swapped out the sample for another.

"This is mine," he said and, looking through, I found myself in a different universe to the first sample. Where there had been a shimmer across the first, this one had a trail of incandescent stars dancing through it. It sang to me, took my breath away; it was entrancing.

"And this one..." He put a third on the platform. I lowered my eye to the scope, but before I had even focussed I could see the glow. It was utterly breathtaking. The joy of the bright stars glittering in the blood was like looking at the sky on the clearest new-moon winter's night. The previous sample was more like a summer's night at a full moon: stars were visible, but the full beauty of the celestial heavens was not on display. This time, where there had been a hundred stars before, now there were thousands. "Her blood is beyond compare."

Gideon snarled behind me, and I stepped in front of him as he made to attack.

Marcus stood frozen, like prey before the predator.

"Don't." He looked casually out at the watching sentinels. "There are more outside in the corridor."

"You—" I stopped short, wary of the city's invidious big brother, I knew the charms we wore weren't infallible.

"There are no microphones in here," Marcus said quickly. "And the masks make it impossible for the cameras too."

"Where is she?" I breathed. That blood, that blood belonged to my daughter.

"She's safe."

"*Where is she*?" Gideon gritted from behind me.

"I can get her to you," Marcus said quickly. "I have a plan, but I need your help."

"Ha!" Bronwyn scoffed, her pitch high.

Marcus and his bargains, always trying to trade lives, like it was some big chess game.

"I will get her out. We'll get her outside the walls just before the delegation exits. She'll be waiting for you."

"That's impossible. Nobody gets out without papers," Bronwyn said, continuing to speak for the group, fully filled in on the information Linus had shared with me.

"She will if she's with the right escort."

"You?" Bronwyn's eyes narrowed.

"No. I go nowhere without guards." His eyes shifted to the sentinels on the other side of the glass. "But a praetorian guard won't be stopped."

"The one who brought us here? How can you trust him?"

"His wife and children, they got ill. He approached my father, thinking he would make an exception, that he would help them," his eyes lowered. "He was wrong."

"Did they die?"

"I don't know. I think so. Kasen never speaks of them," Marcus sighed. "But he will help. He is fond of her."

He really was going to do this.

"What do you want?" Bronwyn gritted out.

"Take a seat. I need to take your bloods," he said, picking up a tourniquet. None of us moved. "I told them I could persuade you to let me take samples. We can only continue to speak if you are seen to comply."

"Mine is all you get," Gideon said tightly, pulling off the lab coat and outer jacket to reveal the fine leather armour he wore underneath. Baring his forearm, the healthy veins pulsed with life as they ran under the oathbinding tattoo he wore there.

"I'll need Bronwyn's as well," he insisted. "I have a vial prepared to pass off as Cassandra's."

And there it was. Utterly in the open. He knew who I was. Had taken precautions to ensure my blood, if taken, wouldn't give me away.

"How?" Bronwyn asked.

He didn't pretend to misunderstand. "I wasn't actually sure until now."

He tied off the tourniquet around Gideon's arm. "I know that Gideon is Rion's man, and if Cassandra was here she would be closely guarded. Last night I thought maybe I was wrong, that the woman he shadows truly was just his wife, but I had to take a chance."

So that must be why our joined hands had thrown him.

"At the very least I knew you could both be trusted to get a message to her," he continued as he went about his work. "Féile is well. She is happy, but she wants to go home, and I want to help you take her there."

"Your deal?" I prompted.

"I need you to treat the ley lines. We know that's what you've been doing in the north. The Empire has spent centuries stamping out all trace of magic, but the ley lines left untended have become corrupted, and the land is failing. Calchas has been tending the line here under the Strand. He's using the latents," Marcus explained.

"Using the latents how?"

"I don't know exactly. I've never been there. They say it's not safe. They give me pills that cut me off from my magic to shield me. I'm not even permitted to help people that way anymore. Féile is also given the suppressant." His hands clenched at his sides. "When they figured out the technique to identify magic in the blood, they were excited, but research on how to treat the illness stopped. He's using latents to heal the ley line, I think."

Thousands of disappeared latents, Linus had said. That's where they were going. He must be throwing untrained latents at the problem. The ley line had to be burning them up; it would be like throwing cups of water at a firestorm. Desperate for magic, it would burn through the little they had in moments. I remembered Elsa's lifeless body after the incident at Keswick.

"Thousands," I said hollowly.

"What?" Marcus asked. "Thousands of what?"

"You think that's what happening to them?" Gideon asked as Marcus stuck the syringe in, the pinch earning him a glare from the warrior.

"There are thousands of ill disappearing across the city; it's been going on for years," I caught Marcus up tartly. "All of them, I'm sure, have a little vial all neatly labelled somewhere here in your labs."

I frowned. Where there were blood tests there would be records. Why had Linus's hackers not been able to find them?

Marcus dabbed at the prick of blood that surfaced as he withdrew the needle. Taking Gideon's other hand, he bent it to press a small ball of cotton wool over the puncture wound, earning himself an offended glare from the hardened, muscular specimen on the chair in front of him.

"So many." Marcus looked at me with horror in his eyes. "You have to stop this."

"How am I supposed to stop this?" What could one person possibly do against Calchas and his legions?

"You're strong now. I've heard that you healed the line that runs through the borderlands."

"I did," I confirmed absently as I evaluated what of Avalon's power remained in my veins, calculating the level of corruption I had sensed in Glastonbury and how much the May line had needed. Was there enough left? The line under Londinium would be in a far worse state than the Keswick line which at least had been tended by Fidelma and the druids all these years.

"No." Gideon's eyes glowed above his mask. "We are here for Féile. If we can't take her with us, we will need everything you have to get back in."

"Gideon," Bronwyn censured, casting a slit-eyed burn at Marcus who had begun his task of eliciting her blood. She was right. We were foolish to speak freely in front of Marcus. We had trusted him before and look where that had got us.

Marcus cast a look at the waiting sentinels.

"Cassandra, I need you to take a seat. They must see me take your blood."

I sat uneasily in the chair Bronwyn had just vacated. Gideon subtly manoeuvred himself so he obstructed the view of our audience.

"You take one drop of her blood, and I will end you here," he threatened. Having seen Féile's blood under the microscope, my blood would leave no one in any doubt of my identity as Lady of the Lake

"I'm not. We just need it to look as if I'm taking her blood, the same as you and Bronwyn," Marcus gritted, showing us the vial he had prepared in his lab pocket.

He took my arm and went through the motions of tying a tourniquet on, turning over my wrist to reveal the same dara-knot tattoo that Gideon wore. He lifted the syringe off the counter, but instead of putting it in my skin, he leaned in and allowed his lab coat to obscure his actions and instead held my hand.

"Please," he begged. "You must trust me. I promise I will get Féile to you."

"How can we trust you now?" My chin crumpled as I

looked into the eyes of the man I had called my friend. "We trusted you before."

His eyes dropped and his shoulders hunched over. "I'm sorry."

"What is he apologising for, do you suppose?" Bronwyn directed her question at Gideon, her tone one of utter contempt. "Lying to us over and over? Or killing Devyn?"

Marcus flinched at Devyn's name.

"I didn't know they planned to kill him," Marcus's eyes locked with mine. "My father... You know why I did it. Citizens were dying. I know you don't trust me, but you know me, you must believe I am trying to help people."

I looked at him clear-eyed. I did believe him. He had dedicated his life to trying to make other people's lives better. I had come here for one reason only, to get my daughter back, and I had brought an army to do so. But people here were dying. I looked at Gideon. I could help; I could do both things.

I stood restlessly, meeting Gideon's gaze once more. I was going to do this. A familiar look of exasperation crossed what little of his face I could see above the surgical mask.

"When can you get me in?"

"Tomorrow night," he said.

I frowned. The autumn equinox was only days away, the closer we were to Mabon the more effective it would be. "The last night would be better."

"The night of the masquerade ball? Too risky. Your absence would be too noticeable," Marcus dismissed.

"I'll try," I said. "There are no guarantees. I may not be able to fix it, but I will do what I can. Whatever the outcome, you bring me my daughter."

"Agreed," Marcus said quickly.

"I am not the girl you left behind. I am trusting you not to betray me again. I am trusting you to give me back the most precious thing I have. Do not fail me." I met his gaze directly. There was no explicit threat, but if he let me down again, I would end him.

"I will make it right." He extended his arm and took mine in the Briton clasp, hands gripping high on the forearm, inner wrists aligned. Blood to blood.

A tingle ran through me as he gave his vow unprompted.

"I swear."

Chapter Twenty-Two

There were several events the next evening, and we each made a brief appearance at one before excusing our early exit with vague talk of interest in other events. I chose the recital I had attended four years ago, an impulse which I knew wasn't entirely unconscious that this was the one Camilla and Graham Shelton worked hardest to attend.

When I got there, I spotted them straight away. It was strange. While I had never been close to Camilla, I had adored the man I'd known as my father. They had, as far as I knew, abandoned me as soon as my feet touched the sands of the arena. Had they felt any sadness, any heartbreak as I had faced the justice of the city, or had they been indifferent? Their task had been to raise me, to prepare me to marry Marcus Courtenay, to obey the Code – which they had done.

Camilla held court, as aloof as ever, while Graham worked, busily networking, which I now appreciated was why they preferred the recital. Less noisy, less movement than other events where their targets were more difficult to engage in discussion on whatever business they were about. Their social status appeared to have remained intact, despite my disgrace, if appearances at the recital were anything to go by.

Bronwyn caught my eye from across the room, and I slipped away, my breath quickening as I made my way down to the transport that would whisk us across to the livelier entertainments to be found at the forum, and Fidelma's tent, where we had agreed to meet Kasen. Was I strong enough to do this? Was I expending my energy for the greater good at Féile's expense? Could Marcus be trusted to deliver? Was I risking my life and that of Fidelma and Marina on a fool's errand?

I exited the basilica and took a porticoed corridor through the forum. What choice did we have? Ultimately even Gideon and Rion had been persuaded that this bargain was our best and only chance of rescuing Féile. Once outside the walls, our only recourse was a military assault on Londinium. Many Britons, including his father, cared only about finally leading the Britannic provinces in the war that had been brewing since Anglesey. For Gideon, only one outcome mattered. And the chances of recovering our daughter diminished the moment we were on the other side of those walls.

Kasen arrived in Fidelma's tarot-reading tent bearing gifts – or rather, outfits to enable us to travel to our destination.

"Mary le Strand is guarded." This was the entrance to the ley line, a ground-level church from earlier times that still stood towards Charring Cross. He handed a sentinel's uniform to Gideon and citizen clothing that had seen better days, to the rest of us. "You need to appear to be latents, there to tend the line. Just put this stuff on and keep your heads down."

"That will get us in, but how do we get out?" I asked. "Won't being alive attract notice?"

"Not all latents die on their first visit. Only the strongest are taken to the circle itself," Kasen clarified grimly, before turning to eye Gideon. "Don't suppose you could be persuaded to sit this one out? You're a little oversized for a city dweller; you'll draw attention."

Gideon snatched the uniform out of his hand.

"I won't," he said shortly.

We made our way separately across the city – Fidelma and Marina walking with me while Gideon strode ahead with Kasen – only regrouping as we neared the end of the Strand, at which point Kasen led the way with Gideon bringing up the rear.

The Christian church of St Mary le Strand stood on an island of its own in the middle of the stream of traffic at river level. The architecture of the building was not entirely a fit with others at this level. It had been built sometime after the Treaty, an unusual enough fact as Christianity had been popular only briefly and religious building of any persuasion had dropped off altogether in the technological age and a spire at this level was highly inconvenient to the highwalks above. Kasen led us through an iron gate and up the steps of the columned entrance. He halted in front of a great wooden door and knocked.

The door opened and he saluted the young sentinel standing within.

"Tonight's lot," he stated, tilting his head in our direction.

The guard seemed happy enough, and we trailed past, Gideon not even meriting the salute that Praetorian Kasen had received. In fact, when I thought about it, Gideon and Kasen had attracted little notice as they walked ahead of us which, given the atmosphere in the city and the customary levels of respect that passing praetorian guards received as they patrolled, was in itself noteworthy.

Kasen led us behind the altar and unlocked a metal door in the floor. I raised an eyebrow at Gideon.

"You've got very good at that," I commented. He had totally mastered the Griffin ability to blend into the background, the one that had so confounded me when I first met Devyn.

"Practice makes perfect." He smirked.

"Nice," I approved, before my stomach lurched at the impact of the oily wave that rolled over me as soon as the door opened.

Gideon steadied me as I swayed on my feet. Fidelma and Marina both cringed a little at the foetid, discordant hum that crept up from the opening.

Kasen waved us down the steps into a brightly lit cellar which seemed to be coated in a dull grey metal, and through another door at the back. I had to force myself to put one foot in front of the other. No wonder people were ill; the corruption of the line was thick in the atmosphere as we descended down the grey circular stairs that plunged deep into the bowels of Londinium. Moisture ran down the walls, giving them a darkly glistening aspect. The electric lights gave way to fiery torches as we went lower and lower, until we must have been below the river itself. The cloying stench in the back of my throat made me gag as I pushed on, closer to this thing that clawed at me.

It was a desperate need, a dark, despairing, ugly thing. This was what had been leeching off me when I had been unprotected by the suppressant pills, it wasn't use of magic that had made me exhausted and dizzy but this. The medication had created not only a barrier between me and my magic, but also a shield. I wanted a shield of lead now to wrap my body in as it pulled and tore at the edges of my magic, desperate and dying.

We came at last to a cavernous room with a standing circle in place, niches in the rocks with ancient offerings still strewn beneath them and the faint traces of a Celtic symbol on the floor. I staggered back against Gideon as the onslaught battered against me. I laid a palm on the wet granite surface of the stone nearest to me, attempting to soothe the clamouring maw of need that came at me. It receded a little.

"I will close the door while you interact with the line. When the latents are brought here, there is a spike above ground in the deaths of those afflicted with the Maledictio. I don't know if it helps, but..." Kasen trailed off, exiting the room. "Knock when you're done."

Fidelma looked haggard, every bit of the toll that tending the line had had on her over the last twenty years etched on her face. Marina held her hand, even as she lifted her chin to face the battle ahead.

Gideon watched me intently as I sat down on the ground and closed my eyes to prepare to descend.

"I'll be okay," I said to him... or to myself – I wasn't sure or entirely convinced. I reached out and took Marina's hand, which clutched at mine, while on my left Fidelma held a steady hand out for me to take.

"I feared we would be too late," she said, almost to herself.

"Maybe we are," I replied, as I compared this damaged and corrupted thing that flowed under the city to the slightly fractured harmony of the Belinus line or even the pain-twisted May line as it had been before Avebury. They had been damaged but this, this thing was unrecognisably mangled. No wonder lines across Europe had died. Better death than this, this thing that sucked at us.

I braced my body and then let my spirit free, let myself float down or let the ley line float up to me. The slimy, foetid, corrupt energy swirled around me, over me, testing me, judging me. There was no song, no flow, only a deep pool into which I sank.

I recoiled from the line that tangled and caught at the souls of those who died above it. As we descended, the horror of what had been done here swirled around us. The mawing pull wasn't from the line but from the hundreds upon hundreds of darkly brittle souls trapped here at this node. Trapped, sacrificed, they were the souls of the latents who had been fed to the ley line. For that was the only way to describe what had happened to them. The souls felt burnt from the inside out, empty, hollow things detached from the lives they had led, from the people they had been. Their energy, their magic, had been given as sustenance to the deeply corrupted, coiling ley line that pulled at us as if we too were to be consumed.

Marina's white light was the one pure thing in this sludge; Fidelma's battered golden light was wavering, so many years of holding this line where it intersected at Glastonbury had made her energy brittle as it damaged her defences.

I could help it, and so I sang to it as I had sung at Keswick, giving the malevolent notes a new essence, a cleansing tone. I sent wave after wave into the abyss, which took me further and further in as I tried to untwist the line.

It pulled me further and further adrift from the shore of my life. So quickly... Devastatingly malevolent, overwhelmingly swift currents... The mists engulfed me, obscuring the line that connected me to who I was, to who I am, to who I wanted to be.

Everything was corrupted, nothing was clean here. The taint spread its darkness over my life.

The lies and deceit clawed at me, the swirling contempt and fear, whispering that the world was there for me to use, that I should take what I could get, that the other was to be distrusted, that my beliefs, my needs, my wants were all there were.

My mother had betrayed me. She had disregarded my safety and for what? I had been left alone, undefended. Taken in by others who wanted me for their own purposes.

My parents had raised me, had tucked me in and fed me, and told me they would be there for me. Then they had quickly left me when my beliefs and needs had diverted from their own.

My protector had come for me, had risked everything for me. He had loved me, I was sure of it. But had he really? He had wanted me to go to his home, to be with his people, to save his people, to restore his honour, to be the proof of his worth. But he had rejected me again and again. How had I not seen the truth? He had never wanted me, had never loved me. He had left me and allowed himself to be taken, to die, his mission accomplished. He had left me.

My friend had deceived me, had accused me of not being more, of being selfish and of only seeing the world for what it could do for me. Of letting my own needs and desires lead me. Of failing the gifts with which I had been bestowed, by not putting them into the service of others, that I was not worthy of them. That I did not deserve them. I did not deserve anything. And then he had deceived me. Abandoned me.

My brother had lived the life his birthright had promised him; he was connected to the life and land of our ancestors in a way I could never be. In a way of which I was not worthy. He was loved, by the friends who would do anything for him, by the people who he served and who loved him in return. He had everything, was everything, that I had never had, could never be. When I had returned to him broken, he had failed me. I was only useful to him as a piece on his chessboard. He used me.

The waves of self-loathing and disconnection swept over me, pulling me down deeper and deeper. My worst fears, my deepest, darkest thoughts wound their claws into me, digging in, drawing blood, taking hold.

I had to fight it off, to push it back even as I allowed the corruption in the line to go through me, a cycle of negativity swirling inside my mind, my heart, my soul. I pushed out towards the line all the light, the clarity, the positivity, the love, the synergy of a better world, a kinder world.

And there, in the darkness, was the flicker of Marina's light. A light that still shone.

Devyn had risked his life for Marina. He hadn't done it for duty, for his oath. He had helped her because he could. He had loved me. I knew it. He hadn't wanted to leave me and he had died protecting me. He had loved me.

The poverty and pain of the city had seeped deep into the line. Despair and hopelessness were the core of the corruption, the lies and manipulations of the powerful were both the symptoms and the cause.

The burned-out, dark flickers were trapped in the deep – tied here, but not here. The connection that held them was not to the circle here and I could not reach it. So much pain. So much loss.

My daughter's soft baby smell, her sweet touch... I had been a terrible mother. I had never had a mother, so what chance had I had? She had turned to another for love, for care.

I felt the bitter twist of seeing her in Gideon's arms, snuggling in for comfort, never looking to me. I didn't deserve her love. I hadn't been there for her. I had failed her.

Marina's light pulsed in the grime. It was white, bright in the darkness. The world was made up of light, and sun, and clean, clear water, cleansing, purifying. I had to stay in the light where the energy felt less fractured, less brittle. I focussed on the simplicity of that.

Light.

White.

Hope.

Joy.

Clarity.

Fading in the shadows.

The thread I held felt gossamer-thin, it wasn't enough but maybe it didn't matter. Maybe none of it mattered. I floated suspended in darkness. The ley needed me and it wanted me to stay. None of it mattered.

I felt the energies of the ley flow, cycle through me and around me.

There was a tug on the thread. A touch. A call. It nagged at me.

It was pain, and I didn't care for that. I didn't care for anything. All of the fractured shards had floated away. I was free.

Gideon's touch seared through. He didn't care for me. I used him, I needed him. Féile needed him.

My name twined around the rope that secured me to shore. I didn't need it. Didn't need him. He didn't need anyone. Didn't care for anyone.

Not true. Féile. He cared for Féile. I cared for Féile.

I should follow the thread.

I didn't want to.

I could just let go and float free.

But he had been there for me time after time. I didn't deserve it.

And yet he had done it anyway.

I could sense my body, my being... worthless, and I sank in the familiar dark. It had always been there pulling me down. I should just let it.

And then he called me again.

I owed him, didn't I? He had earned my response. But the effort was too much.

It didn't matter, nothing mattered.

The flow was life and life was eternal, endless. This was why I felt so little when I returned. It wasn't that the energy didn't care, it was just beyond such things. Bigger than such things.

Féile sitting on my lap. After everything I had done, Féile coming to me and curling her warm body into mine.

She needed me.

Warmth inside. A spark, a connection.

Gideon calling me.

Pleading. Why?

I felt no pain, no weakness here. The corruption and despair were truth.

The dark shadows, I couldn't help them.

My skin, my arm, a warm body embracing mine.

Warm lips on my cold ones.

My name.

They didn't belong here.

I didn't belong here.

I frowned. I held on to the tether.

The darkness wasn't all there was.

It was substantial. It was real.

I hadn't set them free.

All that power and I couldn't set them free. I was needed back there.

The ley line had calmed, its fraught greed had lessened, the song was clearer, but the poor souls were caught fast.

I couldn't help them.

"Come back."

"Come back."

"Please, don't leave us."

"Come back."

"Don't leave me."

"Don't leave me."

"Don't leave me."

Whispered urgent words were pulling me back, luring me up. I couldn't feel anything, didn't need anything, but I followed that voice. Felt the warmth of that touch. A body curled around mine. Hands on my face.

It didn't matter. None of it mattered.

I existed. The thread was there to help me find my way home. I loved. I needed those on the other side.

I was loved. I was needed.

That was the truth. That was my truth.

I had to hold on. The thread flowed on in the darkness.

I had given all that Avalon had shared with me back into the line. I could do no more. The shadows railed against their fate. I couldn't reach them.

The rest was me. I was giving myself up to it.

If I did that they would be lost.

I would be lost.

I held the line.

For them.

People gave to each other all the time.

Oban had given up the future for which he had risked everything so that his sister could have a new life.

Gideon had given up his independence from others, first for me and then for my daughter.

Rion had given everything to make a better future for his people. When his family had come back to him, he hadn't disregarded my feelings in insisting I marry Marcus. He had disregarded his own.

And Devyn. He had loved me; I had come before everything for him. He had given his life for me. And left me with a precious gift.

Féile, my darling brave, beloved daughter. Despite years of neglect, she had let me back in.

I opened my eyes.

Gideon.

His face swam into focus. Desperation in his eyes... loss... pain.

I put my hand up to touch the man in front of me.

He hurt.

I hurt. The darkness called me back.

No.

I snapped out of it.

And drew breath.

I pulled out of the arms that held me, too in my space, too needy. I needed to breathe.

The room was still as I sat there, looking at the three pairs of eyes that watched me.

Marina's eyes filled with the horror at the trapped souls we had left behind.

Fidelma was busy assessing what had been achieved.

Gideon watchful, evaluating. Why was he evaluating? What did he see?

"It wasn't enough." Fidelma's voice was disappointed.

Our one chance.

We had failed.

Chapter Twenty-Three

A rms wrapped around me, holding me, keeping the pain and sorrow that filled me from breaking me apart. Thousands of souls left behind…

Gideon's strength and determination poured into me. Around me.

He so often appeared to be utterly uncaring about everything around him, disengaged from the outcome of any given situation, but at his core, at the truth of him, he was determined. Focussed. Caring.

I let it pour over me, through me, I let it heat the cold recesses of my tattered soul. Was this what love felt like?

Remote. I was too remote. I could recognise it now. Beyond pain, beyond fear, I could feel him. I would hold on to him. He would bring me back.

It was enough for now. We had things to do. I squirmed out of his touch. He released me, and turned, lying flat on his back.

"Good evening."

"Evening?" I had lost a day then.

His eyes slanted to mine, assessing.

"Yes, evening," he said. "The masquerade ball starts in an hour."

The ball, the last-night ball. I had lost a day and a half. I sat up. We needed to get ready. My body was unable to respond to my demand so quickly and I swayed. I stopped and gave myself a moment. The room was softly lit with lanterns and candles.

"There was a major power outage. Most of the city is restored now, save here and I believe the Strand area."

I nodded, familiar with the outages that were a regular occurrence during the Treaty Renewal.

"Have you spoken to Marcus? Is it all arranged?"

His jaw hardened. "We haven't spoken to him."

"What do you mean? Why not?" I felt panicked; we were out of time. We needed Marcus to uphold his end of the bargain and it was the last night. We would have to leave tomorrow. And we possibly wouldn't be back until spring, until our army was ready, and both Londinium's great walls and an army stood between my daughter and me.

"Nobody has seen him since the other night."

"You can't track him?"

"Maybe. I couldn't look for him because you needed me."

"I didn't need you."

His face tightened.

"Really?" he asked. "Are you sure about that? How do you feel, Cat?"

I searched inside myself. I felt drained, exhausted. In all honesty, I wasn't sure that I could stand. But I did feel. I was worried for Féile. I was angry at him for putting me first.

He had put me first. That's why I could feel at all. The line had exhausted me but hadn't burned me out. I still needed him – not as much as before, but Nimue had said that I would need him as much as I should, and so I did. Not fatally so as before. But I needed him. His presence strengthened me; that was our reality, our truth.

"Thank you."

His eyes softened, and an almost smile put some fullness back in his thinned lips.

"You came back," he said. The simple worlds held a depth that I had never known from him.

I felt raw. Flashes of the fractured corruption that had washed through me hit me. I pushed them away.

"It wasn't enough." I hadn't been able to free those souls. Time was running out. I wasn't strong enough.

We needed to find Féile. There was so little time.

"You did all you could."

But not enough. I pulled away to get ready for the night ahead.

I stared at the unfamiliar features of the Mercian stranger in the mirror, clothed in shimmering silks that left my shoulders and arms bare. My skin felt like porcelain once the heat of his touch wore off. Delicate and cold, fragile, like I would shatter if touched.

That was the lie.

I almost flinched at his touch as he placed a torc around my neck. He ran steel-calloused hands across my shoulders and down my arms, threading his fingers through mine, and the pressure eased. I gripped tightly and then relaxed.

I threw him a tight smile.

"I'm not fully myself yet. Stay close," I said, and then I took a mental step towards where I wanted to be. "I need you. You are all that connects me to the world right now."

His eyes widened but otherwise he kept his expression carefully blank.

"I feel like a balloon on a string." Another deep mental breath. "Don't let go."

His eyes locked with mine, unblinking. He lifted our entwined hands and pressed his lips to the back of mine. They were gentle and warm.

Was this his truth, and not the indifferent facade he so often presented? Rion was right; Gideon's actions said more than his words. He had selflessly been what I needed time after time.

"Do you mind?" I asked, looking down at the cosmetics spread on the dressing table in front of me, the elegant glass bottles and myriad creams. I plucked at a nonexistent mark on the silks of my dress, weaving the cloth between my fingers. I had done what I could to set him free, to ask Avalon to make me independent of him. The corruption of the line had been more than I could handle alone – he knew that. Was he angry to learn I still depended on him to restore my strength?

He shook his head, not following my question.

"I tried to set you free," I reminded him, guilt knotting me. He came to my side. His fingers cupped my chin, lifting it so I had to meet his eyes.

"I never asked you to do so," he said in a hard voice. His lips descended, pressing warmly against mine. "Now, let's go and hunt Marcus."

I stepped forward into Marcus's waiting arms slowly, not looking around for Gideon or Rion. Where had he been all evening before he had invited me to dance? The night was nearly at an end; we had only hours until our departure in the morning. He had sworn he would make it right, that he would deliver Féile to us, but there had been no sign of him since I had tended the line. Rion and Bronwyn had tried everything to locate him. Had he deceived us into getting what he wanted? Had he never had any intention of giving my daughter back to me?

We swirled into the crowd, my feet light as I danced in his familiar arms. It was funny, despite the anger unfurling within me I could do this, I could act like I was nothing more than a visitor to the city, flattered to be having a twirl round the dancefloor with the charming, handsome Marcus Courtenay.

"Have you enjoyed your visit to the city?" he asked politely, his face obscured by his mask.

"Yes," I kept my answer brief.

"I trust it has been successful," he added.

Keep moving, keep dancing. Had the others realised yet who I danced with? Gideon was over by the exit to the balcony, his height making it easy for me to locate him. He was at Rion's side in a group of overdressed babbling elite men and women, fussing and flirting as they had all week.

"As much as it could be," I assured him. The line was not fully healed as it had been at Keswick or Avebury, but it would hold for a time. At least for the months it would take our army to gather to its maximum strength, for now that I had spent all the Avalon power we would have no choice but to wait for the Albans to join us. "We have kept our side of the agreement. I trust you still intend to uphold yours."

"I wanted…" He paused, lifting his head to look around us, twirling me deeper onto the dancefloor.

His head bent as he swung me around. "I'm sorry, Cassandra."

My heart ceased beating in my chest. I stiffened, but his hands held me firm.

"Keep dancing." He smiled down at me with that brilliant white smile that said he hadn't a worry in the world.

My heart stuttered back to life. Gideon's head was up; he was scanning the room for me. He could sense that I felt in danger. I saw that odd flicker that I had seen in the borderlands, the aura of the Griffin.

"It's too late for you," he said. His eyes lifted in the direction of the exits where I could see several oh-so-casual guests were rather well-built and watchful for elite party guests.

"Then why let me know the trap is closing?" I asked, my anger at his second betrayal temporarily restrained as I assessed our options.

"It's not closed yet. There's still a chance, if some of your friends leave now, that the council will let them go without a fuss."

I smiled up at him. The smile did not reach my eyes as I looked fully into the face of my former friend.

"Who?" I asked casually.

"Marina." He knew I cared for the girl I had helped escape the city over four years ago; Fidelma he also knew but to him she would be unrecognisable in her current form. "Bronwyn."

Ah. So that was why he was risking his neck.

"Will that unburden you of your guilt when they execute the rest of us?" I asked. "That is how you live with yourself, isn't it, bargaining this life for that many lives?"

He swallowed, the inference not lost on him.

"I didn't know they would kill him," he said blankly,

348

repeating the weak defence I had let him have that night in the lab.

"Well, they did," I said curtly. Unforgivingly. "My brother, will they let him go?"

"No. He's too much of a threat."

"Right," I said bleakly. "Gideon?"

He loosed a black laugh. "If you were on the opposite side to Gideon, would you let him live to fight you on another day when you had your chance to take him out?"

Gideon had spotted us and knew the source of my growing dread. I shook my head slightly: *don't interfere, please don't interfere.* If he drew attention to my dancing with Marcus, whatever slim chance I had of getting some of my friends through the closing trap was over.

I saw him detach himself from the group he was with, leaning down to speak to Marina, her exquisite mask turning my way before she edged toward the door.

"Did you ever plan to let me have Féile back?" I asked bitterly, saving my darkest anger for myself, for being taken in a second time.

His jaw tightened, and he looked over my shoulder as he continued to twirl me around the dancefloor. I caught sight of Governor Dolon in conversation at the edge of the room, his eyes catching mine, a thin smirk lifting his lower face beneath the mask. He knew.

"They know it's me. How?" I asked lightly.

"They've known it was you from the start. The cameras can see right through the illusion. It might look like I'm dancing with a Briton to the rest of the room, but the tech sees through the glamour. It sees you," he explained.

They had known the whole time.

"Why let the charade continue?" I asked.

349

"You know Calchas likes to play with his toys," he said hollowly. "And they wanted you to feel safe so I could persuade you to fix the ley line…"

"But, in the lab, you didn't seem sure I really was me." He had been so convincing.

"I knew you had seen my slip, my surprise that you and Gideon were together. I had to explain it somehow."

They had played me. Again. Féile had been the bait, and the failing line had been the hook. The process had sapped me of the power I needed to prevent the net from closing around me.

"How long do we have?" I asked, scanning the room and the fancily dressed sentinels circling ever nearer.

He shook his head, his face tight. "I don't know. Minutes."

I smiled up at him and dropped into a deep curtsy as the dance ended.

Fidelma was closest, seated in a dark-navy gown at the edge of the dancefloor, her black and silver hair looped up in a graceful shining swathe.

"Are you enjoying the ball?" I asked her as I took a seat beside her.

She gathered her gown and repositioned it out of the way of some passing guests. "Not as much as I might have when my bones were younger." She smiled wryly back at me.

"Can I refill your drink?" I asked, leaning in to retrieve her half-full glass. "We are discovered," I whispered to her urgently. "Tell Bronwyn. Try to get Rion out of here. We'll meet at your tent. If I don't make it, head for the Bishopsgate. I have a friend; he'll find you."

If I could get them out to Linus, we stood a chance. We had a network that might be able to hide those who got out. Marina knew the city; if she got out of the palace, she would be able to blend in. I had last seen her with Gideon.

I made my way hurriedly towards the tall, dark head; he was already stalking towards me. He pulled me into his arms as we met on the dancefloor, swirling me close.

"What is it?"

"They know it's us. They're coming to arrest us," I whispered urgently. "They'll never let me go, but Fidelma and the others may have a chance if they leave now. Fidelma is warning them."

Gideon stopped moving. "No, she's not."

I followed the direction of his gaze. Fidelma stood beside Praetor Calchas. Neither wore their masks anymore. They saw me, and I them.

"We need to get a message out." We needed the army here, now. "Where's Marina?"

"I told her to get out."

Amber eyes glittered down at me through his mask. "The abilities from the Lake. They stayed with me."

Those odd flickers I had seen... I hadn't imagined them.

"More than just the tracking? And you're only telling me this now."

He didn't answer, his eyes scanning the room, the exits.

"You can transform?"

He nodded sharply.

"You can still make it... the balcony," I urged. Gideon stood unmoving and his lips twisted as he emitted a low snarl, his stance preternaturally still as he surveyed the approaching threats. I punched him in the shoulder. "Bring the army. Gideon, go. Now."

Across the room, I could see sentinels moving swiftly to surround the delegates. On the dancefloor, we were the furthest from any of them as they streamed in through the doorway. I didn't have a spark left within me, still barely recovered from our efforts of the other night. I stood helpless yet again as the sentinels poured in and attacked the people I loved.

Gideon still hadn't moved, transfixed by the sight of his mother shoulder to shoulder with the praetor. Governor Dolon began to move towards us, his lips spread in a supercilious smile of satisfaction. Citizens in their finery milled around us in confusion, half-startled at the movement of the sentinels against the delegates, backing away to ensure they did not get caught up in it, the rest lingering to watch the drama unfold.

The dancefloor cleared and we were left standing alone. There was something about Gideon that made the sentinels slow to approach. Many were busy securing the other delegates – Rion was fighting them off, but he was outnumbered, and they used batons to subdue him. I could do nothing as they cut him down.

Another battle caught my eye and I watched as Richard Mortimer went down from a blow to the head. There was a growl beside me that vibrated through the room, a flicker as Gideon's amber eyes glowed and there interlaid over him was an almost holographic version of a lion, a great beast that he was... and yet also was not.

"No, no!" I cried, pressing against him, laying my hand on his chest, the chest of a man... no, not just a man anymore. "Gideon, please, eagle, eagle... I need you to fly."

His amber eyes moved in my direction, his brows drawn together as man and beast were transposed, interlaid one on top of the other.

"To save me, to save us all, you must fly."

Feline eyes blinked slowly, in what I hoped was

understanding. I backed away to give him room. The air shimmered again as the transformation continued until wings spanning many feet flexed wide and strong.

"The windows!" yelled Calchas, directing his soldiers to block the Griffin's escape.

I felt hands grabbing me from behind. I looked over my shoulder to find that the hands belonged to Matthias Dolon. I pulled away, every fibre of my being repulsed and furious. Out of the corner of my eye, I could see more sentinels approaching, some with syringes in their hands. I was powerless and so there was no need for their drugs, I had emptied myself voluntarily. I screamed, fear and rage ripping through me, and I managed to catch the governor with my fisted hand. He weathered the blow and held on to me, his own anger and disdain writ large across his face. I struggled in his arms, writhing like a wild thing as my emotions got the better of me. I would not suffer the touch of this man. I would not.

Then he was gone, and so too were the sentinels who had been coming for me – a flash of golden brown, but whether it was the eagle or the lion I couldn't tell. The floor around me was covered in blood, flashes of the Griffin roaring in its anger, enraged by my own anger and fear. It all happened in mere moments and then there was the pop-pop of shots. The beast was felled. My knees gave way, and I collapsed on the floor, the beautiful silks of my gown spread wide, a shimmering island in a lake of blood.

Gideon. I couldn't think, I couldn't...

I blinked slowly at the sight of my fallen Griffin, his glimmering bronze wings fading to arms once more, the lion veil pulling back, leaving the prone unmoving man in his wake, his clothes, his hands covered in blood, the broken bodies of the sentinels beside him. Governor Dolon, a great gaping gash across his chest, lay beside me, his unseeing eyes staring sightlessly back at me.

I lifted a hand towards Gideon. I needed my feet to work, I needed to go to him. There was so much blood. I couldn't breathe. I scanned the room for Marcus. Marcus could help. Marcus could save him. I could hear the dull background noises, the screams and terror of the fleeing guests. And then Marcus was there, holding me, pulling me into his arms.

"It's all right, Cassandra. He's alive. They shot him with a drug. He's unconscious but that's all." His hand swept across my hair in calming strokes. "Breathe, Cassandra, shh. It's all right, he's alive. I promise you."

Marcus's mask was off and his pupils were dark in his shocked face. His father was dead. And he really was dead this time.

"So much blood," I whispered. "Not Gideon?"

I knew it. I could focus on it now, reason leaking through the sensory overload of the last few minutes. I had known what it felt like to lose a Griffin before, to have that connection severed. He was still here. But I needed to hear it.

I gripped Marcus's jacket and looked up at him.

"Not Gideon?" I demanded.

"Not Gideon," he confirmed, looking over my head and then there was a pinch on my arm, and I knew no more.

Chapter Twenty-Four

The room I found myself in upon waking was familiar. My head felt woozy as I waited for my eyes to adjust to the light streaming through the windows.

It was morning then. The windows were set in a stone wall, familiar from years in the north, yet the style of the window was strange. But I had seen it before: criss-cross patterns with stained glass set in it, old but angular in the way the Empire's lines were. My eyes hurt, and I closed them again; my mouth felt dry. I pushed myself up off my pillows, and the blankets dropped to reveal the beautiful ruined gown Oban had made me for the masquerade ball discarded on a nearby chair. My mask lay on the table by the fireplace, as if waiting for me to pick it up and whirl off to the next party.

I knew this room. My heart stopped beating in my chest as I looked around and took in the granite walls, the elaborate bed, the cacophony of city noise outside. The beat resumed at double pace as I named it: the Tower. I was in the White Tower. The very room that I had escaped from on my previous visit –

a coincidence for which I could no doubt thank my twisted host.

The same copper bath lay waiting in the middle of the floor. It had been a novelty the last time, an odd anachronism from a previous era due to the lack of encroachment of Imperial technology into the home of the praetor. I was all too familiar with such anachronisms now, after years beyond the walls, living without conveniences I had previously taken for granted, like hot running water and steam rooms.

Those who had knocked me out and transported me here had at least removed my gown, leaving me in my slip so that I hadn't been forced to lie in the blood-stained dress all night. My charm too had been removed.

I had to get up. I had to meet this day.

Some white clothes were waiting on the chair. That wasn't right. Where was the regulation black of the accused? For surely that was where this day ended: on the sands facing Calchas and his mob.

I stepped out of the bed and padded softly across the room. I was sure there were guards outside the door – no need to alert them to my wakened state until I had to. Shaking out the clothes, I discovered a plain floor-length white dress with long sleeves. A clatter on the gleaming wooden floor alerted me to the presence of a new mask.

Picking it up, I ran a finger lightly across the natural symbols etched around the edge of the top right half of the mask, swirling liquid greens and blues that evoked nature in a way that almost echoed the Celtic style, but not quite. There were also openings for the eyes – if I was bound for the arena then the mask's eyes should be closed to keep me blinded until I was freed of the mask and revealed to the mob. Nor was there any sign of the mechanism that prevented the accused from hearing.

There was fruit laid out, and a pot of tea sat steaming on the table where my elaborate masquerade mask lay looking blankly back at me. Was Gideon receiving such hospitality? I couldn't imagine the fierce, enraged warrior waking to such urbanity. After the events of last night, it seemed more likely that they would have him restrained behind as many bars and walls as they could find.

Gideon's reputation as a fighter was well respected, but what I had witnessed last night had been something else. The overplay of eagle and lion as he had lashed out at all around him, had been... had others seen it? He had gashed Matthias from waist to neck with his hand. How was it possible? Had the talon been real? How else, though? He couldn't have done that with his bare hands.

The way he had explained the transformation when we had been at the Lake, it had sounded like it was a literal metamorphosis, but last night it had been as if he had coexisted with a shadow that had merged into him. Had he known he could do that?

I reached out to touch and check the food as had become my habit but I was still so depleted even such simple magic was beyond me and so the mango and strawberries remained undisturbed on the plate. I disrobed and washed quickly, anxious to remove any last trace of the night before. After the bath, I dithered over which dress to wear. It felt wrong to comply with my host's choice of outfit, but the layer of blood splashed along the skirt of last night's dress made me reluctant to put it back on. Was it Matthias's blood? Or did it belong to another, one of the sentinels perhaps?

I dressed in the white and lay back on the bed, barely

rousing when a couple of girls came in and cleared away all traces of my morning's activities. What was the point? They wouldn't tell me anything, and I just didn't have the energy. Without Gideon, I was slower to recover. But even depleted I could still feel a connection to the world; they hadn't dosed me like before. It was a mistake for which I would make them pay.

At the girl's request, I took a seat at the dressing table. One of the girls swept my hair up, rather plainly for an imperial event. The reason became clearer when the other wrapped a white cloak around my shoulders and pulled the deep hood over my head after the new mask was in place. One of the girls surveyed me before turning and nodding to the waiting guard; apparently, I was just as ordered.

More food was brought and sat untouched on the table. The wait was killing me. Where was everyone? What was Calchas's next move? Had Marina escaped? Last time I had been marched out onto the sands – was that what I had been dressed for today? Time drifted heavily by; there was little activity outside in the courtyard and only stillness inside the room.

When at last the door opened, it was to Fidelma rather than my expected escort to my trial.

Her face was expressionless. She entered with the same authority and entitlement she'd had when I had known her as the premiere druid in the land. There was no sign that she commanded any less respect than that now.

"You need to go to Gideon," she began, without any explanation of her part in last night's events. "He remains overtaken by the Griffin. When he came to, he was taken by the berserker form once more. They dosed him again, but it wears off quickly while he is in this state. As soon as he gains consciousness, he is overtaken once more. Calchas is displeased."

A fact which didn't appear to alarm Fidelma unduly.

"So Calchas's theatrics are impeded. You can imagine my dismay."

"You must help. If you do not, he will kill him now." Her eyes met mine, her chin lowering some, as she pleaded her case.

"Gideon will not be leaving the city alive. What is it to you? Why should I facilitate whatever charade the praetor has planned?"

"He is my son, and where there is life there is hope." Her eyes flicked to the ceiling and upper corners of the room. No doubt our exchange was being observed.

"I want to see my daughter."

"I can't." Her hands lifted, spreading aimlessly.

"Then the praetor will just have to present his little production minus his guest star, won't he?" A fleeting expression of irritation flashed across her face, similar to the one I was used to seeing on Gideon's... I needed to go to him. But this was my one slim piece of leverage and I couldn't miss my chance. I had to hold out. Féile was here, in the city. My path led to the sands no matter what, I was sure of it. This might be my only chance...

Fidelma nodded curtly, knocking on the door, and speaking briefly to someone on the other side.

We sat in silence while whoever she had sent to Praetor Calchas came back with a response.

"How long have you been working with them?" I asked eventually, unable to help myself. Had she been in league with them all this time?

She didn't turn her gaze from the window, reminding me of her son. All too often he conducted conversations he didn't want to face like this. I had always supposed it was because he didn't care enough to face me. Maybe that wasn't the reason.

"Fidelma?" I prompted. She owed me this answer. I still used the name she had taken when she had become a druid, but had her betrayal been earlier, when she had still been Elizabeth Mortimer of York? "Elizabeth? How long?"

"Since before you were born." Her voice came low.

My breath was stolen by this revelation as surely as if it had been a physical blow. But why, why would she do that? My mind reeled as the impact of her words hit me.

"You're the one who betrayed my mother?" My words were flat. I could barely manage to say them. She didn't deny it. "Why?"

"Magic was becoming extinct all across the Mediterranean, the lines were dying and with it the land. Refugees from all over fled here, and they helped us keep the lines flowing, but there were fewer and fewer of them. And the bloodlines were also thinning out..." She spoke slowly, as if she was exhausted.

I saw again the map on the wall in Oxford. Scholars in the Wilds had been tracking the progress of the failing ley lines across the Empire for decades. Creeping ever closer to this island on the edge of the Empire.

"I attended the Treaty Renewal with Richard back then. I met the new praetor and he convinced me he wanted to help, that he understood, as we did, the danger of leaving the Strand line untended, as it had been for centuries. Our husbands objected, but Viviane jumped at the opportunity to help. I went to meet her in the borderlands, and we were to enter the city together." She finally turned to face me, her eyes hollow as they met mine. "I was nearly at our meeting point when I felt it."

Her fists clenched and unclenched in her lap, her entire body vibrating with the anger as if it was new.

"She was gone."

"But why did they kill her? She was coming to help them."

Fidelma shrugged miserably. "I don't know. Maybe Actaeon learned of it. He was a zealot, no matter the evidence that the Strand line was dying and that the curse laying waste to the Empire would inevitably arrive here."

Her motivations had been honest; Fidelma, or Elizabeth as she had been then, like my mother, had only wished to heal the land. I believed her when she said she hadn't known my mother would be murdered. But since then, she had colluded with my mother's killers. "You let everyone think I was dead?"

"I didn't know they had taken you," Fidelma said earnestly, her eyes pleading with me to believe her. "I swear it."

They *had* taken me though, and my family, and Devyn, had been left without both of us. All those lives destroyed. I focussed back on what Fidelma was saying. Now that she could talk, it appeared she wanted to explain it all.

"Once she was gone, I did everything I could. The impact on the ley line was small at first, but then more people grew ill... it was my fault. I tried to compensate. I gave my life to it. I spent time at Holy Isle as they worked tirelessly to find a way to treat the ill."

Gideon had told me that his mother had trained at Holy Isle when he was a child, and that she had taken him with her on occasion.

"I travelled from one circle to another, aiding where I could. I didn't go to the next Treaty renewal; the high druid at Glastonbury was dying, and I never wanted to see Londinium again. And for a while, it seemed as if I was enough." Her hands twisted in her lap, even though her face had become devoid of expression. Or rather, devoid of hope, as she relived those years. "But then all of a sudden it grew worse."

"What happened?

"Poor Lady Courtenay." Fidelma sighed. "In the years after the Lady of the Lake died, people started to fall ill in Londonium. Then Aurelia Courtenay fell ill. The line had drawn energy from her. She was the strongest magical source within the walls, so she lasted longer than most latents do, because she was from such a strong bloodline. Once she was gone, the Strand ley line declined sharply."

The line here had been drawing on the energy of those with magic in their veins for decades; that was what caused the illness, the death throes of a dying line. With Lady Courtenay's death, a major energy source would have suddenly disappeared and the corruption would have gone in search of more energy further along the line. This was when Fidelma would have sensed the sharp deterioration.

"The corruption surging up the line was worse than I had ever known it, and I had to come and see for myself. I returned as part of the Treaty delegation. I had changed my appearance when I left York and tending the line had aged me. I thought it would be fine, that neither Richard nor Praetor Calchas would know I was here." She cast a glance upwards to where the expected surveillance sat, though I knew, as she seemed not to, that the praetor's home, unlike others, was camera free. "But somehow they did."

"The cameras can see through a glamour," I informed her.

Her face fell. "So I walked straight into their den unmasked. I approached the new Senator Dolon to confirm it was the Mallacht that had claimed Lady Courtenay and to see whether their son, the last of the Plantagenets, showed any signs of ability."

"Why? I thought you had just come to treat the line?"

She rubbed a hand across her face.

"I had, but the bloodlines had grown so thin. If Marcus could be trained in magic, could help to tend the lines, then he could be heir to the House of York. I thought there was a chance his father would listen. That he would help protect him." Fidelma's voice was barely audible as she tried to defend the choice she had made so many years ago. Having been betrayed once before, she had attempted a different approach but I could already see the praetor's next moves and the further betrayals ahead.

"Matthias despised Wilders. He would never have been interested," I informed her. I knew, as Fidelma hadn't, that Matthias Dolon would never have done anything purely for the sake of helping others. "Marcus was only ever a means to an end to him. The only reason he would help would be if it increased his own power."

Fidelma's eyes met mine in wry acknowledgement, and she continued wearily. "He told me that Marcus was experiencing some vertigo and he seemed desperate to help him."

I snorted at that. Saving Marcus would ensure he retained the Courtenay senatorial seat; that was the only reason he would have been desperate.

"He helped me to sneak in to Mary le Strand on the last night of the Treaty Renewal and work on the ley line. I was able to do a little to tend it on my own. It caused a terrible blackout, but when I returned to Glastonbury I could feel how much better it was."

"Matthias couldn't have got you in without help. Praetorians guard the church over the line. They answer only to one man." I saw again the sentinels on the banks of the Tamesis riding down my mother, their insignias the silver of the praetor's own guard. Actaeon hadn't been the one to kill her and take me. The truth had been staring me in the face from the beginning; my very first vision had told me who was behind it all.

It had always been Praetor Calchas. He had Marcus, and once he had taken me he would have been happy to play the long game in order to have magic under his control.

Fidelma's hollow eyes met mine again, her mouth set in a straight line. "I was such a fool. I thought I was helping. My only thought was to save the ley line and Matthias had every reason to help me. Or so I thought." She shrugged wearily. "Marcus inevitably started to sicken again, much worse this time, and I smuggled in some of the mistletoe medication. It suppresses the magic in the blood, so the line would no longer seek its energy from him."

"No. It moved on to others, to the latents in the city. And to me." At least until the vertigo in my early teens had been held off by the same medication Marcus was being fed. Which was also how Matthias knew the Britons had something that held the illness at bay, knowledge he and Calchas had failed to act on until it served them.

"I didn't know. There were no reports of illness at that time in the rest of Britannia. We heard no news of it from Londinium. I thought the Mallacht only affected the strong."

"Because the council kept it quiet. You had to realise that people here would be sickening, dying."

She turned her head to look outside once more. There was still no sign of the guard returning. What if Calchas called my bluff and refused to let me see Féile? What if he decided that he didn't need Gideon after all? I squashed down my rising panic. No, I knew him. He lived for this, for the big stage of the arena. He would want to present the mob with the new governor's murderer. What better way to quiet the unrest that was sweeping the city? The citizenry already felt that somehow the Britons were to blame, but those in the lower classes also knew that the elite had kept the Wilders medicine for themselves. Right now the city was teetering on the edge of civil unrest. What better nudge to give them to ensure they fell in line behind him? No, Praetor Calchas needed Gideon on the sands.

"By that time, I had become thoroughly washed out. I didn't feel, didn't want; the only thing left was tending the line." Fidelma's voice shook.

"But you seemed so kind," I said abjectly. The woman I had met here and on every occasion since had been so gentle, so compassionate. No sign of the burnout that had all but killed me. Callum hadn't gone to her for help when I had been near death because we'd thought she didn't suffer the burnout. We'd thought that my affliction was particular to me.

"I learned to," she said. "I lost my family and turned away from my children. I could see how it hurt them, especially Gideon; he was so young. I didn't care then, but over the years I noticed that people had stopped responding to me and it compromised my ability to get people to aid me in tending the line, so I learned how to appear as if I still cared for others."

My soul shuddered. How close I had been to becoming as single-minded, as ruthlessly focussed as this woman. I could hardly imagine the impact of the years of tending the line on her, emotionally and physically, and she'd had no one to help restore that balance. She should never have given so much of herself to the line, had not been strong enough to do so.

"When you came, you shouldered the heaviest elements. Marina also took on more. I was able to take a rest. I started to allow more of the corruption to leak northwards, and you were every bit as strong as your mother." She smiled tremulously. "Oh, if she could see you, she would be so proud. And once I'd stopped, I started to feel again."

"But you kept helping them."

"No, no... I refused. They wanted Féile. I told them I wouldn't do it. I was going to tell you the truth. I was going to tell you everything."

I wanted to believe her, but she'd had plenty of opportunity.

"If it wasn't you then who?"

"I don't know."

"And last night, you told them we were trying to escape the ball?" I could barely look at her.

"No. I swear it. When I tried to alert the others, Clachas intercepted me; it was already too late."

I saw again how she had stood with Calchas. It had all happened so fast. I hadn't been able to see her face... It was plausible. And if she really had defied him then the praetor would have delighted in having a close-up view of her face as the noose tightened.

"The first day we met, did you know then who I really was?" I tried another tack, another weak point in her defences.

"Yes. Your magic was fractured, buried. I didn't at first but then there it was, like a bell, ringing clear and pure. So I lied. It seemed like you weren't directly under Calchas control and The lines in Kernow and Anglia were starting to fade and we needed you. I knew Devyn Glyndŵr would get you out, somehow. The Griffin's powers... whatever it took, somehow..."

She glanced around the room, afraid of saying too much. She had told me everything, Why hesitate now?

The door opened and a praetorian guard stepped into the room.

"Come."

"He has agreed to let me see my daughter?" I checked.

The praetorian nodded, stern faced. "Yes. Now come."

"They're keeping Gideon here?" I had expected to be taken to the arena, or somewhere secure. But rather than the curved sandstone walls of the amphitheatre, we drew up short of that landmark, at the rear doors of the Governor's Palace.

They hadn't managed to get very far before he recovered. When they shot him a second time, they must have opted to secure him here rather than try and cross the city.

Alvar. I recognised the long-faced praetorian guard the moment his jeering gaze met mine as I exited the transport. He escorted me through the deserted kitchens and back corridors of the palace. On an ordinary day, these halls would be bustling with those who worked here, but now our footsteps echoed back to us.

We came at last to the ballroom. The blood had been removed and there remained no trace of the events of the night before. Crossing to the large glass doors that opened out onto the inner courtyard, he indicated we were at our destination. His lip quirked as he looked me up and down before opening the doors out onto the day. Sunlight streamed down as the Governor's Palace was one of the few buildings in the city that had open sky above it – no highwalks, no extra levels of the city over it. This empty space was a luxury retreat for the few, while so many lived in the dark warrens of the city. Alvar nodded to the walls where cameras no doubt now sat.

"No theatrics this afternoon," he advised. I assumed he was referring to our previous encounter in Richmond. "We wouldn't want to have to punish anyone for your bad behaviour, now would we?"

I was exhausted from tending the ley line and couldn't have summoned a storm even if I'd wanted to, but I could do something. I would find a way to punish them. Loathsome eel.

He pushed me out into open space and, taking the path, we curved around the high foliage to the great tree that sat in the centre... where Gideon stood poised, waiting, his amber predator's eyes trained on me as I rounded the corner. Those glimmering wings unfurled, gold and bronze where the sunlight hit him. There was restrained power in the image that overlaid his own form. He was the Griffin, but he was also Gideon. And both beings were furious at the shackles that bound him to the trunk of the great tree, restraining him from attacking the guard at my side and those that I could glimpse hovering at the perimeter of the courtyard.

His neck swivelled in a preternaturally smooth movement as his focus moved to something he spotted in a window on a floor above us. An eerie cry loosed as his entire being strained to go to what he saw.

Féile.

There, through the large window above, we could see her with Marcus, who stood stiffly by her side. She was chatting up at him, her dark curls long and streaming down her back. She looked happy and well, and so much bigger. As we watched, a woman emerged from behind them and spoke to Marcus before taking Féile's little hand in her own and drawing her away. Marcus's attention turned to someone we couldn't see, his shoulders bunched and his chin turned slightly toward the window before he too left our view.

A growl reminded me of Gideon's presence.

"No, bring her to me. That's not enough. I won't help you," I said angrily.

So close. She was so very close. Could I get to her before… before what? Breathe. I could do nothing. I could possibly use what little power had returned to get to her, but what then? Gideon was bound, the others were imprisoned somewhere in the city, and the army was too far away.

"Prove you can control him first."

I blinked at Alvar. Right, Gideon. He was trapped somehow. I started to go to him but was held fast by the guard at my side.

"Gideon," I called, but his attention was still fixed on the window where she had been, "Gideon, she's gone."

His stare was brightly intense as he turned his head with that uncannily smooth movement back to me. I had to prevent myself from taking a step back.

"Gideon," I said softly, imperatively. His gaze tracked beyond me, continuing to take in his surroundings in a calculated way. He looked like he hovered on the edge of attack.

I pulled again at the hand restraining me and then glared at Alvar until he gave the nod for the sentinel to release me.

I approached the tall, broad-shouldered warrior slowly. He showed no sign of attacking me, his gaze not moving from those he perceived as threats. I laid a gentle hand on his chest, expecting to find his heart racing with adrenaline, but I was unnerved to find it felt steady – if anything, it was slower than normal.

His clothes from last night were torn and covered in blood, one sleeve shredded as if it had been sliced by a sword.

I ran my hand up along his arm, tracing his tattoos as I had many times before. His muscles were taut and poised, a fresh scar across his upper shoulder. Had he been wounded? How had it healed so fast? It looked weeks old, yet it had not been there before last night.

"You get him under control or we will. Are you clear, Donna Shelton?" Alvar stated, his threat less convincing with the cringing of the guards posted at a safe distance. One had a black eye, and another seemed to be favouring one leg.

"Leave us. You're setting him off."

They had Féile though. What was driving Gideon into attack mode was also what compelled me to call him off. We had to do what they wanted.

"She's well, we've seen her – that's a good thing." Whatever had manifested last night was in charge right now and I needed to put Gideon back in control. "Shhh, she's okay. We just need to do what they ask."

As I spoke soft, calm words, I continued to run my fingers up along his arms and felt his muscles relax slightly under my fingertips. I pushed his long hair back from his temple and I could have sworn he curled slightly into my palm. He was responding.

Reasonably confident he didn't seem to perceive me as a threat, I ran my hands down his face until he was receptive enough that I could pull his head down to mine. He allowed it, more interested now in me than in the guards at the perimeter of the courtyard.

I pressed my lips lightly to his, a simple touch to the corner of his mouth, then full against his mouth, a nip to his lower lip, and then with a groan he was with me... responding, kissing me back.

The world faded away to just the touch of our lips. Fierce

and then gentler. He pulled up, confused, questioning eyes looking down at me.

"Usually works for me." I smiled up at him, my words low and only for him. Whatever magic had overtaken him, touch and sensation seemed to return him to his own body, to his own senses.

With the amped-up predator alertness dropping away, Gideon looked tired and a little dazed.

"You back?" I murmured against his lips.

He rested his forehead against mine, a slight pressure that I took for assent.

"We have time. Let's sit."

Gideon nodded, his knees seeming to fold of their own accord.

I lay back against the ancient tree. Gideon's head was heavy, his dark hair streaming across my lap. Once, long ago, Devyn had held me like this, exhausted as I had been from the vision I had seen of the attack on my mother – one of my first frightening experiences during which I lost myself to magic. I'd had no understanding then of what it was or how that magic would impact my world beyond my expulsion from the city I called home once I was discovered.

"Are you okay?" I asked, moving my hand to cup the side of his drawn face.

His lips tugged up at one side. I glared back at him. Yes, it was a stupid question.

"You mean because I turn into some kind of monster or because I'm in chains and likely to be killed?"

"I dunno," I said in return, shrugging flippantly. "Pick one."

His eyes glinted in dark humour back at me.

"Well, turning into an actual griffin was a bit of a surprise," he said.

"Not as much of a surprise as it was for those sentinels," I tossed back.

He swallowed an unexpected burst of laughter. "That's true."

"Did you know you could do that?" I asked a tad more seriously.

He gave me one of those exasperated looks in which he specialised.

"No." He drew the word out as he said it. "At the lake, I transformed into one form of the griffin or the other. I thought after that first night it had stopped. Then, when I was training with Rhodri in York, we discovered I could trigger it at will."

"Why didn't you tell me?"

He shook his head. We were barely speaking in York, much less exchanging confidences.

"I don't know. We were told there was more to the Griffin, that my gift would be in answer to your need. Maybe this is it, the secret revealed."

"Too late," I said mournfully. Though in truth, had we known earlier, what help would it have been? He had some traits of the Griffin, but what good did that do us now?

"Unless you think you could fly us all out of here?" I asked, hopefully. His new form was substantially larger than the more lifelike version in which he had escaped his lakeside confinement.

I surprised another laugh out of him.

"Is this how you feel after the ley lines?" he asked.

"Yeah. Using that much energy can leave you a bit drained," I said.

"A bit drained?" He huffed.

He pulled himself up and surveyed the courtyard as we sat shoulder to shoulder.

"I spoke to your mother," I told him. "I don't think she intended things to turn out this way."

No response.

"I think she set out to do the right thing for the right reasons, but Calchas manipulated her. She tried to—"

"Enough," he cut across me. "I have little time left. Don't fill it talking about her."

I took his hand in mine, interlacing our fingers. "We'll get out of this."

"How?"

"I don't know, but this is not how it ends."

He had used those words to me once before when all hope had been gone. I believed them. Somehow I would figure this out. I would find a way to be one step ahead of Calchas for once. Just one time.

He laid his head back down in my lap, his breathing grew steady, and the events of the night drifted away. I looked up into the leaves of the tree above me, a mighty oak here in the centre of the jewel of the imperial outpost, the beating heart of their power here in the city. The dappled light was waving through the colours, turning in the growing dark.

The golds, oranges, and reds of summer were fading.

My mother run down by the sentinels, a younger Rhodri fighting to turn back to reach her, the oncoming red robes riding her down, riding them all down, the wise ones, the priests, druids, and doctors in the lands north and south of the great Mediterranean, the rivers flowing red and dark with their blood: illness, the great curse sweeping across the Empire.

Grapes withered on the vine, crops rotted in the ground. Lights were extinguished across the lands, and crops were failing year after year, fields growing fallow as the people starved, gripped by famine and the desiccation of the land.

Darkness, illness, famine, death. Grim, unrelenting, creeping as the light in the spirit lines faded and quenched. The music in the songlines silenced. Growing darkness, until a glowing light appeared, transforming into a boy on a horse riding away, a sword lifting from the water, great bronze wings unfurling and taking to the sky. Soaring on the down draft across the great walls...

Devyn's dark eyes looking straight at me, a familiar smile on his face,

"I found you."

I saw the sword broken on the sands... red seeping across gold.

Dark curls glistening, his head bowed as he fell... Blood splaying across the pale grains, whirling around, droplets becoming a shimmer then a point of light, then a pair of lights, sucking down into a great dark vortex. First a few, then many.

So many, coming out of the warrens seeking help at the great doors of Bart's Hospital, more and more of them swirling down into the darkness.

Twinned swords in the vortex, each a counterpoint to the other, swinging ever faster down into the growing darkness, so many lights now, singing, swirling, a Celtic knot, looping, bonding, so many lights growing dim, screaming, held fast, dying in the dark...

I jerked awake, the muscle spasm disturbing the sleeping Gideon. I breathed in, steadying my heartbeat. The darkness was waiting. It was coming for us all.

Was what I had seen true?

Gideon's hand held mine, his calloused one warm despite

the cold of the breeze that swept through the courtyard. I gathered myself. The sword broken... was that in the past? All those people hunted, the Mallacht spreading across the land as their light was extinguished. This was what Fidelma had spoken of, the growing darkness of a world out of balance. She had spent her life pushing back the tide; she had sacrificed everything to it.

I had seen it when we went down into the circle below Mary le Strand.

Gideon startled and was already standing when Alvar and fresh sentinels appeared.

"All right, love birds, you have an appointment." Alvar's voice sounded much surer of his own authority now that the worst of the danger had passed. Not so much that his face didn't fail to blanch when Gideon slung a narrow-eyed glare his way though. "No funny business, mind. You best behave, or it won't go well for your friends."

He indicated that the sentinels should step forward and I noticed they were carrying fresh clothes and a bowl of water and a cloth.

Alvar curled his finger to me, not acknowledging the Briton at my side at all.

"No, we stay together." I looked up at the open sk. It was difficult to judge but it couldn't be much more than late afternoon. It was early in the day for a Mete, but perhaps things had changed since I lived here.

Alvar raised a brow, looking in the direction of the empty window. "Do as you're told and I will take you to the child."

I turned back to Gideon. He was still poised as if every person in the courtyard and beyond was merely potential prey.

"Does your Wilder understand?" Alvar asked me. I

couldn't blame him for directing his question to me. Who would threaten Gideon in this state?

Gideon resumed a casual seat on the ground under the tree, slanting Alvar that obnoxious insouciant smile that he reserved for those he really wanted to piss off.

I matched it with one of my own as I raised a brow at the praetorian in response to his delay in taking me on to my prescribed place in the next scene.

I sauntered out of the courtyard in Alvar's wake, turning back for one last glance at my smirking husband. His eyes were closed, his head leaning back against the oak, and his long legs were stretched out in front of him.

I would see him again.

This was not how we ended.

Chapter Twenty-Five

Alvar led me back through the ballroom and up through the mosaic-tiled corridors until we came to an empty room hung with portraits of governors of the province and a large dining table where he took his leave with another horrid smirk. Power still ran through me, faint but unmistakeably there. No attempt had been made to cut me off from the magic in my blood, but while they had my family and my friends, I could do nothing. Leaving me armed but helpless was a taunt that highlighted how truly powerless I was.

I was startled as the door opened and two women entered, one carrying a tray of food, which she set down on the chair by the fire, laying out multiple plates and glasses on the table.

The smaller of the two tutted at the smudges of dirt and grass on the hem of my still otherwise pristine white dress. She took a cloth and removed all evidence that I had spent much of the day sitting on the ground in the courtyard, while the other washed my hands and sat me down at the table in front of the plates of food I couldn't imagine touching.

They finally left, and I sat as they had arranged me before

restlessly pushing back my chair and going to the window, watching the traffic move up and down the river below. In addition to my own, three empty places waited. Who were they for? I dared not hope that I would be rewarded as promised for Gideon's recovery.

When the door opened again, I didn't look up, but my stomach tightened.

"My dear, it's been far too long since I've had the pleasure of your company."

Calchas.

He stood in the doorway, a pleasant smile on his face as if he had stumbled upon an old acquaintance.

I could feel a snarl that the Griffin would be proud of take life within me as I turned to face him. I loathed this man with a depth of feeling that almost had me swaying on my feet.

"Now, now, Cassandra." He stepped aside, smiling broadly, the sound of my old name grating coming from his lips. "Best behaviour."

The door opened wider, and he was followed by Marcus, another whose mere existence on the earth was enough to—

Féile.

My daughter entered the room hand in hand with Marcus.

I froze. I looked back to Calchas, who lifted his hands as if he stood in the arena addressing the crowd, gracious and giving, his hands spread as he bestowed his gift.

My head swung back to Féile. She looked so perfect and I drank in the sight of her. I smiled tentatively at her as she looked unblinking at me. Her only reaction was to step closer to Marcus.

I took a step towards her, and she looped behind Marcus's leg.

I dropped down to my knees to be on her level.

"Féile," I whispered, holding a hand out to her.

She averted her eyes. I looked up at Marcus in confusion. Why would she not come to me? I lifted a hand to my face. Was the illusion back? Could she not recognise me?

"Féile, you know who this is, don't you?" Marcus squeezed her hand encouragingly.

No response.

Calchas let out a delighted chuckle. "Ah, the fickleness of the young," he remarked. "How quickly they forget all you have done for them."

He swept across the room and took a seat at the table, the reason for the abundance of dishes and extra glasses becoming all too clear. My eyes followed Marcus as he also took a seat and Féile scrambled into his lap, burying her head in his chest and refusing to look at me.

I lifted my head and pulled myself back to my feet. My heart squeezed in my chest as my daughter refused to acknowledge me. I pushed the pain down; she didn't mean to hurt me, I knew that it was a lot for her to process – she had been gone for so long. How would she have interpreted our failure to come for her? Did she blame us for not coming sooner? Had she turned for comfort elsewhere? I had let her down before; had she decided that I simply wasn't worth her trust, her love?

"Come, my dear, join us." Calchas indicated the seat nearest to him. My skin crawled as I took my place.

His cold eyes surveyed me. "You have grown into a beautiful young woman," he said. "Your parents would be so proud."

"Which parents? The Sheltons, who you paid to raise me and who threw me to the curb as soon as I was no longer an asset?" I asked. "Or my birth parents – the mother you murdered and the father who died of heartbreak at her loss?"

"Tut, tut, such insinuations, and within hearing of one of such tender age, too." Calchas reminded me of Féile's presence as though my entire being wasn't aware of every breath she took, every minor emotion that flickered across her face. I didn't need him to alert me to the flinch that had overtaken her entire body at my bitter words as she curled further into Marcus.

I exhaled a shuddering breath and mentally shook off the pain and anger that made it almost impossible to think.

Calchas would be looking to extract every possible ounce of drama and reaction out of me. I needed to stop playing into his hands. He would have a purpose behind this visit and I needed to figure out what it was and how I could thwart it, for the mere satisfaction of doing so. I took another grounding breath.

I drank in Féile, her dark curls glistening, her cheeks showing less of the baby roundness that had still plumped them when I saw her last. Her eyes held that same shielded wariness that had been there before. I had let her down again, and it made my heart break.

"What do you want?" I directed at the figure at the head of the table.

"Why, to catch up. Marcus and I are most interested to hear everything about your life since we saw you last." He laughed. "Though of course, you and Marcus have already done a little catching up without me."

I narrowed my eyes at Marcus. "Traitor."

Marcus smiled tightly. "To who? You?"

"I trusted you," the words left me as if from a blow. "Again.

How do you live with yourself? How can you justify your lies and deceit to yourself? Genuinely, tell me, I want to know."

Calchas looked on delightedly. I couldn't care less what he wanted. Marcus had been my friend once. Someone I admired. Someone I trusted.

Marcus's teeth were clenched, his knuckles white, as he stared at me glassy-eyed. He glanced at Calchas before his eyelids lowered.

"I did not lie to you, Cassandra. You are the one who betrayed this city." His voice was oddly strangled. "I've spent my life trying to help others, bargaining bits of my soul to make others' lives better. With my father. With you."

"You compare me to your father?"

"Why not?" He shrugged. "You both had the power to help people, but there had to be something in it for you before you would do so."

"You stole my daughter."

They had never asked for my help. That opportunity had never been offered to me; instead, they had manipulated me into doing what they wanted. Would I have trusted them enough to treat the ley line if they had asked though?

"Your mutant killed my father," he countered, practically rising out of his seat, every muscle and sinew taut.

"Good," I spat. "And I will end you."

"Now, now, there is a child present," Calchas chided, chuckling at our traded accusations.

Féile was stiff with anxiety as I promised to kill the one man who was likely to have been kind and caring to her since she arrived.

"Forgive me," I said, as outwardly calm as I could manage.

"It's healthy to have everything out in the open," he said,

popping a piece of cheese into his mouth, his eyes closing as he enjoyed the flavour. "Marvellous. Here, you must try some."

Complying, I picked a piece off the plate he offered me, well enough now to check that it was safe to eat, and bit into the orange cube, the sharp tang bursting to life on my tongue. I expected it to taste like sawdust but the salty crystals brought my mouth to life, reminding me that I hadn't eaten since sometime the day before. I smiled tightly as I took a second piece, buying time.

"Delicious," I offered.

Calchas poured out three ruby glasses of wine, one for each of us, and then waved a hand at me.

"What would you like to know?" I asked, smiling, my cheeks stretching at the forced movement.

"Have you enjoyed your time in the Wilds?" he asked, as if I had been out of the city on some kind of holiday.

"Yes, very much. The land beyond the walls is incredibly beautiful," I said, responding in kind. "The sky is vast, so much more sky than you can see here in the city. In the summer it is a great expanse of blue with cotton-ball clouds as far as the eye can see. In the winter, the mood of the day changes with the roll of grey clouds, with sun that leaks through, lighting up the hills and forests and lakes. There are miles and miles of countryside, greens and golds and blues, stretching out endlessly."

I could see Féile listening, so I spoke for her, describing the castle we lived in and the countryside of the Lakelands. Her eyes lifted to mine as she soaked in every word. I had grown up in the city feeling hemmed in, all the concrete and glass closing in about me, and I had never even known the freedom, the wide open spaces that she had

"Ah, wonderful," Calchas applauded, Féile startling at the

sharp sound, the light in her eyes dimming. "Why, it sounds as though you didn't miss us at all."

I levelled a dead-eyed gaze at him.

"No."

"Surely you must have missed some things about your life here?" he pressed, as if he was an uncle disappointed to learn his beloved niece had nothing good to say about the privileged life he had funded.

I shrugged. I didn't know what he wanted me to say and now that Féile had retreated, my own energy had dropped.

"I'm glad that you enjoyed your time away, but you know that we felt your absence deeply, didn't we Marcus?"

Marcus nodded in response, his green eyes miserable. He didn't seem to know any more than I did what Calchas's game was.

"You must have learned so many valuable things in the north," the praetor commented casually. "I believe you have done all you can to heal the ley for now?"

My lips twisted sourly. Fidelma must have told him everything.

He stood and went to the door, speaking to someone outside then returning to the table and rubbing his hands together.

"Do eat, my dears. It's important to keep one's strength up," he urged with the concern of a parent. We ate in silence, Marcus's eyes catching mine once as Calchas lifted his glass to his lips, his look beseeching me, but to do what? To say what?

I lifted a piece of fruit to my lips, nibbling at it in an approximation of enjoying the meal. The rest of my life could be measured in minutes and this was how I was to spend my last afternoon before my inevitable condemnation. But at least I could see Féile, spend what time Calchas allowed with her. Suddenly I wished for this meal to never end.

"Fidelma and my mother tried to help you heal the Strand ley line." I returned to our conversation casually. Calchas loved to talk and all I had to do was engage him. What better way to prolong the meal than let him bang on about his clever machinations? "Why not accept?"

Why murder my mother?

Calchas's lips curled up and the eternally convivial host paused before he began his tale in order to refill Marcus's newly empty glass as he considered my question.

"I was young, newly appointed as praetor of the city, and I was made privy to the truth of the curse of the Maledictio that was spreading across the Empire. When Fidelma approached me and explained the cause and the cure that she and the famed Lady of the Lake could provide, I accepted. I promised them safe passage." He shrugged. "I went to the governor, but he was less than pleased to learn of my plans. What could I do?"

"You killed my mother to redeem yourself." I stated starkly but without the venom that spewed inside as Féile looked on.

"Just so." He popped a grape into his mouth. "Things continued as before, on the inevitable slide into a disaster that Acteon was too pompous to address, for to heal the land would require working with magic wielders, and that would never do."

"But you never intended to just let the city follow the path the Empire had taken," I said. I knew him; he had a contingency in place. He'd been gathering strength, collecting senators who he could bring round to his own point of view until Marcus and I came of age.

"No." He smiled at my comprehension that having lost the

first round he had settled in to play the long game. "When Elizabeth finally ventured back into the city under her flimsy disguise as Fidelma the wisewoman, and approached the newly widowed Senator Dolon, Matthias came to me and suggested that the Britons were there for the taking, that now was the time. I wasn't so sure. The Empire would send in reinforcements if it looked like we could take the whole island because the land here was still healthy; we would expand the available farmlands and the last thing we needed was to become the refuge of an Empire in its death throes. Why share today when you can have the whole cake tomorrow? It was only a matter of time."

Calchas leaned back in his chair, pushing his plate away with an air of satisfaction. "There was no rush. We just had to hold on. The corruption of the ley lines steadied as Fidelma took over at Glastonbury. Matthias had her tend the Strand line at the Treaty Renewals, and that would have to suffice until you came of age."

Calchas stood, thoroughly involved in his story. He went to stand behind my daughter, his hands playing with her curls as he continued his tale. It set my every nerve on edge. Marcus didn't seem too pleased either, sitting mute and stiff beside her. Calchas sent him an amused glance.

"Then Marcus started to sicken. Matthias sent word to Fidelma, and she sent some marvellous concoction that they had started producing somewhere in the Wilds and that fixed Marcus right up. It also had the unfortunate side effect that it blocked his magic. Then, as you came into your magic, you too began to sicken. Fortunately, Marcus had a steady supply of suppressant which also kept both of your abilities hidden from the authorities. By this time, we had started to look for alternatives to Acteon's insistence on allowing the ill to die according to the same foolish policy that had already destroyed the rest of the Empire, dried up the leys and then the land. We started to examine the ill, to see if something could be done. And as you have seen, with the right application of technology and magic, we have managed to treat the ley line sufficiently ourselves.

"How?" I asked. I thought he was burning latents up. What application of technology? "I thought magic and tech don't work together?"

"That's what we always thought. What everyone thought. When the wars finally came to an end and terms were agreed, the ley line here had already been untended for generations. The industrial and technological revolutions had swept away the last traces of magic use within the walls. We saw that the more magically gifted Britons grew ill when they came and would recover once they left. Of course, we know now that it was the ley line drawing on them that made them unwell, but they resolved to avoid the fate of the Empire and Londinium by avoiding technology. To ridiculous lengths, I believe. Is it true that there isn't even indoor plumbing?" he laughed. "In the Empire, they believed that where there was magic, technology did not advance, so it was stamped out. Exterminated. Everyone stayed in their own corners. Here-be-dragons, superstition, and tradition became reality."

"But the blackouts?"

"During the Treaty renewals?" He raised a brow.

"Fidelma treating the Strand line," I realised.

Calchas bowed his head in acknowledgement of my correct guess.

"So, technology and magic can live side by side."

"Oh, yes. Fluctuations in the ley lines can cause blips, but that is manageable. Disruptions can be managed – not at sea and such, but for the most part," Calchas dismissed. "In fact, we discovered that not only can they live side by side but… well, in truth, we only figured it out after we caught the most interesting hacker. He was gifted in magic and tech. Actaeon, of course, clodhopper that he was, tried to have him killed. I persuaded him that we might find out more if we threw him back into the world to see how he was doing it."

Marcus looked up in recognition of this part of the story.

"And what a find. Not only was Devyn Agrestis using magic but he had discovered our little secret and persuaded her to stop taking her pills. And she didn't sicken. It turns out our naughty doctor had also decided he didn't need his meds though he was starting to show signs of illness."

They didn't realise that I had been ill. I had been unwell in Richmond, which I had put down to magic use and done everything I could to hide it. Then I had returned to Londinium and Devyn. Without realising it, in being with Devyn I had done the best thing I could for my wellbeing.

Calchas continued his crowing, barely needing my encouragement, so delighted was he in his own cleverness and at finally having an audience he could boast to, even if that audience were the victims of his manipulations – or perhaps this just added extra relish to the performance. Marcus's face was grey and expressionless as he listened. How much had he already known?

"The time was right to make our move. The Empire is crumbling. We just needed to win over the mob and get Actaeon out of the way. And Fidelma provided the answer. She was rather put out to learn that we'd had Catriona Deverell all this time, untrained and underemployed while the ley lines continued to fail. She demanded that Matthias help her get our little Cassandra and the Griffin out. Matthias bargained with her, promising to return Cassandra to the Wilds in exchange for more of the medicine that Fidelma had been supplying for years. She informed us that the raw materials would be useless without someone trained in assembling the medicine. Fortunately, a likely candidate was easily found. The illness was spreading and when Matthias let slip to him that the Wilders had something, well, you know how these scientific types are. He tried to help you escape the night of your prenuptial revels so he could try to discover more." Marcus had told the truth; he hadn't been part of it all along. His jaw clenched at learning that far from being the one to suggest we be freed to allow him to go north and discover the cure, he had never been anything more than a rather naïve pawn pushed about by his father and his puppet master. "The good doctor to the rescue of the masses. He put forward quite a compelling proposal, and Matthias and I were all too happy to help you slip Actaeon's noose. So Matthias engineered your escape, and, well, the rest, as they say, is history."

"Except you never had any intention of aiding the masses." Marcus's tone was bitter. "You were all too happy to drain their essence and feed it to the ley line."

"Oh yes." Calchas beamed. "I'm forgetting the best part. Not only did your would-be rescuer nearly get you executed, but he gave us the key to strengthening the ley ourselves."

"What?" I asked numbly when he paused, waiting for the prompt. It wasn't enough to monologue his triumph, he had to make me engage, to ask for more. "How?"

"Actaeon putting Devyn Agrestis on the sands against my wishes was a stroke of luck." Calchas was practically hovering off his chair. "His blood hit the sand…"

Marcus brows drew together, reflecting my own confusion.

"The start of the epidemic," Marcus crowed, his face grey.

Devyn had been whipped in punishment for his hacking offence. His blood had sprayed across the sand at my first Mete. In the weeks afterwards, the illness had grown worse.

"Over the summer, by coincidence"—my fingers clawed to scratch the glee from his expression—"we had a few capital offences of people who also happened to be afflicted by the Maledictio. Guilty, I'm afraid. The results were spectacular."

This explained the crowds outside Bart's by the time I had become handfasted to Marcus. Hundreds of people had become ill and the hospital had been unable to cope. The blood sacrifice in the arena was what had corrupted the line. The leaching that occurred as it faded had twisted it, horrifically strengthened by the blood draining directly into the sands. It was then able to draw even more energy from the population above, causing illness in latents in unprecedented numbers.

"You're sucking the life out of people to feed to the line?" That was what I had felt; that was the snarl that I hadn't been able to untwist. Why I couldn't release the burned-out souls trapped in the ley line. The blood on the sand was binding them somehow.

"Well, they were dying anyway. Clever science people figured it all out, and they've even managed to hook the ley line into the city grid, so its health can be monitored," he sniggered at his own joke. "Like I said, magic and tech working together."

Tethered together more like. He had somehow harnessed and sickened the ley line and now he was calculatedly feeding it the disappeared. He had turned the line into a grotesque parasite.

"Then why go to such trouble to get me to treat it?" After all, that was why he had taken Féile. To lure me here. But it was strong, even if in the most appalling way. I had unsnarled it some but if his intention was to ensure its strength and avoid the fate of the failing Empire, he already had that in hand.

"Well, we can't very well go to war while suffering what the people suppose is an epidemic. No, we need the full support of the population. You did such a fantastic job for Marcus and we can't thank you enough. There are all kinds of reports sweeping the city, rumours of the ill recovering overnight. Isn't it wonderful? As long as you keep it healthy, no one else has to die. But it's no matter if you choose not to. We have options."

I pictured the stacked vials of blood in the lab again. He didn't even have to wait for symptoms to reveal latents. He would systematically test the entire population and feed their life-force to the ley.

He spoke of orchestrating the deaths of thousands as if he was arranging a party, and halting those deaths only so he could begin his war. He had waited until the Empire was weak, Actaeon had been dispensed with, and the Britons... they didn't stand a chance. Calchas had figured out how to balance magic and tech. With an arsenal of reliable tech weaponry, the Britons would be annihilated.

"How could you be a part of this?" I asked Marcus. His shoulders were hunched, his body frozen as he digested the reality he had helped construct.

Calchas was leaning back in his chair, smiling broadly as if it was the most entertaining play he had ever seen. Our reactions were a validation that he had achieved the impact he had sought. I saw it all now, how my mother's death had occurred and the pieces that had fallen or been manoeuvred into place. It did seem, though, that Fidelma had never purposely acted against me. She truly hadn't known that I had been stolen until we met at that first Treaty Renewal, and she had tried to bargain for my freedom, had sworn that despite appearances she had not alerted Calchas that we were trying to escape.

"How did you get Féile? Was it Fidelma?"

"Lady Mortimer? No, once you were on the other side of the walls, she became most intractable. But there's always some way to thread the needle," he said, his eyes lighting up in amusement. "You just have to tailor the solution to the problem."

Who? If it hadn't been Fidelma, then who had betrayed us? Who would have helped Calchas? Who could he have got his claws into? The praetor's crowing was oddly worded...

Oban.

I had barely seen him in York because he had been busy putting together a wardrobe for Gideon and me, but still, he had been in a strange city and he was shy, usually drawing close to me when ill at ease. But he had kept his distance. I had seen him only from afar, my daughter's dog at his heels.

"You threatened Oban's family," I said flatly.

"Just so. He was in our control before he ever left the walls. Always advantageous to have a few carefully placed people on the other side of the border. We thought he would be useful but it worked out beyond my greatest expectations when he went north with you." He beamed, spreading his hands wide. "I think he hoped Carlisle was beyond our reach. It wasn't.

He held out longer than I thought, so very loyal. Information was one thing, but to get him to bring the girl to us we had to use a little more persuasion."

I frowned.

"Yes, he was down one mother and one younger sibling before he agreed to do our bidding." Calchas laughed delightedly.

I recalled the timid woman in the corner of his old home, the young children he had left behind with her to go with Marina. Calchas had killed them. Poor Oban. All this time.

I had hoped to prolong the meal in order to spend precious moments in the same room as my daughter, though she sat out of reach, hunched in her chair while Calchas spewed his triumph. But even for her sake I could endure this no longer. I could not enable his delight at our misery for even a fraction of a second more.

"Why exactly are you telling me all this?" I asked, disgusted.

He threw a shoulder up in a shrug. "Why not?"

Much as he loved an audience, I knew there must be a point in explaining all this. He always had a plan; he did nothing without an underlying purpose.

"What is it you want?" I asked through gritted teeth.

"Haven't you been paying attention, my dear? I want everything."

Everything? What did that mean? He had me. The most I could do was tend the line.

"What do you want from *me*?" I needed to know. Was there a chance he wasn't going to kill me?

"All in good time, my dear." Calchas smiled, the overly solicitous pull of his lips as if he was a benefactor waiting to bestow the gift of a lifetime on me.

I glowered at him. I loathed him. Fidelma and Marcus too. I didn't care that they had been motivated to help others; they were the reason my daughter looked at me warily, and they were why Calchas held us in his power.

"Some things in life are so precious. One must savour them while they are available to us." He sipped his wine, closing his eyes as if to savour the moment itself.

"Now Marcus, let us leave these two lovely ladies to enjoy each other's company," he said abruptly, putting his wine down and sweeping out the door.

Marcus untangled himself from Féile who gripped on to him on learning she was to be left behind.

"Shh now, your mama will look after you. I'm not leaving you. I'll take you home before I go to the Mete, okay?" He unhooked her arms from around his leg as he turned to me. "She'll be okay, she's just... it's just a lot for her. I didn't know he was going to let her see you. I wasn't able to prepare her."

I nodded tightly, holding it together with everything inside me. The last thing Féile needed was for me to fall apart. They were going to let me spend what time remained before the Mete with her. I should have seen it coming; this was totally Calchas's style, every last drop of drama to be squeezed out of the steps he was making us dance.

Marcus was miserably stooped as he left the room. Féile sat tensely in her chair. She stubbornly refused to look at me, her chin tucked into her chest, her arms wrapped around herself.

"Féile, darling." I went to her and knelt by her chair.

She ducked around me and ran over to the far corner of the room, sitting down in between the wall and a great chest, tucking herself into a ball and putting her head down between her knees so she wouldn't have to look at me.

I sat on the ground in front of her, measuring my next move.

"I've missed you," I said to the dark curls. "We looked for you," I tried again. "We looked everywhere. We looked up in the attics, and in the cellars, and in the stables. We searched all the houses in Carlisle and out in the forests. We even looked in the birdhouses."

A dark eye lifted to glare at me in scorn at my poor attempt at lightness.

I widened my eyes. "We did. We thought maybe you had magicked yourself small and hidden away somewhere to have a sleep."

Féile lifted her head a little more and shook it. Her mouth set.

"Oban gave me to a man," she said.

"We didn't know, baby," I explained. She must have thought we had sent her away. If Oban had taken her, then she hadn't been pulled away against her will; she would have gone with him willingly. He was a friend, and she would have thought he'd done it at our request. "We couldn't find you anywhere. We came here looking for you."

It was too much to tell her that we had amassed an army to get her back.

She contemplated me, her jaw still set, mistrust in her eyes.

I heard the door open behind me. *No,* I screamed silently, *too soon, too soon.* I hadn't had enough time with her yet. I drank in every piece of her precious face, storing it in my mind, desperate to experience every last second.

Her face was blank as she looked behind me and then her face disintegrated inwards and she started to convulse in sobs.

I reached for her as arms appeared from behind me and did the same. They were taking her from me! Panic beat furiously inside me, even as her little fists started to beat at the man who knelt behind me and pulled us both into him.

I pushed at the arm that was enveloping me, even as I heard Féile manage to blub out between sobs, "Dada, Dada."

Twisting around, I discovered it was indeed Gideon. His strong arms pulled us both close as Féile broke down and released all the grief and anger in her little body.

We were here.

We had come for her.

Finally.

She wept until she was weak from it, the whole time Gideon murmuring soothing words to her, telling her how much we loved her, how much we had missed her, even as his helpless eyes looked over her head at me. Because what he couldn't say, what he couldn't promise her, was that we would never leave her again. That wasn't a promise we could make, no matter how badly we wanted to, no matter how badly she needed to hear it.

Eventually, she quietened. Gideon gathered her up in his arms and stood up from where we had remained huddled together on the floor. She whimpered at the movement and clutched tightly to his shirt, her little fist holding on to the open neck as if she would never let him go.

Gideon surveyed the room before finally settling on a wide embroidered couch that sat in the pale autumn sunlight that streamed through the window at their back. He let Féile curl up in his lap while he put his arms tightly around her.

My heart split at the sight of them. This, this was the knife throw Calchas had aimed for my heart. Bravo, clean strike.

"Have you eaten?" I asked.

Gideon shook his head, seeming as disinterested as I had been earlier. But needing to do something useful, I busied myself preparing a plate and brought it back to the couch.

"You need to eat," I insisted. He gave me a bleak look.

I picked up a piece of food and put it to his lips, realising with disgust that it was the same morsel Calchas had tempted me with earlier. It had the same effect on Gideon as it had on me though, and he allowed me to feed him the rest of the plate, never moving his arms from their tight hold on our baby girl.

When he was done, I put the plate back on the table and, returning, sat on the couch beside them.

"She's asleep," I whispered, running a gentle hand down the side of her face. Her skin was red and blotchy from the outburst of emotion, her cheeks sticky from her tears. I used the hem of my sleeve to dry them.

Then I turned my attention to the solemn-eyed warrior who held her.

"We don't have long; they'll come for us soon."

I savoured the warmth at my side that ran the length of my body as I sat beside Gideon. Spread across our laps, the snuggled body of our little girl exuded a warmth that went all the way through me like a golden shaft of light, heating me from the inside, bathing me in joy. However fleeting it might be...

Spread out around me was the white gown, my dress for the arena. The seconds sped by; we couldn't have much longer. My tightening arms disturbed Féile, and she stirred grumpily, her body twisting to scowl at me before her eyes widened in recognition and remembrance.

"Mama." She beamed, and tucked herself further into me. Her eyes shut tight again immediately.

"Féile," I said, but her eyes remained fastened. A snag caught in my throat. "I won't disappear."

Not yet.

Gideon's arm behind me moved and the fingers tickled at her belly, making her squirm and giggle. She pulled away only to relaunch herself at Gideon on a counter attack. I pulled myself out of the way of the ensuing battle.

The door opened, and our laughter ceased.

The two girls from earlier entered and frowned at me reproachfully in my now crumpled dress.

We stood to meet them and I finally registered that Gideon was no longer in the ruins of his attire from last night's ball. Unlike me, he was wearing the regulation black, but it was tailored differently to the standard uniform of the accused. There were no sleeves, thus leaving his arms bare and displaying all those swirling tattoos. His collar was low and tailored in a slightly more Briton fashion, revealing his strong collarbone and a glimpse of the muscles of his chest, but I had a feeling that the purpose was again to show off his tattoos, to emphasise his wildness.

One of the women stepped forward silently and handed me the mask I had left behind in the White Tower.

I swallowed, looking back behind Gideon to where Féile had curled herself into a tight ball on the wide couch.

"Do we all need to go?"

They shook their heads in unison.

"Just me?" I asked.

They nodded and moved forward to help me get ready.

"I'm fine. I don't need help." But my protests had little effect, and they set to fixing my dress and redoing my hair and makeup.

While my costume didn't appear to fit a trip to the arena, I knew that was where I was bound.

Gideon and Féile sat watching, blank-eyed, all the joy sucked out of the room. Finished, the girls exited the room as Praetorian Alvar and the other sentinels arrived.

Gideon rose from the couch, poised for attack.

Alvar grinned over at Gideon as if daring him to come at him. I glared at Gideon warningly. *Don't fall for it, stay here. Stay with Féile.* He nodded grimly and hoisted her up onto his hip like a shield to prevent him from doing what his warrior's instincts would be demanding of him.

I casually crossed the room and gave Féile a peck on her forehead before I locked gazes with Gideon. I gave him a small smile and kissed Féile again.

"If Marcus comes, you go with him, okay, poppet?" I said, as much for Gideon as for our daughter. Marcus had promised to be back for her; the last thing she needed was to see her Dada gut the man she looked to for comfort here behind the walls.

"See you later..." I said hopefully as I followed Alvar and his group of guards out the door. I surveyed the heavily armed contingent. "It's a little much," I observed drily as he handed me the white mask to put on. Then we retraced our steps to the discreet entrance at the back of the Governor's Palace and the car that awaited to transport me to my fate.

Chapter Twenty-Six

I trailed behind Alvar through the all too familiar golden sandstone corridor that ran underneath the arena, coming to a halt just inside the entrance to the waiting sands.

The thrum of the crowd poured through as we waited, but there was no indication from Alvar as to the reason for the delay. Another group of praetorians approached, red cloaks not entirely obscuring the tall, dark-haired man they had in their custody and from whom they kept a wary distance. The noise gradually grew to a pounding, vibrating roar, the mob indicating their impatience by stomping their feet on the floor of the amphitheatre. It was a sound that had hailed the arrival of a great many accused over the centuries.

I felt the anxiety inside me begin to pulse in response. An angled eyebrow was slanted my way in inquiry from where he was held on the other side of the entrance. Gideon had never been all that interested in learning more about the city – during the good times we had stuck to safer subjects like Féile, or the men he trained. My life behind the walls rarely came up, and when it did it was innocuous stuff – mostly my surprise at yet another primitive Briton tool compared to whatever was used instead in the Empire. I had wondered whether his lack of curiosity was inherent or whether it stemmed from his disdain of the Empire or his dislike of any mention of Devyn. Whatever the reason, it left me a little short of time to explain the justice system in which he was about to be tried.

A guard handed me a second mask; it was black, and the eyes were sealed. Whatever courtesies were being provided to me, Gideon was not to receive them, it seemed.

"It's where we hold our trials. You won't be able to see and you need to do what they ask." I looked back at Alvar. "Does he stand or kneel?"

"Kneel." Alvar smirked.

That meant he was declaring himself not guilty and begging the mercy and judgement of the city. It was to be a full performance then.

"You understand?" I asked Gideon, who didn't seem too concerned. "You'll be asked how you plead and you must kneel; it means you defy the accusation and wish for the evidence to be judged by the city."

"Deny murder?" A dark eyebrow quirked. "Why would I deny it? I did it, he deserved it, and I have no intention of saying otherwise."

"It doesn't matter anyway." The tempo of the pounding was getting faster. I didn't have time to explain. "It's not about that; it's theatre. It's all for show, a show that the praetor is directing. And we have to dance to his tune."

Gideon looked mutinous, he was used to making his own choices; he had a code he lived by, and once you knew what it was, he wasn't as unpredictable as he at first appeared.

"Why?" He shrugged. "He's going to execute me anyway, right?"

I stared at him. Had he not been paying attention? Comply and you were rewarded. Did he think he had been granted my company and that of our daughter for free? That there hadn't been a threat implicit in the gift?

"For Féile's sake," I said.

A small line appeared between his brows but he nodded grimly. "Anything else I should know?"

I lifted a shoulder. I knew as little as he did.

"You won't be able to see until the vote is done." I showed him the black mask in my hand.

I looked down at my white dress; this was a stark change in protocol. What it meant I had no idea. As always, Calchas was way ahead of us, manipulating us like puppets, orchestrating the mob to whatever end he desired.

Despite all my efforts, all my new power and abilities, I was in his clutches once more. As I had been the last time, from the moment he had stolen me from my mother's arms. By working on the ley line, by prioritising the many over my own daughter, I had played right into their hands. All that work for nothing. I had weakened myself – and I had failed my daughter.

I returned to the moment and placed a hand on each side of Gideon's face. I loved him. Not as I had loved Devyn. Not in a way that could be measured as greater or lesser, because that was not how love worked. But fiercely, truly. It glowed inside me.

I bit down hard on my lip, I couldn't tell him here, surrounded by guards and about to take the sands. No, I would see him again. There would be a better time.

I placed the mask on his face and then I was pulled back by Alvar, and he was led out to the waiting crowd, his arms in chains behind him.

The roar of the crowd erupted as the accused made his entrance. They would be able to tell he was a Briton from his bare, tattooed arms. The speculation today must have been rampant. Even if news of the events of last night hadn't got out, there were so many things that were out of kilter. I could only assume that the rest of the Treaty party hadn't been allowed to leave the city this morning. Some, I knew, had got out of the ballroom before the net had closed, but had they made it out of the palace? If they had, where would they go? It was as difficult to leave the city as it was to enter it. There would have been nowhere to run.

Traditionally, there was no regular Mete while the Britons were in town. So to have a Briton starring in one, centre stage, would have the crowd frenzied. There was a noticeably ugly tone to the noise: here was a Briton, one of the Britons they held responsible for the illness ripping through the province. And he was at their mercy

Calchas had never planned for us to leave. He had always intended to throw one of us to the mob – it was so obvious. A sacrifice would confirm that the council were right, that the natives were to blame for all the citizens' woes, and vengeance was being served up. My work on the ley line would confirm this narrative. We had played right into his hands. Or rather, Marcus had manoeuvred us into doing precisely as Calchas wanted. As always.

A tug on my arm told me it was my turn, and the exquisite mask was dropped down over my face and my hood secured. As I stepped into the arena, the tone of the crowd changed to mirror my own confusion at my role in this particular presentation.

The baying for blood ceased as I made my way onto the

sands. I lifted my chin, and moved to join the figure in black who was standing alone in the centre. But then I was tugged to the left, and led to the side of the arena, adjacent to where Gideon stood in front of the council's balcony. The crowd's roar dropped to a murmur as whispered conversations broke out. I pictured the image I made: a woman gowned in white, the colour of innocence, with a vague hint of the exoticism of the Celt in my outfit, and a whiff of magic in the robes that enveloped me. On the one hand, he offered the crowd a demon to condemn, but I was being presented differently. That sneaking suspicion that Calchas did not mean to have me killed grew.

The council were already in place and alongside them sat the most senior of our delegation: the King of Mercia and the Steward of York, Bronwyn, heir of Gwynedd, and the Prince of Powys. There was no sign of Marina or Alec; perhaps a few others had also slipped the net. Fidelma – Elizabeth of York – sat on the other side of the balcony with the senators to watch her son face trial in Londinium, the city for which she had betrayed us.

Rion looked stonily ahead, not acknowledging me, or Gideon, or the crowd. Richard Mortimer and Fidelma were transfixed on the lone figure below, a shadow on the golden sands, his blood already as good as spilt.

The praetor made his way into the arena and the roar amped up as he was greeted by the mob, ready to watch the drama unfold. He stood at the edge of the balcony with no one at his shoulder; he was the single power in the city now.

His arms dropped, and the crowd hushed to hear him speak.

"Friends, people of Londinium," he began, "I come to you today with a heavy heart and wicked news."

The pause for effect was perfect. Even the wind flapping at the banners ceased in anticipation of his next words.

"One of our city's most beloved sons has been cut down. A member of our council. A man who raised his son alone when his wife was tragically taken from them by the dreadful illness which has blighted our city. A man who grew to become a true leading light, the saviour of so many."

The hush remained, confirming my suspicion that last night's events must not have hit the feeds, despite the many witnesses.

"My people, I speak with great regret of Governor Dolon, who was violently taken from us before his time."

The crowd's roar was a curdling bay for blood. They would suspect now who waited upon the sands, because who else could it be but the governor's murderer? The average citizen probably cared very little for Matthias Dolon, but Calchas's eulogy was perfect. The arena was a slavering hound as it quieted, waiting for the familiar words. The din dropped.

"Gideon Mortimer, son of the Steward of York, man of the King of Mercia." There was a mass intake of breath as the pedigree of the Wilder who waited their judgement was revealed. Not just any Briton, but one who was in his own way an elite, a noble of the untamed lands to the north. The mask he wore was for optics and nothing else as his anonymity was stripped away.

"You are accused of crimes against the Code. How do you plead?"

Gideon hesitated. It was not in him to bow, much less to kneel. Frustratingly independent, he marched to the beat of his own drum, the world be damned. Calchas's threat was explicit though, and he called the tune, so for Féile's sake Gideon sank slowly to his knees as instructed and the mob was jubilant.

They had been informed that this man was the murderer and there was no pretence at justice. Now they wanted to see Calchas's greatest ever production play out on their screens.

Idly, I wondered how many of the accused who had taken the sands during Calchas's reign had been somehow manipulated here by a change in fortunes, or a chance temptation tripping across their path. Accused Codebreakers presenting the mob with a case that quieted unrest at just the right time, a rival cut down before he could become a real threat. My only surprise was that I hadn't seen it before.

The screens high above the arena began to play out the events of last night. The lack of cameras in the Governor's Palace had not persisted into Dolon's reign, it seemed. Dolon's choice or the praetor's?

The evidentiary reel rolled, showing Gideon ripping through the sentinels. A nightmare come to life as the camera captured the flicker of the otherworldly Griffin, the ferociousness of his attack and a close up of Governor Dolon bleeding on the ground. Followed by me in Marcus's arms, for all the world looking as though he was protecting me. My face was disguised by the mask I had worn, my gown unmistakeably in the Briton style though. My identity seemed not to be part of tonight's reveal. No, Calchas would be waiting, but the seed was sown; a woman in Marcus's arms would be noted, commented upon.

I looked up at the Imperial balcony to find Calchas smiling in my direction. This, this was why my mask allowed me to see. So I wouldn't miss the show. He couldn't see my face, which at this point wouldn't reflect much more than my confusion. No, it was so that I could see what he was doing, so he could show me how clever he was.

And he was clever, for I had yet again done precisely as the hidden puppet master had decreed, and yet again I'd had no idea what he was doing until it was too late.

The reel stopped and the focus moved back to Calchas once more as he raised his hand, his thumb to the side as the voting commenced. The seconds moved heavily by. Blind under his mask, Gideon would have no idea why the deathly silence had descended. I swayed slightly, my legs giving way because my body was still not fully recovered; the endlessness of this moment was truly too much to bear.

The gong finally sounded.

A sentinel stepped forward, his movement hurried, jerky as he reached up and removed Gideon's mask. Gideon stood up, at some unheard direction, revealing his impassive face to the crowd which had stood in judgement over him.

Calchas spoke, a thin, satisfied smile on his lips. "Friends, you have seen the terrible events that took place, and your eyes have been clear. Gideon Mortimer, son of York, for the heinous crime you have committed upon the body of a citizen of this city, you have been utterly condemned and are found guilty by every last man and woman within the walls of this proud city. The only pity is that you can pay for this crime but once. But that payment must be made. You will return to this place and in full sight of the city pay the ultimate price of your life as a forfeit. The sentence is death."

No! My burst to run to Gideon was sharply halted before it could begin as strong hands gripped me from behind.

"Now, now, Donna Shelton," Alvar's voice whispered in my ear. "None of that. I believe we had an agreement."

My legs threatened to go from under me as the adrenaline was sucked out of me, leaving me sagging in the praetorian's arms. He was the only thing holding me upright as I watched Gideon being marched from the sand.

I had known the outcome from the moment I had woken this morning, but inevitability was no protection against the shock of hearing those words condemning the man you loved.

The crowd was subdued as I took my place at the centre of the arena. The atmosphere was one of curiosity, the mob intrigued by the accused presented for judgement. Their lust for vengeance on the Britons they blamed for the illness had been quenched for now. Today's offering was something new, something different, and they were willing to let it play out.

The council were seated, dignified, not chatting among themselves as they usually did at a regular Mete. As I stood facing them, I was grateful not to be standing here blind as was traditional. I felt stronger today. Spending the afternoon with the Griffin had restored me somewhat – physically at least, though my magic was not yet fully returned. But it was getting there. They had captured us when I'd been at my weakest, and every moment that had passed had allowed me to regain my strength – and exponentially so in Gideon's arms.

The distinctive music was played again as the pieces were reset, and Calchas stepped forward once more, but instead of standing alone as he had earlier, now he had company. My brother.

Rion looked regal and handsome in a dark-blue Celtic-style shirt, his bright hair flowing free onto his shoulders. He had a gold circlet on his head, and no sleeves concealing the flow of tattoos down his biceps and onto his forearms.

Calchas stood on the edge of the balcony and held his arms wide to begin his speech.

"Citizens, people of Londinium. We call you here today to judge yet another who has wronged you, one who is accused of crimes against the Code. However, our esteemed guest has pleaded to be allowed to speak on her behalf."

Incredulous murmuring began with sections of the crowd booing as they realised that the praetor intended to allow the Wilder lord beside him to speak.

Calchas held his arms high until the noise stopped.

"We are a just people, and when presented with a case, a merciful people. Let it not be said that we do not extend this justice," his voice rose, "this mercy, to all within our walls, be they citizen or guest."

Rion bowed his head slightly in acknowledgement of the wise and generous words of his host.

"People of Londinium," he began, "I am Rion Deverell, King of Mercia. As a child, my sister was lost to us. She might have perished were it not for this great city. She was found and raised here among you, as one of you."

A murmur began, speculation rippling across the amphitheatre.

"She returned to us, and there was great rejoicing among the peoples of this island, for my mother's heir was restored to us, and once again a Lady of the Lake walked amongst us."

He looked toward the praetor as he continued to plead my case.

"She was still a young girl, and she mistakenly gave her heart to a young man who deceived her, and who led her to commit crimes that were judged by you, the friends and family who had given her so much. He led her away from the safety and security of Londinium. She returns now, and she offers her life for the wrongs she has done you. But I would plead with you not to judge her harshly, for she was young and led astray." He paused. "I would beg you to forgive her. To show her the mercy for which you are famed."

He bowed his head to the crowd and, reaching up, lifted the circlet from his head and laid it on the balcony, an offering to the mob. His kingship for their mercy. What was he doing? He couldn't do that! What did it mean? Was it just a gesture, or did it have some greater significance?

Calchas stepped forward and picked up the crown with a smile.

"You do us great honour, Lord Deverell," he said, inclining his head slightly. It was an acknowledgement, but not in any sense intended to be mistaken as more than that. Even his term of address was less than it should be. "Who amongst us does not understand the waywardness of youth? Such a sad tale."

He stood silent for a moment in contemplation.

"I will speak to the accused."

He turned and left the box. There was uproar in the crowd; this was unprecedented. The councillors were all looking at each other and some were standing. Rion had backed up and taken his place with the rest of the Britons where Bronwyn was whispering urgently to him.

I waited on the sand as the figure clad in ceremonial robes emerged from the tunnels and made his way over to me in what I supposed was meant to be a dignified manner. He came to a halt a few feet from me – a large man facing a smaller white-robed figure on the otherwise empty sands. I suppose, given the carefully arranged image of it all, I should be grateful my delicate mask concealed my terribly inelegant snort.

"You don't like my little show?" the praetor asked, splaying his hands to take in the amphitheatre.

"Am I supposed to?" I threw back. Here on the sands, I had defied him before and I would do it again. I would defy this man until my last breath.

"Your brother pleads for your life," he said. "I myself found it most touching."

Calchas raised his hands, and the crowd grew quiet, so silent as we stood there waiting that you could hear a pin drop.

"Citizens, people of Londinium, people of the Province of Britannia. One amongst you stands accused of crimes against the Code. How do you plead?"

The roar was deafening. Some cheered for me to stand – possibly those who had been swayed by the handsome king begging for my life, believing the council would show mercy. Most urged me to kneel. They wanted their fun, they wanted to see my crimes played out on screen. They wanted to judge my guilt for themselves.

Once I would have stood. I would have thrown myself on the mercy of the crowd, to see, to judge, but I knew better now. There was no justice. The evidence would be curated, presented to sell to the crowd whatever predetermined fate the council had decided upon.

I tilted my head at Calchas. Which way did he want this to play out?

"Kneel," he said, smiling beatifically.

Despite my awareness that Calchas had already decided how every last moment of this played out, I couldn't bring myself to bend my knees. My fists curled at my sides. This man had sentenced Gideon to death, had stolen my child, had killed my mother. Fury filled me, and I could feel the essence of the earth beneath me, and the sky above me, begin to seep into my bones, into my soul. I was not the same defenceless girl I had been the last time I had stood here.

"Tut, tut, Cassandra," he said as I failed to comply with his direction. "So very many lives in my hands. Do you care nothing for theirs, if not your own?"

I glared at him from behind the mask. He smirked a little

and then I did it. I knelt, bowing my head to the man I hated most in this world.

The last time I had defied him, revealing Devyn to be Briton, I had been alone. Devyn had already been condemned, and there had been no one else who mattered. Now he had my daughter, my brother, my friends. My shoulders dropped.

"There, was that so very hard?" he asked, his fingers lightly touching my shoulder.

The crowd was alive with anticipation, an electric hum rippling around the arena and across the city.

He put his hands down in front of me.

"Give me your hands," he said softly.

I did as directed, and he raised me to stand. The mob screamed, beside themselves at being robbed of their entertainment. Calchas released one hand, raising his to silence the crowd once more. He was like a conductor, playing each hum and roar with the flick of his hand.

"We have been asked to show mercy," he called to the crowd. "While I understand the foolishness of youth may be owed some blame, and I might wish to grant some leniency, I do not, *cannot*, because this girl has been judged by you before. It is your right and her fate that she be judged by the great citizens of Londinium here today."

He was a virtuoso now, whipping them up, and for the crescendo he pushed back the hood of my white cloak, and my distinctive bright hair fell in a wave down my back. The talented hands of the girls this morning had somehow bound it in such a way that the hood coming down had freed it. Then he reached for the delicate mask concealing my face and revealed me. The crowd erupted as they recognised me.

I stumbled back as the force of their emotions buffeted me. The noise of the roar was unlike anything I had ever

411

experienced. I blinked as I attempted to absorb what was happening, to stay in the moment. Up on the screens flashed the devastated faces of Camilla and Graham Shelton. Unlike last time when they had been all too quick to disown me, tonight they were in the crowd and my father's arms wrapped around his crying wife as she reached for me. That made no sense; she had barely cared for me when she was raising me and I had been gone for years. This show of motherly grief was entirely out of character.

Then the screen showed Marcus's face – not in the Courtenay box though. No, he must have taken his father's place with the council. He was standing, his green eyes gleaming in his gaunt, shocked face – very shocked for someone who had sat and partaken of a meal with me only hours earlier.

I looked back at Calchas. I didn't understand.

The notes rang out, heralding the start of my evidentiary reel. It played scenes which had been shown the last time I had stood upon the sands, but this time they were interspersed with other scenes from that time. Not evidence of Codebreaking but geared towards whatever slant Calchas was playing out.

Marcus and me dancing in the ruins at Richmond, us walking hand in hand along a street, the night of my graduation as he shielded me from the paps, a close up of our entwined hands as we stood here on the sands facing trial the last time. A shot of me pushing Devyn away when he attempted to kiss me in the White Tower the night of our trial, when I had been wearing the handfast band and before his proximity had reminded me of my true affections, Marcus busting in and me running from the room with him.

They showed another scene on a beach far beyond the city.

412

It was the Holy Isle raid, the sentinels loading the mistletoe onto boats, Marcus jumping onto a ship and then turning to look at me. Then me again, screaming, reaching out to the camera as I was held by Gideon and Rion. Screaming for Devyn, but that wasn't apparent to the crowd; as far as they were concerned I was screaming for the boy they had last seen me handfasted to. The boy who was returning from his mission to find a treatment for the illness – successfully, though the cost was our separation. I remained behind on the beach, held against my will by the Wilders. Or at least, that's the story that was being broadcast across the city.

He was twisting everything. There was a last look at Marcus's devastated face as the ships carried him away, and I fell to the sands. Then, more recent scenes, me looking stressed and unhappy in the company of the Briton delegation, arriving for the masquerade, dancing in Marcus's arms. Then finally me in Marcus's arms at the end of the ball, his father dead in front of us.

The whole thing had rushed by. I was still trying to process it as Calchas raised his hand, his thumb extended to the side, and the seconds until my fate was decided began to count down. He had twisted everything, changed it to look much more sympathetic to me.

"Why?" I asked, dazed. But I knew already.

"Why make you look as if you can be redeemed?" he whispered into the silence. "Because I have use for you, dear Cassandra. Why else?"

The gong sounded and we waited until a runner finally came to whisper the results in the praetor's ear.

"Citizens, your vote displays your loyalty to the Code, the Code by which we live and by which you have already judged this accused. However, I sense, like me, that you are moved by her brother's words, that you are torn by the love you once held for this child of our city. One who strayed but now returns to us. To her mother and father, a lost daughter returned. To her betrothed, who after the loss of his father glimpses joy in the return of the love he thought stolen from him. Your verdict is 60%. I hear your cry for mercy, for leniency." He projected his voice up into the audience, up to the balconies above, turning so all could see his great wisdom in interpreting the vote. "But I must weigh our desire to show clemency while still recognising the importance of adhering to the Code and the severity of crimes committed against it. I will take this night to consider the sentence, and we will return here tomorrow and right all wrongs here upon the sands, as we have done through the ages."

He looked back at me and laid a gentle hand on the side of my face, smiling with his dead eyes. "Now, we discuss terms."

With a whirl of his robes, he was gone, and I was left alone on the sand.

Chapter Twenty-Seven

T here was no sign of Gideon by the time I made it back to the tunnels. After the crowds had dispersed, I was led out to a waiting car under cover of a canopy. Calchas was taking no chances; I wasn't entirely sure what he was guarding against.

There was no chance of anyone coming to my rescue. The Britons were at a severe disadvantage this side of the wall; there was no resourceful, tech-savvy Devyn to give me hope of escape. The few Britons who remained loose in the city would have no idea how to aid me. Though it seemed I was not entirely in need of saving, Calchas having confirmed my suspicions that he had a use for me yet. I frowned. I needed to figure it out, but I was still too tired from the ley line, too worn and numb by the emotional tumult of the events of this day. Gideon's sentence was death.

I was returned to the empty room in the White Tower where a new evening gown was waiting. I pulled off my penitent's white robes, recognising them for what they were now.

Calchas had never intended to let me die on the sands. He needed me to heal the ley line, to keep it in check from the imbalance that threatened the destruction of the land. I had done what I could, but it hadn't been enough to heal it and he planned to keep me. His very own pet druid, and he would do it by rematching me with Marcus.

Eventually, I was led down the hall to the dining table for the negotiations. The Steward of York, seated beside a frozen Fidelma, looked fit to explode. I was led to the foot of the table where Gideon, at his most indolent, sat beside his parents. Facing him, on my left was Marcus beside Bronwyn and Rion.

Praetorian guards were positioned at the walls where usually servants might wait in attendance.

The praetor entered and took a seat at the head of the table facing me, waving to a guard to fill his glass and those around the table. He waited until they were all filled and then took his glass, raising it for a toast.

"To friends and treaties old and new," he said. When no one responded, he looked around the table. "I see one of our most important guests is absent. But it is far too late in the evening for little ones to join us, don't you think?"

Message received, we all duly raised our glasses and drank to the toast.

Calchas sat back in his chair and proceeded to eat his meal while we all sat stiffly around the table, a set of players waiting for him to give us our lines. But the praetor proceeded to blithely eat his meal as if us sitting down to meals was a daily occurrence.

Eventually, Richard Mortimer was unable to restrain himself any longer.

"What did you do?" he snarled at his former wife.

Fidelma's expression was bitter as she explained again her

discussions during a Treaty renewal over twenty years ago with the seemingly friendly new praetor. "I told him what would happen if the city continued to deal only in technology and ignore the ley lines, that it was not sustainable. That the Lady of the Lake could help."

"There was a reason the lady didn't attend the Treaty Renewals," the steward growled, his expression thunderous as he listened to the woman he had once called wife attempt to explain the indefensible. "You persuaded her to come here, to tend the line, to put her trust in these..."

Rion sat in stony silence, his eyes hooded, looking down at the table.

"She trusted you. You were her closest friend." He spoke in such a low voice that it was difficult to hear him. "She brought the children."

"I don't know why she did that," Fidelma responded. "At the time, I thought it meant she knew she would be safe."

"But she wasn't safe," Rion roared, rearing up out of his seat, the veins pulsing in his forehead.

Calchas waved back the sentinels who had taken hold of Rion at his outburst, delighted at the drama. Rion's magic must be suppressed, or Calchas was awfully confident that none of us would defy him while he had Féile. Which was all too true. Apart from the Steward of York, whose concern would be more for the legacy of the lake gift and less for the beloved child, but of all of us he had the least magic in his veins; as a Mortimer his bloodline was ancient enough that he would be stronger than the average latent, but nowhere near as potent as the other bloodlines that sat around this table.

Fidelma's lips were bloodless as her body seemed to curl in on itself and Rion shrugged off the sentinels before stiffly sitting down once more. The heaviest of silences resumed. Nobody wanted to provide further entertainment.

"What do you want?" I asked baldly. I was sick of him. Sick of his games.

"What we all want," Calchas smiled. "A happy ever after."

I flicked a glance to Gideon whose gaze met mine. Did such a thing even exist?

"Oh, my dear," he said, catching our exchange. "I'm afraid that won't be possible. But perhaps something with a little less tragedy could be arranged if you so wish it?"

"What does that mean?"

"Perhaps Gideon's— You don't mind if I call you Gideon, do you?" he enquired, moving on without waiting for an answer. "Perhaps Gideon's ending might be delayed."

"Delayed?" I asked.

"Hmm, so abrupt. Let's say his current sentence was to be lifted. What might you be willing to pay?"

I was confused. Was Calchas really offering to let Gideon live?

"You will let my son go?" Fidelma asked.

"Why not?" Calchas smirked at our disbelief that Gideon's life was on the table despite his recent sentencing on the sands.

"But I killed your friend," Gideon pointed out unhelpfully.

"Matthias Dolon was hardly my friend. You did me a favour." Calchas's smile encompassed the entire table, including Marcus who sat gauntly quiet. "Matthias was a thorn; he truly hated everything about the natives. Though he also enjoyed power, and was torn between restoring his son to the York throne and clearing the land of vermin and replanting it with citizens fleeing the Maledictio. What grand plans he had. But I had my own plans, and isn't this more fun?"

He splayed his hands out to take in the room, the city, the

country – who knew? As far as he was concerned, it was all his. And with magic and technology at his command, who would be able to stop him?

"What is it you want?" Rion cut across him, as annoyed as the rest of us by his games.

He licked his lips. "I want her power," he said.

"That's not possible," I protested.

"No." Calchas sighed. "So I must make do with you. In my power."

My gut clenched. As predicted, I was trapped, but I was going to make him pay.

"You'll let them all go, including Gideon?" I asked. It was more than I had hoped for. "And I have to stay? That's it, that's the deal?"

"Ah, well, I already have everything I need right now," the praetor said smugly. "So it's going to take a little more than that."

What more could he possibly want? What more did we have to give?

"I want you to marry Marcus as before. And then, all of you," he said, lifting his knife from the meal he was the only one currently enjoying and waving it around, "are going to swear fealty to them, to Londinium."

"No," the steward baulked.

Bronwyn swung to Rion at her side. As the representative for the princes of Cymru and her father in Kernow, she would take her lead from Mercia. Rion sat stone-faced. He couldn't contemplate this; he had given his life to protecting what he had left, to his country. Surely he wouldn't agree to this, even to save the life of his friend.

Fidelma put a hand on Calchas's arm. "Why to Londinium?" she asked. "Why not to you?"

Calchas was always one step ahead, and yet I could see the twisted logic. Unlike Matthias Dolon, it wasn't the appearance of power that satisfied him. It was the control of that power.

"This way he gets everything," I said. "And everyone."

"No resistance – he gets the whole island," Lord Richard concurred.

Bronwyn was horrified. "The Albans will never agree. They aren't even bound to the current Treaty."

"Of course they will." The praetor smiled. "They very badly want something I've got."

"Féile," I provided to the group, as they tried to figure out Calchas's cryptic smugness. Life in the south with its failing lines was hard; how much harder would the failure of crops be in a land that already required hardiness to survive? "He has Féile and she is the next Lady of the Lake. What we had hesitated at, the praetor has no problem giving: the hand of a child in marriage. Do you?"

"None at all," he said.

"Why would we agree to this?" Bronwyn asked, with a sideways glance as Rion continued to stay silent.

"Well if you don't, your tribes will be leaderless, your land will be without the magic that is keeping the curse at bay, and I will still rule the entire island, just with a great deal more dead people in it than there are now."

Right.

A stunned silence fell over the room as the alternative was laid before us. Calchas would see the world destroyed rather than share it. He had worked towards this goal for decades. If he had to let the ley lines die and hundreds of thousands starve then he would.

"We have no choice," Rion finally said.

"You can't agree to this." Lord Richard spoke slowly, his eyes trained on Rion alone.

"He already has." Calchas beamed.

The crown on the balcony. Rion had seen this coming. Had already bargained his country for my life. For the lives of his people, the life that flowed through his lands. Sacrificing their freedom. And mine. If Rion saw no way out, then the others would not find one.

"I'll do it," I said. "But you let Gideon go free. And he takes Féile with him."

Calchas's eyes narrowed. Féile was part of his plan.

"You get what you want, just not yet," I said. "You'll still have me. They'll bring her back when she's of age. I want this for her. I want her to grow up with a parent who loves her."

"You don't love her?"

I threw an evil eye at Fidelma, a sour taste in my mouth. "I do love her. She is my world. But I won't after a while, isn't that right, Fidelma? In a few years, I'll be…"

I petered out, in apparent horror at the fate that awaited me. I gripped Gideon's hand beneath the table, begging him to remain silent. He knew, as the others did not, that I still needed him as I had before, that the lady of Avalon's words had been fork-tongued. I needed him. But I would not have Féile grow up here with me when she could have so much more.

"I assume letting the Griffin stay with me is something you have considered?" I asked, unsure if I was pushing to distract him from the question of Féile or whether some part of me was begging to have him remain with me. If Gideon was with me, there was still a chance, together we would find a way to break Calchas's grip.

"And dismissed. Maybe before, but his gift has grown stronger. It's enough to have you here; his presence isn't even useful for leverage, or soon won't be." Calchas sighed. "Shame you won't be as delightful as you are now. So reactive, so emotional. Always in love. But this one, no, no, he must go."

"And Féile with him," I demanded again.

"If you insist. After you've married Marcus," he reminded me. "A proper marriage, mind you. You know how I've always dreamed of you two having a family."

Children strong in the blood, with magic that he would own. Once he had them... He had promised the Albans Féile, the Lake bloodline was strictly matriarchal, but if anything were to happen to her before she came of age... Would the gift pass to another? One Calchas had not promised away? Horror filled me.

But then another option whispered to me: the ley line would take me if I let it. Everyone would be free; once they were beyond the walls I could just let go. Calchas's leverage would be gone. I closed my eyes and nodded.

"Excellent," he said, "a celebration. Bring me champagne. A rare treat, as the lands across the channel increasingly fail, these are precious bottles indeed but we have a betrothal to toast."

"They'll need to divorce," Fidelma pointed out quietly. Calchas looked surprised. For a man who had planned out every step, the fact that he had missed something as obvious as my current marriage was unlike him. He must have been too caught up in celebrating his own splendid cleverness.

"They are married?" he asked coldly. Interesting, so neither Fidelma nor Oban had told him everything they knew.

"It is a task of moments," Fidelma hurried on at the displeased expression taking over Calchas's face. "Divorce under our laws is merely a matter of mutual consent."

"Consent then." Calchas sounded annoyed.

Fidelma came around the table, over to our side.

"Give me your hands." She took our hands and wrapped them in a cloth, binding them together. "Now say the words."

I wasn't sure what she meant. Gideon looked mutinous.

"It keeps you all alive," Fidelma commanded. "Do it."

Gideon's amber eyes met mine, and the emotions glowing in them did not match the words he spoke.

"I divorce thee." My heart felt crushed. I had little memory of exchanging vows, and our marriage had been an arrangement neither of us had really wanted but the words to release us refused to come.

"Say it," Calchas roared across the room.

I jumped, startled. I had been so caught up in the silent communication flowing between Gideon and me that I had barely remembered that there were others present at all.

"I divorce thee," I whispered from dry lips.

Fidelma unwrapped the cloth binding our hands, ceremoniously withdrawing my hand but Gideon snatched his back before his mother could touch him.

"Well done, Lady Mortimer," Calchas offered, his tone revealing that it had not escaped him that Fidelma had withheld information. "You've managed to separate Cassandra from her Griffin more successfully this time."

"What?"

Calchas smiled at my reaction to his bait, his humour restored. "Who do you think warned us to separate the lady and her Griffin? Who supplied a special little concoction so that he would have time to escort you north but no more than that? With the boy gone, why would you stay? Bonus benefit, we needed you to lead Marcus to the healing druids who could tell him more of the cure."

"Why?"

Fidelma's shoulders were bowed, her eyes shut tight against the revelation that it was her poison that had laced Devyn's blood when we broke free of the walls. But not so tight that they could contain the tears that rolled down her face before she covered it with her hands.

"That was how Marcus knew to make his way to the Holy Isle at midwinter," Rion seethed. "It always bothered me, how Marcus knew when the legions were hitting Anglesey, and when to have you there. The poisoning could have happened in Londinium, but to have word in Conwy from the city required help on the inside."

I looked at Marcus whose head tilted in confirmation. It may not have been by her hand, but Fidelma had supplied the poison and eventually death had found Devyn.

"Why?" I repeated. She owed me this.

Fidelma lifted her head, squaring her shoulders, flinching a little as she took in the man at my side before finally meeting my eyes. Had everything she had told me been a lie?

"The Griffin would demand that you stayed safe in the north. I saw how you looked at him. You would have done as he asked. I needed you to come to me, or at least to hold the line here until..." She tumbled over her words, her chin dropping as each word fell into an unforgiving void, the echo of it indefensible. "If he was gone... I felt nothing then."

She had cared solely for the restoration of the Strand line. I knew myself the all-consuming desire to be made whole that the ley line fostered in a person. She would not have cared for anything beyond that. She had played a double game, told me that Devyn would get me out – which he had – but she had worked with Matthias Dolon to make it happen, and that had been the price. I would never forgive her.

I couldn't look at her.

The guards returned with the requested bottles and a tray bearing two handfast cuffs. I recoiled. It had been years, but I hadn't forgotten the suffocation of my own will in favour of the state's until I didn't know that one had replaced the other. I wasn't ready. I swallowed. I needed to speak. Marcus glumly lifted one off the tray. I couldn't take my eyes off the remaining one. It was new.

"Wait," I said. "Not yet."

The praetor raised an eyebrow, displeased at my last-minute baulking. "I thought we had an agreement."

"We do, we do," I said hurriedly. He had stuck the knife in and twisted it with that revelation and was unprepared to grant the request, I could sense it in him. He loved the drama of balancing out punishment with mercy, to give the pain a twinge of sweetness, a delicious twist of the knife in the wound. "Just let me have some time. Let me have tonight."

Calchas narrowed his eyes at me. "There will be no escapes tonight. Féile is not in this building, and she will not be given to your erstwhile ex-husband until that cuff is on your arm."

I wouldn't get to say goodbye to her.

"Please—" I started.

"No, Cassandra. This is what you asked for, and this is what you will get." He was annoyed because he had already allowed more than he had planned to give me.

"At least let me have tonight. I never got to say goodbye to Devyn." I sent a dark, unforgiving look Marcus's way. His green eyes met mine, but not in guilt; something else glittered there… Defiance? I looked back at Calchas. He thrived on drama. Surely he wouldn't refuse me this? My pain, Marcus's guilt, and possible jealousy, Gideon's anguish at leaving, this was all catnip to the praetor. "I would like tonight to…"

Calchas's eyes widened in faux sympathy at me across the

table. "What terrible luck you've had with men. Let's hope third time's the charm."

He waved a hand in Marcus's direction who, with a bland smile, casually took a sip of his wine, his robe dropping below his wrist, revealing the flash of a wristband.

"Then I can have tonight?" I pressed. I wasn't sure why I was pushing this so hard. What were a few more hours? But my soul shuddered at the thought of that metal going back on my arm. My heart hurt at the thought of not getting to see my daughter one last time. I turned to look at Gideon. His eyes met mine steadfastly, burning with the anger he was burying inside for our daughter's sake. He would live. She would live. I needed to get him to take her far away from here. Once I was gone, Calchas's hold over the island would be too.

The praetor rolled his eyes, bored of my demands. "Once you have bid your prospective husband an appropriate good night."

Calchas was giving me this one thing, but only at the cost of adding an extra flourish to tonight's production. I smiled and nodded tightly.

"What guarantees will you give that you will treat our peoples well?" Rion asked. Now that the crux of the negotiation – my surrender – was over, the kings and princes of Briton were pushing for what terms they could get under the new Treaty which would leave them as nothing more than puppets on thrones.

I stared at the handfast cuff on the sideboard. My one advantage lay in Calchas underestimating who I was now. I was not the naive youth he had manipulated before, nor was I the fragile burnout that Fidelma saw me as. She didn't know that Gideon's presence restored me, or he wouldn't have been permitted near me. And I was already partially restored.

But that advantage would be gone once the cuff went on my arm. I had no way of knowing if I would be strong enough to resist its compulsion. Each further hour spent with Gideon gave me a greater chance. I looked again at Marcus. His jaw was locked as he stared at the table while the negotiations continued around us.

I had just given my life in favour of the hundreds of thousands who would die if I did not – was he satisfied now? For a second time, I had to give up the man I loved and agree to marry him. Would I remain compelled after our marriage? If Calchas had permitted Gideon to remain in Londinium I could have hoped for some moments of lucidity during which we could do something, find some way out of the binds in which Calchas had entangled us.

Marcus, aware of my gaze, looked up at me. His green eyes were direct, as they had been when he had promised to make it right only a few nights before. I had believed him then. He had tried to warn me at the ball, had accused me of being like his father in front of Calchas at lunch, but he hadn't known the extent of the disappeared, I recalled. He hadn't known. Calchas was making it appear as if Marcus had been knowingly part of their plans all along. But had he?

"Cassandra will journey to the ley line at Glastonbury once a year only and none of you will be there. She will be heavily under guard."

"The lines in the Lakelands must be tended, or the north will fail and if it fails your Albans will not be too happy," Rion bargained.

"You will have Fidelma, and her pet city brat, as soon as she is found," Calchas countered. He didn't have Marina then; she had managed to get away. "Of course, I have her one remaining sister and with such bait most rodents will eventually surface."

I nodded to Rion. If I was here in Londinium, then Marina was more than capable of tending the circles in Keswick and Penrith. The steward said nothing. If I didn't know him better, I would say he looked defeated, stunned by Fidelma's revelations and bound by the fealty he owed to the Plantagenets, and therefore in no position to deny Marcus's restoration to the throne of York. He'd been neatly outmanoeuvred. With Rion and Richard Mortimer taken, Bronwyn had no choice; the western Celts would be crushed if they stood alone.

"Then we are agreed. I will have the terms of the Treaty drawn up, and we can sign as a way to celebrate the marriage of Lord Courtenay and your princess tomorrow, just as we did at the last treaty. I do love a little historical symmetry, don't you?" Calchas delightedly surveyed the sullen faces of the leaders of the Britons at his table. He had finally achieved what centuries of praetors and governors had failed to do. That he would be doing so outside of the Empire and under his direct – if hidden – rule would only be the salt enhancing the flavour of the meal.

"As enjoyable as this has been, we have a big day ahead. It's important to look our best," Calchas commanded as he pushed his chair back from the table. Alvar stepped from his station by the wall to the door, opening it to reveal our praetorian escorts.

Calchas's amused gaze followed me as I made my way around the table to Marcus.

"We were friends once," I said. *I see you.*

I took his hand in one of mine as I leaned close. It would

look to the others – and most importantly, to the praetor – as an offering of reconciliation and nothing more, I hoped.

"We exchanged gifts, and were true." I gripped him around the wristband that I had not failed to notice earlier and pressed. "I hope in the morning, that is something I can find again."

Marcus's eyes met mine, soft in relief, his fingers brushing the tattoo on the inside of my wrist – the triquetra I wore in Devyn's memory, a symbol of the charm he had given me long ago. "I would like that too."

"Charming, brava." Calchas applauded, and at his signal, we were each escorted from the room.

Chapter Twenty-Eight

G ideon's hands were on me as soon as the door clicked behind us, whirling me around.

"What are you doing?" His eyes were furious. "You can't possibly mean to go through with this?"

"What choice do we have?" I gritted back. He had suppressed his true feelings so well during dinner, I should have realised it wouldn't hold.

Gideon pushed his hands through the black wings of his hair, his mind busily tearing through the possible scenarios, just as he had at dinner, just as we all had, and came up empty. There were no choices here.

"He has us. We walked right into it; at least this way you and Féile will be happy."

He looked at me nonplussed and then he lifted one of the chairs by the table and smashed it against the wall. The door opened, and several sentinels rushed in, weapons raised.

"No, no, it's all right," I said, raising my hands to fend them off. Well, one hand anyway, as the other hand was directed at my former husband, warning him to stay where he was. "It was an accident."

The lead praetorian was my once sympathetic guard Kasen. I smiled slightly at the sight of him, my eyes pleading. He nodded before ordering his men out.

I turned back to Gideon. His golden eyes simmered with the anger inside him.

"It won't be so bad," I said.

"You are the Lady of the Lake. You need the Griffin," he said.

"I can live without the Griffin," I said. Maybe. His eyes shuttered, and he turned away. Here we were, our last night, and I still didn't have the strength to tell him how I felt. *Tell him, you fool.* What would be the point, though?

"Gideon," I called to him softly. I hadn't meant for my words to sound like a rejection.

He turned to me, and where words had failed, our bodies did not.

He pulled me into him, and his mouth descended on mine, desperate and hungry, alive. So alive. I kissed him back fiercely, my hands tearing through his hair, under his tunic, across the warmth of his skin. Skin to skin, touch to touch, I was in the air, on the bed; he was over me, inside me, and we spun higher and tighter together. Frantic and heated, unable to feel, touch, smell, taste enough of each other as we came together.

We collapsed as the storm faded, wrapped in each other's arms. I fell onto his chest. Surrounded by the salty, woodsy scent that was uniquely Gideon. I closed my eyes and imagined myself back in Carlisle, the clean Lakeland air sweeping in through the open window, heard the laughter outside, the patter of small footsteps coming up the corridor.

I would never know that again. I would never be there again. My heart was sore inside me. Maybe it would be better once I could no longer feel. Once I no longer needed this. Them.

His hand travelled down the length of my spine, slowly, as if we had all the time in the world. He twisted me across his body until I was underneath him, his strong arms bracing himself above me as he looked down directly into my eyes.

"How could you agree to his terms?"

My lips trembled and I felt tears heat the corner of my eyes. I couldn't speak. I pushed him away, and he let me. I turned my head away while I gained my composure.

I bit my lip and breathed for a few moments until the tear in my throat grew less painful.

"Why did you do any of it?" I threw at him the question that had been swirling inside me for months, years.

"What?" he asked, thrown by the lack of context.

"Why did you sign up for any of this? You didn't have to. You didn't even like me," I reminded him.

He huffed. "You really want to do this? Now?"

"Yes, why not? What have I got to lose? I'll never see you again." I turned to look at him. "In fact, I wouldn't worry about it too much. By this time tomorrow I won't even care."

He flinched. His jaw tightened at the reminder. He had given up the last four years of his life to remove the previous handfast cuff.

"What exactly are you asking, Cat?" He propped himself up on one elbow and looked over at me in the flickering light.

I shrugged. "I'm not sure. I used to worry that you were forced into marrying me, but then you were angry at my asking Nimue to free you. It doesn't really matter anymore.

You will take care of Féile, right? That hasn't changed – you still love her?"

His eyes flashed.

"All I've ever wanted is to have..." He stopped and started again. "My mother left when I was a child; my father never seemed to love me either. I told myself I didn't care that I didn't need anyone. Then that little girl wrapped her tiny fingers around my heart and, well... I would lay down my life to keep her safe, to ensure she always knows that she is loved. That will never change."

I nodded. I knew this. But there was one answer I didn't have, one that gnawed at me.

"Were you with me because Rion ordered it?"

"You keep saying this. You think I slept with you out of duty?" He laughed out loud, turning sombre as he looked back over at me, a finger reaching out to trace my bare collarbone. "I was so angry at you for not being there for Féile, angry at what you had said before... but I couldn't watch you drift away again. From the moment I first set eyes on you, you were so alive, so vivid. I pushed you, you pushed back. I was yours from the moment you stepped into that glade fit to kill me."

The day he had shot Devyn, magic had swelled up inside me to strike him down.

"I thought you didn't like me." He had been horrible from the first moment we had met.

"You walked into my life in love with another man."

"How did you know?"

"I put a hole in a man's shoulder, and you looked like you would raze the world in retribution. It wasn't too hard."

A smile widened across my face.

"You liked me."

Silence.

433

"You liked me, liked me."

I nudged his ribs with an elbow, and he huffed in response.

"But I was with Devyn."

"Mmm. You were so busy trying to convince everyone you were with Marcus, but I saw you. I saw where your heart was given. Not only were you in love with someone who wasn't me, but it was Devyn bloody Glyndŵr. Oathbreaker. The legendary Griffin."

He looked at me. His eyes were dark with the past.

"If he had lived, I would have stayed in my place. I knew you would never look at me as you did him. Until I discovered that there was a fate worse than that one. That you would look at me," he breathed deeply, "and see him."

I gnawed at my lip, remembering back to the times when he had kissed me and frozen when I responded. Was this why? He hadn't been recoiling from me, but afraid that I was only kissing him back in the hope that I might find some essence of Devyn within him.

"I never saw him in you," I said softly.

He had told me his worst fear of that time, so I offered him mine in return.

"I thought you hated me, resented me for stealing your independence. For needing you."

"Maybe I did for a while there." He touched my chin lightly, turning my head back to face him so I would see in the golden depths of his eyes his pain, his darkest fears. "I married you, I made promises but you did not want them, did not want me. I know you were in pain so I stayed away. For as long as I could. I stayed away."

Promises? Our wedding vows. He *had* given me his vow, and I had never acknowledged it, had crushed it beneath my heel.

"Then when you became so ill, I couldn't stay away any longer." He took a deep shuddering breath. "I lay on the other side of the bed, watching you fade away. I just wanted to be near you before you were gone. You turned into me, your head on my chest, and your heartbeat... it began to keep time with mine. I could hear it, feel it grow stronger. When you woke... I have never known anything like that night. And then you came to me at the ball like I lit up the world. You came to me, you were alive... but I was afraid it was him you sought. The next morning, what I said was unforgivable."

He had attacked me, had said horrible things to me, had pushed me away before I could do the same to him. As every woman he'd ever cared about had.

"When Callum discovered that you needed me, needed me to be close to keep you whole, I felt like I had cursed you, like my need to tie you to me, to bind you to keep you from leaving me was something I had done to you. It was my punishment to be there for you but not touch you. How could I touch you? So I sat there night after night, so close, so needed, and not give in to my need."

"I thought you didn't want me," I said. "That you suffered my presence."

He gave a bitter laugh. "Oh, I suffered all right. I experienced the agonies of the damned. To have what I wanted so close but not be able to touch you. When I was weak and thought I might break, I would sit outside in the hall, hoping I was still near enough to be of use but needing to put a stone wall between myself and temptation. "

"You weren't with other women?" I asked. I had been so sure, and then all the more humiliated when I had to track him down the next day to ensure I had spent enough time close to him that I didn't lose the fragile emotional health that allowed me to be near my daughter, unaware that he had never been more than a few feet away.

He frowned. "Other women? For me, since that day, there has only been you."

That day? The day we had first met?

"Are you telling me you haven't been with another woman in five years?" I scoffed. Not if the tales I'd been told were anything to go by.

"Like a Christian monk." He smiled at my incredulity.

"But I was with Devyn." Was he really saying that if Devyn had lived, he would never have touched another woman?

"I don't have the healthiest relationship with love."

His amber eyes met mine solemnly, hollow at the future he had foreseen, and his lips twisted.

"What a waste that would have been," I teased. "So, all that time, after Féile was born…"

"You were healing. I never looked elsewhere. I never really hoped, expected… this."

"So you didn't marry me because Rion asked you to." I smiled at him; it had always seemed out of character that this was the one order he had followed.

"I married you because you would have died," he teased, my noble knight.

"And I've divorced you for the same reason – so we're even," I threw back flippantly. If my aim had been to keep the mood light it failed dismally as his face darkened.

"Even?" he said bleakly. "We'd barely started."

Then he kissed me. A soul-deep promise of a kiss. A promise we both knew he couldn't keep.

I sat in the window, staring out as the pale dawn light crept slowly over the city. I felt cold despite Gideon's tunic and the warm arms wrapped around me. I leaned back into him, holding on to every second.

He squirmed as my cold fingers traced the winding Celtic swirls repeated through the oak tree on his thigh, up and across his hip.

My lips curled in a smile. "Does my big, bad warrior find my fingers too cold?"

He snatched up my fingers and lifted them, trapping them in both of his and blowing his hot breath into the space. "Your big, bad warrior finds your fingers an affront. How do you get this cold?"

I laughed, and once he had freed my sufficiently warm hands, began to trace the dara knot on his inner wrist.

I then drew the four-sided knot in the window, misted by the condensation against the cold glass. Beside it I drew the triquetra from my tattoo for Devyn, and beside that the triskelion I had received in Avalon, the three arms spinning to reach each other.

"What do these three symbols have in common?" I asked him.

"They're all pretty common symbols," he said, examining the three shapes on the window.

His thumb rubbed against the Dara knot that had transferred from his inner wrist to my own.

"Two sided, three sided, open, closed," he muttered to himself. "They have nothing in common."

"They are all different, but they are all intertwined." I retraced the intricate knots, different numbers of loops but all combined to make a single knot. When we tended the ley lines, we usually did it with three people; three is a significant number in druidic tradition. "Mother, maiden, crone. Earth, water, air. Past, present, future. "

"What are you saying?"

"I think that there are many stones at each circle, and they are each significant, but they always combine to make a single circle." I traced the circle in the triquetra. Was this the answer? When I had descended at Mary le Strand, my anchor hadn't been one of the three, it had been Gideon who had pulled me out. What if my reach could go further? Could I heal the fracture at the heart of the Strand line, free those souls trapped within? Once he left, I would never be as strong as this again.

"When I started to tend the ley lines, I had this recurring dream that I was tethered to the shore, and when I come back, it is because you hold me here. I asked Nimue to set you free so that I didn't need you and I think she said that whether I needed you was up to me but that the Griffin responds to necessity. After the Strand you restored me; having you close still felt necessary. I've had time to think carefully about what she said – that I have all I need and need all I have. Maybe the reason I have needed more of you than any lady that went before is because the ley line needs more than it ever did before? Maybe I've resisted using all the tools available to me."

"You think this is why it didn't work before?"

"It's part of it." My gut clenched. "But there's something else, something I haven't seen before. Why couldn't I free those souls as I did in the borders?"

"The last souls were trapped by war, a war fought with magic and technology; their deaths bound them to the land they spilt their blood on," Gideon mused.

"But the latents that were fed to the ley line here, their blood wasn't spilt, their energy was drained. How are they bound? If I can't free them, their pain will continue to twist the line."

How would we have a second chance? *We* wouldn't, but *I* would. I would be taken to Mary le Strand to tend the ley line, but never at full strength, and never with others. I could never go deep enough alone to heal the fracture in the Strand line.

"It's too late now."

Was it? Without the Griffin I couldn't go deep enough and come back, but could I heal the ley line?

The sound of steps in the stone corridor alerted us before the door opened, and my helpers laid out a breakfast we didn't touch and dressed me as Gideon sat in trousers and tunic in the window seat, watching dead-eyed as the simple white dress I had worn to the arena only yesterday was replaced with a more elaborate version of the same.

"Donna Shelton," one of the girls said as she handed me a circlet of flowers with a smile. I shook my head and waved it away. I needed no crown for my hair; the dress was travesty enough.

"Please, donna." Her hair fell messily onto a face that seemed somehow familiar. She offered the circlet again and numbly, I took it as she knelt to fuss with the hem of the dress while her colleague pinned the last of my hair. The ring of flowers and foliage in my hand was bright against the white of the dress, a fiery autumnal selection of crimson berries and white flowers set in orange and gold leaves. What an odd choice. I stared down at the odd selection, the bright colours taking me back in time to the bunch Devyn had sent from Richmond. Acer and oak, the leaves were exactly the same choices Devyn had made, gold and crimson leaves with berries. I felt something being tied around my ankle and pulled my foot away. What stupid accessory were they foisting on me now?

Wide eyes looked up at me from under the dark-brown hair falling into her eyes as she gripped my ankle to prevent me from displaying my new piece of jewellery to the room. Miri, that was her name, the nurse I had been friendly with at Bart's. She lifted the white lace to give me a peek at the rose-gold disk that now lay there, a disk that had been lost to me the night I had fled this room and left the city behind. Marcus had found it, after all this time. And he had returned it to me now. Marcus keeping his vow. He hadn't promised not to betray me I had realised – but he had vowed to make it right.

I closed my eyes in silent gratitude. To Marcus, to Miri, who he had trusted to bring this to me. The girls had only just slipped away when there was a knock at the door. Kasen entered the room, many guards behind him in the hallway. Reinforcements.

I stood and braced myself to take one last look. To imprint my scarred warrior on my brain for the years ahead.

"I would choose you."

Gideon sat, his legs stretched out, that half-smile playing on his lips, pretending to the world that he was entirely unaffected by our separation.

"Your father said that you were the second choice. He meant after Devyn, right?" I prompted him. His lip quirked in amusement in answer.

"You weren't. There was only Devyn." I said softly, reaching to take his face in my hands. "And then there was only you."

All pretence at indifference dropped away. He stood, his hands at my waist pulling me into him.

"I never had to choose between you," I explained, "but

know this: I would choose you as Devyn never chose me. He never... I was never first for him. He chose his duty, his oath over me. Repeatedly. He only chose me in the end because of the baby, so was he really choosing me or was he yet again choosing duty first and me second?"

I smiled at Gideon. Was I only this brave because now, at the end, I could speak freely? I looked over my shoulder back at Kasen to assess how much longer the praetorian would grant me.

"You chose me even though you owe no fealty and loathe following orders. I see you now. You choose me, I know you choose me. Damn duty and damn the world." I could see the confirmation in his eyes. Through the anger, this was his truth. "He chose duty over me, time after time, and I couldn't understand it. I understand now. Because I must choose duty this time. I can end this. I can save so many lives. But I can only do it if you and Féile are safe."

I stepped forward and laid my palm on his chest. I could do this. I could say goodbye.

I locked eyes with his. "Know that if I had a choice, you would be my first choice. Always."

Viviane had warned me of the pain of separation for the Griffin. My mother, as she lay dying, had ensured that Devyn and I would not know that pain. Once the handfast cuff went on, I would no longer feel the pain that was tearing me apart. I focused inwardly, going down, deeper and deeper into my core until I found the shining thread that bound us, that gave me strength. I had to set him free. I snipped the bond clean through. The Griffin had provided what I needed. He had to leave, and I could need him no longer.

I felt the absence immediately. Devastation flowed through me at the loss of the connection. I opened my eyes and through the shimmer of unshed tears, found that Gideon had fallen to his knees before me. I had been prepared for the impact of my action, but he'd had no such warning.

His golden eyes looked up at me in shock. There was a flicker across his features as the Griffin reacted to the broken bond and started to surface. The guards raised their guns as they too noticed the change.

"No," came a voice from the hallway. "Hold."

There was a disturbance as guards were pushed aside. Marcus pushed through, the steward in his wake.

"His father will subdue him." Marcus took position in front of the kneeling, shimmering Gideon while I was held back by the sentinels who were taking no chances. Their orders were to bring me to the arena at all costs, no doubt.

Lord Richard knelt by his son, reaching out, holding him by the shoulder, grounding him, whispering to him. Using whatever damaged connection they had, trying to help him resist the change.

Slowly those whispered words seemed to relax him as he looked up and fixed his gaze on his father's. Pain filled them as they flicked over to me. He was back.

I relaxed in the grip of the sentinels, looking at them pointedly until they released me and then I turned and walked through the door without turning back.

I could do this. Féile would be safe. Gideon would be alive.

I could do this.

Chapter Twenty-Nine

The city passed by in a blur, the route heavily guarded despite the short journey and the walls that stood between me and freedom.

Fidelma rode with us and Calchas relaxed back in his seat; he had won. I sat there, finally fully charged, and there was nothing I could do.

My gown flowed around me, a creation that sold me as a princess of the city as if the last years had never happened. The tattoos on my arms were the only indication I was not the same person who had left here three years ago. I traced them lightly, the dark ink embedded in my skin. The three loops of the triquetra with the circle through it. My mind turned over the infinite Celtic trinity: earth, water, air; past, present, future; mother, maiden, crone; life, death, rebirth; mother, daughter, wife. I was a wife no longer, but the blue veins that pulsed underneath continued to push the blood around my body. Where there was life, there was hope. Who had said that? Cicero. I was comforting myself with the words of a Roman consul.

Today was Mabon, the autumn equinox, the first ceremony I had participated in. I saw again Callum holding an apple in his hand, illustrating the tilt of the earth's axis, the balance of light and dark. It was a time to restore balance. If only I could persuade Calchas to give me access to Mary le Strand today.

I traced again the triskelion tattoo that had appeared in Avalon. *Present in belief, past in trust, future in love, held by courage.* My mother's words. Whatever future she had striven to realise, it was over now.

"Ah, I almost forgot," the praetor of the city, soon to be ruler of all Britannia, held out the handfast cuff.

I stared at it. The energy thrummed in my veins, calling me, inviting me to take a different path, to end this now. But I couldn't, because it wasn't just me, it was Féile, it was the city, it was the people. How many would die if I took that path, if I allowed the power in me to pull the city down around me rather than restore the balance?

Londinium would become the new borderlands, hundreds of thousands of souls torn and trapped. The horror of it swept through me.

I braced. The charm on my ankle would protect me. I extended my arm, and he snapped it in place.

My head bowed under the force of the effect the cuff had on my emotions. The magic stored within me met it, my charm making my will resistant to the dictates of the magic contained within the band. I could feel its intention, its pull to comply with the Code, the desire to be with the bearer of its partner. But I was no longer the blank slate I had been the last time the cuff had wiped me down and overlaid my will with its own.

The car turned north.

"Where are we going?" I asked, curious. I had assumed my

wedding would take place in the Governor's Palace perhaps, but we were headed west through the theatre district.

"The arena." The praetor beamed at me.

"We're going to a Mete before the wedding?" I queried lightly.

"Something like that," Calchas answered vaguely.

"Is Marcus coming?" I asked mildly. I needed to appear as if my wish to comply was paramount. Having my own will was the first advantage I'd had, and I needed to maintain it for as long as I could. Until I had my chance.

"Yes, we thought we'd have the wedding where the whole city could participate."

"How wonderful."

As we stepped out onto the balcony, the mob cheered. Doves were loosed to fly up through the amphitheatre, circling up to the tower balconies and into the sky above. The oohs and ahhs of the crowd were a background to the visual symphony of augmented holographs swinging up and through the layers of seats and crowds of people. It was an indescribably beautiful display that enchanted the whole arena – and the entire city, no doubt.

I looked around the balcony as if to appreciate the shared joy of such an experience. Spotting Ginevra amongst the senators, I gave her an excited wave. She waved tentatively back once she had recovered her surprise at being acknowledged.

The misery in the expressions of my Briton friends was an off note in the otherwise celebratory atmosphere. Marcus stood opposite, his eyes hollow as he ignored the dancing holograms in favour of the sands.

I turned to investigate what was making him so unhappy.

My smile faded.

Gideon. He wasn't supposed to be here. I could feel the lines of my brow pucker together. That wouldn't do, and I ran a finger lightly over my forehead to smooth them out.

I turned to Calchas; the praetor would explain. While I was doing my utmost to keep my reaction from my face, I found that he wasn't watching the display either. Instead, his eyes were on me like I was an exotic substance in a petri dish to which he had just introduced a foreign element.

"Lord High Justice..." I paused to gather my thoughts. I was safe to question this surely; Gideon shouldn't be here. This was not the arrangement. "What is going on? I thought we were having a wedding?"

"We are, my dear," he assured me. "Just tidying up a few loose ends."

"Loose ends!" Rion swore, his usual measured manner entirely absent as he struggled against the restraining hands of the two praetorian guards beside him.

"Yes, well, we are gathered here to celebrate a wedding. We can't begin the ceremony until the bride is free to marry again." The praetor turned to Alvar who was positioned behind him. "Lock it down."

Alvar nodded in salute and waved a hand over his head. The seldom-used roof closed in over the arena, a couple of stories up, just below the giant digital screens, swinging shut to the sounds of protest from the crowds gathered in the balconies above. New metal gates clanged shut, sealing the exits, Calchas ensuring that no one would be getting in or out until the afternoon's deeds were done no matter what their abilities were.

"But they divorced," Bronwyn cried, her head swivelling back to watch the dark shadow of the executioner approaching the tall unmoving figure of the man I had until last night called husband. The Steward of York stood behind her, unmoving, unprotesting, his gaze locked on the arena floor.

"In your laws perhaps, but if she is to be Queen of all Britannia, then there must be no confusion. And here one marries until death does you part," Calchas explained patiently. This then was his revenge for being wrongfooted last night by the news of our marriage.

Gideon stood alone out there on the sand. My breathing shallowed. I willed myself not to react beyond what was expected of me. I arranged a mildly petulant expression on my face, as if put out that Gideon's approaching doom was completely ruining the mood, ruining the day for my friends and no more. Distracted, I allowed myself to act as if compelled by the effect of the handfast cuff, reaching out to hold Marcus's hand for comfort, but he pulled away and took a step back from me.

I frowned as my mind took in the implications. Calchas was reneging on our deal. *Don't react. Don't show your true feelings. Blood on the sand.* I saw again the blood that had seeped into the sand when Devyn had been beaten. When he had died in my arms on that beach in Cymru. Red seeping down through the golden grains. I had to stop it. Had to find a way.

Blood on the sand.

That was what I had seen, that was the key.

Calchas had crowed that Devyn's blood on the sand had been the key. That was what had allowed the ley line to feed off people. That was the strange element in the line, the discordant note that entangled the souls: they were bound by blood. Not their blood, but all the blood that had been spilt here.

All this time, centuries of accused dying on these sands, latents burning out slowly. There was always a second node to counterpoint the primary nexus, Keswick had Penrith, Glastonbury had Stonehenge. And Mary le Strand had the amphitheatre, or whatever structure the ancients had built here before the Romans arrived. I looked down at the circle below and let my senses flow out across the sand. The electromagnetic hum of the circle greeted me, and I was standing at its edge.

"No!" Fidelma broke ranks from the silent Britons. "You can't do this. Please, I'm begging you. He's my son. "

Calchas raised a brow. "That is unfortunate. It's so terrible to lose a child."

Fidelma crossed to him, and the officers surrounding the praetor moved to protect him, but he waved them away.

"Please," she said, almost frantic. "I've done everything you've asked. Everything."

She looked out at her son and turned back to Calchas, falling to her knees and picking up the hem of his robe.

"You can't. You promised to send him home." She looked to me. I could strike now, but the circle here felt wrong, closed. I looked out at Gideon; did I have enough power? I would only get one chance at this. I closed my eyes and swayed at the thought of his blood on the sand, like Devyn's before him. Devyn's blood had been the key that had allowed the ley line to leach power above like never before. The few cases had become an outbreak, and then Calchas had started to sweep the city, hundreds of disappeared, and a paranoid, terrified and therefore unquestioning elite supplied with a treatment.

The number of capital deaths had increased in the last years, not just to keep the population distracted but for Calchas's own callous purpose.

I suddenly couldn't breathe. The blood on the sand. Here at the arena. The line twisted and corrupted by the sacrifices of blood.

"Yes, how untrustworthy of me." Calchas almost snickered down at the stricken woman.

"Without the Griffin, the lady will never be able to fully heal the land." So she did know that the Griffin restored me, knew and had kept it from Calchas.

"Who says I want the land fully healed? I fuel the Strand ley line, I control it now. As it is, I can siphon off its power as and when I want to; our technology has harnessed it. Could I do that if it was in balance? I think not. This way I have exactly what I want." He met my unconcerned, limpid gaze even as my mind turned frantically.

The ley line or the Griffin.

How could I save them both?

There had to be a way.

"Technology and magic together under my control. You think I will ever truly control your Lady of the Lake while her Griffin lives? No, Lady Mortimer, I think not. You were the one who warned me. There is no cage strong enough to keep him from her, no vow he won't break to get her back. You were happy enough to help kill the last one. Once they are outside, the rest of them won't risk their lives to save her, but him. I see him. I know him, and I'm afraid it just won't do."

Dismissing her, he stepped forward and raised his arms until the crowd fell silent.

"Citizens, you have found this man guilty. He has wronged this city, and he will duly pay for that with his life. We can brook no further threat. His act broke the Treaty and now the age of the free tribes of Britannia is at an end. The Maledictio is ended. We have their leaders. Their army lies waiting in the Shadowlands. Tomorrow we take our legions outside of the walls. Tomorrow we will crush the last of their defiance. Tomorrow we go to war and take this land for our own."

The crowd responded to the jubilant words that spoke of glory but not of the sorrow that comes with war, erupting into frenzied applause at the taste of a future where they would no longer be confined behind the city walls. Calchas had promised them the lands beyond the city walls, new territories that they would rule. They knew our army waited outside, but without their leaders, and the advantage of their magic as well as their direction, it would be a massacre. He had what he wanted. Rion and the others had already agreed to swear fealty. Calchas was taking no chances. My stomach swooped. I had to stop him. Time had finally run out.

But I also had to heal the ley line and undo the corruption that Calchas had wrought. That was my purpose. That was what the oak had shown me. I had thought that my life would be the sacrifice that was needed. That my blood would be enough. But his blood was the key.

The stars were aligned tonight, on Mabon. Magical blood on the floor of the arena would unlock the ley line from this circle. I was at full strength and I could save him. But if I did, how far would we get? Could I doom both the living and the dead for this one life?

Devyn had made a choice once and now so must I.

"Executioner," the praetor commanded, and the dark-hooded man stepped forward with his axe, indicating that Gideon should kneel at his feet and place his head on the waiting block.

No. Gideon wouldn't kneel. He wouldn't kneel.

This wasn't supposed to happen. I needed time to think. I had thought that once they were all safely out of the city I could go deep enough to heal the ley. The ley would be healed, I would be gone, and with me Calchas's leverage over the Britons. I thought I had finally figured out a way to best him, but I had been wrong.

Gideon stepped back from the block and I breathed a little easier as he started to speak.

"We have but one life, and it is not to serve ourselves, to bend others to our will, but to serve others, to be a force for good. One person does matter, one person can make a difference."

He looked up at the balcony – at Fidelma, at me. One person could make a difference. It had to be now, today. I would never be this strong again, but I needed to be at the Strand to heal the ley line. Think. I let my power explore the circle in front of me. Would this circle allow me to go all the way to the faultline from here?

No, it was locked. And old blood on the sands was the key. It had to be now. It was Mabon, the autumn equinox, which meant that if I didn't do something, the corruption would flow west and north.

"My lady marries today. Long be her life! Together they will rule this island, and all will be equal, all will be free." Gideon was speaking as he bowed his head. "It is my honour, my privilege, to spend my blood so that they may walk into the future together."

He knew. Somehow he knew that his blood would unlock the circle. But how? I looked again to Marcus, who stood frozen, his jaw clenched, his eyes glazed at the warrior's speech. I didn't understand. This wasn't supposed to happen.

I couldn't save him. If I went now, I would damn everyone else.

Gideon stepped forward to the block.

He was alone. He had spent his life being rejected. I had rejected him. Was this how he faced his end?

No.

"I choose you," I whispered into the wind that swirled and swept around the arena.

"I choose you," I whispered again, and stepped forward.

But Marcus's arm came around my waist, pulling me back into him.

From where Gideon stood, alone on the sand, we would look united, together.

Gideon's eyes blazed in our direction. At me. At Marcus.

Together.

No, this was all wrong.

"People must take a stand, for what is just, for what is right. I give my life in that cause. For the sake of those I love."

And with these words, he knelt.

But what is right? How could I save one man and damn the city, and all the souls trapped in the node?

I felt disconnected from him, from Marcus, from the world.

Marcus pulled me tight against him as Gideon looked up at us again before bowing his head.

I was letting it happen. Knowingly.

Only this morning I had promised him I would choose him. A promise I now betrayed. I had the power to save him… or all those souls and the dying land…

Marcus whispered in my ear. "This is not how it ends."

The axe fell.

Red.

So much red upon the sand, spreading out.

I felt nothing. I was nothing.

My gaze floated across the balcony, unable to look at the fallen Griffin. The uncaring senators, the shocked and furious Britons, Bronwyn in Rion's arms, the frozen Steward of York staring not at his broken son but at Marcus and me. Fidelma's scream. Bronwyn's sobs. This was the only sound in the ensuing silence, the crowd oddly subdued at the death of the nobly spoken warrior.

Calchas frowned at the silence. Ever in tune with the needs of the crowd, he moved swiftly to distract them with his next piece of entertainment.

He grabbed my hand and Marcus's and raised them high until the attention of the crowd moved from the broken body, the blood seeping into the sands on the arena floor below them.

"And so a necessary evil is removed from the world so that the city's future rulers can be brought together." He smiled beatifically at us. "Out of the ashes of our fallen governor rise the future King and Queen of all of Britannia."

The crowd roared enthusiastically as its favourite son and his bride were presented to them as a bright and glittering future. There were no kings in the Empire, but the crowd was delighted with the shiny new vision and seemed not to mind.

"We emerge from the greatness of the Empire that bore us and rise anew, a jewel freshly polished," Calchas announced. "We have been but an outpost of a once mighty Empire. The Empire is lost, while we are renewed. The illness has been cured, our technology has triumphed, and our rulers have the strongest magic in the land. It is a glorious day indeed. And now for the main event."

Calchas stood back and pulled Marcus and me in front of him, joining our hands. Marcus's green eyes held mine. He had sworn to help me. Well, it was too late now. Rion held Bronwyn. Fidelma, on her knees, still wept alone. She had fought to keep him alive, the child she had walked away from; now, at the end, she had tried. The steward still watched Marcus and me, thin-lipped and hollow-eyed.

They waited with the rest of the city for the next event to unfold: my long-delayed wedding to Marcus Courtenay. A marriage that would make me the Queen of York, I realised. Not just York, all of Britannia. The next act after this would be for all the kings and princes here to swear fealty to the puppet rulers that Marcus and I would be.

A breakaway state from the Empire. Calchas had waited for just the right time. The Roman legions would not come; famine and revolt across the Empire ensured that Calchas's independent fiefdom was something they would not have the resources to retake and hold.

Marcus repeated the vows that the praetor dictated. He led them again so that I might also repeat them. The words of the vows were meaningless in their assembly. I tried to focus on him, but my gaze kept returning to the sands where a strange mist had closed in over the fallen body that lay there.

That was new. I once more sent my senses across the circle of the arena. It felt different. Unlocked. The blood. Gideon's blood had opened it. I could sense the ley line here now. It was bound; the arena bound it. And something more... the odd notes were stronger here, the foreignness visible.

If I struck now—

Marcus pressed my hand, pulling me back to the moment.

"We now pronounce you husband and wife." Calchas beamed. "Long may you reign."

The sound of bells pealing out across the city made their way into the arena, as the roof finally opened.

A dull roar sounded through me.

The lights in the tower above us flickered and then went out.

He was dead.

"Thank you," I said, and smiled at Calchas. The handfast cuff released and I was free. What minor impediment the metal band had inflicted was gone. And now the ley line was wide open.

The crowd exploded.

No, not the crowd, the world.

I was only one person and I had never assumed I could be enough. Calchas and people like him, they forced their will upon the world around them, bending everyone and everything to it. But to what end? So that they, who already had so much, could have more. It wasn't right. It wasn't just.

No more walls. No more elites.

The symbols of power would crumble. I would churn them into dust.

I could feel the very walls of the city shake and tremble under my will. I pushed the ley line upwards, closer to the surface, letting it dance and weave through the foundations of the walls that had protected the corruption of the city for far, far too long.

Then there was a dull roar and the walls came down.

The world swirled around me; the promise of the lakes was mine. I was the sword in the darkness.

In my mind, I descended deep into the circle, the darkness of it blinding me, but I followed the foreign element until I reached it and cleaved it in two. The force of the blow rebounded on me, and I was blown out of the ley line. Stunned, I sagged in the arms that held me fast.

And then sentinels crashed onto the balcony.

"My lord," a guard said, addressing the praetor and Alvar at his side. "We couldn't gain entry. It's an illusion."

"Who raised the lockdown?" Alvar demanded, ignoring the report as he looked up at the now open roof.

"Sir, the power is down across the city," the guard reported.

I felt dazed. Fidelma stood staring out at the sand and the stain upon it, but I couldn't bear it; the swirling sand answered me and covered the body, the grains whirling and dancing in a frenzied mania around the amphitheatre.

The crowd was screaming, running for the exits as cracks appeared in the walls of the very structure that had housed the false justice meted out here for generations. On the balcony, senators and their families were similarly scrambling for the single exit, pushing each other as praetorian guards and sentinels poured in and the Britons, unarmed, positioned themselves in front of me, Marcus stepping forward and taking his position beside them.

The winds whipped around us, holding the guards off while they protected themselves as best they could against the buffeting winds. I felt the crackle of lightning answering my call high above the city's soaring towers, crackling across the city, waiting for my direction.

I was free. I bowed to no one. I could take it all, take the city, take the power.

No, I had to stop it.

If I could seal the fracture, then no one would have to die again. The ley line would be healed and it would stop leaching whatever power it could capture from above ground.

Tonight we would finish it.

Chapter Thirty

"It has to be now," I said. "I need to get to Mary le Strand."

I could feel it, the cleaving of the ties here had opened the fracture; I could do it now. But I needed to release my hold on the storm here.

"My lords," said a sentinel carrying swords to the outnumbered Britons... No, not a sentinel! Linus, and behind him Alec, Rion's captain. He made it out of the ball. The Britons were armed now, but they were still no match for the sentinels' tech-powered weapons.

The arriving sentinels weren't as polished-looking as the ones that guarded Calchas. Alvar's expression seconded my realisation that the new arrivals were definitely not from the imperial legions. The praetorian guard discarded their guns in favour of the ceremonial weapons they wore and were trained to use.

"The Code is in chaos; all tech is down across the city." Linus grinned. He had done it. He and his friends had helped, as he had promised.

"It has to be now," I repeated. "I need to get to Mary le Strand."

If Gideon's sacrifice was going to count, it had to be now; there would never be another chance like this. Tonight was Mabon, the tide was high, and the circle was unlocked. I scanned the fracas around me. Marcus growled impatiently and, taking up one of the swords on the ground, entered the fray as the recovering praetorian guard took an attacking position while Calchas was hustled off the balcony.

"Calchas is making for the control room," Linus cried.

"You must stop him. We need the tech to be down for as long as possible," I instructed him. If we were to make it across the city, we needed the chaos of the blackout. Linus nodded, and within moments was back in the fray, yelling to the fighting Britons and dissidents that they needed to stop the praetor.

The storm overhead raged down on the city, the praetorian guards penning us in but the close quarters and the bodies of the fallen, pushing, fleeing council members hampered the fight. The Britons were trained better in hand-to-hand combat, and I watched as Alec cut another down and moved on to the next. Rion's golden head also cut a swathe through the black and scarlet uniforms. There was screaming and grunting as hits and slices were traded.

I spotted Alvar, who was momentarily still in the midst of the fighting. His eyes gleamed as they met mine and he pushed his way towards me. Marcus shoved and sliced at bodies, trying to cut off the threat. Callum had taught me well, and I raised a hand to send a bolt towards Alvar, but there were so many people and I couldn't be sure I would only hit him.

My hesitation cost me, and a knife left his hand. I caught his triumphant grin and then I was falling.

But I fell to the side. Someone had pushed me out of the path of the blade. There was a snarl and Marcus was after Alvar as he fled.

The body on mine moaned. Fine cloth entangled us as I pushed myself upright to meet Ginevra's startled eyes.

"Ow," she said, taking in the knife handle protruding from her shoulder.

"Ginevra."

"I don't know why I did that," she said, looking at me as if I might have the answer.

"Hello, Gin," I greeted my old friend.

"You left," she said. She had missed me. And I her, I realised.

Then Linus was there, helping me back to my feet. The fighting had lessened, Alvar's knife the praetorians' final move before retreating.

"Where is Féile? Marina?"

"We have them, they're safe," a second sentinel said, stepping forward – Rion's captain, Alec.

If this was going to work, I wouldn't be enough. I needed the others.

"I need you to bring them to the Strand," I told him and, when he didn't move I added, "Now. We heal the ley line tonight."

Richard Mortimer had lifted my former best friend to her feet and dealt with the knife before handing her to a senator I didn't recognise who stepped forward, watching me warily as he took Ginevra from the steward.

"Calchas is gone," Rion said as he arrived, a few armed –

disguised – sentinels with him, more having given pursuit with Marcus.

"As soon as the tech is up, he'll be back in control of the city. We need to move," I told him. "We need to get to Mary le Strand. If the ley line is healed before Calchas resolves the blackout, we have a chance."

"Wait until we have the city. You can deal with it then."

"No, it has to be now. The blood has triggered an opening that wasn't there before." Gideon's blood. I shook my head. I couldn't think about that now. There would be time to mourn after it was all over.

I could heal it. We had Féile and Marina. The future and the present, and me as the past. The three of us had to be together to heal the fissure. My mother's words circled in my mind, her counsel to have belief in the present, to trust in the past, have love in the future, and be held by courage. Belief. Trust. Love. Courage.

I took a deep breath.

I wasn't as strong as I had been, and the break was so deep.

But we could do this. I looked out to where Gideon had fallen. I had to do this.

Rion indicated to Alec to bring Fidelma who still sat on the ground, broken, staring out at the arena floor.

We raced across the city, our passage hampered by the panicked crowds that were leaving the arena, fleeing the swirling sands and mayhem within only to find themselves in citywide darkness as lightning flashed overhead. The streets, buildings, and lit towers of Londinium were dark; there was no safety to flee to. Their confusion and fear spread to the citizens that were emerging from their darkened homes, fearful of the outage and confused by the events they'd seen broadcasted from the arena.

Bronwyn took my hand as we were buffeted by the crowd, and I dragged her across the streets I had grown up in. Alec carried Fidelma as she no longer seemed to have the strength to carry herself. Rion pushed himself in front of us to give us some headway through the panicked citizens.

Finally, we turned onto the Strand, weaving between people as we ran. How long did we have until Calchas resolved the chaos, and the tech was back in place once more? My feet hurt in the fancy slippers that were designed for getting married in not for running. I focused on the physical pain as I pushed down the grief that slithered through my focus. I forced it back as we swung through the gate, no sign of the sentinels that had stood guard before.

We paused at the entrance to the cavernous space down under the church; it was an abyss of black now that the lights were out. There was a flicker, and then a sphere of light appeared over our heads, lighting our faces in an eerie otherworldly light. Marcus stepped out of an alcove. Bronwyn gave him a severe look as another and then a third light bobbed over our heads. It was the light trick that Marcus had learned from Devyn so many years ago.

Down the endlessly spiralling stairs we went until we finally came to the flat corridor that led to the room at the end of the hall.

I braced as I looked at the dark oak door, impervious as time itself. Marcus and Linus grabbed the great rings and pulled it open. Great sconces blazed around the room.

"Mama!" My darling girl broke free of Marina's arms and ran to me.

"My baby, oh my baby." I pulled her small body tight to mine, the weight of her the most comforting thing I had ever experienced.

Marina stood quietly, her face pale as she smiled cheekily.

"What kept you?"

"Oh, y'know, this and that," I chipped back at her lightly.

I pushed Féile's dark curls back off her forehead. "Sweetheart, do you know what we're going to do?"

She nodded solemnly. "Marina says we're going to make the song better."

"We are. We three make the triskelion."

Her neat little nose screwed up "What's the tr-trick-salon?"

I rewarded her stalwart effort with a smile. Putting her down on the floor, I showed her the triskelion tattoo that had been placed on the inside of my wrist during my trip to Avalon.

"That's right." I took her finger and traced the three legs that curled towards each other. "You see, Marina represents the present because she is from here in Londinium and her magic appeared just when it was needed the most. I represent the past because I am the Lady of the Lake, an ancient title handed down since the dawn of time to the caretaker of the land."

"And am I this one?" Féile asked, looking up at me. This, this was why my mother had brought me with her. To heal this line would take the power of three; she had hoped I would be that third. And now I would be, except that I would do it as the lady, not as the child.

"You are," I said. "You are the future, the future of the land and the city. Because you are special. You are the child of the only two people who have lived with both magic and technology."

"But Dada hasn't lived here." Féile frowned.

"No," I agreed with her. How to explain this to her now…? I could feel the impatience of the others. We didn't have time for this, but I had to know that she understood what was going on, and why, before we did this.

"Oh, the daddy who died?" she asked, realising.

I nodded wordlessly. The tear inside me threatened to split me in two. How to tell her now that both her fathers were gone?

"Dada told me about him," she said with an air of a child patiently explaining to an adult the obvious source of her knowledge. Gideon had spoken to her of Devyn? A lump formed in my throat.

"He lived here for many years," I explained, "and he was very good at tech."

"So am I," Féile said proudly.

"Catriona," Rion urged from behind me.

"Are you, poppet?" I said. "You must get that from him."

There was a flicker from the open door, the electric power in the stairwell attempting to ignite.

A slight sweat broke out on my forehead. Fear. Once the tech entangled itself in the line again I had no idea how to free it from whatever Calchas had engineered.

"Féile, darling." I steadied myself, ensuring no trace of my fear could be heard in my voice. "I'm going to try to fix the song. Can you hear it?"

She nodded.

"I need you to sit with Marina and me around the symbol, you see." I sat on one side of the triangle as Marina placed herself to my left and I sat Féile to my right. "We're going to hold hands together. You need to hold Marina's hand very tight, no matter what happens."

Marina flicked a narrow-eyed gaze at me.

"If I don't come back up, you need to release me," I told her in a steady voice.

Bronwyn's gasp was the loudest thing in the room as she realised what I was telling them. I wasn't sure if I could come back from this. Wasn't sure I wanted to.

I held Marina's gaze. "It's deep, so much deeper than Keswick, and in a far worse state than the May line. I'm not sure, but I need to know that you will hold Féile, or we don't do this."

"No," Rion said in the tone he used to convey utter finality. "If you're not strong enough, it could kill you. You can't do this."

"We'll never have another chance like this," I said. "It's me or everything you've worked so hard to protect – the land, the people."

"They were all I had left…" His eyes begged me not to do this. My brother, who had me back after a lifetime of being alone.

"You still have Féile," I reminded him. "You are all she has now. I will try to…"

But I couldn't promise. The faultline was severely tainted; the surge from here that had hit Keswick had almost killed me, had nearly consumed me on my previous attempt and on the last descent I had still had plenty of power from Avalon. And this time I needed to go deeper.

"I'll take her place." Fidelma had recovered some from the stupor she had been in since the axe fell.

I turned to take in the face of the woman I had once trusted.

"That's not possible," I said.

I took in my brother's stoic face and Bronwyn's stricken one.

"All I ever wanted was a home, a family of my own." I

breathed shallowly over the shards in my throat that were threatening to cut off my voice. "Thank you."

I took the hands held out to me, Marina's steady grip and Féile's softer one.

"Ready?" I asked, and they nodded back.

I was alone so quickly, descending deeper and deeper to where I had sensed the fissure before, Code-like tendrils spooling down beside me in the dark. There was something still other too, some binary claws sweeping through the line despite the blackout.

Down, down, the panic and fear on the surface dripped like a toxin down the path I travelled. The faint warped notes of the songline guided me further and further.

The ley line itself was flowing, somewhat healed from our previous efforts. There it was, the murky contamination, the tendril leaching streams powered by blood, released by sacrifice, trailing under the city between the two power nodes of the circles. This time I could see them, cauterise them, keep them from merging with the line. A scent of lavender and summer lit up the tangle of Code and it melted away. Somehow, the binary claws held the line no longer.

I drifted further down.

The corruption twined around the flow, causing it to warp and skew, twisting it apart. I pulled and tugged, working to free them.

Harmony and energy washed through me, the white light clearing away the pain, the worry, the anguish of the last months: Féile's empty bed; Gideon's blood on the sand.

The pain faded until I could no longer recall what had

bothered me. The new song lilted and blended with the second but I had to hold it open longer, I had to allow it more time.

I descended again. Just a little bit further.

It was time I didn't have. Never enough time.

Devyn gone. Gideon gone.

All gone, and now I was gone too.

Too far.

Fading and darkness.

Endless down.

"Come back."

Dark eyes. Demanding, always wanting something.

No. No more.

I had done what was asked. I had given up the things I wanted, the future I wanted, in order to do this, to be here, to make it all well.

I had to finish this.

He didn't get to ask for more.

The dark was soft and clean, and there were no more demands.

"Don't leave me."

A tug. A halt.

No. I needed to go deeper. The fracture was extensive but the notes were pulling it together. I needed to go further down.

I still had Féile, a life that could have been.

The notes, the harmony wrapped around me, softly inviting.

So tired. So cold.

I needed to let them go. It wasn't safe for those lights to be here in the darkness with me anymore.

The lights floated upward, like air in water, bubbling to the surface.

Then there was a thread of light.

I closed my eyes. I didn't need it.

"I came for you,"

Dark curls.

I held on for one moment more.

Amber eyes.

"I swore."

The light was stronger and my thread was a rope, amber strands twining with black, lighter strands, lavender and red, pale gold, violet, rich blue, looping around each other, creating a tether, an anchor I could follow back.

I grasped it, allowing myself to fall deeper into the dark.

The fracture pulled tighter, closer, but the last healing note needed to be formed. I couldn't reach, it needed more...

I couldn't hold the anchor and finish it too.

I had to finish it.

Fading voices. Calling me. Needing me.

So many would be protected if I loosened my grip on the anchor, reached a little further.

"No." A tug.

An offer, a pulse of sorrow.

And then one of the threads was free, gold unfurling from the grouped tether, floating down, wrapping itself around that last fracture.

Who?

It was done.

"Come back."

I held the tether as it pulled me to the surface. It was done.

They held me.

I took a shuddering breath.

There was strength behind me. Small hands on my face.

I opened my eyes and blinked in the brightness of the room, lit by torches after the obsidian depths.

Féile was there, flinging herself into my arms. I braced myself for a fall but was held by the muscular chest at my back.

I felt floaty, disconnected, not emotionally burnt out but struggling to focus, struggling to make sense of what was in front of me.

My circle of three had expanded: Bronwyn, Rion, and Marcus all sat in the circle with me.

Fidelma.

Her body lay limp on the floor.

Marcus hurried to help her but her eyes were empty. She had finally done what she had spent her life trying to achieve, had manifested the desire that Calchas had identified and manipulated. The ley line was healed. It was whole once more.

I looked up from her body to the others. They had joined the circle; they could have been killed. There was magic in their blood, yes, but they were untrained in tending the line, little more than latents.

"It was his idea," Rion said, lifting his chin to the person behind me.

"Three sided, four sided, the strength is in the unity." A hand came about my waist, pulling me back into the hard, muscled body. I twisted in his arms, the dark shadow outlined by the light of the torches as he bent his head to mine.

Pressed his lips to mine.

"I told you it doesn't end like this." His deep voice vibrated through me.

I pulled back and looked into amber eyes that glowed bright with an eagle's sight and a lion's pride.

Gideon.

"How?" I asked. I couldn't breathe, couldn't think, my eyes still seeing the blood on the sand.

"How did I have the idea?" he repeated. "It was your idea; many individuals are stronger when they come together as one."

He was here. I raised my hands to his face, needing to touch it, to know that he was real.

"You're not dead," I observed, dumbfounded.

His mouth slanted to the side. "Nothing gets past you, lady."

It definitely was him. Only Gideon would choose to mock me at a time like this.

"How did you do this?" I asked.

"Marcus. He knew that the praetor planned to close down the arena and that since he likes to keep his theatrical flourishes to himself, there was a chance that his guards would not know that what they saw on camera was not playing out as Calchas wanted it too until it was too late," Gideon explained. "All Marcus needed was someone who would trade their life for mine."

"Your father." Richard Mortimer, who had struggled to show his love for his son in life, had not failed to do so in death. The steward hadn't tended Ginevra's wound; the glamoured Dr Courtenay had. Which meant the man I had exchanged vows with was my amber eyed Griffin.

Gideon's head was bowed and he closed his eyes briefly, the lines of his face taut in grief.

I looked at him numbly, unsure what to say, or what words of comfort to offer. Richard Mortimer had not been the most likeable man, and had never been the most caring of fathers, but he had sacrificed his life for his youngest son.

And his mother had given her life for mine.

I looked around at the grey faces around me; they had risked their lives by joining in as they had. For nothing. The fracture was repaired but there was no sign of the souls as there had at Avebury.

"I couldn't free them." I had been so sure that I could.

"You healed the line. The song is pure," Marina chided me.

"No, I think the tech held them there. I thought that once whatever Calchas had done was resolved, they would be free."

"The nasty claws are gone," came a small voice from the child still holding tight to my waist. My brows tugged together as I tried to comprehend what she was saying.

"The technology that bound them to... That was you?" I recalled the summer light unhooking them.

"I told you I was good," Féile piped up, affronted that I had so quickly forgotten, before her face twisted as she admitted, "but it was my daddy who died, he was the one who showed me, and then it was easy."

"The black energy." Marina let out a heavy breath. "It was Devyn."

"He came." I met Gideon's gaze. "He promised. And he came."

I smiled down at Féile, at my little girl for a job well done, and allowed Gideon to pull me up. We made our way back up the stairs and out into the mayhem of the city. I could feel the exhaustion pulling me down.

But it was not over yet.

"We have to secure the city," I said, turning to Gideon, drinking in the sight of him once more. He was alive. "You need to go and fetch the army."

A growl conveyed his disagreement.

"She's right. You need to go and bring the troops; they are waiting for a signal. They can take the city and subdue the legions," Rion commanded Gideon.

"The walls are down," I informed them. In my rage, I had made dust of them. "You need to do this."

Gideon's jaw locked, his eyes showing he was conflicted. He had never been one to take an order he didn't agree with.

"As my lady commands," he said, inclining his head.

I nodded, and there was a sudden shimmer before an eagle took flight in front of us, circled above us once, and dipped low before it burst upwards and was gone.

Chapter Thirty-One

I woke in darkness, candlelight illuminating a familiar canopy and the stone walls of my room in the Tower.

I jolted upright.

What was real? Was I still trapped in this damned room?

Images came tumbling in: Gideon dead, the wall falling, Britons in the streets. Real or dream?

I felt confused and startled, and then warm hands pulled me down and wrapped around me, and a low voice murmured words assuring me that all was well. And I slept.

———

"...Don't know what to do. We must restore order."

"They can wait. She's exhausted." It was Gideon's voice.

Blood on the sand.

His father's.

I pushed my eyes open and drank in the tall figure standing in front of the diamond-paned windows, his hair loose and his frame relaxed as he leaned against the wall. And his head was firmly on his shoulders.

I exhaled, alerting them to my newly wakened state.

Gideon came over and, lifting my hand from the covers, bowed to press his lips to it.

"Good day, my little apple drop," he greeted me with one of the daft endearments he had started using since our arrival in the city.

My heart flipped. I had thought him gone. Had felt the pain of it.

Marcus had made it right.

The touch of his kiss tingled on the back of my fingers. He often hid his true feelings behind a shield of indifference, the worse the hit the stronger the mask. I had chosen people I didn't know over him. He had been let down by all those he had loved and I had proven no different. I couldn't meet his eyes. Flustered, I looked beyond him to my brother.

"The city is secured?"

"Yes, and Calchas was taken," Rion answered me.

"How long have I been asleep?" I asked.

"Three days." Marcus came forward as he handed me a glass of water. I frowned a little at it. "Hydrate."

"Thank you." I meant for more than just his care of me. He had betrayed me again, but because of him Gideon lived. His green eyes were hollow, remorse still evident as he met mine, nodding briefly in acknowledgment before his face twisted. I may be on the road to forgiving him but it would take longer for him to forget all that had passed.

I had vague memories of a drip in my arm. I looked down there was nothing there now. Marcus leaned in and pressed the glass to my lips in a manner that spoke to habit. I waved him away, sitting up.

"Féile?" I asked him. Was she well? Had the ley line impacted her as much as it had me? She was so little and she should never have had to be part of the healing of the line.

"She's fine and she has been reunited with Snuffles so all is well in her world," Gideon reassured me from his resumed spot by the window, his tone oddly flat.

"What happened?" I again directed my question to Rion. I didn't know how to face Gideon. His mother and father were both dead because of me.

"You healed the ley line and now the druids have arrived, and they believe that the fracture has been resolved. With a little maintenance, the line will be fine," Rion offered.

I raised my eyebrows, smiling at him. "Ah, that's the one part I already know."

"Right." Rion smiled back ruefully. "Well, while you were busy healing the ley line below ground, things got interesting up here. With the blackout, the city's defences were pretty much non-existent. Gideon fetched the army, and as you apparently were already aware, the walls are no more."

"Once they were here, it was pretty much all over," Bronwyn added, strolling in eating some toast and perching on my bed.

"Are there many injured?" I asked. I was tired but they were glossing over events. Surely it couldn't have been that easy.

"The fighting at what was left of the gates was largely man to man. We had few weapons, and theirs didn't work," Rion said, looking over to Bronwyn.

"Calchas and his men went to some control room to try and bring the tech back up but Linus and his hackers stopped him." Bronwyn paused. "They arrested Calchas, though it would have been better for everyone if they had killed him there and then."

"No," I said. "He doesn't get off that easily."

"Mama," cried a little voice, and then Féile was there, jumping on the bed, accompanied by her less than well behaved furry companion. I pulled her to me and hugged her fiercely, resting back in the pillows and wrapping my arms around her. She was safe.

When I woke again, the room was empty. I lifted my head to find it not entirely deserted, a pair of long legs spread towards the fire from a high-backed chair.

I took greater notice of my surroundings now – the canopied bed, the diamond-paned windows set in granite walls.

"Why are we still in the White Tower?" I hated this building. I felt trapped.

Gideon stirred and his head appeared around the back of the chair, dark hair gleaming from the light of the fire. "It's the most secure building in the city."

He seemed disinclined to come to me, and I had been in this bed far too long. I pulled a wrap around me and, levering my legs over the side, I tried them out momentarily to test my strength. I seemed fine.

"I've been here the whole time." Gideon read my concern. "I don't think you need me anymore, but just in case."

I had disconnected us. I had chosen not to need him.

His voice was low, dispassionate. My tread was silent as I crossed the room to him.

"I thought you were dead." I recalled the axe falling. The terrible numbness, like a veil through which I had watched it.

"No."

I laid a hand on his chest, wanting to soften his pain, needing to feel his heart beating beneath my hand. I thought it had stopped forever; I knew he felt guilt and sorrow at his father's death, but all I could feel was joy and relief that he was still here with me.

"I'm so sorry," I said. His father had exchanged places with him.

"He was always more interested in winning than living," he said, his voice tight with pain.

"Did the others know?" I asked.

"No. We weren't sure it would work." His face was all hard planes in the half-light as he spoke to the fire rather than face me. "The city watched a different version of events. We knew the technology could see through the glamour, so we had to ensure that there was a lockdown. Linus incited some unrest in the East End, and there were a few minor cyber attacks against the firewalls."

Marcus had followed through on his promise to make it right. And more. I had only hoped that he would deliver me a charm to give me a small chance to defy the compulsion of the handfast cuff, knowing that if I had that tiny amount of freedom of will, I would have a slight advantage unknown to Calchas should the chance arise that I could do more than directed and heal the ley line. I had hoped, and had asked for no more than that.

He had delivered more. Where he had been complicit in Devyn's death, now he had gifted me Gideon's life.

"What now?" Gideon asked. "You are free to make your own choices."

476

Was I really?

I had never been free, never had the space to truly decide my own fate.

"Rion will want me to rule Londinium." To become queen of the former imperial province. Rion had control of the board now, the Steward of Anglia was gone, the princes of Cymru and Bronwyn's family in Kernow would follow his lead. My brother would lose no time in making sure the future of the island was positioned in our favour. Following through on at least this aspect of the Praetor's plan was the most obvious strategy. My throat felt as though a band were around it, restricting the oxygen, a heavy hand pressed on my chest.

I had spent my whole life following the path laid before me, a path carved out by the will of others. Before all of this, I had wanted nothing more than to marry Marcus and have a family. To comply with the Code and make my parents and my society happy by keeping to the boundaries they had laid out for me for the type of life I would lead, the needs that would be fulfilled that would make me happy. Devyn had taken me on a different path that had opened up the horizon and showed me a world beyond the confines I had grown up in. In Cymru that cage had conspired to close in around me once more and I had fought for the one thing I wanted even when Devyn himself would have given in. Once he had gone, I had bowed to the weight of expectations once more. I had served my brother, my teacher, the country, even when it had almost cost me my daughter.

"Rion does not get to decide. You are tied to no one. Not even to me. You don't need the Griffin anymore. The Belinus, May, and Strand lines are all well. Tending them now will not be as difficult."

"But we're married," I said absently. Yet he was right. Rion might have plans, but I did not always agree with my brother.

"We're not," he corrected me quietly.

I blinked at him, surprised. I focussed on his words, replaying the sequence in my head. We were. The first time we had married had been a matter of survival, the second time I had been blackmailed, compelled, and he had worn another's face, but we had still exchanged vows. The cuff had dropped away. Had it been tricked as I and everyone else in the arena had? I had exchanged vows, the contract completed *but* the name had been wrong. I wasn't married to Gideon, nor could anyone argue that I was married to Marcus.

"I'm free," I realised. Truly free.

No one was going to choose a path for me; nobody was going to dictate my life. The ley line was healed, and I was bound to nothing, obliged to no one but my own free will.

A laugh broke free and, unable to contain the emotions within me, I raised my eyes to the sky above and twirled in place. *Devyn, can you see me now?*

The door snicked as Gideon left the room. I stilled.

I danced while his family lay dead. How could I be so insensitive?

I made my way back to the bed and stared blindly at the darkness until dawn began to break over the city to begin a new day.

As soon as I was respectable, I left my room. My hand hesitated as I turned the wrought iron to release the latch. Too often, I had been restrained in this room.

My very bones eased as it turned and opened into an empty hall and I went in search of Rion.

Asking a passing grizzled, tattooed beast of a warrior who, I learned, had joined our march on Londinium from Powys, I was guided to a study. Of course. Trust my brother to find the stuffiest, bookiest room in any building and make it his own.

He stood and came around the desk and enfolded me in his arms as if he would never let go.

"I thought we were going to lose you," he said into my hair.

"Never." I laughed. "Who would annoy and defy you if I wasn't here?"

"Féile shows great promise." He laughed, releasing me. The darkness in his eyes was not quite gone. He had been in the circle, had felt me start to leave – they all had before Fidelma had taken my place to heal that final fissure.

"I want to talk to you about the future," I said, taking one of the leather armchairs.

Rion smiled a welcome to continue.

"I don't know what you've been planning—"

"I have made no plans," he cut in mildly.

My head went back in surprise. "What?"

A wry smile twisted his lips. "I would not be so foolish, dear sister."

My eyebrows felt like they would hit my hairline and keep going.

"What do you want?" Rion asked, leaning back against the back of his armchair, one arm laid casually along the top.

"I want Féile to be free to make her own choices," I began after I had recovered from my shock. Rion was actually conferring with a piece on his board. "Alba cannot have her; they were not needed anyway."

479

"The deal was made." His mouth twisted. "I will see what can be done though. Is that all?"

"No," I began tentatively. "All I ever wanted was a family and a home. I don't want to be..."

"Queen of Londinium?" he finished for me.

"No," I said flatly. The thought filled me with horror. Trapped on a throne, so much power, but power warped, as the history of my line attested. The Lady of the Lake throughout history had been powerful, but for every Nimue there was a Morgan le Fey, for every Elizabeth there was an Anne. The lady could be a force for good, but my line should not be the only source of power – both magical and material. It was too much.

"There was a reason that when the lady returned she only supported the Kings of Mercia and didn't rule herself." I tried to explain my feeling that I was not the right fit.

"You're worried that you might let all that power go to your head." Rion's voice was teasing, but he was also checking.

"I don't think so, but what about my daughter, or her daughter?" I said. "There must be a balance in Londinium, just as in Mercia, so the lady does not ascend the throne on the occasions she has married into the royal family."

"Then who?"

I raised a brow at my brother. "Who do you think?"

I wasn't so foolish either. Rion would have already considered all the pieces on the board.

His cobalt eyes gleamed. "It must be someone both city and country will accept. Someone that the Empire accept as the ruler following an outright rebellion. The Empire is failing but we must tread carefully so as not to give them a focal point to make an example of us. Marcus is the obvious choice, but with the steward gone, as heir of Anglia he will have enough to do to keep that house together. Nor do I think the commons here would accept him; he broke their trust when the treatment was kept exclusively for the elite."

He contemplated the fire before crossing to pour us drinks before retaking his seat.

"There was a reason why Calchas wanted you," he said as he took a sip. "You have healed the lines, the people of all tribes would kneel to you, and you were raised here behind the walls and you know their ways. Are you sure you won't consider it? Even for a time?"

I shook my head resolutely. I had no interest in running a country. I had seen Rion in action in Mercia – all the paperwork and organisation. But Rion would never be accepted by the citizens of Londinium.

There was one other who knew the ways of both worlds. Born and raised behind the walls, but steeped now in the Celtic lore of her ancestors, caught in the robes of a druid but too worldly to be confined by them.

"What about Marina? Marina knows the city. Is of the city. She should rule."

Rion ran a hand over the stubble on his chin. "It might work if she was a figurehead but would the elite accept an urchin from the stews?"

"They might if she had somebody they considered important alongside her," I prompted.

"A senator?" Rion choked on his drink.

I shook my head slightly, smiling at him over the rim of my glass. "Oh no, someone far more important than that, someone dashing, and regal, and oh so serious…"

"Me?" Rion looked at me as if I'd lost my mind. "She's barely more than a child!"

"Not to marry." I tutted. "Why do you lot always have to resolve everything by locking people into lifelong relationships they might not want?"

Rion's brow wrinkled. I had succeeded in truly bamboozling my brother.

I sighed. "As steward. Take a couple of years to advise her and help her while a council is arranged to support her. That's all."

"It could work." My whole body relaxed. He was contemplating this aloud, was listening to me, and was not insisting on trapping me under a crown I did not want.

"Work? It's brilliant," I said, not terribly humbly. "Briton and citizen together."

Rion took a couple of sips of his drink and swirled the firewater around in the cut glass a few times before nodding. "And what about you?"

"I told you, all I want is a family and a home." I shrugged. "We can mind yours while you're busy down here, if you like."

"Who is we?" he asked carefully.

"Féile, Gideon, and I." I frowned. "Who else?"

"Who else indeed?" He raised an eyebrow. "Does Gideon know about your happy-ever-after plans?"

"You think he won't forgive me?" Was it too late. Had he already spoken to Rion?

"Forgive you for what?"

"His parents are dead because of me," I said in a low voice.

"That's not your fault."

"Isn't it? I let the axe fall," I said earnestly.

Gideon had been off with me since I woke up. Distant.

"I let the axe fall believing it was him. He must hate me."

"I don't think that's the problem." Rion leaned forward.

"Then what?"

"Catriona Deverell, as Lady of the Lake you are powerful, but you've never been able to see what's right in front of you."

"Hey," I objected. "I figured out how to fix the ley line and get one step ahead of Calchas. I'm not entirely... What am I not seeing?"

"You are free now. Free to make your own choices. Free to choose your own path in all things," Rion said slowly.

"Why would that make Gideon unhappy?" Gideon was the one who had reminded me that I was no longer bound by the ties and obligations of the past.

"Free to choose who to marry," Rion said pointedly.

"But why would I want to choose to marry anyone? I already have a man I consider my husband."

"Does he know that?"

Oh.

Chapter Thirty-Two

The question of what to do with the praetor was to be settled the way it had always been in Londinium: in the arena, by the people of the city. Calchas had served his fake justice, had run his theatre long enough, and now the city would know it all. They would judge.

The crowd was hushed, silent. There was no drumming of feet and many of those in the amphitheatre tonight had never had the privilege of attending a Mete before. Those senators found to have had no knowledge of Calchas's doings retained their seats, which amounted to less than half the council. The rest of the seats were taken up by the Briton delegates. The majority of the arena had been filled by lottery. Linus had argued that the families of the dead deserved to be here to witness Calchas face justice in person, but I disliked the idea of stacking the mob so heavily against the accused. It felt wrong. Too similar to what had gone before.

I was last to enter, with Rion and Marina at my side, at his orchestration. Oban had supplied me with a suitably symbolic outfit, tones of city and country combined in one look. Féile had forgiven him on sight as soon as he had presented Snuffles to her. The others were disinclined to follow suit, but Oban had lost a mother and a sister before he had capitulated. He was my friend and would remain so.

The crowd was subdued, the citizenry, despite our assurances, unconvinced that we genuinely meant them no harm. My eyes scanned the balcony, restored from the damage of recent events, for a tall, dark-haired warrior. Gideon had picked up an old Griffin speciality: elusiveness. He had been with the army keeping order and the like, and I had barely seen him since the night I had woken. Féile, it seemed, was able to find him, as I knew when she wasn't with me she wandered off to be with him.

But today, in the arena, I couldn't see him. He wasn't here, and then I felt a dark shadow position itself behind me, my looming protective guard, and my tensed muscles relaxed.

"Friends, countrymen," Rion opened proceedings. "We are here today to bear witness to the crimes committed against this great city, and against the very land itself by one whose role was to serve you, and to serve you better."

The figure that walked out on the sand was dressed in his ceremonial robes. He would be judged as praetor, as a representative of the Empire, as keeper of the city, and it was fitting that he be attired as such.

"Hello," I whispered over my shoulder.

He was close enough that I could feel his huffed breath. "My lady."

That was how it was then. Formality was never a good sign with Gideon.

Calchas took his place on the sand below the balcony, flanked on each side by former praetorian guards. Kasen was on his left and another guard was on his right; they had witnessed up close the atrocities, had carried them out; not all had liked their orders.

"You are accused of crimes against the people of this city and province. How do you plead?"

Calchas, of course, with a mocking tilt to his lips fell to his knees with great ceremony. Even cast as the villain, he would want every last moment juiced for maximum drama. The crowd muttered amongst themselves, surprised at the traditional turn of events as the familiar tones rang out and the evidentiary reel began. Linus and his team of hackers had outdone themselves.

There was no footage of my mother's death of course, taking place as it had in the borderlands, but there was an infant, blood on her robes, being handed to a younger Camilla and Graham Shelton. Then there was Aurelia Courtenay's death, the higher incidence of illness, Marcus ill as a young teenager. There was a view of the circle below Mary le Strand, an explanation of the ley lines for the benefit of the citizens who were only mildly aware of their existence. Next we saw Devyn being whipped, the blood on the sand, and then the blood in the labs. There were images of us together that I had been able to hear but not see at the Mete four years ago when Devyn had stood on the sands below. How young I looked. How young Devyn looked, and so he would forever remain. I pushed away the wetness from my cheeks. I had forgotten that here there were pictures of him captured forever. Rhodri was whispering to Féile who looked up at the big screen, enraptured. Next came our escape from the White Tower, then Marcus and Matthias returning with the cure that had been stolen from the druid community of the Holy Isle.

There was the cure doled out to the elite, while praetorian guards entered houses located between the inner and outer walls at night, house after house; sometimes one person, but increasingly whole families, were pulled from their homes.

Those people were brought to the old church, entered the circle, then there was nothing until more footage showed the dried-up corpses being carried from homes, and from Mary le Strand, out of the city to great mass graves. So many bodies. The noise of the crowd swelled, hissing in reaction to what they were seeing. Many in the arena were not elite and so they would know people who had disappeared. Knew now that this had been their fate. There was more footage of the arena, of blood identified in the lab, its owners accused of capital crimes and blood spilled on the sand. This blood was on the hands of those who had judged, on the hands of the citizens who had believed the so-called evidence placed in front of them.

Then there were images of Féile arriving in the city, filthy and wild, struggling against her captors, held in the hospital until she responded to Marcus's kindness and he took her to his home, which was heavily guarded. Marcus had begun to make it right earlier than I knew.

Next was our arrival in the city and our search. My first attempt at Mary le Strand was shown, and then images of me being carried out in Gideon's arms and the ill in the stews recovering overnight. There was a replay of our arrest – events the mob had seen before but this time with context.

There was no video of the bargain made in the Tower, but enough pieces were there to tell the story of what had happened. Calchas's plan to keep me weakened, to ensure the ley line remained unhealed, kept leaching off the magic in the blood of latents above. Finally, we saw the axe falling, the cameras capturing what I hadn't seen, the last moments of Richard Mortimer.

I reached behind me until I found Gideon's hand. "I'm sorry."

"For what?" the low rumble came as the reel played on. "I don't blame you."

"You don't?" I asked. "I let you die."

This time I could hear his huffed laughter. "You've done worse."

Worse? What on earth could be worse? I turned to him as Rion glared at me to pay attention. There was Linus and his contingent arresting Calchas in the control room and the armies of the Britons entering the city peaceably.

I was up. I stood forward.

"Citizens of Londinium, you have seen now what the praetor has done. He allowed the ley line to die, to feed off the magic in the blood of those living above. His actions were... No, it is not for me to sway you one way or the other. You have seen what was done – it is for you to judge."

I looked down at Calchas on the sand below.

"Let the accused speak in his defence if he wishes it," I said. What Calchas had done was horrific, but the systematic control given to the city in the Mete gave no right of defence to the accused. That changed now.

Calchas's penitently bowed head snapped up at this. He took a step forward, appearing to gather his thoughts.

"People of Londinium, citizens. I am one of you. What I have done may appear defenceless, but it was done to save so many more." Calchas raised his hands as if offering his words to the mob who had for so long hung on his every word, but this time his words were met by hisses and shouts of abuse.

"I have wronged you in seeking to protect you from the dangerous magics that flow under our very city, magic that now appears to offer to solve all your wrongs. But it was magic that wrought this misery from the start." He clasped his hands to his chest. "My own son and daughter were amongst the first to sicken and die. We lived on the Strand, so close to the epicentre of the corruption that sucks life from the city. How could I stand by as other fathers, other mothers, watched their children sicken and die?"

I caught Marcus's eye. Did this mean that Calchas himself was a latent? Marcus returned my querying glance with a half-shrug. It was possible. All this time, he had been killing people for having the same blood that ran in his own veins.

"This known traitor will have you believe that she has healed the ley line, that she can rule our city and force you to live under the rule of the Wilders who believe in magic and superstition. They would have you live in the dark ages once more."

The crowd hummed at this, but the mob were his no longer. They had seen the evidence of his actions and the truth of the past. Why would they believe the truth of the future he painted now.

I spoke again.

"Friends, whatever the future holds will be your choice. If you wish to remain in the Empire, you may do so. But our worlds here on this island do not need to be so very different; magic and technology may live side by side. Our belief that they could not is yet another lie."

I pulled in some power. My control of simple magics was not always perfect and yet the flames from the torches flickered and swirled together until a Griffin appeared in the air above the arena. He dipped around the amphitheatre before soaring high up though the towers.

"Cheap theatrics," Calchas spat.

I laughed out loud. He was one to say so.

"A Griffin, huh," came the murmur behind me.

"My new favourite thing," I whispered and found our hands were still joined as he lifted mine and pressed his lips to it, to the sound of an exasperated sigh from my regal brother.

I raised my hand until the crowd fell silent once more.

"If you choose another path, a new path, to be sovereign to yourselves, to form a new state of your own as part of Britannia, I propose Marina, daughter of Londinium, one of you, who has the power to tend the ley line but who also knows and loves this city to rule until a new system can be found. One of your choosing." Marina stepped forward, taking her place beside me. Our eyes met and held.

How far we had come from that first day we had met on the threshold of her home in the stews – her flinty gaze assessing me – to the escape through the tunnels under the docks, and now her rise to become one of the finest druids in the land. Her braids were bound in as elaborate a style as I had ever worn, her grey eyes were bright, and the ruby red of her dress flattered the dark tones in her skin. Oban had outdone himself. And I had no doubt Marina would outdo herself in this role, more than my brother would see coming. I grinned as I continued. "Until that time, my brother, Rion Deverell, will act as steward; this and more will be decided upon in a future vote. But now we must turn to the matter at hand."

I looked down on the sands, my smile dimming as I contemplated the arrogant man who stood looking for all the world as if he were still up here, pulling the strings. "This is the final Mete. After this we will find a new way. But to close this chapter we must judge the citizen before you."

I raised my hand, thumb pointing to the side as the minute ticked by. We had discussed Marina calling the count but she had not wanted her first act to be what was effectively the closing act of the past.

At the final bell, Linus rushed to my side and whispered the result. I wasn't sure if I felt relief or regret at the result.

"Citizens, you have chosen mercy," I said into the hush. Change comes slowly. I had not believed the truth. How could I have expected the people of the city to believe the evidence placed before them? We told them that what had gone before was untrue and yet expected them to accept our truth. People needed time, time to adjust, time to sift through the evidence themselves. Time they would be given.

"The results are: 68% guilty."

Calchas's grin was one of triumph. We could do nothing; most of the people believed him guilty, but given the low rate of conviction the punishment would not fit the crime. We had discussed the potential outcomes and had agreed upon scenarios based on the vote. I looked to Marina and Rion now, stepping back to allow the soon-to-be new ruler to pronounce the verdict.

"The sentence is not death, despite the countless innocents that you have sent to theirs, nor is it imprisonment, as we would not have you here acting as a taint on the land." Marina's voice was steady, her accent revealing her local, if less than elite, origins. "Former Praetor Calchas, you are stripped of all titles and property and banished from this land. If you ever return it will be to face your death."

I met Calchas's eyes, which already gleamed with fresh plots, and then his eyes suddenly widened. His body fell forward, crumbling onto the sand, blood spilling from the knife wound in his upper back. Kasen was standing over him, his fellow praetorian rushing to tackle him to the ground as Gideon pulled me behind him protectively.

"What?"

Calchas wasn't moving. His blood would be the last to seep into the sands of the arena.

"Kasen's family... that's why he helped us," Marcus explained.

A light materialised out of the ground beside Calchas's fallen body, then another and another. Now there were hundreds of dancing lights lifting into the night. The souls. They hadn't escaped when I had healed the ley line, but they were free now, released by the death of their murderer. The darkness of the blacked-out buildings was illuminated by golden lights as hundreds – no, thousands – of bright spots swirled upwards.

Free. They were free.

"This is how it ends," Gideon said from beside me.

"No," I said, facing out over the arena as the souls lit up the sky. I turned, seeing them reflected in his eyes.

"This is." I stretched up and pulled his mouth down to mine, pressing my lips to his in a promise – a kiss he had given me a hundred times. If I had been paying closer attention I would have seen it, felt it, known what it meant. He pulled away to look down at me, his amber eyes glowing.

My choice. My future. My match.

"Marry me," I commanded.

His lips tugged up at the corner.

"I live to serve."

Acknowledgments

I never set out to write a book, many of the early scenes in the book began life as no more than daydreams scribbled down, then something more than doodles. As time passed more was teased out, first as a challenge until I eventually became invested in discovering what happened to these characters.

I had no idea what I was doing, and somewhere around 80,000 words in realised I had to learn more of the craft to fashion these pages into a tale worth reading. The author community is amazingly generous, there are books and podcasts and articles and sage words all around, many of which I seemed to find at just the right time. I'd like to particularly thank *Writing Excuses* whose fifteen(ish) minute nuggets were so helpful.

They say you should write what you wish to read, like many fantasy readers I grew up on Tolkien, Lewis, Eddings, Jordan, Martin, et al and longed to read these type of stories with different types of central protagonists and for me, more romance. In the years since I started doodling there has been an explosion of books in this genre that go well beyond what I could ever have imagined when I was a teen – Cole, Collins, Harkness, Maas, Bardugo, Pasat, Lu, Deonn, Kuang and so many more - it's been a golden era, or the beginning of a new one. Had these already existed I'm not sure I would have had a go. But I would like to thank these authors and all the rest for the wonderful worlds they've created. And add that there are so many more stories to be told so if you have one... give it wings!

But this journey was not taken alone, special thanks always to Kim, for encouraging me to keep taking another step. To the wonderful team at One More Chapter, Bethan, Charlotte, Melanie, Claire, Lydia, Tony, Laura and Andrew. Thank You.

Author Q & A

What were the most difficult world-building challenges when it came to creating **Legend of the Lakes?**

Creating an Alternate History

Merging and mixing the real, the mythical and the alternate has been both a challenge and great fun. Growing two parallel cultures with two different starting points that diverge even further at the start of the industrial revolution was at times befuddling and at others wonderfully organic. And in other plot points I seem to have been overtaken by real life which hopefully hasn't detracted from your enjoyment of the books.

What ifs give a delicious viewpoint onto the world we live in today as we get to examine what might have been, or what we wish could be.

In a world where the discipline and resources of the Roman Empire continued uninterrupted by the dark ages, technology and science have advanced further. On top of which the physical constraints caused them to use their resources to create what seems a futuristic city but is merely our own amped up a little. Much of the technology described here exists today, we are already much more observed by the state and large companies than we like to acknowledge.

The Celtic kingdoms meanwhile are the legacy of Arthurian legend and Celtic myth and magic, and the avoidance of technology. More complex on this side of the wall was including the touchpoints in history that took known ruling families and gave them a role in this parallel timeline. It was fun for me and enriched the depth of the world, but if the tangle of Plantagenet, Tudor and Glyndwr is too much, don't worry. These are easter eggs there for the enjoyment of those so inclined, if not, drive on, they are only background rather than material to the story.

What were some of your foremost sources of inspiration?

Calendar and Festivals

The year in the Briton world is a blend of traditions and eras, as is our own today. Roman gods still star in January (Janus) and June (Juno), Latin numbers name November and December, while in Irish some months are still named for the pagan festivals celebrated here May (Bealtaine), August (Lúnasa), October (Samhain).

The calendar used is the eight point wheel, which incorporates the Celtic fire festivals of Imbolc, Beltaine, Lammas and Samhain. The second four points are the cross quarter days, made up of the solar events of solstice and equinox especially given the importance of stone circles, which the ancients built in alignment with these points in the year.

Light and dark was how the Celts measured time. The dark

half of the year began at Samhain and summer was greeted at Beltaine. Entry into the Celtic world of book II took in the first of these festivals while many more featured in book III.

Samhain, 1 November: The beginning of the new year for the Celts. The most celebrated today is the evening before, but for the Celts and Christians it was three days. All Hallow's eve, All Souls and All Saints.

Winter Solstice/Midwinter, 20-23 December: The shortest day of the year, to which Newgrange and Stonehenge are aligned, speaks to its importance in ancient times.

Imbolc, 1 February: Halfway between winter Solstice and spring equinox, the first of February in Ireland is the feast of St Brigid (or Brigid the daughter of the Celtic god Dagda) and is the traditional beginning of Spring.

Spring/Vernal Equinox,19-22 March Ostara: This day marks the crossing of the sun's path over the equator. For the ancient Greeks and Persians it marked the beginning of the new year.

Beltaine, 1 May: Traditionally the beginning of summer and is still celebrated in some places with Maypole dancing and the cutting of green boughs. Like its counterpoint in the year Samhain, Beltaine sees a weakening of the veil, rather than the dead the other world can cross over. My grandmother used to leave a bowl of milk for the fairies on May eve to keep them happy.

Summer solstice/Midsummer, 19-23 June: The longest day of the year in the northern hemisphere, when the north pole is on its maximum tilt to the sun, is still marked with bonfires and floral wreaths in many countries of the world.

Lammas/Lughnasadh,1 August: The first of the harvest festivals, Lugh was the Irish god of the sun, while Lammas is Old English for mass of loaves, and is still marked by a fair in many parts of Britain and Ireland. In many parts of Europe this was the grain festival heralding the beginning of the grain harvest, with fairs featuring circle dancing, corn dollys and loaves.

Autumn Equinox/Mabon, 21-24 September: The second of the harvest festivals is a time of plenty, named in recent paganism for the Welsh god of light, Mabon. The last of the cross quarters when day and night are roughly equal as the sun is over the equator.

Ley Lines

Leys are paths of energy that are conjectured to run beneath the earth's surface connecting prehistoric and Christian sacred sites and monuments. Many areas of the world have similar beliefs – the songlines of the Australian aboriginal Dreamtime, the fairy paths of the Irish, the dragon currents or feng shui of the Chinese, the energy lines of the Aztecs of Peru and many more. The lines explored here are in England and Scotland and abound with churches, barrows, stone circles, and other significant sites, they are generally regarded to have a straight masculine line, which is interwoven by a meandering feminine line.

The May Line: Or Michael and Mary line for the number of monuments built in their honour along it, is aligned with the path of the sun on the 8th of May, cutting from Great Yarmouth through Abbey Bury St Edmunds, taking in Glastonbury and Avebury, to St Michael's Mount in Cornwall.

The Belinus Line: Or Elen and Belinus line, is named for a British road-building Iron age king. This line runs from the Isle of Wight, taking in both ancient capitals of Winchester and Dunfermline, multiple prehistoric monuments including the Penrith stone circle, on through Inverness, and aligns with the Dark Rift of the Milky Way, which the ancients believed was a gateway to the next world.

Exploring the World of The Once and Future Queen

MONUMENTS AND CAPITALS

The Monuments of the Ancients

Keswick Stone Circle

Castlerigg stone circle or Keswick Carles is a 5000 BC circle in the Lake District near the town of Keswick, known for being visited by Keats, Wordsworth and Coleridge, who wrote of it as *"a Druidical circle* [where] *the mountains stand one behind the other, in orderly array as if evoked by and attentive to the assembly of white-vested wizards"*. It has alignments with the autumn equinox and winter solstice, as well as various lunar positions.

Penrith Stone Circle

Is one of the largest in northwestern Europe and may have had as many as 70 stones, of which 27 remain upright, including Long Meg, a 12ft high monolith of red sandstone. There are a variety of colours including four non-local quartz stones which align with the solar solstice and equinox as well as lunar events. There are a number of local legends surrounding the stones including one that says if you count them correctly and put your ear to the red monolith you'll hear Long Meg herself whisper to you.

Avebury Stone Circle

The largest in Britain and is part of a wide network of Neolithic sites, including a wide henge/ditch, barrows and West Kennet avenue, made up of about 100 paired stones.

The Capitals of the Kingdoms

Carlisle

As far north as the Romans successfully held, Hadrian's wall ran from just north of the city all the way to the east coast. The Deverell home depicted here is a sprawling castle for the royal family of Mercia. Carlisle castle in reality is much more similar in style to a bunker, testifying to its position on the hostile England/Scotland border, but here far from the wars a more elaborate home was possible.

York

A city which seethes with the past, the walls still circle a city that inspires Winterfell of *Game of Thrones*. York's history is dotted with rebels and it still defends the sons that history have much maligned, Guy Fawkes and Richard II of the House of York. Medieval times echo through the narrow passageways of the Snickleways and the Shambles. I couldn't resist making it the capital of Anglia.

ONE MORE CHAPTER

YOUR NUMBER ONE STOP

FOR PAGETURNING BOOKS

One More Chapter is an
award-winning global
division of HarperCollins.

Sign up to our newsletter to get our
latest eBook deals and stay up to date
with our weekly Book Club!
<u>Subscribe here.</u>

Meet the team at
<u>www.onemorechapter.com</u>

Follow us!

 <u>@OneMoreChapter_</u>

 <u>@OneMoreChapter</u>

<u>@onemorechapterhc</u>

Do you write unputdownable fiction?
We love to hear from new voices.
Find out how to submit your novel at
<u>www.onemorechapter.com/submissions</u>